Stephanie Dowrick

Running Backwards
Over Sand

Viking

VIKING

Penguin Books Ltd, Harmondsworth, Middlesex, England
Viking Penguin Inc., 40 West 23rd Street, New York, New York 10010, U.S.A.
Penguin Books Australia Ltd, Ringwood, Victoria, Australia
Penguin Books Canada Ltd, 2801 John Street, Markham, Ontario, Canada L3R 1B4
Penguin Books (N.Z.) Ltd, 182–190 Wairau Road, Auckland 10, New Zealand

First published 1985

Typeset in VIP Garamond
Typeset, printed and bound in Great Britain by
Hazell Watson & Viney Limited,
Member of the BPCC Group,
Aylesbury, Bucks

British Library Cataloguing in Publication Data

Dowrick, Stephanie
    Running backwards over sand.
    I. Title
    823'.914[F]   PR6054.08/

ISBN 0-670-80368-5

For all those people
who took me out of the woods
and showed me the trees

PART ONE

Morning in the Land of the Long White Cloud

The common cormorant or shag
lays eggs inside a paper bag.
The reason you will see no doubt
is to keep the raindrops out.

Anon

One

Here she comes, our hero. Zoë Delighty. This is her story. The true story of Zoë Delighty.

She is young. Tall, dark, radiant this evening with a vivid light, a lit-up sense of herself that she wants to share, wants, most of all, to have reflected back to her. She wants others to bask and therefore to confirm that there is light coming from her. That will make her light real. That will be her pleasure.

There is no single source of this light she holds, our lighthouse, this light she is eager to share. It is made up of fragments, polished by a journey still continuing, flaring now with the rare excitement she feels at finding herself, for this moment, bright light in a dull room in Chelsea.

In this speck of time she has no task but to be alight. This seems to be her way, her role: to brighten, to be bright. And what grey woman or man working overtime with grey-cell work can offer more than radiant Zoë? Tall and straight, dressed in long black broken with red, caught for this instant as a single image: long black red-broken not-breaking lighthouse.

Where has she come from, this moment of light?

Bent in close, it might be possible to hear her say:

My name is Zoë, Zoë Delighty. It's an improbable name; you would not be the first to think so. My mother meant much better than well, but there was a dreadful time, I suppose it must have been during the middle 1950s, when most people confused it with the names I would now describe though not dismiss as being of the tap-dancing variety: Annette, Lynette, Gayleen, Debbie, Vickie, Tracy. (Their brothers are called Aaron, Troy and, later, Jason.)

We learned ballet, not tap, my sister and I. She low-profiled with Rebecca Delighty. Rebecca Alice Delighty, which would have given her wonderful initials for the late 1960s but by then she had sacrificed Delighty for Callan and was rationing Valium in an Auckland flat, scornful of such nominal wonders in the harsh reality of long hard days with her ever-present children and short tense nights with her mostly absent husband.

Ballet kept us with a crowd of Helens, Beverleys, Sallys, Andreas. No fashioners of high romance were their Mums, no dreaming on Lynette's behalf of rhythmic taps, gorgeous smiles, hairless armpits, stiffened bra beneath tight bodice, full skirt swishing to the floor in a glorious moment of sashay, sashay.

Zoë Delighty could fashion her own romances. *Down by the sea I lost my shoe oh what a funny thing to do a little wave came up one day and took it stealthily away I saw it go upon the tide and float towards the ocean wide and there perhaps another wave will wash it to the mermaid's cave.*

To be a mermaid, scaly-tailed, to sit waiting on cold hard rock: that was no part of my dreams. But to cross oceans and find my way inside the darkest, deepest caves, I dreamed of that. And of the moment when light would burst into a dark place and make bright, subtle and varied what had been lost in dense shadow.

Apart from that brief time when, mistaken for the tap-dancing set, Zoë Delighty seemed interchangeable with Lynette Long, I have been pleased with this gift from my mother. My Zoë-Delighty-name has delighted me, and most of mine.

This gratitude is confined to my mother, Jane. Her husband, James, present — tenderly and passionately — at the moment of my conception, was truly established as absent by the very differently tender and passionate moment of my birth.

Zoë's mother had known her father for some years before her birth, before her conception. They had been formally bound together by God and the legal system of New Zealand for five years or so when on a mild October evening an unexpectedly warm note of spring led Jane to feel unexpectedly warm towards James who, by then, more often inspired in her a kind of autumn feeling. Not winter, no frost white-binding the branches of trees, but not summer either. No full blooms blooming. No bees humming. No honey.

James had often read to Jane in their early years together. She would choose a work and listen to him read it aloud to her. She had taken great pride in her ability to introduce him to her fine repertoire of literature, her prize from years of solitary, voracious reading on the isolated North Island sheep farm where she had grown up. His obsession with architecture, boyhood hobby become manhood profession, had kept him from making any but the most obvious discoveries for himself.

As well as listening to his reading, she fuelled his spoken dreams of transforming his high ideals of architectural design into liveable, practical realities. She shared and encouraged his belief that he could use the multi-faceted landscape of their much-loved country as inspiration, not blight it with monstrosities savagely at odds with the unique range of shapes and shades of the land. But as plan after innovative plan was rejected by the blind, the prejudiced, the envious, in favour of what was familiar, predictable and immediately understood, he gave up: reading to her, sharing his ideas, even complaining about the ironies of having to design government projects, forced to follow the orders of bureaucrats in whom any incipient sense of aesthetics had been crushed, just as bulldozers would crush the foliage, the birds, the lizards to clear the land on which 'his' cheap, short-life, unrewarding buildings would rise. His failure hummed discordant in the silence between them.

Yet now a sweet brief renaissance was taking place in the small wooden house they rented on a bush-covered hill in a small town some miles outside a large city. Jane lay in the bath, enjoying the water, the soap, the lavender smell of crumbled bath salts, the quiet of the house as Rebecca slept, the pleasant memories and distraction of her husband reading to her again, from *New Statesman and Nation* as he sat on the down-turned lavatory seat a few feet away from her. He read well. The water relaxed her. The unusual quiet of the house gave her a sense of peace and control.

The article was finished as the water began to cool, as the skin at the tips of her fingers began to crinkle. She stood up. A pleasantly ordinary body, stretched a little by her pregnancy with Rebecca but

11

satisfied in its memories of much pleasure given and received in those summer days and not yet close enough to winter to care about the droops, the hairs, the veins. Why should she? It would not have occurred to her to ask.

Her husband's eyes saw two women who merged quickly into one exactly resembling neither the girl she had been when he first knew her nor the woman who stood now – short, firmish, warm, dripping – before him. But the woman he saw stirred him. Her receptivity to his reading suggested a receptivity of a more general nature. He moved towards her. With the smell of lavender in his nostrils he nuzzled her neck, drew his fingers around her nipples, enjoyed the mixture of bath and natural wet as he stroked briefly between her legs; then they both lay down and he entered her in their way for all seasons, he on top, she beneath, lying on the bathmat, faded now, which celebrated the Silver Jubilee of George V, while he shot into Jane the seed which was to fuse with her ovum and was eventually to grow into what could, for a moment, be named as a lighthouse.

Before Jane's body had dried, with bath water there to be seen even in the fading light, James stood up, tender still but with all passion, like the sperm, shot. He picked up the *New Statesman* from where it lay by the lavatory on which he had sat during those last seconds before the beginnings of Zoë's existence, rolled the journal up into a satisfactory tubal shape to hold in his strong hand and patted it against Jane's bottom as she bent to dry between her toes, her foot resting on the edge of the bath.

She acknowledged neither the tap nor the door closing behind him. She was communicating with whatever ancient inner instinct might tell a woman she has just conceived. That new life has again begun. That her body has been invaded. That a miracle of renewal is to take place. The skin will be stretched, veins and nights broken. She knew, her generations of foremothers had prepared her to know, that she was again pregnant.

She was sure it would be disastrous.

She was sure he would be unable to bear it.

She was sure it was to be a boy.

Nine years later she was dead. Dead Jane. Dead and burned. Ashes to ashes. Unearned urn. Zoë used to make jokes like that. They came from the same impulse to hide which would overcome her when people, ordinary helpless people, would say as she stood in bus queues, in shops, parks, school yards, at dentists and at doctors. 'Tell your mother . . .' and she would reply, loudly, coarsely, 'I don't have a mother. My mother is dead.' Impassive. Not a twitch then nor for many years, until she couldn't love Gabriel enough (or could she only love him too much?) and he left her and she began to twitch and ache and rock and eventually but oh so hard to cry for them both and for all the ashes, the dust, the dirt, the pain, the screams, the darkness she must do battle with. Screams that tore, dark that battled, lights that threatened to go out.

These images disturbed ten-year-old Zoë only in her dreams. What obsessed her by day was the insensitivity of the people with whom she was forced to live. Not her sister, Rebecca. The two girls were true to each other almost always, lapsing only when Rebecca passed into puberty-land and Zoë was left in the courtyard outside, canny enough to punch Rebecca hard on her poor unwelcome tiny breasts, unkind or perhaps confused enough not to understand that Rebecca's pain was more than a reaction to physical attack, well-aimed though that was.

Rebecca loved Zoë. Zoë loved Rebecca.

They had secrets together, times together no one could touch. They both remembered Jane, though rarely spoke of her.

The household to which they went to live when Zoë was nine and Rebecca twelve did not or could not love, nor understand what lay behind the jokes and vulgar, loud remarks made by two small girls looking at the world through cracks, dancing on a hollow globe as it turns, turns, goes on turning, even when its centre has long ago dropped away.

Zoë's mother wrote to her father as Zoë, a tiny fishy creature, swam behind the sweet flesh of her body in the pool beneath her heart:

Dear James
I don't have words, nor interest to search for them, to describe the sense of betrayal I feel. That far outweighs anything else. Your strange request that I shouldn't miss you – surely a decision which can't be advised about? – is totally redundant. There's no way I

can concern myself as to whether or not I 'miss you'. What I do miss is any sense of reality. Yet Rebecca's tea needs to be got as usual, her story needs to be read as usual. That's real enough. But I'd also thought it real enough that although 'romance' and 'excitement' probably had gone out of our relationship that we had a life together which we'd chosen, together, to begin. A life which was to have created its own reality. An illusion, it seems, which makes it hard for me now to be sure where other lines hover between reality and illusion.

I cry to myself sometimes and say, 'I miss him'. But James it may not even be true. And anyway, what the hell does it matter?

Come on Sunday to see Rebecca. She asked me last night if she'd been naughty. It was hard for her to ask, poor little girl. Evidently she's confused in her own measurement of reality. She can't remember being 'naughty' but had got it into her mind that she must have been, or why else would you have gone away. I hated you then. That was real enough.

I've already phoned Bill King about the window. His estimate should come next week.

Jane

After Jane died James was confronted with a very awkward decision.

He had, ostensibly, left Jane for Caroline whom he couldn't contain himself from describing at the time as 'much more fun than dear Jane'. It wasn't surprising. Caroline's sense of fun, her magical allure, was little more than a sparkling mirror in a most attractive surround which reflected back to James his witticisms and old jokes transformed by being newly heard. But the mirror faded. Caroline's blonde beauty grew mousy. She had her own set of stretch marks. Two pregnancies for Jane, two for Caroline. Caroline looked sad, and confused. Her allure had been too briefly experienced, too quickly lost.

When Caroline no longer sparkled, when she frowned and looked down instead of gazing up with adoration and respect, James knew that further change was hopeless. Nothing would allow it. Not confidence (who was he, twice married, twice disillusioned, to offer a spark of passion to make a new fire?), not money — two wives, four kids, drained the slim resources of an unsuccessful man; not lust. Winter had set in. His igloo was cold, but familiar.

What James was prepared to do, what he silently hoped poor Caroline was prepared to do, was to make what he would, if pressed, have described as 'the best of it'.

Jane's death, and the ensuing responsibility of Rebecca and Zoë, was not part of the best of it.

James had left Jane because he was bored. Autumn was not what he wanted to share with a woman for whom he continued to have, albeit rarely, summer feelings she did not appear to share. Her second pregnancy could only exhaust him. Rebecca had at least been a novelty. There would be nothing novel about Jane's absorption in another baby. The idea of a son disturbed him.

Jane had told him, had woken him out of a most satisfactory and immediately forgotten dream, that she was expecting a boy. Did she think that would help? They hadn't even discussed the possibility of another child. It seemed to him a long time since they had discussed much at all. He had become irritated by her pragmatic optimism in the face of his failure. They had once talked at length, diving into the other's being not just through sex but also through words and jokes and shared allusions. Oh long ago.

Jane's calm assumption about the child's sex revolted him, disturbed him more than the news itself. It seemed symptomatic of Jane's femaleness, this irrational 'knowledge'.

James struggled to fight his desolation at the loss of the dream which increasingly seemed to have contained within it the very symbols of freedom. He struggled to suppress images of swelling flesh and piercing cries. He knew Jane was tense. Proud, distressed, she lay separate from him at the far side of her half of the bed.

He wanted to cuddle her. He wanted to be cuddled by her. Wanted her breasts against his chest, her arms around him. He wanted the eternal, maternal solace: all will be well.

He patted her, or the blankets which lay over her. Oh Jane. And spoke, 'Christ, what a time to tell me! Let's talk in the morning.'

The morning, noon or night for talk didn't come. Nor the sweet embraces to suggest even the possibility that all might be well.

Jane's pain and possibly her anger were hidden behind quiet eyes in her competent face.

James pushed his pain away, irritation returning again and again at the loss of his dream, scratching at it until he had almost forgotten any other event of that night.

Within months, before the swelling had really begun, long before the first piercing cry could be heard, James had found Caroline. Sweet Caroline, blonde Caroline, so young so good so innocent of the dreary future in which her star would dim, flicker and go out. She enraptured James. He cast off the old net, fled the old nest, went rolling in pastures new. He allowed a rush of blood — the last of the kind he would ever experience — to his head and to his penis to tell him that Hope Lay Ahead. With Caroline. *Nothing could be finer than to be in Carolina.* The refrain did not leave him. Surely this meant something?

Good-bye Jane. This isn't easy.

No James.

No Rebecca. Daddy isn't coming back.

No Caroline. Of course she won't blame you.

No Caroline. Of course Jane can cope.

No Jane. It's not that I don't care, I just want.

No James. I wouldn't have you back if you crawled in here and begged.

No Rebecca. Mummy isn't really sick. It's just the new baby brother growing in my tummy.

No Rebecca. That isn't why Daddy went away.

No Rebecca. Mummy won't ever leave you. You're my big girl, my beautiful big girl and I love you and you love me and we'll both love the new baby boy when he arrives.

No, darling. I won't ever go away.

Zoë Delighty was born on 4 June 1947. She startled Jane by arriving in a rush and by appearing to lack the necessary genital confirmation of Jane's belief in her maleness. It was not that it was difficult for Jane to adjust to her son being a daughter. Zoë's charms were immediately clear. She cried a lot, loud lusty cries, but she responded quickly to Jane's efforts to soothe her. The rush with which she had been born made Jane feel, just a little, taken over by Zoë. Rebecca had taken hours to push steadily down through the birth canal as Jane breathed and heaved and held back and pushed, as was appropriate. Rebecca had behaved as expected, looked as expected. Jane had been waiting for a Rebecca; a Rebecca had arrived.

Jane's reaction to the unnamed boy who emerged a Zoë was initially full of contradictions. This was the baby who could have been the final straw to send that camel James out with a broken back. This was the baby she would have to cope with alone. This was the baby who was her last chance to have a son.

But Zoë Delighty smiled and dribbled and grew and held Jane's fingers tightly and nuzzled at Jane's heavy milky breasts and loved Jane with such passion that Jane melted, melted into the infant as the infant melted into her, knowing that she could feel this tenderness for Zoë with a completeness not possible when Rebecca was a baby and she had shared her body and time between shy Rebecca and demanding James.

She had found it hard, the switch in rhythms from baby to man, and without being able to acknowledge it in any conscious way, had simmered with anger that she was the one who should move, bend to the demands of one, then back to the demands of the other. Now, with Zoë, she could sit for hours, cuddling, feeding, talking, cooing, and when Rebecca joined them their circle was complete. No new ball game was asked for.

Twenty-five years later Zoë was to say, for the first but not the last time, to a group of friends gathered around a large table, 'My mother breast-fed me for fifteen months. Life can only go downhill after a start like that.'

Most people at the table laughed. They thought she was joking.

Jane stayed in the small wooden house on the bush-covered hill when James had left for a flat with Caroline. She felt safer there, knowing the streets, the shops, the time the post and milk would be delivered, knowing she could ask neighbours for small favours, to keep an eye on Rebecca, to hold Zoë for a few minutes when Rebecca needed her complete attention. Husbands rarely left their wives in those days, especially when the wife had a small child and another baby on the way. People cast pitying glances at Jane, asked in leaden tones if she was *all right*, and she hated that pity most of all.

Hated James for causing her to be the recipient of it. Almost better to be the shamer than the shamed.

But time passed and Jane obviously coped and the little girls looked lovely in their hand-made clothes: appliquéd dresses with stories on them, knitted cardigans with animals emerging from pockets, brightly coloured shoes, multi-coloured ribbons. Oh yes, Jane could cope.

James sent Jane money. Never enough. How could he, with his new love and first one baby and then quickly another? Plumbing a bottomed pool, scraping, carping, knuckles raw, so many ways to deliver a blow. To bloody.

When Zoë was four and Rebecca almost seven – and able to read as well as any ten-year-old, the teacher told Jane proudly – Jane went back to work. She had worked hard before her marriage to James, and as long as possible before the birth of Rebecca. She had been a teacher, a good one, a woman from the country who understood the ways of city kids, who loved the noise and exhilaration of tiny children beginning to make sense of their world as fuzzy outlines on pages or blackboards became words, magical signposts towards new discoveries.

Now, returning to work, she was exhausted by the thought of giving herself to any children other than Rebecca and Zoë.

The options to teaching seemed few. She had to be at home for the girls after school, in the shorter holidays at May and August and over the long summer months of Christmas when she would return with them to the farm where she could again be a girl herself. No office working eight to four-thirty would accommodate willingly the reality of her life: total responsibility for two small precious girls.

When she had almost despaired of finding a solution, had tried to animate visions of herself as tea or cleaning lady, as someone who would welcome piles of washing or broken zips to mend, a solution raced to her faster-beating heart, to her working-overtime brain: it had to be right. Without waiting to finish the task at hand, she ran to the local library, poured out her story, her plight, to the woman long familiar in her function as librarian. She would work hard, knew the books, knew the people. Yes, said the librarian. Simply, yes.

The library was almost next door to the school which was prepared to lower its entrance age to absorb bright, loving, thoroughly breast-fed four-year-old Zoë. Zoë, proud of her bigness, eager to be liked, willing to be sat in the front row right under the teacher's eye.

This was the start of an important new period in the lives of Jane and Rebecca and Zoë Delighty. They had a different routine now which began with breakfast together at the big kitchen table, tender with each other at the beginning of a day in which each would be out in her separate world. Occasionally one of them would be cross. Rebecca would often delay Jane and Zoë. Absorbed in a book she would sit, half-dressed, hunched over a page, one shoe on and laced, the other lying beside her, and would grump and grumble when Zoë or Jane would screech that it was time to go, time to walk down the two long rows of houses, past a short burst of shops, each with its wooden awning, protection against inflated drops of tropical rain, to school and library.

In the evenings, just sometimes, Jane went out and the big girl from next door came in to sit with Zoë and Rebecca. Jane went to pottery classes, to films, to occasional parties when she would look and smell especially delicious. More often friends came to her, especially her dearest friend, Maria. She came more than once a week, glowing with pleasure at being with Jane, apparently even with pleasure at being with Jane's daughters. Their conversation was seamless, a flow of gossip, politics, jokes, reassurance. Words begun by one then picked up by the other then returned, deepened in meaning, or lightened and bounced: women's talk.

The sound of the women's voices was good for the little girls to hear. They could have stayed to listen in the kitchen, or out on the back porch, wherever the women were, but didn't need to. They felt very little curiosity about most of what was discussed, and no anxiety. Maria came, kissed them all with loud smacking kisses, distributed chocolate-covered buzz bars or sticky yellow lumps of hokey-pokey, talked, laughed, kissed again and left.

James also came. Every other Saturday his old Austin would pull up outside. Jane would go out to stand on the edge of the footpath as he emerged, tall and awkward, from the car. On fine days she would stand there with him, chatting before he came in. On wet days the two adults would talk in the kitchen while Rebecca and Zoë played, tried to play or to sink more deeply into a book, in their shared bedroom. James and Jane rarely laughed and their talk had a scratchy quality to it which reminded Zoë of fingernails on a blackboard.

Jane wanted to make James's visits pleasant for the children, perhaps pleasant for James too so he wouldn't give up coming. And she continued to care that he came.

She would cook special meals for when he returned with the girls from their outings. Zoë, who noticed such things, knew that her mother made certain dishes only when her father, or another male guest, was to be present. Her friends' mothers did that too. A kitchen peopled by a woman and assorted kids had an atmosphere very different from that where a woman, a man and assorted kids sat together. Table manners, table settings, especially table conversation and atmosphere changed when there was a Dad around. The atmosphere grew more charged, energy flowing in lines rather than in circles; rights and wrongs fought it out, rather than collapsing in a muddle in the middle.

Zoë liked it that their Dad came only every other Saturday. She quite enjoyed the outings he took them on. There was nothing to object to unless you count a certain boredom, sensed but not fully understood by Zoë and Rebecca, provoked by his inability to get the point of their true-life accounts, by his failure to respond to the games of fantasy at which they and Jane effortlessly excelled.

Between those Father-Days, Rebecca and Zoë almost always had Jane to themselves. Maria didn't count. She added to the atmosphere they enjoyed. She was so like Jane: warm, soft, funny, caressing easily, listening with real interest.

Friday nights before James's visits took on a special quality. The small town close to the large city where they lived itself seemed large and impressive to Zoë and Rebecca. It had one main street where the 'big' shops were. None of these shops had more than two storeys, most had only one, but their floor space appeared vast. The girls and Jane had a routine that allowed for only slight variations. After school and library and home-for-tea they set out, not in their usual direction, but cutting through the churchyard. Each girl held one of Jane's hands, and her head would turn first one way and then the other, and sometimes straight down as the girls leant across her to talk and to giggle at each other. They looked remarkably alike, this woman and her daughters: firm bodies, dark hair bouncing in short unruly curls, light eyes – blue behind glasses for Jane and Rebecca, green for Zoë – bright faces, not pretty but mobile, curious and open. All three talked a lot, excited by the outing, familiar though it would be.

The churchyard contained a number of graves, mostly very old from the beginning of the settlement of the town in the later years of the nineteenth century. Brave English people buried in the new land they had come to with such high hopes for better lives. Dead now, anyway. A new cemetery lay just outside the town, a mat of tended green broken by shiny, ugly slabs with an occasional concrete erection tortured into angel shape. Most people preferred that distance, preferred not to be reminded of cold grey marble over deep dark dirt hugging pale, unlit bones.

On how much better ashes. Light blowy ashes. Translucent, soft, disappearing from the ends of fingers. Now you see them, now you don't. Gone for ever. High, high. Sky high.

Jane's warm live fingers are caught on either side by Rebecca and Zoë as they make the first of their ritual stops. Yvonne Lee is in Zoë's class. She speaks English for her mother who presides over their shop, nodding, smiling encouragement at the customers but totally reliant during her husband's frequent absences on this sombre girl, her daughter, who has managed to learn what is for Mrs Lee the eternally unlearnable English. The regular customers point, pick things up, or wait for Yvonne's help, tiny Yvonne, tinier than Zoë despite two extra years, confident of her place at her mother's side in the life of the shop. Poor Mrs Lee. It is her clever stock-filling which makes of this small place a magic cavern: birds on sticks, paper lanterns, kites, exquisitely embroidered towels and clothes, boxes smelling of camphor. Most thrilling of all are the objects which can be wound into life, to whirl, to walk, to cluck, to coo. Mrs Lee's smiles are lively too, but what does she feel with no adult chat to break up yawning days?

From the long racks under the high ceiling hang the most dazzling of the whirling, whizzing, cooing objects. Sometimes, when she sees favourite customers arriving, Mrs Lee will drag a small step-ladder to the centre of the shop floor, will climb onto it and wind up the objects, making a wild cacophonous display which enchants the onlookers and perhaps Mrs Lee herself who laughs and bobs on the steps of the ladder.

On the tables beneath are the more practical items to be bought on everyday occasions after your eyes have soaked in the glories above. Here are the rubbers, pencil-sharpeners in all kinds of disguise, pencils and pens and small and large notepads. There is always some item that Jane or one of the girls needs.

Zoë is respectful as Yvonne takes the money. The Chinese girl barely reaches the till but delivers back perfect change with a seriousness that separates her totally from the classmate who's only too pleased if Zoë nudges her through the hard words at reading time.

There are other Chinese store-owners in the small town. Mrs Lee's own sister is married to the town's greengrocer. She'll be dragging and heaving sacks of onions, of potatoes, of sweet purplish lumps of kumara, lifting boxes of watermelon, of peaches, grapes and apples throughout the nine months of repeated pregnancies. Her husband's brother sells fish and chips, fish freshly dipped in batter then fried in huge vats of boiling oil while customers wait, wet-mouthed in the narrow, hot shop, for their precious parcel wrapped in newspaper which can be torn across the top to dive into the goodies beneath. But even the most delicious fruit and vegetables, or fish and chips, can't match the magic of Mrs Lee's cavern.

Zoë loves Mrs Lee, and though she is made shy by her limited comprehension that Mrs Lee cannot think or speak in English, she makes a special point, each visit, of smiling hesitantly but firmly at the woman, occasionally telling her things, noting Mrs Lee's careful attention and sure that some of what she's saying is reaching her. She is rewarded, always, with a returned smile and a nodding bow.

Sometimes Mrs Lee will rustle behind the counter, producing, always scrupulously fair, two tiny goodies; strange sweets which taste as odd as their smell; brilliantly coloured fluffy birds, wonderful to stroke; sticks of incense which Jane will light when they get home and which will allow Zoë, eyes pressed tightly shut, to imagine herself all the way to Hong Kong where Yvonne was born.

Whatever the outcome of the visit to Mrs Lee's 'Hong Kong

22

Paradise', Zoë is always surprised, always enchanted. They all say thank you, thank you and goodbye and see you soon. They bow and smile just as Mrs Lee does. They want her to feel at home.

Spirits lifting, spirits soaring. Zoë remembers: the smell of Jane, the touch of Jane. Safe at her side, my face rubs against the pocket of her grey flannel coat and when she bends down over me her scratchy scarf tickles and I push it away and she rubs me on the top of my head and I look up into her face and I see her wide mouth move and I see her eyes behind her glasses do a little jiggle as they look at me and I am safe safe safe in my world and I swing back on my arm, swing back behind her, make my arm long to hide these giant's feelings I have inside me that I don't have names for but they make me giggle and now I press my giggle into her back, my face against her soft bum and she can feel my hot dragon breath sieved through her clothes and she turns around and kneels down so that our faces are at equal height and she looks at me and she has those giant's feelings too, I can tell I can see them and she doesn't know what they are either and she laughs her lovely laugh and calls my Zoë name, Zoë my zoo creature she says, and she puts her face in my neck and snuggles beneath my ear until I shriek and laugh and then she stands up and we all walk on. My mother, my sister, and I.

Jane has structured their route with care, making a large world of this unremarkable place, creating possibility where others might have seen only dreariness. Jane learned early, as a small child among many on an isolated farm, to watch carefully, to note delicate changes, to rejoice in subtlety rather than novelty.

Jane knows that no other shop could compete in magic with the Lees', but their next stop – perhaps the most important of all – is into Jane's other world: her work world, filled with treasures to be discovered by the turning of pages, not the winding of keys.

This is the local public library with rows of books on offer, free, bought for its citizens by the local council, a priority for every small town in this country which prides itself on its cultural heritage, its refinement, its interest in the rest of the world which lies so far away. Each book has a different story to be absorbed, hugged, bits to be read aloud when clever or funny, or best of all, rude or magical.

Some stories will be read again and again; others will be forgotten after the last page is laid to rest inside the covers.

There's double magic here. Not only all the books, familiar rows occasionally broken by the thrilling sight of a new acquisition leading to the pounce, the chance to experience the splendour of a new book, your date stamp at the back, your library number to head the list on the card left behind when the book goes out under your arm. Not only all that, delight enough, but also everyone nodding and smiling at Jane-who-works-there, come back to her work place with her two little girls.

Rebecca and Zoë love the merging of Jane-at-home and Jane-at-work. That Jane's work is with these books which can be borrowed and shared by them, that Jane can bring them to her work place with such pride and even, leaving them to browse, put on her work face and talk in quiet and serious tones to borrowers or other library staff, seems to them a glorious aspect of their Delighty life. They are proud to be welcomed by Miss Durham, the chief librarian, always at her post.

Tonight, this typical Friday night, she emerges from behind the desk where she's been sorting books, looks over the top of her rimless glasses to see them better and greets Jane the Mother with an enthusiasm which is remarkable as she farewelled Jane the Worker only hours before. But Miss Durham is touched. It's her Friday treat to see Jane with Rebecca and Zoë. She's already anticipating the pleasure with which the girls will choose their books and she knows they will, if she has time and asks them, be only too pleased to give her details of the stories they are now returning. Sometimes she allows Rebecca to stamp the books which she and Zoë have chosen, just as if Rebecca were a grown-up on the staff. Rebecca does it with great care, the stamp always newly inked then pressed down in a straight line as her tongue presses against her bottom lip. Rebecca likes to be the oldest.

Miss Durham moves towards them slowly across the polished floor of the library. She is much smaller than Jane and speaks with an English voice after all these years, suggesting more hallowed halls than any she'll find in this raw place. Her blouses are always lacy-edged, with delicate round collars and pearl buttons, each one done up, right to the neck.

Fridays mark the end of the week for almost everyone in the small town. For Jane the days begin with a precious hour alone, reading or just thinking in the big bed before it's time to wake the girls and get them off to school for nine o'clock and herself on to the library. School ends on most days at half past three and Jane leaves the library at four, carrying the shopping she's done in her lunch hour, hurrying home to make sure the girls are there, glasses of milk emptied, biscuits and apples eaten.

Workers here usually begin at eight and have knocked off by four-thirty. Still time for a swim, a run, a game. Time for an hour and a half in the pub before it closes, if you're a man.

Friday nights are gala nights before the barren weekend stretch when nothing is open except the Returned Servicemen's Club, the fish and chip shop and the sweets and ice-cream shop owned by the poor woman rumoured to wear a wig which all the children pray will fall as she bends to scoop for the ice-cream to fill their cones. Cold air comes up to the woman as she bends, once more, once more.

There are other kinds of ice.

In that great land mass which is New Zealand's southern neighbour, winter is beginning.

Antarctica. Nine months of temperatures that could fall to more than $100°$ below zero. It's impossible for most human beings to imagine how cold, how dark, how unsupportive of life that is.

A small group of penguins waddle across a tiny corner of those icy tracts. They seem to be in conversation with each other, but each disappears, apparently separately, into the water which remains to testify that summer is still echoing. The water scarcely moves but soon it will tighten, as though pausing. Drops of water will grip their neighbours, then freeze into a nine-month-long embrace. There will be no more dripping, dripping, splashing or sloshing. There will only be ice, stroked or whipped on its surface by winds that move through the darkness. The sun will neither rise nor set. Morning will not come. Night will fall, and will settle where it lies.

Two

Under the sheet, pulled up over her head, Zoë tries to block out the sounds made by James and Caroline's household, of which she and Rebecca are now a reluctant part. James and Caroline have begun the day as they will end it, fighting. Their children are crying. James shouts first at Caroline and then at his sons and then back at Caroline again for having failed to deal with his sons or, anyway, to silence them. It is morning. Zoë is ten, and must get up.

She escapes to the sea and stands beside it. To her left is the beach running up to meet the wall which binds and encloses it, separates it from the footpath, holds in the sand so that it will not creep across the whole surface of the town, covering it up, causing it to disappear as though it had never been. None of the low wooden buildings in the town is much more than fifty years old, despite the ignorantly hideous memorial strutting out between two sections of the wall which proclaims to any pausing passer-by that here landed early boats which brought pale sick doubting travellers from the other side of the world, looking for a quality of life that would still not easily be found in this unfinished place.

The sea is very cold. Icy. Zoë stands beside it, not waiting to go into it but because here is the place, the only one, where she can be alone but not like that dreadful aloneness she feels when she's crouched beneath the tent of sheets she pitches on her bed. Here, on the deserted beach, in the cold, beside the sea, she sucks deep on the luscious taste of freedom. Ten years old and she knows she is free to brave the cold, to throw herself into the freezing embrace of the sea, to ride the waves and then to dive deep deep beneath them, to let go, to drift, her hair like seaweed, to drift, weightless, like the foetus she once was in that other watery place inside Jane's body. Her mouth would fill with salt. The fish would nudge her and, numbing, she would not mind. She would swell, gently, as water went in to all her secret places inside. *Down by the sea I lost my shoe oh what a funny thing to do* . . .

She savours her freedom to choose the sea. And to reject it. There will be other days yet, she knows, when she'll laugh and race into the water and it will be warm and she can enter and leave it whole and alive. Zoë still wants such days.

The wind is loud in her ears. It blows sand which stings her face. The sound of the waves is also loud. These sounds engulf her. She pulls the rubber bands off the ends of the neat and ugly plaits required by her neat and ugly school and her hair springs into its natural curl and begins a feverish dance in the wind, whipping across her face, mixing with sand and the taste of salt. Her body is braced, bent slightly at the middle. She has lost all her little-girl roundness. She's tall for her age, slim as the smooth driftwood, worn white and beautiful by lifetimes in the sea, which she loves to collect. The tide is low and pieces of driftwood are scattered along the beach, helpless as to their fate. They will be carried in the mouths of dogs, then dropped, or collected by a rare passer-by, or gobbled back into the sea as the tide rises to move across the beach now dry beneath Zoë's feet.

She crouches down, clasps a stick in her hand and begins to draw, pulling back the veneer of dry white sand to reveal the darker wetter sand beneath. Pat Boone has advised writing love letters in the sand and Zoë hums his tune as she carves a huge 'Darling'. And then stops. Runs. Leaps forward and, landing, grinds her heel into that spot where she landed.

Her breaks alone are too few. She is finding peace, and then only elusively, by the sea, where she can exercise her choice to stay alive.

There seemed to have been no such choice for Jane. Her first feelings of disquiet were easily pushed aside by the demands of daily life with Rebecca and Zoë. It was only at night, when the girls slept in their bunk beds next door, that Jane looked at the pain. She felt afraid.

One early evening, when Rebecca and Zoë were involved in a loud game out on the back porch, she stood in her kitchen beside Maria. Both women were chopping vegetables. Jane chopped more

27

and more slowly. Maria continued to peel and chop but was aware of Jane's distraction and willed her to speak.

'Maria.'

Maria stopped at once, turned and looked at her friend, but Jane was again chopping, apparently fascinated by the sight of large string beans becoming many small bean pieces.

Maria's heart beat just a little uncomfortably. This wasn't like Jane. She was deeply reserved but ever to the point if there was a point to be reached. 'What is it?'

'Oh nothing really.' Jane continued to chop, then put down the knife and ran a hand through her thick hair. She glanced at Maria. 'I've had a pain, quite a severe pain really – nothing like I've ever had before. It seems to move around my abdomen in the strangest way. I thought it was heartburn which made me smile a bit as I only ever had that when I was expecting each of the girls . . . then I told myself it was some new variety of period pain. But it's not either of those things.' She picked up the knife again and turned it over in her fingers before running her thumb along its dull edge.

'It seems silly to fuss, but it's the uncertainty really, more than the actual pain. I can't afford to be ill. Not even for a week or two. The girls . . .'

Maria moved to put her arms around Jane though the two women didn't often touch. After a few moments she stepped back, rather awkwardly. 'Look, if you're anxious then you've got to do something. You know as well as I do you're the last person to fuss about nothing. I'd swear you have the word "stoic" imprinted like a cattle mark on each of your bones. You're not going to help those precious girls by neglecting yourself. Are you afraid that it might mean staying in hospital? Something as serious as that?'

'I'm not sure. Maybe that's what I *am* worried about. You know I've never left the girls . . .'

'Well you could now. Good God, Jane, what are friends for? This might be my big break to take care of them and show you what childrearing should really be about! Dr Spock, you've had your final round of applause. Move over for Miss Maria Gilroy, lightening the load for mothers of the world.'

Jane laughed, as Maria had intended her to, and asked, 'What would I do without you?'

28

'Waste your pearls on swine, darling,' came Maria's swift reply.

They gave themselves a feast that night.

The wooden table in the kitchen was covered with an embroidered table cloth bought from Mrs Lee at the end of a delicious hour of indecision and kept in the dresser for special occasions. Rebecca floated white camellias in glass bowls next to each place setting and arranged tall sticks of furry pussy willow to make a centre-piece. Zoë disappeared to the bedroom and emerged minutes later holding aloft Christmas hats which she was insisting that everyone must wear. There wasn't any reason for this celebration, Jane had told the girls, except that she and Maria had decided it was much too long until the next birthday gave them a reason, so to fill the gap they'd have a non-birthday party of roast lamb and potatoes and kumara, string beans, mint sauce and lots of gravy, and for pudding, a mound of pavlova with layers of crisp meringue separated by thick whipped cream and topped with sliced green Chinese gooseberries, smooth orange peaches from a tin, and slimy dots of passion fruit. To wash it down they raided their supply of home-made ginger beer, which tasted of the danger that sometimes refused to be contained by jar or stopper so a jar would explode, its contents shooting high like fireworks at Guy Fawkes time.

Food eaten, table cleared, dishes stacked to be dealt with in the morning: the women and girls laughed and boasted their way through rounds of charades, finding, dividing, acting out and guessing new words, creating a spiral of excitement which could only be unwound, slowly and with pleasure, by each alone in her separate bed.

Next morning Jane woke to a cloudless sky, the first for weeks. A good omen. 'Enough blue in the sky to make a new pair of pants for every sailor in the the world,' she called to the girls as she woke them.

A huge weight seemed to have gone from her shoulders. She knew it was difficult for her to share her anxieties. At home, as a child and young woman, she had seen her own mother with so much to worry about she'd not wanted to add her frets to the load. Her role as James's wife had quickly been established as listener, not talker;

as soother, not complainer. She had grown used to keeping everything inside when it concerned only her, even with Maria. But sometimes keeping it all in, keeping cheerful for and with the girls, was harder even than talking. She would learn to speak up more readily, she told herself. And the pain certainly was gone this morning. Perhaps she had imagined it after all, or it *was* simply worry, indigestion or period.

The pain didn't come back for several weeks, but then it was much fiercer and Jane went at once to Miss Durham to ask for a couple of hours off to visit her doctor, a dull but seemingly capable fellow she had got to know through rounds of mumps and coughs and occasional flu.

She had to sit for some time in the waiting room, flicking through tired copies of the *New Zealand Women's Weekly*, barely distracted by earnest admonitions as to how to get longest use out of her bottling jars, or how to embroider perfectly feminine dresses just like those the tiny Princess Anne was wearing. When, at last, her name was called she went in, closing the door behind her as she began to speak, to say that it was probably nothing at all, but that . . .

The doctor interrupted her, asking her to go behind the screens and take off her clothes. He called in his nurse so that all proprieties should be seen to be observed and then carefully examined Jane, who lay silent now on the narrow high examining couch, who spoke only when spoken to, to indicate more, or less, or yes, here, or no, not there. When he had apparently finished pushing and kneading and considering, the man withdrew to his desk while the nurse waited, watching Jane in silence as she dressed. With her clothes and her coat on, Jane went to sit on the unwelcoming upright chair opposite the doctor's soft swivel armchair and listened to his voice as it said, 'Routine tests . . . hospital . . . just as soon as we can.' Heartier now, 'No need to worry, Mrs Delighty.'

Jane's mind dashed out of the room to make plans for Rebecca and Zoë's safekeeping. Maria was changing clay into pots in the hot North. Damn. It was only to be a couple of days, perhaps James and Caroline . . . although the girls had always protested and whined on the rare occasions when asked to stay overnight there. Only two days. She would talk to them, explain that it would help her most if they could grin and bear it. And afterwards they would all have a treat together which they would plan in scrupulous detail, which would get them through the week which lay ahead before the hospital was ready to admit her.

'What's wrong, what's wrong?' Zoë shouted at Jane, sitting on her knee, her arms around Jane's neck, her face only inches from Jane's, unaware that her voice was high and loud, pulling tighter the band of pain around Jane's head until she feared her scalp would lift to expose the mass of brains beneath.

Rebecca was hanging back, standing like a stork, scraping the back of one leg with the foot of the other, oblivious of the angry red mark with which her leg was protesting. Her eyes were fixed on Jane, her mute request for explanation and reassurance even more desperate to be answered than Zoë's loud demands.

'It's nothing. Really, darlings, it's nothing. But sometimes, especially at night, there've been pains in my tummy bad enough to keep me awake and make me feel tired and grumpy in the morning. The doctor thinks I should find out once and for all what they are and get them fixed. Then I thought, when I come out of hospital – and I'll only be gone a very few days – we could all go camping for a week or so. Maria should be back by then or we could travel up to meet her. The tent needs a good airing – and we do too.'

Rebecca's eyes had left Jane's face. She was staring hard through her glasses at a place on the floor where an ugly stain had interrupted the neat pattern on their rush matting. She couldn't bear to watch Jane, nor listen to her any longer. She cannot tolerate Jane's attempts to cheer them up and distract them. She doesn't want to hear Jane's camping plan which Zoë was attaching to with such excitement. She has never told Jane how much she loathes being away from her on those rare occasions when it has seemed necessary, or when James and Caroline – struck by conscience – have pressed especially convincingly. Their small bright house was enough for her, was all the womb she longed for after a day in the world outside. What mattered to Rebecca, what was real and engaging and safe, was the life she and Jane and Zoë shared together.

After her mother died (R.I.P. Jane Alice Gilroy Delighty, 1917–1955), Zoë found that she could from one day to the next

31

speak Russian – and did, whenever possible. What made it possible was to be out of earshot of adults, who, failing to understand the particular dialect she relished and rolled around her fast-moving pink tongue, laughed and called it names: gobbledygook, rubbish, lies, nonsense, deception.

There was a great deal that Zoë found herself able to express in Russian. She recognized it as a tender and subtle language, without the boundaries and restrictions of English, without 'good' or 'bad' words or words that were suitable for adults but not for children. She could even speak about her dreams and nightmares in Russian, and about those precious dreams she had when she was not actually asleep but perhaps not really awake either. In some of those awake dreams she imagined herself asleep, imagined that having slept she would wake up in her bottom bunk bed in the small house on the hill and Jane would be there, making breakfast for her and Rebecca in the kitchen, calling to them to hurry if they didn't want to be late for school, telling them this was no time to dawdle, coming into the bedroom meaning to be cross but then laughing and kneeling down for a last-minute cuddle.

Zoë believed there was an indescribable place between awake and asleep and that she spent more and more of her time there. Pictures raced through her mind night and day and were as compelling with her eyes open as when her eyes were shut. Her sense of time expanded and spun. She knew she could move backwards and forwards at will. Her sense of so-called reality, never very strong, slipped from its mooring and drifted

She tried to talk about these things, but when she saw incomprehension or pity fill the listener's eyes, she closed up, put up shutters, pulled on that face which cracked jokes, teased and laughed. And how people liked it! Happy-go-lucky Zoë. How quickly she's recovered. What a little toughie. *She'll* be all right.

The girls at school found her Russian highly impressive. They were different girls and no boys at all from those she'd gone to school and played with before her mother died. Now they were Catholics. Catholic girls, little pearls of Our Lady, giggling, studying, above all praying, behind the convent walls which not only kept them in but also protected them from the world outside whose major characteristic was its lack of Catholicism, a world in which, if vigilance was not constantly observed, unmentionable and even unimaginable acts could be perpetrated by those non-Catholics who, empty of faith and goodness, might clutch at little girls. Despite the brown scapular hanging back and front and the silver medal of Our Lady of the Immaculate Conception worn beneath the singlet, beneath the blouse, beneath the gym slip. Their buds are precious and vulnerable to bruising. These girls could too easily fail to grow into perfect white unbruised untouched blooms.

It is, after all, only Catholics who know why little girls must have their legs covered in 30-denier putty-coloured stockings in the South Pacific summer. Who know why blouses must have sleeves, why even a cap sleeve jutting over the shoulder is not enough. Who know why dresses must touch the ground while kneeling. Who know why little girls should never be seen in the floppy navy bloomers they wear for gym. Who know why hats must be worn, white gloves kept white. Who know that it is only desperate envy which makes those non-Catholics laugh at their badges with the precious Sacred Heart of Jesus on them, why they yell *Catholic dogs stink like frogs in their mothers' bathing togs!* in the streets as packs of Catholic girls pass by, panama hats bouncing against each other, occasionally giggling or whispering behind hands, more often turning their eyes, soft with pity, at those sad people yet to be given the gift of faith.

The transition from being a non-Catholic to a Catholic passed in a dream for Zoë. It was more acting, a drama played out in a new language, Latin, which was stranger and less beautiful to her than her recently acquired Russian. In this new drama there was the smell of incense, the sounds of choirs and organs and deep priests' voices and higher altar boys' voices. There were the rich sights of vestments, altar drapes, massed flowers and holy pictures. There were constant reminders, in Latin, in English, and in the oblique language of symbol and imagery, of the central theme: she, Zoë, was essentially bad and had ceaselessly to struggle to rid herself of her desires for worldly pleasures, even for those pleasures she did not yet know she desired, and to move humbly, one step at a time, one hand in the Blessed Virgin's and both eyes on the priest, on the painful glorious road to salvation. But only if she had not done . . . so many things. And had she? The searching, the probing, the

33

vigilance which were all part of the daily examination of conscience were hard for Zoë to learn. Life was richly complicated. She could see many pictures, hear many voices: which were those of saints or guardian angels? Or of devils? The Ten Commandments were soon carved as deeply into her mind as the illustrators' renditions on holy cards of the words themselves, carved by Moses in English onto tablets of stone which he was to carry down from the mountain so that women and men would know the rights against which so many wrongs could be committed. Even in that secret no-words language of the soul. Unto eternity.

To Zoë the two years since Jane died already seem like an eternity. She is two years away from the mother who gave her life. It is one year since she was offered the consolations of Our Holy Mother the Church. Her relationship with this Mother will, she is assured, last for ever. If only she avoids sin, and eternal damnation.

James Delighty began to take instructions in the teachings of the Roman Catholic Church shortly before Jane's death. Caroline, his wife, had, as the consummation of the single act of rebellion in her life, married James 'outside the Church'. This marriage was celebrated beneath a photograph of Winston Churchill in a registry office at four o'clock on a Friday afternoon, in time to drink a very small amount of extremely expensive imported French champagne before catching the overnight sleeper north. There the newly-weds would spend a week in the vacated flat of James's only brother before returning to the cramped flat they had rented three years earlier in a quiet street in a nice suburb not far from where Caroline's heart-broken and prayerful family lived.

Caroline had always been such a joy to them. Small, fair-haired, and blessed, truly blessed with the loveliest of natures, the only daughter among five sons, she was the pearl in the oyster of their lives. When she married James in the registry office, when she effectively continued to live with him in a state of sin as that was no marriage which they could recognize, they blamed themselves: they had spoiled her, indulged her, petted her too much, prayed for her too little. They had given her a first name chosen for its prettiness rather than its saintliness. Why, she could easily be mistaken for a Protestant.

Until she met James, Caroline had strictly obeyed their injunctions about avoiding non-Catholic men. There were few temptations in the building firm where she worked as a valued assistant to the manager, and outside the office all the social events of her life revolved around her family or the Church. But James had been so persistent, so persuasive: incarnate of all that was forbidden.

The experience of rebellion was brand new for Caroline, and became confused for her with her first experience of sexual desire.

James pressed her for not just more kisses but more touches and then more and more until she was touched all over and still wanting more and not just on the outside of her body but on the inside too, in those places where she had never ever touched herself, where she washed with the face flannel folded into four, where she dried quickly and without affection, and now that place was not dry but wet and open. Her back is flat on a strange bed. Her knees are bent, not pressed together but apart. James looms over her, his face is strange. It must be love oh what would my mother think oh God oh God: stop.

And when Caroline saw the pain on her mother's face, as she was with James more and more and with her family less and less, she didn't know what to do with her own twin pain except to bury it and return to James for more touches, more caresses, to allow him more bites at this apple of her daddy's eye until, at last, that daddy told her she was either to pull herself together, to behave with the modesty he expected of his only daughter, or she was to leave, to get out and find some other place to call home.

Telling James about this, describing to him her father's words, unconsciously mimicking the melody of his voice, Caroline had grown righteous. How could he possibly throw her out? Mother of God, she was his daughter, was she not?

By allowing that righteousness in, she began, just faintly, to loosen her grip on her brief, energizing spasm of rebellion. This would lead, soon, to a lessening of sexual passion too, until even the memory of that wholly-felt unholy sexual desire would be difficult, and abhorrent, to recall.

35

Three years after James had left Jane, three months and one week after her marriage, Caroline's second and last son was born. She named him Brendan after her father and his. This gesture of family solidarity was seen as reconciliatory, and gradually brought Caroline's parents and four of her brothers back into her life. The fifth brother, a priest, knew that it would be wrong to see a sister living in sin with a non-Catholic person of the opposite sex and her two bastard sons. Though he prayed for her.

Caroline's initial reunions with her family took place on neutral ground, in the tea rooms of one of the larger city department stores where women dressed like inelegant, late-Edwardian maids brought them pots of strong tea and delicate white-bread sandwiches and plates of mixed iced cakes. Caroline could manage only one child or the other in these places, so had to arrange the meetings for times when she could persuade James to be home to babysit for her. Conversation was strained by Caroline's need to suggest an exalted state of happiness, a rediscovery of Eden, even if she had entered that garden through the Gate of Sin. But after some months Caroline went, without her children and without prior arrangement to her mother's home and sat again in the kitchen where for most of her lifetime she had sat among relatives and priests and her own brothers, and she put her head on her arms, folded on the big table, and wept. And when her mother, for the first time in years pulled her towards her until Caroline's tears were falling on the older woman's cotton print dress, Caroline thought James could keep his hot touches, his demanding fingers asking for things which couldn't be right and her a mother herself, now, and his shocking words in her ears asking her to touch him down there. She had chosen that, had traded in these fine embraces from a mother who was at six-thirty Mass every morning of her life, a daily communicant who would have died before agreeing to do the things which she had done and even liked. Her mother would not be *asked*. Anyone could see she was a woman to be respected. Did James ask her because he did not, God help her, any longer respect her?

Caroline cried and cried. For her mother and the grief she had caused her; for her sons, to whom she would never be the good, the unselfish, the positively saintly mother her own mother had been to her; for James, still the most attractive man she had ever known, despite his increasing lack of attention to her when they were anything but horizontal. Most of all, she cried for herself.

When the front of the print dress was thoroughly soaked, her mother said to Caroline, 'We'll have had enough of that by now, will we not? Here, dry your great self and I'll make us some tea and tomorrow we'll go together to see Father O'Reilly about you and your wee boys and that so-called husband of yours, and we'll ask the good sisters to make a novena on your behalf.' She picked up the kettle and filled it before turning back to her daughter.

'Dry your tears, Caroline Rosaleen Delighty.' Caroline's mother acknowledged her married name for the very first time. 'It could be that we'll be bringing new souls into the Church, not losing one at all.'

It was not the words themselves but her mother's sense of conviction and authority that won Caroline. Her longings for James had been fuelled not only by rebellion but also by pride in his apparent sophistication, much greater than that of any man her schoolmates might have married, and by the intense feelings of flattery she had experienced that he would leave a clever older woman like Jane for someone like herself.

All her life Caroline had been told what to do by her father, her mother, by the nuns at school and by the priests interpreting for Our Holy Mother the Church. That pattern of subjection had been briefly set aside for the novel experience of being told what to do only by James. Now, listening to her mother, needing to find some sense in the confusion she increasingly felt about her importance in James's life, she slipped back inside that pattern as a snake might long to slip back into a once-shed skin, wriggling a little, aware of the occasional new wrinkle, but content inside a familiar place.

James listened without any perceptible interest when Caroline came home and told him she had made the beginnings of peace with her family, but, as he thought it over, he realized he was rather pleased.

He did occasionally acknowledge to himself that he and Caroline had cheated each other, but that his was the greater blame. He knew he had been genuinely moved by Caroline's charm and her eager belief in his superiority. He knew he had been deeply aroused by that sexual innocence which he had speedily made a thing of the past. He also knew she deserved better. That she would – in the not much longer run – have been considerably happier with a man of her own background, with whom her brothers could watch rugby, and play pool or cards. Most of all, she would have been happier with a Catholic whom her parents could have welcomed into their home with affection and pride.

It gradually became obvious to James that the relief Caroline was experiencing from the renewal of contact with her family was becoming complicated by the re-emergence of her Catholic conscience. She was beginning to see herself with increasing pain as a woman living in a state of mortal sin with a man to whom, in the eyes of the Church, she wasn't married, and with sons who were neither legitimate nor baptized.

The strain between James and Caroline grew as quickly as undergrowth in a rain forest, and was as damp in its sadness. James felt it most acutely when he returned, every other Saturday, from his outings with Rebecca and Zoë, knowing that Caroline had spent the time with their sons at her old family home.

He wanted to speak, to find words to say, he was not quite sure what – but it was Caroline, nervous and pink-cheeked, who forced him to confront their uneasy situation.

'James,' she began, 'I can't go on sleeping with you. Well, not making love, anyway. You know what I mean. I want to go to confession, to be able to go to Mass and take communion again, and that would mean being able to say I won't sleep with you until we're properly married. I mean, married in the Church.'

She paused, waiting to test his reaction, saw none, and started again. 'I do still love you. It's not that I don't. I love you more than ever.' She didn't stop to test the truth of this last remark. 'But I can't see what else I can do. I'm sure this is right. I've been thinking about it for ages.'

Still James said nothing, sat unmoving in his chair as she continued to stand above him. Caroline grew desperate. Her voice rose. 'I know I can't explain it well. Perhaps if you saw Father O'Reilly it'd all make more sense.'

James finally directed his mouth to move, words to emerge, and they stunned her. 'Right Caroline, I will. I'll phone your Father O'Reilly tomorrow.'

38

He did not. But he did take care to put as little sexual pressure on Caroline as he regarded as humanly possible. He did offer to mind the two boys when she went to Mass, although Caroline usually refused the invitations to her mother's house for breakfast afterwards so James would not be exhausted by prolonged child care.

James also began to read, privately and without comment to Caroline, books by Ronald Knox, Teilhard de Chardin, pamphlets sent out in plain brown envelopes by the Catholic Truth Society, biographies of great male philosopher saints, even soldier saints. He also began to recall moments in his life when an individual had offered him a kindness or an insight he had badly needed. As he searched for clarity among his memories, it seemed to him that a significant number of those individuals had been, themselves, Catholic.

When their sons were old enough to begin to shape questions and to wonder, Caroline wanted to take them to Mass with her and it made perfect sense for James to offer to accompany her, as how much praying could get done with two lively kids to handle? So it became a habit. And also a habit that after Mass, at which James would stand and sit and kneel and turn the pages of a missal along with everyone else, they would go to Caroline's former home for breakfast and talk, to read copies of the *Tablet* and the *Zealandia*, and it would be almost afternoon before they returned to the sad discomfort of their own flat.

James liked these new habits. They provided an oasis for him in a bleak week which offered little else in the way of consolation. He knew himself to be an outsider in the large steamy kitchen with its array of faded sentimental portraits of saints, but he appreciated the many ways in which Caroline's family tried to make him feel at home, almost one of them. He was genuinely fascinated by the sense of belonging they had, with each other as immediate family, and with their apparently real sense of Church as family. He envied their certainty.

He had neither the intention nor the desire to become more securely part of that world. He had recognized the disappointment of his own life and in the face of that was grateful for this unexpected possibility to 'borrow' a culture which distracted him, a set of feelings, references, convictions which he had barely known existed.

It was Jane's illness that threw him into a chaos of uncertainty. He was overwhelmed by sensations of guilt and anger, betrayal and fear. He imagined that he knew how it would feel to be marooned on quicksand, to be sucked down quickly quickly, to disappear forever as a ton of fine sand filled in and smoothed out above his head.

Jane had always been strong and dependable. Could she really be that ill? He had met her when she was in her first uncertain year at teachers' training college and he was in his final, marvellously optimistic year of architectural studies. She had been shy in a way that only a country girl newly come to the big city can be shy. Yet even then she had an air about her of confidence that needed no display and came from a deep safe place. That was what had attracted him. He had wanted to know that place.

But if that safe place was not inside Jane, and certainly wasn't inside Caroline or himself, perhaps the only way he would find it was in something larger than a human body: in the body of the Church.

His reading began again. His attention to the detail of the ritual of the Mass increased. When his head was bowed he began, tentatively and with great self-consciousness, to string words together in the manner of a prayer. Within months he found himself praying whenever he could wrench out time alone: in his car after he'd parked in the yard and before he went in to face the frustrations of the day; at night in the bed he shared, without sexual intimacy, with Caroline; as he sat on a bench in the park while his sons raced with a ball before him, calling in vain for his attention.

Caroline noticed his distraction and put it down to his worry about Jane for whom she herself was certainly prepared to pray, if only to assuage the guilt she continued to experience at having 'stolen' that woman's husband. She wondered, often, if James was still a little in love with Jane. Things were so bad between them, in this hollow place of their own marriage, yet she knew James wouldn't leave her as he had left Jane. Without being able to name it, she could sense his defeat. She regarded his weekly attendance at Mass only as a link in the weak chain between them.

When James at last told Caroline he had contacted one of the diocesan retreat houses, had met a priest, a retreat master, whom he

40

liked and who was prepared to work with him through the months of instructions, she had to fight back surprise. She knew she should have been thrilled. Hadn't she and her family been praying for this for years now? But she also noticed other thoughts darting into her mind like the arrows that darted into the body of St Sebastian, the holy martyr. If James became a Catholic, if Jane died – Jesus, Mary and Joseph, let that not be – they could, they surely would get married in the Church. She would, then, be with James until death did them part. Forever. She had never thought of leaving James. There had, almost at once, been the babies, and anyway, she loved him. Of course she did. But their life together was empty, not only of physical love which could always start again when they were joined anew by priest and God, but also of any real interest in each other. Even their boys were a source of irritation rather than pleasure to James. Perhaps he blamed her for their existence, though she'd left all that side of things to him. He was the one who'd been married before. She hadn't minded when she became pregnant. That was what marriage was for and even if they were not, strictly speaking, married at that time, they were as-good-as.

Ian and Brendan had become fine boys, both of them, with her fair colouring and James's strength and height. But her pleasure in them was constantly under threat. They seemed to displease James, sometimes simply by their presence, and she had constantly to be alert to keep them, as far as was possible, out of their father's still-lustrous but fast-thinning hair.

Three

The roundabout and swings sit high to the side of the big recreation grounds where on weekdays teams of high-school girls practise the marching that will transform them into a uniformed, vivid mass of non-individuality, a multi-girl creature of yellow, red or green when the team competitions are held and bands bellow and parents applaud.

This is where weekend rugby is played by the talented and the yearning, acolytes all in the great New Zealand religion. This is where track races are held, faster faster across uneven grass, and where seagulls sit to squawk and shit when they tire of the littered beach.

Zoë loves the swings. At ten she is almost too old. She must hold her legs out high in front of her if she is not to scrape her feet as the swing carries her down from that high soaring place where she longs to stay. This is not her only way of flying. She can also fly down stairs, hardly touching the carpet. She has little access to stairs, however, in this country of single-storey buildings. The stairs at school are impossible. They are crowded with girls forbidden to talk between classes who make eager compensation, pressing heads or hands together, or, if pious, pausing before niches set into walls which contain plaster-of-paris statues of Little Saint Theresa or of Jesus with His Sacred Heart displayed, to nod their heads in deep respect and ostentation.

Zoë loves the roundabout too. One foot hits the ground only long enough to keep the rough wooden structure whirling. Both her hands grip the iron divider between sections, in one of which sit little children. As Zoë whirls them under the hot sun she shouts and sings to them in Russian and they catch her jokes and laugh with her.

Ho, ho, ho. Zoë hasn't a care in the world. She has penetrated the mysteries of foreign languages. Out of no named place words tumble to create stories which make people laugh and admire her and ask for more. And when any kid, new to school or playground, says, 'I bet your mother . . .' Zoë can look that kid straight in the eye and without a blink say, 'I haven't got a mother. My mother's dead. I'm an orphan. Russian.' (And probably royal, she adds under her breath.)

My mother, my other. I am in her bed, my favourite place and hers. Pillows are piled high behind us, her head rests against them. My head is lying at her side, against one of the breasts which she likes to tell me I ate from for so long, her nipple in my mouth, joined together as warm sweet milk trickled down my throat and into my tummy which was round and fat.

I stretch my legs as long as possible for I am a tall and graceful knight who can tame fierce dragons and ride like north winds, but they only reach beneath her knees. I want to lie on top of her so, talking to her, I clamber up, crowing, calling aloud, making a play: 'Let me ride on you my snow white beastie. Take me fast to London town.'

She wriggles and moves down in the bed and I pretend to collapse; then I can lie down too with my face in her neck, lying along the length of her body so I can feel her under every inch of my front, can feel how she's much wider and longer than me. I press my body down onto hers, though gently; she mustn't get squashed. I shut my eyes and I am on a raft. She is my raft, my safe place, and we are floating floating on high seas, then gently in a lagoon, hardly moving at all. If I were to open my eyes now and look down I would see brilliant coloured coral beneath the raft under the bright blue sea, speckled by the movement of fast and tiny fish. I want to be able to stretch my arms down on either side of her to keep her in this place beneath my body forever, to go on feeling the way her heart is beating. I want to touch her soft breasts with my hands. I want to hold them. I would like to suck her breasts again, just like I used to, but I know that I can't, that she won't let me, even in a game.

My cheek is against the beating pulse in her neck. I bury my toes

43

into that fatty place above the inside of her knees. I burrow in. I don't breathe so that I will be as light as a feather so that she will hardly notice that I'm here, so that she could even get up and walk around without noticing I'm now a limpet attached to her from neck to knee, heart beating against heart, beating with hers, joined to her, soaked into her, part of her. I am the warm fat keeping her from feeling cold. My mouth dribbles. Water comes out of it making a little puddle in the hollow of her neck. Oh Zoë, she says, pretending to be cross. You baby, dribbling all over me. And I am a bit ashamed as it's true that only babies and very old people let water fall from their mouths but I'm feeling so relaxed here that this little flow didn't seem like something to dam behind my teeth. I put my mouth on the place where the dribble is and suck it back in. All gone and clean now, I say to her. And she wriggles some more and isn't really cross, but after a few minutes she pulls herself up, her back is against the pile of squashed pillows and my bottom sits on her tummy and my back is against her knees which are bent high like a book-end and she bounces me and we begin to sing, begin the same words at the same moment: '*And when he was up he was up, and when he was down he was down, and when he was only half-way up he was neither up nor down. Oh the Grand Old Duke of York . . .*'

Hearing us singing, Rebecca comes in and climbs into the big bed too beside Jane who hugs Rebecca to her side and I lean forward, scarcely breathing, to give Jane butterfly kisses, my eyelashes moving up and down, up and down against her cheeks until she is laughing and wriggling and calling out to her big girl Rebecca to save her. Until she is begging me to stop.

At her Catholic school Zoë was, initially, a novelty. Not just because she had no mother and spoke Russian, but because she was a convert. A special person, not born with the gift of faith like the other girls but someone who had the gift of faith brought to her. Rather like the Angel Gabriel brought the news of her Immaculate Conception to the Blessed Virgin Mary.

James had, he believed, offered Rebecca and Zoë a fair choice after they came to live with him and Caroline and Ian and Brendan in the old house he had bought to accommodate them all.

No one would dream of *forcing* them to become Catholics, he had said. Anyway, Catholicism wasn't like that. It was a gift offered to some, not all, to accept or not, though the refusal of this gift could lead to a lifetime of unhappiness. He was only asking them to visit Father Malley on Wednesday afternoons after school so that at least they would understand what was so important to the rest of their family. (Not our family, not our family, Rebecca and Zoë each litanized, in silence.) Having listened to what Father Malley had to say, James went on, they could then make up their own minds.

So two little girls, reluctant emigrées from their former religion and father-free home, sat with a young priest who loved God deeply and experienced great awe that he had been blessed with the vocation which meant saintly women three times his age called him Father, looked at him with respect, stood up for him when he entered a room and knew that he would have the answers, should they want to ask the questions.

Of course Father Malley also understood that when they saw him they were seeing Christ's humble representative on earth and not someone who had once wept and cursed and almost turned his back on prayer when, in his last year at school, despite three weeks of daily rounds of the Stations of the Cross, he had failed to make a place in the First Fifteen and thereby win the love and admiration of his father on earth for ever. His father on earth had been an All Black, had played rugby for New Zealand in Wales and South Africa, had kicked hard balls through high goal posts, with nothing on his feet but browned calluses. He had made of himself a glorious legend and young Danny Malley could not even make it into the school First Fifteen.

Oh how he had wept in the dark privacy of night, and then had gradually come to understand that God might have other intentions for him and when he told his father that he would enter the seminary if it were God's will they should accept him, he had at last seen the leap of proud joy into his father's eyes, and his father hugged him as he'd not done since Danny was a tiny child and told him how blessed the whole family was by this event and had gone at once to the Returned Servicemen's Club to share the good news with his mates there, and was helped home only when his celebrations had been brought to an end by his passing out cold, flat on the lino-covered floor.

Lamb of God who takest away the sins of the world, pray for us.

Rebecca liked Father Malley. She blushed when he spoke to her and sometimes he noticed and blushed too, uneven red blotches rising to spread over his sandy skin and travelling up beyond his ears where his hair was cut short. Rebecca remembered from one week to the next the stories he told them and when he began to ask them to learn by heart the answers to catechism questions she always had them right, though sometimes she hung back to let Zoë give the wrong answer first.

Zoë wondered if Father Malley would prefer to see Rebecca on her own but when she suggested that she could wait for Rebecca outside, or at the swings, Rebecca looked shocked and reminded Zoë in a voice not entirely her own that they had promised James they would at least listen to what Father Malley had to say.

Father Malley lent Rebecca illustrated stories of the saints and urged her to read with special care the stories of young girls, scarcely older than herself, who died rather than letting men have their sinful way with them. These girls became virgin martyrs and their souls went straight to heaven where choirs of angels sang at the tops of their voices and jubilant saints thronged to welcome them.

There were no boy virgin martyrs. It was something special, just for girls, a prize for holding back the vast tide of male lust.

There were also stories of girls who had been visited here on earth by the Blessed Virgin Mary, Jesus Christ's own mother who brought healing water up through a spring in the ground, or gave them warnings for the world which the world has ignored, warnings so dire that the Pope himself fainted and his hat fell off when he peeked into the envelope that contained the note on which the warnings were written. Since which time he has had the hiccups constantly, even in his sleep.

Father Malley didn't tell them all of this himself. He shared with them only the bare bones. The flesh was added by Ian or Brendan or any one of their million cousins who liked to whisper in a creepy voice to Rebecca or Zoë that their family always included a nightly decade of the rosary for them, offered up for their conversion.

46

Zoë was unimpressed by these stories of visions and voices. None of this was new to her. But the drama of martyrdom appalled and compelled her. She and Rebecca spent hours in bed discussing what they thought they would, or would not, be able to bear. Being squashed between doors as rocks are placed on top like St Margaret: no. Being burned at the stake like Joan of Arc: maybe. Being eaten by starving lions, having limbs torn from a still-alive body as carts pull in opposite directions: no. Being stabbed to death while clasping a crucifix and a bunch of roses to your barely developed bosom and protesting your purity: yes.

Yes too, eventually, to Father Malley's suggestion that if they were baptized now he could prepare them to take their first holy communion when their brother Brendan did, on the Feast of the Ascension just six weeks away. (Not *our* brother, Rebecca and Zoë each silently contradicted.) After all, how could they possibly disappoint all those people who had knelt, and prayed, rosary beads slipping between steepled fingers, for just this Yes? After all, if they refused, would it seem they had not been *offered* that precious gift which everyone around them regarded as their most prized possession?

Zoë wondered if Rebecca really did have the gift. She knew all the answers to the questions in the catechism. She could have earnest conversations with Father Malley while Zoë wriggled and searched in increasing desperation for a moment of distraction or escape, no longer amused by even the deepest red of Father Malley's blushes. Sometimes Rebecca even asked *James* to explain to her what a story or answer meant.

At other times Zoë was pretty sure Rebecca simply wanted to please Father Malley, the first man apart from James they had ever spent time alone with, and a much nicer man than James on the whole. At least he listened to them without always interrupting, and seemed to find what they had to say of some interest. Zoë longed to ask Rebecca outright: 'Do you really want to be baptized? Do you really have this gift of faith? And if so, what does it *feel* like?'

But since Jane died, since they left their home and came to live in this strained household, Zoë and Rebecca have found it increasingly difficult to talk about many things that matter. They learned to avoid each other's eyes when Jane was dying and this has become a habit, reinforced by the inability of any adult to mention their dead mother, except in sanctimonious flashes of such piety that Jane herself is entirely lost and Zoë is frantic, furious, cheated of the flesh and blood real person drifting off far and fast, even from her memories.

Four

Two little girls sit at opposite ends of a closed-in verandah at the front of a wooden farmhouse. Rebecca is lying flat on her stomach, her nose buried in an ancient rug stretched out over loose-fitting floorboards. Beneath the cracks, if she was to look, she would be able to see the hard-packed earth below. Her fingers are pressed tight into her ears. She can hear a humming inside her head, high pitched and constant. Her glasses lie on the floor beside her. Her eyes are screwed up as tightly as her muscles will allow, so tightly that nothing, not a single tear, can escape. She is on the alert, tensed for escape. But there is no escape. She is scarcely breathing.

Zoë sits as far from Rebecca as the length of the verandah permits. Her back is against the wooden wall of the house. Her knees are drawn up to give her forehead a resting place. This end of the verandah smells mouldy, perhaps from the boxes of old books and faded copies of the *Freelance* and the *Auckland Weekly* stored there in wooden boxes for re-reading on a rainy day.

Zoë is muttering to herself, counting, again and again. She is changing her rhythm: *one-and-a, two-and-a, three-and-a.* She repeats this chant and feels comfortable with it. She begins to sway, back and forth, hitting the wall behind her. She will not cry, whimper, ask for sympathy. She is growing a mask, one that will become many. Today the mask exists only in its most embryonic form. Her chanting and swaying is interrupted by a flash of terror which takes persistent, repeated swaying and counting and counting and swaying to overcome.

Jane's first two days in hospital were unremarkable. The girls had gone off reluctantly to James and Caroline but Jane had asked James to be sure to spend some time alone with them, to take them to the pictures perhaps, which would be a special treat for them, though

49

she emphasized how helpful this would be to Caroline, getting the visitors out of her way.

The pain was so concentrated and constant now that Jane was experiencing it as part of herself, but the tests provoked new pain as hospital staff pushed and pulled and invaded her body with tubes and liquids and needles. When her second day of tests was over she was exhausted, more tired than she could ever remember feeling, even after giving birth.

She was relieved, almost euphoric, to get back home and longed for James to arrive to return Rebecca and Zoë. A neighbour had sent in some cold lamb which, with pickles, tomatoes and fresh bread, would do them for their evening meal. She certainly didn't seem up to cooking, not this first night.

As soon as James had parked his car the girls leapt out and ran up the path and the steps to the door, shouting with pleasure as she stood there to meet them, to bend down and kiss them, to hug them both and kiss them again. James closed the car doors and followed slowly, pausing to inspect some shrubs as his daughters and their mother reunited.

'How was it Jane?'

She looked at him. 'Oh, much as you might expect. No results yet of course. I won't know for about a week. I'm not too worried but I've been really quite off-colour. And I hate that. You know me.'

James squirmed. He had no wish to be reminded that he does, or did, indeed know Jane.

He glanced back at his car, vehicle of escape, then to Jane again. 'The girls were fine. They missed you, of course, but I took them to the pictures as you suggested. I think they enjoyed that.' He paused. 'You should rest now Jane, or at least get an early night. You look tired. Let me know if there's anything . . . well, you know, if I could be of any help?' He kicked the step with his scuffed tan shoe. 'I'd better be off, but let me know.'

To Jane's surprise he leant forward and kissed her, somewhere between her mouth and cheek. She grew warm, uncomfortable. Oh well, she thought, I guess the bugger has some feelings after all.

The next time Jane had to go into hospital it was to undergo major surgery and she had been warned she would have to stay there some weeks. There was no question of the girls accepting several weeks exile with James and Caroline. Besides, they would then have to go to a strange school. That would certainly be too much.

She walked around for several days with the uncomfortable knowledge of this impending hospital stay a secret known only to her, to her doctor and to anyone else who might wish to look at her file and see the words, 'suspected malignancy'. Jane knew how seriously ill she was but out of love and long habit her uppermost concern was what to do with Rebecca and Zoë while she had to be away from them. How could she make it easiest for them, most tolerable, most nearly normal?

There was also the problem of telling Miss Durham, knowing that in her absence extra work would fall on Miss Durham, already at the library for such long hours that Jane has secretly wondered if she has anywhere else to go, despite the visits she has made to Miss Durham's tiny tidy flat by the sea.

Miss Durham first, and then the girls: she must pull herself together and take some action.

Before Jane had a chance to speak to Miss Durham, Maria came back from the North, tanned, vigorous, longing to see Jane, to share every detail of the time away, of the skill she had developed in her craft, of the man – married of course, but – with whom she had been spending blissfully unrestful nights.

Maria had almost forgotten the single conversation she'd had with Jane about the mysterious pain. Jane had seemed much brighter after that evening, really, her usual self, and nothing more had been mentioned. But now, as Maria walked into the house, Zoë was saying to her, even while she was still being kissed, 'Mummy's been away, in the hospital, and we had to stay with Caroline and James.'

Maria stared up at Jane from the place where she was kneeling on the floor by Zoë. Jane looked away, laughed nervously, and coughed as Maria asked, 'My God, what the hell was wrong? Why didn't you tell me? When was this?'

'Oh good heavens, you'd only have come back, and it was just for a couple of days. The girls were wonderful. They came back from James and Caroline's claiming to be suffering from advanced maternal deprivation but still able to beat me hollow at our first game of charades. So much for suffering!'

51

'Jane, I can *see* the girls are fine and hear it too.' She turned to grin at Rebecca and Zoë who were dancing around her making what they thought were attractive whoops of welcome. 'But what about you?'

'I'm fine too, just fine.' Jane didn't meet Maria's intent gaze. 'And do we have to wait forever to see what's in those huge parcels in your basket? I know they're for us.'

Maria had no choice but to accept Jane's postponement of any discussion she might be willing to have, but when Jane left the library the next day she saw Maria's stylish old blue Jowett Javelin standing outside with Maria leaning against it, opening the door for her.

'Get in Jane, no arguments. I'm taking you home but first we're going down to the beach for a bit of a walk and a talk.'

Jane was astonished, and touched. She knew how important Maria's job was to her and how rarely Maria would voluntarily cut her day short. Maria and Jane had met at teacher's training college. Jane had known no one and it had taken her all the courage she could summon to walk into the great hall where the first-year students had been told to gather. At the country high school she had attended, been head prefect and dux of, there were never more than a hundred pupils, despite the many miles over which children were brought in by bus. She had known every one of them, every one of them had known her, and her brothers and sisters.

She had felt completely alone in what she had perceived that day as a huge crowd of faces, all animated as they talked to friends. When the room was called to order she slipped into the end of a row as inconspicuously as possible. A roll was shouted out from the stage and when 'Gilroy' was bellowed Jane was astonished to hear not only her own voice but that of the girl next to her call 'Yes' in unison. She had turned with curiosity to this namesake, and had been delighted when the girl giggled and passed her a note asking if she was the daughter of the long-lost Marmalade Marmaduke Montgomery Gilroy.

Jane had to reply that this glamorous father was not hers; but all was not lost as, when the assembly came to an end, the girl asked Jane if she was there alone and, seeing Jane nod reluctantly, gathered her into her crowd of city friends.

52

From that first day Maria and Jane had been 'best friends', sharing a great deal more than mere surname. What they did not share was a love for teaching. Jane had taken to it at once, but Maria was constantly searching for alternatives, hating the chaotic classroom setting and unable to reconcile herself to sharing her time with so many youngsters at once.

At about the time that Jane had given up work to wait for the imminent birth of Rebecca, Maria finally landed the perfect job. She was taken on by the Department of Education's Correspondence School, teaching children in areas too remote for school buses to gather them up to a catchment country school. She was to deal with each of these pupils on a one-to-one basis, sending them out assignments and notes, and receiving back from them finished assignments, drawings, long newsy letters filled with detail of their lives in isolated backwaters. Like all the other teachers at the school, she made radio broadcasts too, for those pupils who lived within radio reception areas. Invariably her broadcasts would bring a new shower of letters as her pupils responded to their imagined picture of her in the big city talking to them through the microphone, telling her what their Mum had said as they had listened together, or their Dad if the whole family had gathered for the event.

After her holiday Maria would have been more caught up with it all than usual, keen to begin working through the precious life-line of mail that would have continued even over the holidays, and to meet up again with her colleagues.

Jane was thrown offguard by Maria's arrival. Like many women who have learned early to lean on no one, Jane was almost absurdly moved to have someone else take charge. Before they reached the beach she had told Maria the worst, or what she then believed to be the worst.

She had cancer, there could be almost no doubt. But of course it was operable. She was, in fact, to be operated on by the very best surgeon available in just a couple of weeks, as soon as she had time to arrange her affairs . . . to see to the girls. The few days she'd already spent in hospital had been unpleasant, but not much worse than that. Really, she couldn't complain. Even James had been quite decent.

Maria stopped her car and parked it by the beach restraining wall. The women got out and walked down to and along the sand, in silence. Jane was leaning, just slightly, towards Maria, though neither woman was aware of this. It was, Jane was experiencing again, such a relief to *tell*. But Maria looked dismayed.

'Please don't worry. Of course it's a shock and I must admit to having been through a fair few "why me's" in the dark of the night, but good heavens, I'm only thirty-six and as strong as a horse. I'll be fine in a month or two, you'll see.'

The women stopped and stood where the water began to lick the edge of the sand. Maria took Jane's hand and traced a circle in the palm with her fingertip, breathing deeply from her stomach and attempting to calm herself. Jane was at the very centre of her life, had always been a dear and good friend, but since James left and they had been able to spend more time together, Jane had become the central pivot of her existence, crowded and happy though that was with work at the Correspondence School, with other friends, with occasional and usually unsuitable lovers, with theatre and pottery. She grew calmer, holding Jane's hand. Touching Jane was like that; it seemed to settle Maria, though she would never have embarrassed Jane by mentioning this.

Maria kicked aside a piece of driftwood then said in a relatively cheerful voice, 'Perhaps the simplest thing would be if I got someone to come in to water my plants and feed the cat so I could move into your house while you're in hospital, and perhaps for a bit after that too. Then I can take care of the girls: they'll be able to go to school as usual and when you've had your op and are home again we can all take care of each other until you're entirely well.'

Jane's habits of self-sufficiency rose up and she wanted to protest against this disruption to Maria's life, but stronger than that impulse was her knowledge of how much she needed her friend. What else could she do but thank her, accept, hug Maria swiftly and fiercely, then race her, a sandal hanging from either hand, along the sand and back to the parked car.

The night before Jane was scheduled to have her operation, Maria arranged for a neighbour's daughter to stay with Rebecca and Zoë. Jane had insisted on taking herself to hospital, carrying one small bag and travelling by bus, so Maria saw the room for the first time with Jane already settled in the high, hard bed. The hospital had allocated Jane a single room on the ground floor. The wall beyond Jane's bed had huge, floor-to-ceiling glass sliding doors. Although it was dark the silky curtains were still open and Maria could just discern that in daylight Jane would look out from her bed onto flowers and bushes. She noticed an easing of tension within herself. It could be worse. At least Jane would have some privacy in this room. She had dreaded being in a ward. She was such an intensely private person and would hate to be ill and vulnerable in front of strangers.

Maria pulled up a chair and sat down, but within seconds was standing up again, fidgeting as she began to pace the room.

'For heaven's sake, Maria, do sit down! Tell me how you're finding motherhood. Have they worn you out already?'

Maria perched on the edge of her chair. 'Not a bit of it. Rebecca's bringing me cups of tea on the hour and Zoë was drying dishes tonight as though I were Brown Owl testing her for the Brownie badge in shiny cutlery. They're quite okay, a delight actually. Enjoying the novelty of getting away with almost anything, I should think. We all read a story together before the sitter arrived this evening, taking it in turns to read. I noticed they hardly needed to refer to the text at all. It was *Wind in the Willows*. I love it too but those girls of yours seem to know all their favourites off by heart.'

'We do seem to be like that, all three of us. Reading favourite books over and over again, giggling over jokes we've heard, or made, innumerable times.' Jane smiled. 'I'm very lucky Maria. We're quite astonishingly alike, it makes it really easy for me.' She paused. 'Yet when I look hard at the girls, or think about them a bit, I know how different they are from each other too. Rebecca's frighteningly proud. She'd hang back and hang back, burning away with frustration and misery but unable to move forward and speak up, or come out of herself. Zoë, as you know, will push herself at me without any shame at all, but I worry about her too. She needs such constant reassurance behind that tough little face and her terrible hair cut. I did my best to talk her out of it. And now everywhere we go people say to me, "What a *sweet* little boy", and old Zoë simpers and carries on or, worse still, winks at me and *I'm* supposed to keep my face straight! She claims it's her disguise. Some disguise!'

A nurse came into the room, smiling possessively at Jane and nodding at Maria, letting her know she was superfluous to the drama of hospital life in which she – and now Jane – were central actors. The women fell silent until the nurse had left with Jane's thin collection of notes anchored to a giant clipboard clasped securely under her arm.

Jane wriggled down in the bed, her hand picking at the white bedcover as though looking for something precious, even vital. Maria examined her own hands, lying in her lap.

'You know,' it was Jane who interrupted the silence, 'this is going to sound somewhat absurd however I say it, but I find that I mind dreadfully about the scar.'

Maria gaped at Jane. This was certainly not what she'd expected.

'Well, who would there be to see it, you might ask! And it's true. I've not thought much about sex, or about me and sex, well, probably not since James left.' She continued to pick at the bedcover and Maria stared at the place too, fascinated as to what Jane might eventually discover with her restless fingers.

'It was such a shock James going, though I think that's only partly true. Maybe if I'd been aware myself that I wanted another child, or if I'd discussed it with him . . . but until Zoë was conceived I'd not discussed it even with myself. That seems odd when I think about it. And then when he went off into the moonlight with Caroline I was insulted more than anything. God help me, I know I'm more useful than beautiful but at thirty I wasn't exactly past it and anyway, what do they *want*? We flatter ourselves that we have someone who wants an intellectual equal, a fellow adult to share their days and nights with. They tell you – or at least you let their flattery tell you – they want someone to talk with and be excited by above the neck. But you know Maria, I've come to doubt that any of that's true. When it came to relationships I thought James and I were of the brave new guard. In retrospect I wonder if all that early talking wasn't just another aphrodisiac for James. That he saw our great meeting of the minds as fuel for his next erection.

'It's a wonder really,' Jane paused, laughed a bit, then went on, 'how women can sustain the almost full-time job of massaging ego, cock and back to ego again. It's more monotonously demanding than milking cows and only half as rewarding. I mean, the curds are there but where's the cream?'

She laughed again. 'Still, what do I know of cows? We only ever had sheep. Our milk came in great buckets from the farm next door. And if it comes to that, what do I know of men? I only ever had James. I suppose we'd not been talking much, not even that, not for ages. But I did love him still, in my way. Couldn't he have understood what demands Rebecca was making on me? But of course he didn't. And I didn't. So here we are.'

Maria took Jane's hand. To hell with Jane's reserve. She would sit here and hold it.

'I never thought though that what I had with James was my *lot*. You know how I love my life with the girls. In every conceivable way they're a joy to me, but vaguely, I suspect foolishly, I'd assumed that when they were bigger and I was less tied to them some gallant knight would ride up to the library on his white charger, tether it to the power pole outside and stride in, searching for great literature and finding – me!' Both women chortled at the incongruous image.

'Maybe I'll just have to settle for a scar fetishist. The doctors have warned me the scar's got to be a long one. One of them's a Ceylonese woman and she's been particularly kind and frank. She's here on some kind of exchange, bless her. Oh damn it Maria, I don't *want* this.'

'I hate to say this darling,' Maria prayed her tone was bright, 'as I know how you adore clichés, but the last thing you need worry about is some unknown man's opinion of your scar. Knowing your ingenuity you'll turn it into an asset. A tasteful embellishment from a tattooist? It could set a new rage. But what you've got to do now is get a decent night's sleep – and get well. Please Jane, try not to worry. You are beautiful you know. You don't know of course and I could tell you until I was blue in the face and you'd still not know. But there it is. And I'm renowned for my eye for beauty. Except when it comes to men . . . when all that glitters is not soul.' She looked at Jane, grimaced, and said, 'Sorree! The jokes don't get better with age, do they?'

Maria paused. This wasn't the time to hold back. 'You're not only beautiful, you're strong and funny. And I love you very much. In

57

fact,' she grinned, 'as one of the three leading lights in the Jane Delighty Fan Club let it be my task and privilege to pull up your blankets and wish you a speedy journey to dreamland.'

'My, aren't we just the little mummy! Well, what can I do but what I'm told.'

Jane sat up high in the bed, in happy contradiction of Maria's suggestion.

'Kiss the girls for me won't you. Tell them I'm fine, that I miss them already but I'll be home soon. And tell them I expect them to take good care of you and to pick up their own wretched clothes. You must insist they do it, Maria. They're such slobs and charmers to boot. I won't have you running around after them.'

'I should think not. Does it look as though I can come in tomorrow?'

'Ring first, don't waste a journey. But if you can.'

'Ah well. Fingers crossed then eh?'

The two women hugged, briefly, and Maria charged out, not looking back at Jane who had turned to gaze through the glass sliding doors into the darkness outside.

The public hospital where Jane had first been sent had a policy to give, whenever that was feasible, the same room to a terminally ill patient so that she or he could feel as much at home as was possible in a medical institution.

Each time, over the next two interminable years, that Jane went back into hospital and Maria went to visit her in the room with its glass sliding doors, and saw the flowers in the gardens beyond bud, bloom, drop, be replaced, bud, bloom and drop, she remembered that first visit when she and Jane had believed, or tried to, that all that mattered was a scar, a single scar on a healthy body. Jane was covered in scars now, but made no jokes about them. She had endured operation after operation, although there seemed little hope, or point.

Maria was haunted by a memory of someone once saying, 'If I had a pin I would sit on it, and rise to the point.' She would sit on a thousand pins, would have them permanently inserted up and down the length of her body, if that would help Jane, if it would even help her, Maria, to understand the goddamned point of why Jane, of all people, was disappearing before her eyes: withering, juices running dry, hair almost white, lines drawn around sad eyes, mouth constantly parched and asking, always asking, 'How are the girls? Are the girls all right? What have the girls been doing? Tell them that I love them, that I'm getting better. That I'll be home soon.'

Jane was at home, in bed. She spent quite a lot of time at home now, though mostly she had to stay in bed. On her best days she could get up for an hour or two to sit in her special new chair that her own mother had sent her, delivered in a huge truck while all the neighbours looked out to see what was coming. It had been a surprise only Maria had known about. Jane's mother could rarely come to see her since Jane's father had suffered a stroke and needed her constant attention, though she rang whenever she could, despite Jane's protests that the toll calls were more than she could afford.

When she was well enough to sit in the chair Jane would read to Rebecca and Zoë, a girl hanging over an arm of the chair on either side of her. Even when she was too tired she would sometimes try to read to them or tell them stories, but they were embarrassed by her attempts, knowing how hard these were for her and how pale and worn she'd look afterwards.

Maria was almost always at their house. Not only when she was looking after Rebecca and Zoë while Jane was in the hospital, but when Jane was at home too, 'getting better'. Maria and Jane didn't seem to giggle much any more. They had long talks in quiet voices and when Rebecca or Zoë came into the room they would turn sad faces towards them though they tried to pretend they were smiling, that everything was fine or would be soon, just as it used to be. Sometimes Zoë didn't want to go into a room where they were.

Sometimes Zoë wanted to squeeze her beloved dolls, even Eleanor, her favourite. She wanted to squeeze them until they hurt, to pull at their arms and legs or hair. She could imagine them lying in pieces and herself shouting at them to put themselves together again: how could she do it for them? She didn't know.

When she had these feelings Zoë was ashamed. She would hold her dolls gently and ask their forgiveness, telling them that it was all a joke of course she hadn't meant it. But the feelings didn't always go away. Sometimes they grew until they filled her up, until she could have choked with them rising and rising inside her. Then she would have to lie on the floor and push her head against the wall, harder harder until it hurt so much she could think about nothing but that pain. Then she would rub her head on its crown, round and round and round, to make that pain all better.

Rebecca and Zoë were often alone, eating the meals Maria would leave ready before she went to the hospital to visit Jane. They didn't look each other in the eye, nor did they talk about Jane, or Jane's absence, or Jane's illness. Very occasionally one of them would tell the other, in a rush and looking away, 'She's getting better. She'll be all right soon.'

Neither of them believed it in the burrow of her bed at night, but they were learning to blank Jane out of their thoughts and to invite in long, complicated fantasies inspired by their games or reading. They were both reading like starved creatures, ensuring that when one book was finished they had another immediately to take its place. They would run to the library after school, trying not to notice how Jane loomed in that place by her absence.

Zoë also pretended not to notice that Miss Durham was keeping them many more than their fair share of brand-new books. She tried to avoid the well-meant enquiries after Jane's health from the library staff, unable to tolerate the special tone which crept into people's voices when they spoke to her, especially when they asked about Jane. She loathed the cheerful way people would smile at her or help her to do things, or try to, as though she were a baby again.

'She's getting better,' Zoë would say, again and again and again. 'She's much better now. She'll be back at work soon, though first we're all going camping, to the far North with our tent, in Maria's car. All of us, and Maria. She lives with us now.'

James comes to the house. He barely speaks to the two of them, but so what. He closes the door behind him as he goes into the bedroom he once shared with Jane. The girls are living through their ears these days and they know that Jane is crying, that James is shouting, then speaking more quietly but on and on, and still Jane cries.

At last the nurse who now comes every day goes in to interrupt. James leaves. There is silence in the house.

60

Maria tells Rebecca and Zoë they are to go away for a couple of weeks. She tries to persuade them to regard it as a treat, time off school. They are to go to their aunt, their mother's sister, living on a farm with her husband, a top-dressing pilot famous in the family for his daring skill with a tiny plane. They love their aunt and uncle, but this time, without Jane, they don't want to go. They won't be able to *hear* from so far away.

Maria insists. Jane has to go back into hospital, she explains, but the doctors really do think that this is the last time.

'Does that mean she's nearly better?' Zoë asks. Though this is hard to believe, even for her.

'I think so, my pet,' Maria tells her. Then picks Zoë up and hugs and hugs her until Zoë thinks that all the breath will go out of her body and she will be left flat and rubbery like an empty balloon.

Maria helps them to get ready to go, sorts through their clothes and makes neat piles ready to be put into the suitcase they will share.

When they are nearly ready Maria tells them that they should go on in to say goodbye to Jane. They troop in to her bedroom, excited now by the adventure of a railcar journey all on their own, eager to tell Jane what they have packed, which clothes, which books, which pictures to show their aunt.

Jane is sitting up high against a white mountain of pillows. 'I'm feeling much better,' she tells them, 'almost well again.' She doesn't look it. She is thinner even than Rebecca. Zoë can see her breasts under her nightie when she leans forward towards them and they are strange, wrinkly where they used to be smooth, straggly, not comfy mounds any more. Zoë presses her head, though very gently, against Jane's tummy. She is desperately searching for Jane's smell. Jane smells odd now. Where is the smell she is used to finding on Jane's body, which was part of Jane, part of cuddling her, of being held by her? Now there is a smell which is sweet and sickly and rotting, not Jane's own smell at all. Zoë wants to ask Jane where her smell has gone, wants to hit this horrid new smell, smack it, tear it away, jump on it, stamp it to death, piss on it, shit on it, call it vile names, tell it to go away, kill it.

She lifts her head. She smiles at Jane.

Jane tells them she feels well enough to get up into her chair and

61

read them a story before they go. 'My brave girls, going off on the railcar all alone while their mummy lies in bed.' She laughs at herself. She's very proud of them.

'Rebecca darling, you choose the story,' Jane is saying. Rebecca flushes with pride and anxiety. She jumps up from where she's been lying at Jane's side and runs from the room shouting, 'Just a minute, won't be a minute,' as she heads for the bedroom next door.

Jane pulls herself forward in the bed, so slowly that she hardly seems to be moving, then she turns her bottom, puts her legs out in front of her and then, finally, to where they can hang, loosely, over the side.

'Just help your jelly-legged mummy, Zoë,' she asks. 'I'll lean on you and we'll pretend – what? I know, we'll pretend to be Renaissance beggars. I'm leaning on your shoulders and you have your arm outstretched. You'll be asking for money but really – in real life – you're a princess and the reason for your disguise is that you want to see how good and generous your subjects are, and you'll return all the money to them.'

'Yes!' crows Zoë. 'And you're my ancient nurse, well, not very ancient as you love to dance until dawn, but you're wiser than a hundred kings and I make no decisions without you. You came to me at my birth and told me we had a special, magical connection spun over thousands of years which would never be broken, no matter what, not even if I rode on the fastest horse to the furthest corner of the earth.'

'That's it,' says Jane as she painfully eases herself, with Zoë's careful help, down into the chair. 'It will never be broken because it's as strong as a rope woven by ten million spiders. It may be invisible to some, but we'll always know it's there and Rebecca –' she breaks off as Rebecca comes back into the room, sparkling now as the air fills with their old story-telling excitement, 'Rebecca's the stolen daughter of a neighbouring king who's been searching high and low for her and, if she only knew it, she's about to be found by a good fairy who will whisk her back to her homeland where she'll never be anything but happy again.'

'So we'll all be happy!' Zoë interrupts her. 'We all have our magic circle to take us in, keep us high up. We can all fly higher, even than the birds.'

The girls are kneeling now, on either side of Jane. It *is* just like before. All talking at once, weaving words into a magic carpet which will carry them, together, into a land of love and stories and immortality. A carpet woven by them and for them, room on it only for Jane, Rebecca and Zoë: ready to soar.

'And now the story,' Rebecca and Zoë call out in unison as Rebecca holds up the book, read and loved countless times.

'You read first, Rebecca,' Jane turns to her. 'You read so beautifully.'

Jane sits, very still, one hand on Zoë's head where it rests against her knee. In front of Jane Rebecca is sitting cross-legged, her dark brown hair falling down across her face and catching on her glasses as she brings to life the words familiar to each of them.

> *Far and few, far and few,*
> *Are the lands where the jumblies live,*
> *Their heads are green, and their hands are blue,*
> *And they went to sea in a sieve.*

Zoë lifts her head and looks up at Jane. Her face is shining as the words sing from their mouths. Jane will be well again, she will, she will. Zoë knows it. And she touches the wooden floor, for luck.

The silence of the farmhouse verandah is slashed by the sound of the phone ringing inside the house. Rebecca can hear it, even with her fingers in her ears. Zoë can hear it, even above the sounds of her chanting and rocking.

Their aunt is on the phone for only a few moments when they hear the ping which announces that the call is over. Zoë gets up, runs to the sprung fly-door, pushes it open with great force so that it crashes shut behind her, and runs out along the rough driveway that hits the road a quarter of a mile or so from the house. She leaps across the cattle stops and runs as fast as she can, not even noticing how rough and uneven the stones are beneath her sandals. One of the sheep dogs catches her up, runs beside her, wants to play, but she pushes him away, though he doesn't understand it, thinks it's a new game, asks for more.

When her breath is burning in her body Zoë squats down at the side of the drive, on the grassy verge next to the ditch that runs along the length of the driveway. She has her head between her knees, conscious of nothing but the pain of getting the breath back into her body. After a few minutes her breathing has quietened and she stands up, kicks the clump of high waving *toi toi*, feather dusters far above her head, kicks and kicks until her toes are bloody. Then she walks, slowly, the dog beside her, back to the farmhouse, where her aunt comes to meet her and to tell her that her mother is dead.

Five

After Jane died, Rebecca and Zoë stayed on at their aunt and uncle's farm for several strange, aimless weeks. Neither of them would later be able to remember that time very clearly, though Rebecca, who was eleven then, wandered off on her own one day, stayed away from the house for hours, and came back shivering with severe sunburn. It was prematurely baking hot that November. Rebecca's pale skin came up in huge blisters and stoic though she was, her mother's daughter, she screamed with pain each time the blisters were treated.

When the blisters had finally gone there were odd-shaped scars dotted over the top of her body and down her legs. Those scars took years to fade, if they ever did.

The girls did carry faint memories of a particularly uncomfortable kind of embarrassment. People would visit their aunt and if for any reason they couldn't escape they would be stared at by these curious intruders, have faces thrust in front of them which registered odd notes of brightness as if Rebecca and Zoë had just won first prize in the Art Union raffle, not 'lost' their mother, as the favoured euphemism of the day would have it.

Of course they knew they hadn't *lost* Jane at all. There had been no misplacement, not on their side anyway. And on Jane's? 'Taken over' might have been a more appropriate description. Though she was certainly lost in the sense that she didn't win what was, in those early days after her death, grimly and frequently referred to as a 'brave fight'. That made Zoë think of Jane lying in her bed, dressed in some hideous, inappropriate military garb, bayonet at the ready to stick it through the next invading Bertie Germ that might dare approach her wasting body.

Whatever it was that had taken Jane over spread through her fast, clutching at her as no lover would have dared, sucking at her until she grew smaller, weaker, dryer. Until she was, eventually, empty. By the end there was nothing left except a badly scarred, depleted body, lying in a mortuary, waiting to be transformed into a pile of ashes.

Rebecca and Zoë gathered together hints through significant glances and half-heard conversations that some great fight was going on about what was to be done with 'the girls'. They wanted to shriek, 'Hey, that's us. We're the girls!' Though of course they didn't.

Maria had spent virtually all the two years of Jane's dying at Jane's house. She wanted to continue to live there and to take care of the girls there, knowing that for each of them it was the only home they had ever known. People tutted about her giving up her freedom to take on complete responsibility for two girls to whom she was not even related, but Maria shut them up with a glance. She and Jane had never been able to bring themselves to agree explicitly that Maria would go on living with Rebecca and Zoë, but Maria knew as surely as that she and Jane had once shared a surname that this was exactly what Jane wanted, and expected, when she could no longer expect to get well.

The only insect in the balm was James. To everyone's surprise, and embarrassment, he declared that Maria was 'unsuitable' to have the responsibility of bringing up 'his' daughters. The inevitable meetings between Maria and James during the years of Jane's dying had been tense and difficult. Maria hated him for the ways in which he could continue to distress Jane, and for his apparent lack of restraint. But she had never expected him to interfere in what he surely understood were Jane's wishes. She could only conclude, with considerable bitterness, that James thought he had a hot connection to God in this first great flush of his relationship with Him and that God had confided to James His low opinion of Maria.

James fought hard, quickly growing stubborn and entrenched as he encountered resistance to his plan. He grew louder and less inhibited in his declarations of Maria's 'unsuitability' by which he could only have meant that she was not a Catholic, was not married and had, oh God forbid, lovers. Though time was when James himself had been free enough in that department, Maria muttered behind a face clenched into barely sustained patience. After all, hadn't James left Jane in the lurch precisely because he was sexually fascinated?

The girls' aunt went to the city to visit both Maria and James and when she returned the girls eavesdropped while she told her husband in an incredulous tone that James had behaved as if there had been some kind of test of straws offered to Jane and Maria, and that Jane had drawn the shorter one. At some quite bizarre level he seemed to blame Maria for Jane's death or certainly to resent the fact that Maria was still living when Jane was dead.

No one asked Rebecca and Zoë what they wanted. They would have chosen Maria like a shot. Bang, bang James. That failing, they might even have chosen to stay on at the farm, perhaps harbouring some illusion that they were simply on some limitless kind of holiday from their real home to which they might, one day, return. They would have travelled to a new school with their boy cousins on the ancient bus which stopped at the gate by the large mailbox with a little tin flag on it and the family's name and the names of the newspapers to be delivered there.

The gate was a fair distance from the house, at least it would have seemed that way to a child. There were large patches of red-hot pokers there that summer. The boys used to race down the driveway to arrive just as the bus pulled up at about ten to eight, already full of kids from even further away. Rebecca and Zoë would race down with them sometimes, envying them a bit as they got on to join in the games with all those other yelling, fighting, giggling kids, then walking back much more slowly, and in silence, up the path again.

Maria came once to see them, just before they left. She pulled awkward, ugly faces as she told them that, after all, they were to go to live with James. Zoë cried then, for just a moment, and Maria looked as if she might cry too. Rebecca cleaned her glasses with her hanky to.

'Everyone thinks it's for the best,' Maria said, over and over again. 'He is, after all, your father. And blood is thicker than water, people say.'

But try swallowing it, she might have added.

Six

The roofs of the churches are among the highest in this new land. Even the most modest has some sort of tower, constantly erect to show the faithful in what direction lies God.

The church in which Rebecca and Zoë are baptized, make their first confession, receive their first holy communion and are confirmed is not a church at all. It is a basilica. It has rounded shapes, almost breast-like, though Zoë no longer thinks about breasts and she giggles when the priest says 'bosom' or 'succour'. Those words, and her increasingly elusive memories of the feelings Jane's actual breasts stirred up in her, have become confusing. She wonders if she should confess that they make her giggle, but knows she couldn't say what the words are without giggling again, even in the dark, up-turned coffin of the confessional box. She knows the priest on the other side of the sliding panel is looking down at his knees and not at her. She's been told that only God Himself can see into her mind, her heart, her conscience. But perhaps the priest will somehow know that it's her, Zoë, who has a soul smeared with sinful, impure thoughts.

Mother Church is the new mother to replace the old. The eternal mother, mother to millions, yet each one, it is said, a precious chosen soul. Jane was mother only to Rebecca and Zoë. Her time on earth was brief and insignificant. She's gone for good now. Ashes to ashes. The skirts of Mother Church have been encircling the world for two thousand years.

Mother Church is putting marks on Zoë to sink in for life. Once a Catholic, always a Catholic. Zoë's learned lots of right answers to catechism questions. On the top of each new page of all her exercise books she prints, in capitals, *AMDG* so the God who prefers Latin will know that each mark of her pen is dedicated to His greater glory.

Zoë knows when to sing and when to remain silent. She can even pray. She can examine her conscience, and confess. She learns a new system of justice, of weights and balances, of bargaining with God.

Zoë doesn't ask God why He took Jane away. That was His will, the sisters have told her, sure that's explanation enough. His will is mighty, almighty, although he leaves His creatures free to invoke His anger on the road to forgiveness and peace. Zoë's delicate notions of free will are battered by paradoxes. She can stand by the sea and choose to stay alive, choose not to submit to despair, the greatest sin of all. Free will. A wrong picture or thought may come into her mind and looking at it, as it passes, she has chalked up a sin. Free will? She will confess. She is learning to endure her life with James and Caroline by developing the life of her imagination. She is learning to camouflage the unbearable beneath a drape of dreams, fantasies and wishful thinking. Lies. She will confess.

Zoë has always liked secrets. Now there are so many. There are secrets shared by all Catholics, underwater flowers in the moat which separates them from non-Catholics. There are private, individual secrets to whisper under your breath to God or, more often, to His son, Jesus Christ (half human, He'll more easily understand), or to Christ's mother, Our Lady, almost human too but different because she was spared the stain of original sin, recently and belatedly washed with baptismal water from Zoë's own soul.

There are mysteries for Zoë to untangle about why it's necessary to whisper to God when He knows everything anyway, but sometimes she enjoys the intensity of feeling as her thoughts waft upward, like incense, from that place between her steeple-pointing hands where her breath is making tiny droplets against her palms.

There are secrets to be shared too with the saints, especially with the virgin martyrs, and with Zoë's own special Guardian Angel who will take her soul – should she die in the night and not have committed a mortal sin since her last confession – straight to God, with perhaps a brief zig-zag back to purgatory to burn off the effects of her venial sins.

These Catholic faithful measure themselves against ideals of perfection gleaned from the lives of saints who lived and died thousands of miles away, sometimes a thousand or more years away.

They stand small beside measuring sticks of perfection that reach up to heaven, against which they can only lean, bent beneath their consciousness of paltry insufficiency. Oh Lord, Zoë is learning to ask, how much is enough?

But at least they do have a measuring stick against which to lean. Unlike the non-Catholics, flailing in the swampland of ignorance and delusion, waiting, perhaps, for the caring Catholic to say just one more decade of the rosary, to attend just one more non-obligatory Mass, to spend just one more hour in silent prayer with arms stretched out in the crucifix position.

School and Church are two halves of one world. Catholic boys and girls go to Catholic schools. Their parents are proud to be a minority community in a non-Catholic country. They nurture their differences. They cherish the intellectual traditions and the history of their Church in a country that has only the bud of an intellectual tradition to call its own and a mere century of European history to pick over. They pride themselves on the life they give to the so-called dead language of Latin. They welcome the shroud it pulls around their precious central ritual: the Mass. They understand, some of them, the contradictions and tensions involved in placing emphasis on words, forms, rituals, in a country whose European population fears those things.

In this country where a punch on the arm can be a genuine message of sympathy, Zoë is learning what it is to be a small magician dependent on words.

She has many sleights of hand. She has a tall top hat. She captains a fine light craft which moves along the river of language, bouncing on currents of English, Latin and Russian. Standing on dry ground she can toss word-balls into the air so quickly the spectator isn't aware of skill, energy and timing but sees only a dazzle of fast movement, of colour: clever Zoë. Zoë also knows what it is to grow tired of having your arms in the air, hiding your face, hiding your feelings. She knows she is marooned in a perilous place surrounded by the pits of no-words land. What there is no words for must be pushed away.

If she looks back . . . ? She can't. That was Jane and their life together. What happened to that? She doesn't dare ask.

If she looks forward . . . ? There are James and Caroline, bulwarks looming on her landscape. No escape. They see the balls she tosses, hear the noise she makes, recoil at the attention she attracts to herself. What they do not see is that she doesn't know when to stop.

Perhaps she can look to the Church? Many mysteries there, but explanations too. And dramas in which she can be merely spectator. The Catholics are convinced of their dramas. Zoë is wary of her own though they are all she has. But what can easily be created could just as easily disappear. Whoosh.

Zoë's words flow into the sunlight. At night her head bursts with jostling images.

No words come to save her.

Blood streaks the backdrop of Zoë's nights, a thick, indolent blood river widening as it comes towards her.

Mother Church is awash with blood, emptied from the chalice each day down the throat of a priest, dripping from the hands and side of Christ on countless crucifixes and holy pictures. Blood gushes from the wounds of martyrs, virgin girls like Zoë herself, stabbed to death while their mothers never came to save them.

Blood gushes from those other virgins, lured by Bluebeard into his trap, seduced by honeyed promises of love, marriage and eternal happiness, then stabbed and stabbed again in the cellar of his castle, their last sight on earth the bodies of their bloodied predecessors piled in a heap before them.

Zoë wriggles and turns. Death is stalking. Is it her own death or some ghostly image of Jane? Might this ghost Jane loom up beside her bed, wanting to reach out to Zoë, to climb in, to touch and be touched? Perhaps this ghost still thinks she's Jane, warm and comfortable, and doesn't know she is cold and clammy and terrifying. Zoë knows how hurt that ghostly Jane would be were she to turn away from her, horrified and repulsed.

Zoë lies in the dark and begs the ghost not to come, but she also whispers to ask: did Jane know she was dying? Does Jane know she is dead?

Does Jane know she was lifted into a dark wooden box, sealed on all sides and polished and ornamented, with black slimy satin to lie on?

Suppose the doctors were wrong. Suppose it was a mistake? Suppose Jane hadn't been dead at all, but asleep? Suppose she had stirred as they slid the wooden box towards the greedy flames? Suppose the heat had woken her and growing hotter and hotter she had turned from side to side, drops of sweat mixing with her tears of fear and anger, bruising and scraping her poor thin self as she turned in that smallest possible space, tossed in it even as Zoë is tossing in her own bed, but in a space too small to bang her fists against its roof, no chance to call, words choking back into her mouth, flavoured with smoke.

Zoë prays to ask that she won't die in the night. She is afraid to sleep even when her arms are crossed over her chest as her Guardian Angel would like to find her.

Zoë asks James if she can have a night light beside her bed to make a small pool inside which she can lie and keep the dark at bay.

James tells Zoë to ask Caroline and when at last Zoë finds the moment and the words to do so, Caroline laughs.

Caroline tells Zoë that only babies need lights on at night, not girls of ten. Caroline has never heard of anything as ridiculous as a ten-year-old girl wanting a night light.

Zoë keeps Rebecca awake as long as she can.

Even during school she's thinking of games or jokes or stories which she'll begin to tell just as Rebecca is sounding sleepy. But eventually she always runs dry and sometimes Rebecca, lying in her own bed, turns her back on Zoë, saying goodnight in a firm voice which tells Zoë to go to sleep too.

Zoë has told Rebecca she's afraid of the dark, though she's only told her about the things which she fears might be under the bed, behind the cupboards, which might be twitching the curtain, casting shadows, or creeping along the passage towards her at this very minute.

Rebecca always waits to run to turn the light out until Zoë is burrowed deep beneath her blankets. She stands by the switch in the middle of the room and asks, 'Ready now?' and when Zoë, submitting to the inevitable, nods, she plunges the room into darkness then makes a giant leap from the place where the switch is to the middle of her own bed. She's not afraid of the dark as Zoë is, but she knows it would be foolish to take unnecessary risks as to what might lurk in that dusty space between the suitcases under the bed.

Then Rebecca is asleep, a silent mound, just too far away to touch. Even the sounds of James and Caroline arguing, criticizing, shouting, defending, have ended for the night. The radio sits silent. A morepork cries, sounding out its own name. A dog barks at a slow-moving car. Then these sounds too are soaked back into the sponge of the night. There is silence everywhere. Zoë is still awake. Inside the darkness she rocks and mutters.

I am pushing against the dark. It's black and wants to lie all over me. I'm pushing against the dark but it's above me, next to me, all round me. It wants to come inside me, flood me. It wants to make me darkness too. I am pushing against the dark with my eyes wide open to see through to its soft bits. If I push hard enough against those soft bits I can find shapes of familiar things: my clothes making a camel's hump on the back of the chair, books leaning like a Pisa tower against the wall. I can begin to see through the dark and seeing through it I'm growing too big for it. It likes tiny creatures it can engulf. When my eyes are shut I *am* a tiny creature. Perhaps it will know my eyes are shut and send its darkness creatures to crawl in under the cracks where my eyelids meet my cheeks. They could creep all over me, even under the sheets, even under my nightie, covering me with slime. They could go up my nose or in through my ears but not if I turn onto my tummy and bury my head in the mattress and put a pillow over the back of my head where it sticks out above the blankets but then I can't hear anything and I won't know if the darkness creatures are coming. Nothing will warn me. I need eyes everywhere, and ears, but secret ones they can't see. I need to be alert to all dangers at once.

Where is the morning?

Seven

James does not love Caroline. James loves God. Caroline does not love James. Caroline loves God. Each of them is faithful to God, in their own way. And shouts at the human partner in the threesome of their marriage. And wishes themselves different.

Consciences pulled apart under constant vigilant inspection. Such busy lines between heaven and earth. But not much time for human problems. Perhaps there isn't time or love enough to go round?

James and Caroline are stretched to the limits with two near-strangers in the house. Rebecca sulks and won't be persuaded to speak beyond bare essentials. Her private thoughts and feelings are kept as close to her chest as a snake's belly is to the ground on which it crawls. She hides behind her glasses and walls of books. She smiles only at the borrowed bliss of other people's lives. She writes plays in which the true worth of the heroine is discovered during a moment of extreme adversity in the final act by a man of great kindness and honour.

Zoë makes scenes. Zoë shows off. Zoë is rude, ungrateful, unhelpful and disobedient. Zoë won't shut up and must be punished. Who is there to care?

Rebecca.

At thirteen her first period has not yet come but her breasts have begun, tentatively, to move out towards the world. Her eyesight is deteriorating in an apparently matching rhythm: breasts a little bigger, sight a little worse.

Zoë notices these changes and hates them. They frighten her though she can't locate her fears. She wonders: is Rebecca becoming someone different? She hits Rebecca on the breasts, mocks her, calls her names, even in front of other people, even in front of Caroline and Ian and Brendan. She tries to make them laugh at Rebecca and sometimes she succeeds.

When Rebecca can't hide from Zoë's attacks, when she can no longer tell if they're 'real' or 'pretends', she turns from Zoë to hide her pain and her anger. She can find no way to say, 'Stop it, Zoë. We can't afford this. We need each other. We're all we have.' There is no one for Rebecca to turn to and no place for her to go except further into herself. Sometimes Zoë looks for Rebecca. Rebecca is not to be found.

Maria comes to see them, when she can, when she can bear it.

James won't allow Maria to take them away from the house and the girls know how much she hates being there, accepting the tea Caroline meekly offers, taking care not to look at the pictures of the saints, or the heavy crucifix hanging next to the front door.

This is no place for them to talk about Jane. They don't. Maria tells them funny stories about her country pupils and occasionally brings letters to show them. She writes them letters too, and draws flowers or jokey comic strips up and down the margins, remembering that Jane did this. Maria does it even when really they're too old for that kind of thing.

What doesn't change is their love for books. Rebecca and Zoë make stories from the stories, enhancing the authors' notions about girls born to dance, to act, to skate, to *star*, somehow finding their way towards their moment of success on stage, trapeze or rink, brilliant under burning lights, bowing to astonished audiences, scales falling from the eyes of families who stand, dazzled and humbled, in the wings as their cygnet becomes swan, their caterpillar becomes butterfly, their dowdy girl becomes vessel of mesmerizing tragedy.

They contrive their own stories too, though less and less often without Jane to tell. But sometimes on one of the weekend walks to which they are banished they see a house and imagine that it's theirs to live in alone, or with Maria, or they see a car and imagine trips they could take: far far away from the place to which they must eventually return.

It was James and Caroline who decided to make more of an effort. A warm clear Saturday morning inspired them to organize a day out, a picnic, and before the four children were awake, or anyway, up, they went into the kitchen to make preparations.

Caroline spread melted butter on the slices of crumbly fresh brown bread James had been out to buy and then sliced, then together they filled rounds of sandwiches with cold lamb and home-made pickle, tomatoes from the garden and black yeasty Marmite. Caroline threw together a batch of scones and while they baked she put biscuits baked earlier in the week into square tins decorated with scenes of English Christmas. James went out to the carport to check the aged fragility of his car against the potential rigours of the day: hot sun, gravel roads, a heavy load. When he came back inside Caroline was wiping clean the formica benches. They looked awkwardly at each other, wanting to talk, tasting rust.

Ian and Brendan appeared and sat down side by side at the kitchen table, strong wiry boys with reddish-blond hair cut short. They began to argue, then stopped, quickly, the argument unresolved, looking nervously at James, expecting a reprimand. James would not tolerate noise, especially in the mornings.

Instead of a reprimand James told them, as he sat down at the table with a cup of tea in his hand, that they were off for a picnic, just as soon as Rebecca and Zoë had stirred themselves and everyone had eaten their breakfast.

Brendan jumped up from the table. A natural optimist, despite his parents, he saw bright possibilities in every day, denying the monotony of a routine beyond his control. He ran down the passage to bang on the girls' door, shouting, 'Come on you two. Hurry up. Dad says we're going for a picnic. You better be quick though or I bags we go without you!'

Rebecca and Zoë had been sitting on the sides of their beds, reading and talking. They looked at each other when they heard Brendan's message, immediate conspirators. On the few occasions other than church when they have had to undergo excursions with James and Caroline they have been mortified by people's assumption that Caroline is their mother. And yet, how can they avoid this? They stand as far from her as possible, but they know now that in the eyes of the world two adults, one male one female, and four children is a family. Living happily ever after. Where was the banner to wave above their heads and proclaim that they belong only and forever to Jane?

'Oh well, come on Zoë.' Rebecca took off her pyjamas and began

76

to get dressed, turning her back on Zoë as she did so and praying Zoë wouldn't make a fuss. She was utterly weary of James and Caroline's endless fighting and yet, sometimes, even she could see that Zoë really might provoke them with her voices, her inappropriate giggling, her insistence on her own idiosyncratic point of view. She coaxed, 'Maybe it'll be fun. Perhaps we'll go somewhere really nice and you and I can go off on our own for a bit. I'd like that. Wouldn't you?'

Her modesty preserved, Rebecca turned back to face Zoë who was pulling faces at her, mimicking the sweet, quiescent Little-Saint-Theresa-like model Caroline relentlessly and hopelessly held up before them.

'Papal farts,' retorted Zoë, still wearing her simperer's face. 'It'll be revolting.' The girls giggled hysterically at her lack of respect for the Holy Father. But it cheered them up and with a few pauses for silent mouthing of Zoë's blasphemy, they finished dressing and went to eat the breakfast of Weetabix and hot milk and weak tea which was waiting for them.

The car was full with its load of people, inflatable dinghy, picnic hamper, thermos flasks, rugs. Zoë and Rebecca each had a book with them to stave off inevitable boredom though neither of them could read while actually travelling as this made them throw up. Which made James furious. He loathed the smell of vomit.

Brendan sat in the front between his parents but kept squirming around to try to discover what the others were doing in the back. His wriggling disturbed James's concentration. He glared at Caroline who tugged at Brendan, passing on James's command that he should sit still.

In the back Rebecca and Zoë and Ian began to play 'Animal, Vegetable or Mineral?', but without much enthusiasm. Then, unexpectedly, James took up the game, showing himself able to find words almost impossibly obscure. Rebecca and Zoë were exhilarated by his interest in one of their activities and didn't notice Ian fall silent as they vied with each other to amuse James with the cleverness of their guesses.

James had chosen as their destination a beach new to all the children but familiar to himself and Caroline as they had occasionally gone there for picnics in their passionate courting days. Caroline was

77

looking forward to seeing it again though was slightly uncomfortable as to whether, in making this choice, James was telling her something she had failed to understand. He was difficult to read behind the frowns across his face, proclaiming an almost perpetual state of irritation which drowned other more subtle shifts in mood or meaning. And he was wretchedly impatient when she missed what was, to her, quite invisible, and was, to him, neon writing miles high.

The beach was almost empty and longer than the human eye can see. They walked away from the parked car across coarse clumpy grass, past groups of pohutakawa trees just beginning to show the magnificent red spikes which are their gift to a New Zealand summer, then across a band of small rocky pebbles and on to the sand which swept down to the water. The tide was far out. Soon it would begin its journey back up the beach. The waves appeared to be gentle, but Zoë knew they could suddenly splash her right across the face, could sting her and confuse her, even knock her down if she wasn't constantly watchful.

Each child ran behind a separate tree to change into their swimming togs then, emerging, to dump their pile of clothes beside Caroline and to race along the sand, leaving trails of footprints, only theirs to show that this beach had been intruded on by humans. Gulls squawked and flew up towards the sky, furious their sanctum had been invaded. They would return, gradually, to gossip in groups and paddle and peck at the shallow edge of the water. James had told the children they might see pelicans at this beach. 'The pelican, the pelican, its beak holds more than its belly can!' Rebecca and Zoë had chorused, pulling this out of the file of tiny poems each stored in her head from their years of living with Jane, though the file was rarely opened now, and almost never for new additions.

James helped Caroline to lay out the food which they covered with a heavy bead-edged net against the claims of flies and sandflies. He smiled at her, warmly if briefly, then lay back on the edge of the rug to read his copy of *The Horse's Mouth*. Caroline glanced down the beach after the children who grew smaller as they ran then disappeared behind sandhills. She worried for a moment, then turned her concentration onto herself. She took off her sandals, tucked her cotton dress up into the elastic of her pants making bloomers above her pale bare legs, and walked towards the water to paddle out until the waves threatened to wet her clothes, when she went back to sit with the reuniting gulls at the water's edge. Her arms circled her knees which were pressed up tight against her breasts. Her eyes searched beyond the tiny offshore island, a tree-covered, abandoned quarantine base and the single interruption in an apparently infinite seascape. The only sounds Caroline could hear were those noting the mesmeric rhythms of waves rolling in relief to the end of their journey, and of gulls, squawking and squabbling.

Caroline was lulled into a state of peace more restful even than sleep and it was literally agonizing when she was jerked from it by the sound of relentless screaming. She knew that voice, even transformed by fear and distance: Brendan. She jumped to her feet and raced towards the chilling sound, running in the same direction the children had taken, what, half an hour before?

James was running beside her, then passing her. When she reached the source of the sound he was holding Brendan and already his shirt was stained red with the blood gushing from Brendan's head. Jesus, Mary, Mother of God. She choked back her panic. Her heart was pounding with anxiety and the unaccustomed speed of her running. She took the child gently from James, holding him close to her as she looked to James for an explanation, perhaps even for reassurance. He was pulling off his shirt, no time for her, then tearing it into strips to make bandages for Brendan's head. 'There, there, Brendan, you'll be fine in no time at all,' Caroline crooned to her son, again and again, like the chorus of a song from which all the verses have fallen away.

A few feet from the two adults and the bleeding child stood Rebecca and Ian. Rebecca's face was tight. Her hands were clenched into fists, but she was motionless. Ian was hunched painfully into himself. He needed to cry, to run to his parents, to be hugged, but all their attention was focused still on Brendan who had stopped screaming but was now sobbing, deep shakes of grief which seemed to rise from his stomach, toss his shoulders and emerge to drown the words of explanation and protest he was frantic to share. Blood mixed with snot, with sea water and sand and his copious flow of tears.

Zoë was nowhere to be seen.

When Brendan's sobs had slowed to more regular crying James stood up from where he had been kneeling beside Caroline and their younger son and seemed suddenly to notice Rebecca and Ian, shivering in their swimming togs despite the day's heat. 'What happened to Brendan?' he demanded.

The two children said nothing. Rebecca's hands formed tighter fists.

'Ian, tell me, what happened to Brendan? Come on now, boy, you must know. Did you have a hand in this?' James's voice hardened with anger and impatience.

Still Rebecca and Ian said nothing, although Ian glanced at Rebecca as though seeking her guidance.

'Where's Zoë?' Caroline suddenly asked.

Brendan's cries spiralled. 'She wants to kill me,' he managed to scream, between his sobs. 'She threw a rock at me. She hates me. She wants me to get killed.'

The child turned back into the embrace of his mother, wailing, engulfed in the enormity of it all.

Caroline ached with suppressed anger. Sometimes she came near to hating Zoë, though she knew how wrong that was. But she couldn't help it. Things had been bad enough when she had to see the child only occasionally and be subjected to her stares, her giggles, her ridiculous stories and her contempt. But then Jane had died, God rest her soul, and James had insisted that Zoë and Rebecca should come to live with them, should be part of their family, even though she had cried and protested and told him they would all be much better off if the girls were to stay with Maria. He had never lived with Zoë, and had lived with Rebecca only when she was tiny. She had known that it could only lead to more distress, to even less time for herself and her and James's own children. It's our duty, he had said, ignoring her pain. And had done what he wanted, and look now she thought hopelessly, knowing nowhere to look.

James stood directly in front of Rebecca, grabbed her arm, shook it, bent down until his angry face was only inches away from hers and shouted, 'Where is she? Is this true? Tell me where she is, the little bitch. Why can't you make her behave? You're thirteen and she's your bloody sister. Tell me that now. Why can't you make her behave?'

Rebecca was white with anger greater even than James's own. She refused to look at James. How dare he speak to her like that? She twisted her arm repeatedly against his grip. Finally breaking free, she moved back from him, shouting up at him, her voice shrill with fury, 'He tried to drown her, your bloody son. She asked him to stop and he wouldn't, he wouldn't. He knows she can't swim. And now she's run away.'

Rebecca's voice broke and she began to cry and then to gaze, hopelessly without her glasses, in the direction in which Zoë had run. Just after picking up, aiming, and hitting Brendan's head with the largest stone the beach had to offer her.

Oh brave Zoë. Now a tiny ball of hunched-up body. Trembling with fear she is hiding in a cave, no thought passing through her mind of lighting it. She knows only that she is a murderer, alone in a dark hiding place, unable to guess how long she has before the tide rises to drown her there, in the dark, without again seeing the sun high in the blue sky that stretches without limit above the heads of normal people, living with their mothers in ordinary families.

Darkness above her, darkness below; she is freezing cold.

Zoë almost never went to the beach with other people. She knew they might find it funny to mock her reluctance – no, her refusal – to go into the water out of her depth. They might not believe that she can't swim, that she can't bear to be touched in the water, grabbed by her legs which are milky white and weak beneath the surface of the waves. She loves the ocean passionately, but only when she is alone in it, when she can choose how much of it washes over her, when she can bounce up and down in it knowing that her feet can still touch its sandy floor but pretending that she can swim as well as any mermaid and watching her loosened hair trail in it, wild weedy seaweed, and move her hands through it letting water rush through the cracks between her fingers which tell her that she is not a duck or platypus.

What could people know of her fears? Even if she could find the words which seem extra to her powerful vocabulary, could anyone ever understand that if she is forced to put her face under water it's as though the darkness which she fears has rolled right on top of her, has her pinned beneath its weight? More than that, who could understand how strongly she's drawn to close her eyes, to open her nose and mouth, to breathe in that weight, not to push it away but to welcome, welcome it, and going down down, to be embraced by that darkness forever?

And what if she were to find words to describe the whispering voices she can hear in her head when she stands at the edge of high places? Voices that call to her to fly, to soar, to find herself free to tumble, upside down and then rightside up again, until she smashes, splatters, becomes rag doll on the ground below.

But nobody does know because Zoë couldn't tell them.

Though she had shouted to Brendan, yelled at him with all her strength, 'Leave me alone. Don't touch me. Leave me alone.' She had exposed her weakness to him, had laid bare her vulnerability, had asked for his compassion, given him the opportunity to pity her, but he had laughed, ignored her pleas, dived beneath the water, fish-like, fearless, again towards her legs, this time grabbing them, excited by her fear, pulling them from under her until she stood on nothing, nothing. And when her arms flailed out at her sides there was nothing for them either and she knew that she was going down deep into the water, tipping backwards, gulping it in, filling up fast with water and fear and rage.

Bursting up at last to the surface, burning and choking and blind, she could hear Brendan laugh, roar with laughter and call to Ian to share his triumph. Her eyes stung, salt and sand grinding into their delicate surface as she rubbed them. Hearing Brendan's crowing, she sensed he was approaching her again.

Zoë caught her breath and gathered into herself all her strength and forced her way through the water, striding against its great weight until she had reached the edge where she threw herself down, anger knotting her stomach, anger slashing a pain around her head.

Behind her she could hear Brendan call to Ian, 'Look at Zoë. What a baby. She can't even swim. Can't even take a joke. Betcha she's gonna cry.'

Zoë lay still; her eyes stared into the sand. She was throbbing, waiting for Brendan's feet and ankles to emerge from the sea. Blood pulsed behind her eyes as she searched for a stone, the biggest, and as she stood up and aimed at Brendan she knew she had become an angry giant, roaring aloud her intention to kill him as her arm went back and the stone went forward and the red pumping behind her eyes was mirrored in the blood running down Brendan's appalled, terrified face.

She had remained transfixed for a moment, awed by her power, then, seeing Brendan fall, hearing the beginnings of his first terrible scream, she had turned to run. For her life.

It was James who found Zoë. After ordering the children, and especially Rebecca, to stay at Caroline's side, he ran down the beach in the direction Zoë had fled. He hadn't known Zoë was afraid of the water. 'Couldn't swim,' Rebecca had said. It had never occurred to him to ask or even notice if she could swim. All children could swim in New Zealand, couldn't they? But if she couldn't swim and was caught on the peninsula as the tide continued to rise, she could be in trouble. She *is* in trouble, he reminded himself, anger welling up again as he remembered the blood on Brendan's head, the day spoiled, his own good intentions ruined.

James ran, calling Zoë's name. He had little faith she would emerge, or reply. He'd have to find her. 'Fuck you, Jane,' he heard himself say. That shocked him. He rarely swore these days. But, God help him, if Jane hadn't died, hadn't left him with these bloody kids she'd obviously spoiled out of existence, then all this distress need never have happened.

The brutality of his logic did not escape James, but he nursed it, hovered over it like an alcoholic hovering over his last gin at closing time, feeling more and more sorry for himself as he ran, though it was Zoë's name he continued to call.

The water was up around her ankles. She had climbed onto a shelf, but it was narrow and her legs ached dreadfully. Her legs, and Rebecca's, had often ached since Jane died. Jane had told them, when the pains began a year or so before they left their house, that they were growing pains, part of becoming big. She had rubbed their legs, told them how tall and strong they would be, fearless warriors who could leap over fences, over trees, over walls of castles. They had laughed, wondering how much call there would be for such leaps. 'And suppose I landed in a big pat of cow shit on the other side?' Zoë remembered asking. 'What kind of white knight is yellow and warm and smells all over?'

No one rubbed their legs now. No one touched them. Not ever. No kisses. No cuddles. It was strange, funny really. Zoë hugged her pillows, and her dolls. But it wasn't the same. She was crowded by her fears. Were they all that came close?

And now this water, rising higher and higher, slowly but perceptibly, even in the dark.

She heard James's voice calling to her. She knew it was her name, that he was somewhere near, and yet it seemed quite remote to her too. Who was he, this man, calling her Zoë name, the name Jane had given her to make her special, the name of no one else she had ever known, the name which meant, Jane had told her, life itself. She had felt like an arrow when Jane had told her that, straight and proud. She could do anything, fly anywhere. Except with Jane. Except to Jane.

Zoë was shaking with cold and shock and fear. Through the mouth of the cave she could see sunlight. Warm, bright, welcoming: it was shining on other people. She would have to face James first if she went out, be punished for this terrible thing she had done; except she wasn't sorry, just afraid. But she wanted to see Rebecca. She couldn't possibly leave Rebecca alone, with no jokes no stories no secrets no glances to share. Not yet.

Zoë stepped cautiously down from the ledge, up to the tops of her thighs in the water, and walked slowly across the tremendous distance that stretched to the mouth of the cave where she pulled herself, with difficulty, up onto the ledge that surrounded the outside of the cave. She then swung over onto the rocks of the peninsula, thirty feet or so from where James stood, and called his name.

Eight

The Reverend Mother of the Convent of Our Lady of the Rosary, the school to which Rebecca and Zoë were despatched after Jane died, was a woman of small stature, excellent posture and large reputation in the Catholic community for her standards of scholarship and piety.

She was pleased to welcome Rebecca and Zoë to join her pupils. She had known Caroline well when Caroline had been a pupil at the school: an exemplary girl, no trouble at all. When Rebecca and Zoë were received into the Church she sent for them to spend fifteen lifelong minutes with her in a parlour in which each individual article of furnishing shone as brilliantly as the wooden floor uncovered by any mat. Zoë wondered if she had stepped inside a brown icicle, but Reverend Mother seemed kind and Zoë remembered to say 'Yes, Reverend Mother', or 'No, Reverend Mother', each awful time a question was directed expressly at her.

Reverend Mother told Rebecca and Zoë how very, very lucky they were to have been given the precious gift of faith; how very, very lucky they were to have such a wonderful stepmother as Caroline; how very, very lucky they were to have two new families: one with their father and new mother, one in the body of Our Holy Mother the Church.

She did not say how unlucky they were that their own mother had died. How unlucky they were that what had given life, or certainly meaning to their lives had, with Jane, as good as died. She did not offer any suggestions to ease the difficulties of reconstructing a life for yourself, with the help only of your confused and distressed sister. And nor did Rebecca or Zoë expect her to say any such thing. There was now, two years after Jane's death, no precedent to suggest this possibility.

At the end of the interview Reverend Mother bent over and, oh horrors, Zoë realized she was going to kiss each of them, first on one cheek, then on the other, then back to the first again. Dizzying. She then walked to a dresser, unlocked it with a tiny key to reveal an inside as polished and shiny as the out, and removed two holy cards. On the one she handed to Rebecca — older girl first — was a portrait of St Francis of Assisi surrounded by pets, both man and animals looking somewhat tubercular, but at least it wasn't St Maria Goretti. No one had ever mentioned St Francis protesting his purity, or dying for it. In fact, Rebecca had deduced, he had managed both an impure life prior to his conversion *and* a state of sanctity thereafter. If you were going to be given the gift of faith, that seemed a rather better order of things then spending *all* of your adult life in the scramble upwards. Knees on gravel. At least you would know what you were sacrificing by your anguished abstention.

On Zoë's card, handed to her second, was a picture of St Bernadette. She was kneeling in the grass at Lourdes in France, in conversation with Our Lady who hovered several feet above the ground. Zoë would like to have seen her shown sitting down beside poor Bernadette who must have been a bit frightened by this unexpected visitor, perhaps with Our Lady putting her arms around her, hugging her close. But the only hugging that got done on holy cards was Our Lady holding the clean and tidy infant Jesus, and then it was more of a hold than a hug.

When Zoë very occasionally saw Reverend Mother around the school, after that occasion in the parlour, she received only a brief nod and it was impossible to know if Reverend Mother really knew who she was. There were so many girls, all looking pretty much alike in the uniform designed expressly for that purpose. But Zoë didn't mind. Her reputation was growing where it mattered, among the girls. They admired though rarely dared to copy her lack of respect which was discreetly but effectively displayed.

In her third year at the convent, and her first year in the senior school, Zoë's neat white teeth bit into the dark forbidden fruit of sex. The taste was sour.

Zoë was, that year, in the class of Sister Mary Joseph, a possibly younger nun who was considered by the girls to be ferocious, eagle-eyed, almost passionately religious, but low on charity and much given to stinging young girls with her whip-lash tongue. Sister Mary Joseph could bring chills to the warmest spine, but Zoë adored her, fell, for the first time, in love. She was entranced by the nun's cleverness, by her sense of drama, by her use of silence: prelude and pause to the miraculous sentences which went on and on, subordinate clause rolling after subordinate clause, like waves of sheep, brought down from the hills by the dogs at shearing time.

Here was someone who inspired her to want to do her best, for whom she could make discoveries as to what 'best' meant. In combination with all the 'hard' subjects which moving to the third form offered, school could become an exhilarating place of adventure. At last.

Her classmates were bitterly disappointed by this change in Zoë the Bad who now jumped up from the front row to clean the blackboard, who offered to stay behind to tidy the classroom and water the plants, who begged without shame for extra help on those rare occasions when there were mistakes in her homework, who knelt close to Sister Mary Joseph at Benediction and Mass and vainly attempted to pray with a fervour to match the nun's own.

Even James and Caroline noticed the change in Zoë, and prayed that it might continue.

In the last month of the second term Zoë sat down as usual in her place at the front but when the rustle of standing up began it was for Reverend Mother coming into the room, not Sister Mary Joseph. The girls chorused their good mornings, crossed themselves, prayed, crossed themselves again and, when instructed to do so, sat. Reverend Mother was brief. She had, she regretted to tell them, bad news. Sister Mary Joseph's mother was ill and by special dispensation she'd been moved to a convent nearer to her mother's home. This had been done only because Sister Mary Joseph's sister was also a nun but was nursing lepers in the South Pacific and couldn't be brought home.

Zoë sensed the rise of excitement behind her. Sister Joseph would not be missed. Except by her whose heart was already down in her regulation lace-up shoes. Reverend Mother was speaking again.

'So for the rest of the year, girls, you'll be taught by Sister Mary Pius X who's come out of retirement to help us all. I know I can rely on your gratitude and co-operation. Good morning and God bless you.'

At her first sight of Sister Mary Pius Zoë's heart left her shoes and entered some pit in the earth which had no bottom. The nun had been hauled out of retirement with cobwebs hanging from her. She must have been there as witness when the Maori Wars began and was as lost as the slowest in the class when, with arthritic hands, she painfully opened a text book.

But Sister Pius was not too old, nor too slow, to bait the children, to keep them in late to cover pages of blank paper with senseless lines, to set them hours of homework which had Zoë tired every day at school and then to mark it in a way that was totally unpredictable and ignorant of the effort she had demanded. Zoë's resentment grew, as did the pain she tried to fight when she looked up to the front of the class, hoping against hope to see Sister Joseph and finding Sister Pius's frowns instead.

During miserable August school holidays Zoë resolved to take the matter in hand and at least write to Sister Joseph. She cajoled her address from the kind nun who served as porter and opened the front door of the convent with a rope, pulled from behind a grille so that no unknown stranger would see the face of a nun.

When the reply arrived Zoë was ecstatic. It was addressed to her, at the school. She turned the envelope over. It had been opened. She turned the envelope over again. Her name on the front: Zoë Delighty, but the envelope torn behind. It was outrageous, but typical of this place where you couldn't even have a thought in private. She raced to the lavatories, went into a cubicle, slid the lock across and pulled the letter out of its defiled envelope. It had already been removed. And read. And refolded with such lack of care there were now two sets of creases, not one. Zoë reached for the words themselves. There weren't many.

Dear Zoë
It was very kind of you to write such a long letter to wish me well. I miss all the girls but am kept busy with my new class [Zoë's cheeks flamed red with jealousy: missed *all* the girls, busy with a *new* class] and am happy that it is possible for me to spend some time with my mother.

88

If it is God's will, we will meet again. Thank you for asking for this in your prayers.

You are in my prayers also.

God bless you, Zoë.

Yours in Jesus Christ,

Sister Mary Joseph

Was that *all*? Zoë sat on the lavatory and cried. So stiff and empty of any recognition of what she believed had passed between them. Where were the inspiring sentences which had rolled down the hill of knowledge towards her? Didn't Sister Joseph miss her too, or had she forgotten already? Was there some girl in the new school more clever, more pleasing, more devoted than she, Zoë, had been?

Zoë knew there must be some failing in her. First that Sister Joseph had actually been able to go, had *requested* the move away, and then had been capable of sending a letter with just those few cool lines.

Zoë would have been ready to write to her daily, to compose poems and prayers, to press flowers between the pages of her missal until they were dry and faded enough to send. She had, for weeks now, been scribbling *SMJ* on tiny pieces of paper and burning them, hoping that the smoke could somehow carry her feelings of love to that place where Sister Joseph now was. And was now caring for someone else.

Too bad, too bad, Zoë told herself. She was a fool, an idiot; why should she care anyway? For a *nun*? It was ridiculous. The other girls were right: Sister Joseph was cruel. Well, let her keep her sick mother and her God; probably they were all she could love and care about anyway. Perhaps there never had been any room for her, but at least she knew that now.

Zoë ripped the letter into confetti and flushed it down the lavatory, pulling the old iron chain with a force that left it clanging against the white tiled wall. She went to the basins, cupped her hands to the brim with cold water to cool her face and returned to the classroom, late and sparkling.

The next day she moved the long tassle-ended girdle from her waist down to her hips in brave imitation of a swinging flapper, hitched her gym slip above it until her knees were exposed for any

89

stranger to see, pushed her panama hat to a perilously insecure place at the back of her head, took off her white gloves, chewed forbidden gum to give her American courage, and sauntered down town with a select group of followers, to look over the boys from the Marist Brothers school at the place where they gathered, at lunch time, to buy their hot, greasy fish and chips.

As Zoë was famed, within the limited horizons of her world, not only for the audaciousness of her behaviour, but also for her style, she was intensely humiliated when she was expelled from the Convent of Our Lady of the Rosary for meeting with, looking at, surely not talking to, boys. In a fish and chip shop.

The news of this event, which occurred not once but two or even three times, was carried, Zoë would never know how, to Reverend Mother herself. In all fairness, Reverend Mother attempted to discuss the matter with Sister Mary Pius, Zoë's form teacher, but Sister Pius was frightened of all the girls and, having been given this unexpected opportunity, could only lash out with a bitter tirade against modern girls in general, which did not help Zoë, specifically. Reverend Mother realized how little clarity or, indeed, charity, she could expect from Sister Pius and terminated the interview before Sister Pius had said all that she was discovering she wanted to say. But the rule of obedience was as natural to Sister Pius as breathing and, puffing only a little, she left the room, thanking Reverend Mother and God blessing her as she went.

Reverend Mother sat in her study for some time, praying and considering the matter, thinking of her school, its reputation, its many girls and this one individual girl, Zoë Delighty. What a ridiculous name! But, as she was a convert, thanks be to God, it was hardly fair to expect that she might have come to them with a name more appropriate for a pupil at Our Lady of the Rosary. There was an older girl too, with a Jewish name: Rachael or Rebecca? No bad news of her, nor good news either.

Reverend Mother was inclined to be merciful. That was part of her vocation. But the image of the bad apple in the case of good apples lodged in her mind. Rosy on the outside, bad within, spreading to the next, and the next. Reverend Mother walked to her window and looked out, across a shorn green lawn, beyond rows of flowers and tidy paths to the small grotto where girls prayed before a larger than life-size statue of Christ, standing with his arms outstretched, His hands slashed red with the wounds of nails, His heart exposed in raised plaster, bleeding copiously for the sins of the world. Reverend Mother joined her prayers with those of the kneeling girls.

She wrote only a short note to Father O'Donovan, the parish priest, and in his turn Father O'Donovan telephoned James, asking him to call at the presbytery. When James arrived the priest sat him down in the least uncomfortable chair in the best front parlour and offered him a drop of what he called, with some relish, the hard stuff. James was grateful for this as his ignorance of the reason for the meeting was making him feel disadvantaged.

When two glasses had been generously filled with fine Irish whiskey, Father O'Donovan placed his stocky frame on a chair pulled up directly opposite James and told him, man to man and no mucking about, that unfortunately Reverend Mother, fine woman that she was, a saint really, God bless her, had decided, after much prayer and thought and, believe me, it was no easy matter to do, that she could no longer have his daughter, young Zoë, as a pupil at the school.

James stared at the priest, mildly irritated by his mispronunciation of Zoë's name to Zoo-ey. He shook himself. What was the man saying? Zoë had seemed blessedly improved, was doing her home-work, was less difficult with Caroline. Thinking of Caroline, James groaned inwardly. Caroline had taken to referring, through tight lips, to Rebecca and Zoë as 'your daughters', as though by some genetic mismanagement he had produced them to be the troublesome kids they undoubtedly were. Shit.

'What's she done? I've heard nothing . . . I know she's a bit loud, rather a show-off, I know that, but she's not a bad kid. And her mother. Well, it's been hard on her and her sister, Rebecca. Their mother died almost four years ago. Perhaps they still miss her?'

'I'm sorry, James.' The priest was looking James right in the eye, sorrow definitely etched in his own. 'I'm sure Reverend Mother has considered all the facts but she does have the other young girls to think about. You see,' he paused, about to reveal the terrible truth at the heart of this interview, 'she's been playing up. Out of the school, like. And I'm afraid,' he emptied his glass, 'there were boys involved.'

'Boys!' James's memory rolled back thirty years to snickering tales of wild girls who did things in the long grass and emerged smirched of body and reputation. Not Zoë.

'Well, nothing too unseemly mind, but we can't be too careful. It would seem that she and a group of other girlies, but Zoë definitely the ring-leader among them, have left the school grounds, more than once and without permission, to go down to meet with a group of boys from the Marist Brothers school, in the fish and chip shop. We know who the boys are, and it saddens me to say there are senior altar boys among them, but they'll be punished. Of course it's much easier with boys. We can cane them and forget the whole matter. But we could do no such thing to your Zoë.'

The information was dizzying. Part of James wanted to laugh. It was absurd. All this fuss about some skinny, pimply kids gawping at each other in a greasy fish and chip shop. Part of James wanted to save Zoë from the pettiness of the situation, to share with her his understanding that this incident was nothing but a faint comma in the rich rolling sentence of her life. But he couldn't. What the Church, in its many voices said, mattered too much. What the priests said he had learned to listen to. What Caroline and Caroline's mother said seemed to ring true and sound, even though he knew that even now he often heard their voices as if carried across miles of wasteland.

Father O'Donovan was speaking again as he stood up, took James's glass and headed to the handsome crystal decanter for a refill. 'I know how hard this'll be on you, and on Caroline too, God bless her. She's done a real fine job with those two girls.'

James looked away. The priest, riding the waves of mercy now, went on. 'It's hard on everyone that this should happen at such a, shall we say, delicate stage of pre-adulthood.'

He handed James his refilled glass and sat down again, careful not to spill a drop from his own glass as he sank.

'At least we can thank God they were Catholic boys. It could have been that much worse.'

James didn't look relieved. Father O'Donovan had to remind himself that James was, after all and despite his devotion, a convert.

He spoke again. 'I'd suggest you allow me to phone the Reverend Mother at St Brigid's. It's a good school too. Maybe not quite up to Our Lady of the Rosary but I'll be explaining to Reverend Mother there that your Zoë's not really a *bad* girl – indeed, that there's a great deal of good in her – and that we're all praying for her. If the Reverend Mother will take her in she'll start with a clean slate. All this can be forgotten. A clean slate's just what's needed.'

Delighted with his solution, delighted to have concluded the interview, and delighted, too, with the quality of his whiskey, a most welcome gift from a grateful parishioner, Father O'Donovan emptied his glass, shook James by the hand and led him to the front door of the presbytery.

There was no part of Caroline which found Zoë's behaviour absurd, or forgiveable. She felt humiliated by the girl, made mock of before Reverend Mother and Father O'Donovan who would now know how wild and uncontrollable Zoë was, despite Caroline's best efforts. Zoë's behaviour was cheap, of the cheapest kind, no decent girl would flaunt herself at boys like that, push herself forward, go running after them, seeking them out, and only twelve years old. At that age Caroline had known nothing of boys – well, only of her brothers who would always protect her from their friends, as was right.

Caroline could hardly bring herself to look at Zoë, never mind speak to her. Silence was the only retreat open. She had to go on living with Zoë and Rebecca. James had decided that, and clearly it was the will of God (who moved in mysterious ways). She was certainly not one to shirk her duty or question God's will, but in no way was this easy for her.

The eye of the storm, the heart of the maelstrom, Zoë herself, unusually slowly realized with what horror she was being regarded, beyond the level expected for her acts of flagrant disobedience. It wasn't until after a painfully embarrassing interview with Father O'Donovan, unoiled by any alcohol, in which the priest had questioned her, solemnly and persistently, as to her *motives*, her *intentions* towards these boys, that she realized she had, quite innocently, lost her innocence in the regard of those around her.

Zoë was not unaware of the Church's emphasis on the sixth and ninth commandments. She had been taught for more than three years to examine her conscience daily with regard to impure thoughts or acts. She knew, through the oblique sentences in which the information was effectively conveyed, that it was forbidden to touch her own body with pleasure. She knew the rewards for virginity: a happy Catholic marriage or, better still, a vocation to eternal virginity as a nun, a bride of Christ. She knew that temptation would constantly cross her path, in all sorts of guises, laid there by the Devil himself, and that she would grow through her resistance to it. She knew that the God who knows everything was, nevertheless and only because He loved her, keen to test her, to see how she would react when offered a caress beyond the limits of Catholic decency.

But there had been no caresses offered or expected in the heat of the fish and chip shop. It was an adventure born out of anger and loss and created by a need for rebellion which coursed through Zoë with special strength when loneliness threatened. Old feelings, and new ones too, had been aroused when Sister Mary Joseph came into her life, and left it again. She knew she had to beat against that great hulk loneliness, that she had to show — perhaps only herself — how *alive* she was.

There was no lust anywhere, unless it was in the minds of her judges.

At twelve Zoë's longings, buried deep and without name, were for her mother: to be held by Jane, rocked by her, to lean against Jane's breast drawing in the smell and warmth of her and to be told, again and again for the joy of the telling, that she, Zoë, was loveable. Perhaps even that she was good.

Zoë hated St Brigid's when she was first sent there, trailing her sordid reputation, leaving her friends and Rebecca behind.

The priggish girls refused even to speak to her and whispered and nudged when Zoë passed by. But there was a tiny minority who had their own battle scars and who sensed in Zoë the spirit of an adventurer who might possibly brighten their convent lives.

The nuns at St Brigid's were more progressive than those who had taught Zoë previously. The aims of their order encouraged them to fight hard to raise the standards of their school for their mainly working-class students, and despite huge classes and constant debts these nuns seemed to find a little time for all of the girls, sometimes even to play with them, hitching up their robes and growing red-faced and puffed throwing a basketball in their extravagantly unsuitable attire.

The new Reverend Mother had been asked by Father O'Donovan to take Zoë on trial, to give her three months in which to prove herself changed by goodwill and prayers. Reverend Mother had agreed, though privately she'd resolved it would be six months at least before she would pass judgement. The story of Zoë's misconduct, regaled to her by Father O'Donovan with the pauses and emphases of a practised preacher, seemed to her somewhat . . . inflated? When she had met Zoë, brought to her one Saturday morning by the child's father, Zoë had been closed-faced and awkward. She had fallen against a chair as she came into the room and had seemed so painfully embarrassed and concerned about this that there was no possibility of getting to know her. Reverend Mother had liked the girl's face though, despite its expression of painful wariness.

She had hoped that no one but she need know that Zoë had been expelled from Rosary. But news in the small Catholic community travelled fast, via sisters and cousins and good Catholic neighbours.

Reverend Mother's decision to give Zoë an extended trial was quickly tested. During the final ghastly months of her third-form year Zoë hardly spoke yet somehow, through her silence, was inciting the less stable girls to all kinds of mischief. Over the long summer holidays at Christmas, Reverend Mother's thoughts returned often to Zoë. She puzzled about the rapid changes that came over the girl's face when she was unaware of an adult's observation, and worried about the tightness that held Zoë's face in at all other times. Her form teacher had despaired of her and clearly her work was way behind her ability. Reverend Mother wasn't yet regretting her decision to give Zoë the extra months, but she knew that if she couldn't see any improvement she would have to consider asking the parents to send her elsewhere. But where? There was no other day school for Catholic girls in the city. It would have to be boarding school, or a state school, but even those were unlikely to take a girl twice expelled.

Reverend Mother turned to the consolation of prayer.

In the first term of the new school year auditions were held for the school debating team. These were usually open to fifth and sixth formers, but Zoë had made a special request, handwritten and passed to Reverend Mother via her fourth-form mistress, to be allowed to compete.

Reverend Mother considered what it would mean to break an old rule, and the complaints that would come from the older girls who had earlier had to wait their turn. Yet she'd been able to see how proud Zoë was, how 'natural' her rebellion to adult authority had become. She did not know, for even Zoë was only dimly aware of this, that what was forbidden to Zoë became prize to be plucked. This compulsion, growing as she grew, was born from her gift of independence. But the good fairies who had brought her this gift had left no instructions as to how it could usefully be harnessed, or even shown to be a gift at all.

After a long internal debate Reverend Mother's compassion for Zoë won, bolstered by her pleasure that the girl had made this gesture outwards. She decided to agree to Zoë entering the auditions but knew she mustn't be seen to favour one girl over the others. She would have to issue a general invitation to the third and fourth formers to compete to form a back-up team which could practise in competition with the senior team, the lucky few who would go out to represent all the girls of St Brigid's in the diocesan competitions. The more Reverend Mother considered this, the more she liked the plan, and was grateful to Zoë for prompting it.

The day of the auditions came and classes were cancelled for the afternoon. The school filed into the big auditorium to sit in neat rows, humming with anticipatory excitement and pleasure in the interruption to their strict routine.

The girls who were to audition were already at the back of the stage. Each one stood alone, sliding occasional nervous glances at the others, noting that their uniforms too were newly pressed, wondering if their hands were damp as they held well-thumbed sheets of paper on which notes were inscribed.

When it was Zoë's turn to speak someone touched her arm, wishing her good luck. Zoë barely noticed, and didn't respond. The words she was about to share were shaping inside her head, bursting into colour after weeks of intense preparation.

She had not made her preparations alone. Already Rebecca was a veteran of these events, not only in oration but also in impromptu speaking and debating. Seeing the poised girl standing on stage speaking with such control, and with flashes of dry wit quite unexpected in someone of her age, it would have been impossible to guess that Rebecca was agonizingly shy, that she continued to shrink behind her glasses, and to mourn: her mother? her own tentative sense of self? her loss of place in any safe universe?

It was Rebecca who had guided Zoë to her chosen subject: the historical persecution of the Jews and the establishment of the state of Israel, one year younger than Zoë herself. They had spent many intense hours discussing possible subjects, quite unconscious that those through which they ranged were all marked by tragedy and misunderstanding, yet contained the possibility of transcendence.

Their political analysis did not exist. Their knowledge of history was made up of tiny threads of information thinly draped over craters of ignorance. They harvested their information from books written to move the reader to the author's unilateral point of view. They chose these books instinctively, perhaps as a continuation of the wishful fantasies of childhood which had been the stuff of the books they had recently left behind.

There may also have been some stubbornness in their partisanship for Jews. They met few Jews in their Catholic world and Maria, central figure in the future they had lost, was, they had learned from James, herself a non-practising Jew.

Rebecca's style was to lead with her heart and to use her quick mind and tongue to channel her emotional conclusions. With complete trust, Zoë stepped into her sister's footsteps. The two girls were more easily close than they had been for years as they practised and rewrote and argued together.

In front of her first audience, with this carefully chosen first subject, Rebecca's method adopted by Zoë worked without flaw.

Tall, thin, awkward Zoë: her hair grown out long and scraped back into tight unattractive plaits. Her drab school uniform emphasizing the ungainliness of a body growing much faster than she would have wished. Her skin pale with nervousness so that her hated spots stood out. Her chest flat, though she prayed every day to reach that magical moment when she could wear a bra as the other girls did. Her feet turned slightly inward, left jutting against right.

Zoë stood before them, this big audience of nuns and girls, few of whom were yet her friends, and breathed up from her stomach as Rebecca had instructed to quieten the flutterings in her throat and chest. She looked down at her notes for the first and last time and spoke, in a deep sad voice as she raised question after question about persecution, about prejudice, about loneliness: about what it might mean never to belong. Then she attempted to answer those questions with stories of heart-breaking individual experience she had culled from books and found in her head.

She was aware of her audience as Rebecca had told her she would be. After the first few fearful moments she had known the hall was hushed and its space was all hers to fill. She could sense the level of attention rising towards her, stimulating her in an entirely new way. She could see the last page of her notes in her mind, could feel the sweat trickling down, a cold tiny stream under the long white sleeve of her shirt. She could hear Rebecca's voice instructing her to slow down, to keep them waiting, to count to an interminable five before her final plea over which they had argued and worked, and then to let them have it.

'That there should be freedom and hope for all, regardless of religious or political description, and that we should refuse to be torn apart by ancient division.'

After she had finished Zoë experienced that moment of perfect silence which every performer longs for and which she hadn't until then known existed. It came before the first sound of applause, before even the nuns at the front were on their feet, clapping her, Zoë the Bad, and smiling and wiping away tears.

Zoë knew, even in that first incredible moment, that her star was rising in the humblest of firmaments: small school in small city in small country on the other side of the globe from what was usually called 'the world'.

Only Rebecca could have led her towards this moment of being someone, not just a troublemaker failing to live up to adults' notions of her 'promise', but a someone who could, like her sister, engage, move and affect a whole hallful of people at one time. She saw Rebecca and herself travelling the world, going from stage to stage, dressed in garments of sobriety and dignity, with audiences standing to cheer as the two women modestly acknowledged the applause which not they but their subject matter fully deserved.

Zoë giggled for an instant at this vision, and began to walk off stage. The voice of her audience called her back. She blushed now, and then stood still.

Zoë had, for just this moment, grown larger than herself. She was warm, fully alive, high above the waves.

She was glimpsing a beacon. And catching its light.

PART TWO

Upstream

All countries are going to be exactly alike
unless I find the secret of making them new again
by renewing my own self.

Colette, *The Captive*

One

It is five months since Gabriel left. Five months of waking up each day to measure the degree of pain and uncertainty which I would need to disguise.

Not that I blame him for going. I don't. He had to leave, to save himself. I am no life-saver. I can't swim, can't bear even to float out of my depth. I need to be able to put my feet on the ground and to run, when *I* need to. Never mind saving anyone else.

They met at a party in Chelsea, Zoë and Gabriel.

It was a very ordinary party. They were bright in a pale room, there apparently by chance.

Most of the people were older than Zoë: married, settled, conservative, resigned. Zoë, who was none of those things, was involved with all the surface of her being with a newly reformed speed freak at the time, a man of translucent twenty-year-old beauty with mad dancing eyes. But he was gentle and funny when he spoke. Mostly he and Zoë would just lie together in his almost empty room in a kind of stupefied silence which Zoë found most restful. He could spend hours stroking just one part of her body, or another. The unmarked skin of her inner elbow where a blue virgin vein throbbed, the lobe of an ear, the curve of a breast, not the nipple. His attention was curiously lacking in personal direction. That is, he enjoyed the skin, the ear, the breast, not especially Zoë's skin, ear or breast. Which gave her space to drift and float, both cossetted and free. It was very nice for each of them.

The weekend Zoë was to meet Gabriel, her gentle stroker went home to Sussex to visit his Mum and Dad. Zoë saw him off at Victoria Station. They had made unusually vigorous love the night before and she was somewhat distracted, wondering if she might have cystitis, but they managed an excellent, tender imitation of

Celia Johnson and Trevor Howard kissing goodbye at the station in *Brief Encounter*, though Zoë doubted this was the image in his mind, and didn't bother to ask. She felt uplifted enough to have it alone, yet she also tasted the melancholy of that parting and as she waved the stroker off she was quite sad, lonely almost, although, by then, she had quite a number of friends in London, and no need really ever to be lonely.

From Victoria Station Zoë walked to the Tate. She liked to go to art galleries alone. She knew little about painting, except that it mattered to her, and she was embarrassed by her ignorance. Her father had an amateur's well-chosen library of books on fine art, and an excellent collection of books on architecture and design, but as they were his Zoë would rather have gone blind than show any interest in them. Anyway, she had left home when she was sixteen, despite her father's threats to prevent this by having her made a ward of the court.

Zoë walked through the gallery, nodding to favourite paintings, her greeting to them an unconscious hangover from her childhood when she had anthropomorphized almost every supposedly inanimate object in almost every room she entered so that she would need to undertake an exhausting round of touch, unable to be calm until she had reassured chairs, tables, pictures, rugs that she had, indeed, noticed them, even if she could sit, was about to sit, on only one among them.

She sat down today in front of a Gauguin painting of several women, sitting together, on a bench. There had been a reproduction of this painting in her mother's bedroom. Zoë knew for sure she liked Gauguin's work, and the memories of the clash of colours and harsh soaring light of the South Pacific that his paintings stirred up in her. She thought she probably appreciated Gauguin in a way denied to the English with their life-long experience of passion-bleached colours under low grey skies. With other painters she was much less confident, wondering what the English could see, trained as they were by generations of unbroken access to what was, as she was constantly reminded, absent in the life of the colonies: Culture.

Back in her room at the South Kensington flat she shared with a random group of young women and men, Zoë lay on her double bed and contemplated the rest of the weekend. The brief melancholy of the railway station farewell had entirely left her. She felt only the closeness. She was happy, more than happy, buoyant. It seemed unlikely now that she did have the dreaded cystitis. It usually showed its ugly acid face within twelve hours, punishment for the vigour and power of her body. Punishment, sometimes, when there had been no power no joy no thing that was good at all. Oh Mother Church: one hand stretched out to offer gifts; the other to pinch and slap. She was relieved at her escape and full of energy to be out in the world again. She'd been invited to a party this evening by a man she hardly knew, someone brought to the flat recently by one of the other girls, a friend not a boyfriend, who had finally reached Zoë after several thwarted attempts and had asked her to this party, this evening. Zoë had told him it was unlikely but, leaving her foot in the door, that she'd let him know. And now she would, if she could find his number, if he was in.

His name was Craig. Don't be vague, think of Craig, she giggled to herself as she dialled, barely able to recall what he looked like but flattered and relieved when she heard the pleasure in his voice, when he told her that yes he was still going to the party and that no, of course he hadn't given up on her and asked someone else. He'd collect her at nine.

Zoë stood in front of the alcove where her considerable array of clothes hung from a battered wooden pole. She loved to dress up. It was part of the magic she wove to create her world. It was part of saying aloud, 'Here I am, here I am.' It was part of pretending, of hiding behind a chosen effect.

She took down a new dress, long, close-fitting, black crepe edged in red satin, bought some weeks before which had hung since, waiting for a really special occasion. The party this evening was unlikely to be special enough. It was her own good mood she was celebrating.

With total absorption she applied her dark make-up, her tongue pressing down her bottom lip just as Rebecca's had done when, as a child, she had stamped their departing library books. Then she brushed her thick curly hair hard to make it stand out to frame her face, bending deep from the waist as she did so and singing tunelessly to herself. Finally she was ready to put on the new dress and fasten the red satin-covered buttons that ran down the length of its front.

Zoë looked at herself gravely, critically, from all possible angles in the full-length mirror. She had only recently learned to trust the possibility of feeling any genuine pleasure in her appearance. Memories of her skinny, awkward adolescence sat just behind her shoulder. She seemed always to have known that she could pin on a mask to fool the world and often enough herself. But to feel joy rise up from within to radiate out, that was something rare, precious, real for herself as well as for others. She felt it tonight. She felt lit up: by the day that had just passed, by the dress she had chosen well, by the adventure that could lie ahead.

The clothes she'd worn all day lay in a pile on the floor. To hell with them. Zoë lay down carefully on top of her bed. Here she was, in London, alone, damn near a woman of the world, good at her job, good in bed, a survivor, making it, making out, making do, doing better than she could have hoped, than she ever dared to hope when she left New Zealand, propelled by her need to leave that place, puffed up with dreams and plans but not far behind that laughing joker's face, dwarfed by her fears of what might follow.

Craig was pleasant, and nervous. Zoë loved putting him at his ease, making him laugh, asking him pertinent, even impertinent questions about his work, where he lived, where they were going. It was a skill she'd learned early, recognizing it as the perfect means of apparently making contact while hiding behind the screen of your questions and their answers. It was the skill that had been the basis for the beginnings of her professional success as a journalist in New Zealand. Craig was thriving on it and Zoë began to relax, enjoying Craig's Morgan and the sight of her long legs stretched out in front of her. One day she'd drive a car like this, not just sit and grin in the passenger seat.

Craig moved into full swing, treating Zoë to the climactic details of a recent boardroom coup in which he had, apparently, played a central role of stunning originality. Well, she had asked. 'How *fascinating*,' she encouraged not once but several times. 'How absolutely fascinating.'

Men like Craig were easy for her to be with. She was far more mystifying to them, she was sure. They dimly perceived her as offbeat, odd, eccentric, according to their adjectival preference, and she doubted very much whether they would have begun to take her seriously even if she had, for one moment, allowed that possibility to occur. Certainly they regarded her as likely to be promiscuous. She was so frank, so disarmingly *funny* about sex. That had to mean she liked it, didn't it?

Craig took Zoë's elbow as they walked into the crowded sitting-room of a mansion flat in a tall 1930s block in one of the less attractive streets away from the river in Chelsea. Zoë could see there were about equal numbers of women and men in the room, older than herself, probably in their late twenties to middle forties. The men seemed to look like Craig though some were wearing roll-neck sweaters under sports jackets, rather than a dark suit as Craig did. The women were wearing small-flowered fabrics in various shades of mud, dresses mostly, but some long skirts topped with fake-Victorian blouses, high at the neck, long at the sleeve.

With the antennae that grew ten feet above her head, Zoë received the approval that came to meet her as she moved into the room. It was not simply eyes drawn towards a young, attractive woman. It was an acknowledgement, at a level beyond a rational description of her as visually pleasing, of her energy, her excitement, her incandescence. Without knowing why, the voices of her acknow-ledgers grew more animated. Drinks were proffered, muscles relaxed.

Craig noticed people noticing Zoë and was proud of his choice. Still holding her elbow he steered her towards their hostess, introduced them, then left Zoë to go in search of drinks. With relief her arm fell to its place at her side. As she talked to the older woman Zoë was rising on her inner toes, stretching tall inside to enjoy the warmth radiating through her, seeing it reflected in the woman's face too as she welcomed Zoë and told her with genuine feeling how glad she was that Craig could bring her.

Safe, she was safe here. So far, far away from New Zealand. She was her own woman, unencumbered by the weight of James's disapproval, free of Jane's absence. She treasured the moment.

Zoë turned a beaming smile on poor hapless Craig as he returned, white knight, with a glass of frightful Spanish wine for her to drink.

He bent near and touched her hand as he lit her cigarette. She smoked St Moritz menthol cigarettes, even though she knew it was rather a New Zealand thing to do. She had quickly learned to recognize such things and effectively to eliminate them from her vocabulary of behaviour. But she liked these best. She was sensitive to taste. Especially in the mouth.

Craig was obviously impatient to have her to himself and to share with her more of the background to his jousting on the business plains. He backed her against a wall and she stared at him in amazement at his skill and daring while calculating how long she could inflate her modicum of real interest and listen, before asking to be excused to go to the lavatory so she could, discreetly, cruise the room. Not that she expected any great surprises, but she loved to meet new people when she felt so good, and surely the whole point of a party was to be seen and to see who, even in the most unpropitious of places, might be waiting to be discovered. Remember the good fairy, she told herself, the glass slipper, the pumpkin, the pea.

With a gentle smile and a little pressure to his upper arm which he had, he was relieved to note, automatically and effectively flexed, Zoë excused herself as Craig began to unfold the possible outcome to his coup. 'I'll be back in just a moment,' she probably lied. Craig turned away in search of his host, a former colleague with whom he still shared an occasional evening of beer and city gossip in the King's Head.

Zoë left the room and found her way to the bathroom. She locked the door, checked her face, sucked in her cheeks to make unlikely hollows, then grinned at her reflection. As she came out, a small-flowered woman was waiting to take her turn. The two women looked at each other, instantly assessing their very real differences in self-presentation, aware that each of them was likely to be here as appendage to an identikit coup-maker. Zoë felt somewhat embarrassed. Had she still been grinning as she came out? She looked the woman in the face and smiled at her, grateful when the woman smiled back, in a seemingly warm and open way. It was sometimes hard still for Zoë to read the English. They were so, was it subtle?

She moved back carefully into the sitting-room, checking where Craig stood, relieved to see he had his back to her and was engaged in conversation. Picking up an empty glass, she made her way forward, sensing that as she moved people's eyes followed her.

She edged in the vague direction of the drinks table then noticed, between heads, that on one of the walls was a reproduction of the same Gauguin painting she had seen today at the Tate, the same painting which had hung, in reproduction, on her mother's wall all those years ago. She paused, then eased herself past groups of people towards it. She stood in front of the spot where it hung on the wall then, forgetting the party, the people, even herself, she leant towards it as though she might step into it, be there, be part of that moment, on the bench, with those women, hot and slowed-lazy under the sun, her hand reaching up to stroke the sweet-smelling oiled hair of the woman in front of her on the bench, even as her back is rubbed, gently round and round, by the woman behind her, the one in the dark blue and white flowered *lava lava*. And if she leans back, just a little, she can feel the weight of the woman's breasts against her hot sticky back, and if the woman laughs as Zoë throws her head back and tickles her with her hair, she can feel the woman shake as breasts and belly join in the laughing.

She remembers Charles Olson: 'When the attentions change/the jungle leaps in.'

'Do you care for a drink, or?'

Zoë is startled by the voice. She is not in Tahiti. She is in England. She is not leaning back against a large laughing Polynesian woman. She is standing alone in a Chelsea sitting-room filled with people she doesn't know. A man she doesn't know is asking her something, and again, 'Your glass is empty. Perhaps you will allow me to get you something?'

His accent is odd, as is his appearance. No coup-maker this one. He has small, very dark eyes, moving fast in a high-cheek-boned chiselled face. Englishmen's eyes don't move that fast. It's part of a level of excitement to which they do not care to rise.

His hair is very dark, as dark and curly and as long as Zoë's own. She has a quick involuntary flash, seeing her cheek against that hair. No no.

'Well, yes, thank you, how nice, a drink would be, yes, nice.' She slides some smiles across her face, wondering why he continues to stare, why she suddenly feels so uncomfortable, so put out of herself.

Perhaps her mascara is smudged; could she have dandruff on her shoulders that he has noticed even in the poor light of this room? Perhaps too much of her breasts are showing? She puts her hand to the neckline of her dress while he continues to stare. How rude.

'You do not need to cover your breasts in this way. They seem very beautiful. How *English* you are.'

Zoë recovers her sense of self. English she is not. 'No I am not. Well, do you intend to get us drinks or are you just going to go on standing there, staring at me?'

The man laughs, and moves away. Zoë breathes out, with relief, but when the man comes back her breathing becomes shallow again. What the hell is going on?

The man is staring again. It is insupportable. She launches into her series of questions. The answers weave between, make a pattern. He is German, from Berlin, living here in London, a sculptor, yes, he loves his work, yes, he loves London, he too lives in Chelsea, quite near here in fact, a worn out flat, bereft of everything but a view of the water, opposite.

He makes her laugh. She is enjoying herself again, parodying herself, liking that, delighted that he is quick enough probably to be aware of it. Yet she is also still uncomfortable. He is so, so foreign. What can he be thinking, and he is staring constantly, his eyes moving all over her face and the front of her body so the temptation to hide rises up in her again and again.

'Who did you come here with?' He is asking her a question now. Zoë waves in the general direction of Craig.

'He's over there, with the group in the centre. Reddish hair.'

The man has lifted an expressive eyebrow. Zoë blushes. 'Oh God, he's not my . . . well, the man I *am* involved with is away for the weekend, you see.' Zoë studies this man's face to see if her piece of news has any effect. Impossible to know. He is looking deep into her eyes as though looking for a mote. Perhaps he likes to swim. Between high walls. Towards castles. Towards princesses.

But frogs, in whom no latent princes lie, also like the water.

'Well, it's been wonderful to meet you . . . ?' Zoë gives the man the benefit of her most dazzling smile, which he does not return.

'Gabriel,' he says, with the kind of long 'ah' produced when a doctor presses a stick to your tongue in order to gaze down your throat, looking for infection. 'Gabriel Bongiovanni. My great-grandfather was Italian. As you hear, it rhymes with Don Giovanni. Please, will you wait here?'

Zoë is stunned. What a glorious name. 'Mine is Zoë Delighty,' she offers, not to be outdone. He is also clearly impressed. They look at each other, again.

'Please, Zoë, just a minute, eh?' She smiles, nods, genuine dazzle this time, then watches in increasing amazement as he moves, Gabriel Bongiovanni, slowly, politely apologizing as he brushes past people, not towards the drinks or the lavatory but towards Craig who looks around, surprised, as this man, to him clearly a foreigner, taps him on the shoulder and gestures, discreetly, towards a slightly gaping Zoë. She shuts her mouth fast, smiles tamely. Craig looks annoyed, startled, then both annoyed and startled. With a shrug of dismissal he turns back to the group, begins to talk again as Gabriel Bongiovanni edges his way back towards Zoë.

'Well, that's all right then. We can go.' He is speaking to her again. Still staring, though perhaps with slightly less confidence than before.

'Go!' Zoë notes the lack of originality in her exclamation. 'But what about Craig? I came with him, I mean.' Zoë stops. She may be alone on her team, but she does play strictly within her rules. Only on the rarest of occasions has she left a party with someone other than the man with whom she arrived. Only when tempted by the most pressing degree of sexual curiosity. Which she does not feel for this man. His cord jacket is such an ill-chosen and unflattering colour. He is certainly very good looking, but uncomfortably odd, and he stares.

'I told him,' Gabriel was speaking again, 'politely I believe and I hope with truth for you also, that you and I had a great deal to talk about and that I wished to take you home — so, we can go now?'

'Oh can we?' Zoë searched the room for a solution. For salvation. Saw none. Put down her glass, picked up her cigarettes and, walking just behind Gabriel and with a somewhat awkward nod to Craig, left the party in Chelsea and walked out into a soft summer night.

Gabriel had the most exquisite hands Zoë had ever seen on a man. She noticed them first when she was lying with him on his mattress on the floor. They had arrived there after a long indirect walk through the streets, mostly in silence. Zoë's unspoken questions were for herself, and Gabriel had not interrupted her search for answers.

Now, solemnly and with great persistence, he was undoing the many red satin-covered buttons running the length of the front of her black crepe dress, even as she followed him with her own rather lovely hands, doing the buttons up again.

This pantomime continued for some time before she rolled away from him in impatience to lie on her stomach. She was confused by her suspicions that she was way out of her depth, also oddly deflated from her high of the evening, but curious enough to stay where she was.

'Do you have anything to eat? I'm starving.' She was not, but was certainly desperate to be, for some minutes, alone.

'I don't think so but, please, one moment.' He left the room and she sat up quickly to win the button war before lying down, again on her stomach.

'Only these, I'm afraid.' He had returned and was holding out a jar of mixed nuts.

'They'll do. Thanks.'

He watched her eat. At least, she assumed he was watching her as he lay without moving beside her while she was attempting to unjumble her kaleidoscope of thoughts by concentrating on her hand moving from jar to mouth, filling it with stale and unpalatable nuts.

'Zoë, I'd like you to stay here with me tonight.'

Here it was, at last. Oh well. She finished chewing, wiped her mouth with the back of her hand and turned to face him. 'Yes, I'm sure you would. But I can't.' She moved and looked away from him. Monogamy was as natural to Zoë as sky-diving, but it made the excuse that men liked best. 'I mentioned already that I'm, well, you know, *involved* with someone. So really, I shouldn't.'

'Does that mean you will?'

It was impossible for her to gauge how much irony there was in his voice, but his answer charmed and disarmed her. Her questions were submerged as the joy of the day rose high in her, tidal wave against doubt. She laughed, forsook the almost empty jar of nuts, and rolled back towards him.

*

Gabriel woke Zoë in the morning, at the last gasp of morning, with a shower of flowers. He had crept out of bed and the room and the flat without waking her, and had returned to find her still, and still sleeping. He knelt by the mattress they had shared on the floor with the flowers in his arms and, when she stirred, sensing his presence, he woke her with small gentle kisses. She smiled and stretched towards him, beginning to notice the flowers, as well as his face bending over her, gazing at her with love maybe, admiration certainly. He stood up and began to drop the flowers down onto her, one by one as she laughed and called his name and told him how clever and wonderful this was, he was, how utterly beautiful, and tried to banish from her waking mind the image of his standing above her, dropping flowers down onto her grave.

Zoë moved into Gabriel's flat exactly four days after she met him. It was 4 July, American Independence Day – more to the point, Gabriel's birthday – and she could think of no better present to offer than herself as full-time live-in lover. She did not warn him, nor come gift wrapped. He was delighted to see her when she knocked on the door. It was the first time in their tiny history she had turned up like this, without prior plan. He was surprised to see the first suitcase behind her, more surprised when she told him there were more, and piles of boxes, waiting to be brought up from the bottom of the stairs.

'But Zoë,' he wasn't staring now, he was looking down and away and only slowly up again. 'You know, I am here for only two more months.'

The cloud on which Zoë had been floating for four days and nights sagged a little beneath her. 'No, of course I don't know that. How the fuck could I? Did you tell me? You said you liked it here, could work well here. You said, if I may remind you, "Against such a defeated background, one has to explode with work." I thought that meant you *lived* here, really lived here.' Her voice was rising but her heart, like the cloud, was sinking fast. These last days had been extraordinary, completely extraordinary. He had lavished her with attention, listened, had really listened to every word she'd uttered, even the most ridiculous and hastily considered. He had made love to her as though her life or his would be saved only if he caressed and appreciated every last inch of her. What the hell had all that been about? She didn't know.

'Oh well,' cracked the joker as she sprang up out of her box, 'I've brought all this junk here now and I'm not taking it back. So, if it's two months, it's two months. I'll be tired of you by then anyway.' She giggled, unconvinced. 'Happy birthday, Gabriel. I am, well, I intended myself to be, your present.' Christ, was she going to cry? Surely not. She never cried.

'And you are. It's a most beautiful present, Zoë. We must celebrate at once with the wine I'd bought for your visit this evening. But first.' Gabriel pulled her towards him, across the space of their first disharmony, held her close as she rested her head against his collar-bone, smelling the new familiarity of him, collecting her thoughts, pausing, then hearing a faint splash as the rope bridge which swung back to her previous life fell. Far down into the deep green gorge, rushing behind her.

Two

The soft evening light to be seen through the wide-opened sitting-room window was cushioning the shapes of buildings, bridges, houseboats, roads and wall. Gabriel stood at the window, pressing those shapes into his memory, bleeding them of colour until they were all grain and texture and matter within space.

On the mat-covered floor behind him lay sheets of dark red writing paper, a gift from his mother, barely touched. The room was almost empty of furniture: a trestle table where notes and books were immaculately ordered and stacked, two huge cream-coloured cushions on either one of which both he and Zoë could sit. On the wall above the trestle table was a dark brown cork noticeboard with photographs tacked onto it of landscapes, of single buildings, or of shapes. All black and white. The single painting in the room was black too, not large, apparently reflecting only the light, make of it what you will. The only colour on the walls came from a postcard, set apart from the photographs on the noticeboard, of a painting by Sonia Delauney: radiant swirls of colour, a dance of rainbow veils, but controlled too, each colour leading on to and saying something about the next, and the next.

Zoë stood in Gabriel's kitchen, her kitchen too now. She was stirring a sauce which the recipe had promised would, by this stage, be thickening. It was thin, and growing thinner. She badly wanted this meal to be a success. Not even for Gabriel, for herself. During these first two weeks with him she had allowed a very clear picture to develop in her mind of a woman serving to her lover food as magnificent as her love for him. Or his for her.

She couldn't seem to find the recipe.

Gabriel's idea of food was even more elementary than her own. He was suspicious of a meal that didn't include green vegetables, but usually ate these raw, adding bread, fruit or cheese or, rarely, meat, according to the time of day or week. He arranged these single items most beautifully on the plate, arranged the plate most beautifully on a tray, with cloth and napkin and a flower in a tiny vase, always in a new combination. Zoë couldn't match his skill in presentation, would grow impatient even watching him as he punctiliously sliced and quartered and bent back and arranged. What she wanted to show herself capable of, more than capable of, was making rich voluptuous meals, excessive with sauce and drenched in mysterious but totally memorable flavours.

She had never had this urge to cook before. She had made a point of quieting any such incipient urge even before it could be named. The girls who had become women with her had shown no shame in the many hours they spent preparing food for Gary, Barry or Brian when he returned home from rugby, surfing or cricket. They neglected their own interests to have perfect meals ready on the dot of the ordered time, but often hours before the hero actually returned, awash with alcohol and complaining and petulant because his dinner was now dry in the oven.

Zoë had always insisted on going out or had produced sandwiches or spaghetti bolognese so unspeakably awful that the hint that she might cook was never made again.

It was not that Zoë was empty of longings to please. These had always been strong in her, and sometimes she'd been shamed by them. But if she could not control the longings, she could determine the route through which they would emerge and anything as ordinary as showing herself to be the good little woman in the kitchen in the Land of the Great Many Bottlers was definitely not for her. Besides, she could, actually, burn soup from a tin.

Yet, here she was, stirring a ridiculous sauce, even as she smelt something – could it be the meat? – burning in the oven.

Gabriel left the sitting-room and came to the kitchen, leaning against the door frame, anxious about Zoë, wanting to help. He also wanted to be near her. He found his attraction towards her was indescribably compulsive. He found *her* indescribably exciting. He had been, at once, transfixed when she walked into the room at the party. He was there quite by chance, or so he thought. Some weeks before he had met the woman who was his host that night at a lecture at the Goethe Institut where he went, occasionally, when a quasi-homesickness came over him, a longing to hear German spoken, not just the words themselves, but the way in which words are used in Germany: to search, to challenge, to break new ground in old arguments. The woman had sat quietly next to him but when the lecture and discussion were over she had turned to him and said she hadn't understood all the lecturer had intended. Could he perhaps find time to have a coffee with her to discuss it further? There was no flirtatiousness in the woman's manner and Gabriel enjoyed the hour they spent together, and drank coffee with her several times again before she asked him to the party which she and her husband, mentioned now for the first time, were giving to celebrate their sixth wedding anniversary.

He had felt shy about accepting. His English was not yet good enough to follow conversation made in a group and he knew he was hopelessly out of his depth in understanding the social dynamics of the unradicalized English petty-bourgeoisie. But he was also curious, a little lonely, and grateful to be asked. He took from his suitcase an old corduroy jacket, brushed it down and decided he would pass. His expectations had been quite modest and even those had seemed unlikely to be fulfilled, and then he had seen this extraordinary, well, he could only name her to himself as this *wild* girl come into the room. It could simply have been that everyone else around him in that room was depressingly muted, but he thought not. She had something utterly individual as she stood there, at the door, beside some almost invisible man. She seemed too big for the room, or for her body, though her body was certainly not small. She was not conventionally beautiful. It wasn't that. She was alive somewhere, somehow, or larger than alive (didn't the English have an expression 'larger than life'?). She glowed, and looked as though anything, anything was possible, with or for her. He had said to himself, as she stood near the door and he, out of sight, near the wall: this is a woman I could really love. He had felt acutely self-conscious, though there was no one to read his thoughts, but stubborn too, and single-minded as to his insight.

The girl had slipped out of his sight for a while and then he noticed her almost lost behind the dark hulk of some man's back. He moved to get a better view of her. She appeared to be staring intently at the man. Her lips were slightly open and moving sometimes to broaden her smile. Did she love this man? And then she had gone altogether, had left the room and the man had moved to talk elsewhere. His heart had sunk. Maybe he had lost her? But she had come back into the room, had moved through it, slowly and alone, and he had noticed the eyes of women and men had followed her. She wasn't especially graceful, but the association with untamed creatures returned to his mind. He wanted to go to her straight away, in case he lost her. He practised some English phrases in his mind. They all sounded ridiculous to him. Oh, if only she were German, but he knew how glad he was that she was almost certainly not. He watched her pause as something caught her eye, then she moved towards it. He had arrived too early at this party, unsure of the conventions, and had used that awkward time to explore each one of the reproductions that hung in the room, so immediately he saw her back as she faced the wall, he knew it was the Gauguin she was absorbed in. He wondered how a young Englishwoman would see Gauguin's work. He was curious that she could stand so still there, unless she was unhappy and seeking an escape? But that couldn't be. She had radiated happiness. That had been what had made her exceptional, her glow, her *joie*. He had to speak to her.

When, hearing his voice, she turned to face him, he was struck at once by the process of focusing he was able to observe in her old-leaf green eyes. She was having to come forward to listen to him from some distant place. She was, in that moment, unprotected, and he felt great tenderness in himself, then amusement as she spoke to him again, brisk now, collected, but still emanating this feeling of great energy. Not only wild creatures were stalking across the landscape of his mind, but images of volcanoes were forming, tall, magnificent, and imminently about to erupt.

He knew he was staring at her in an entirely unacceptable way and he couldn't stop or even guard it. He was avid for the sight of her, wanted to drag her into himself through his eyes. She regaled him with questions and he was grateful for them as he could answer, could find the English words with almost no thought at all, and could use most of his mind to struggle with the central, the absolutely crucial question of how he was going to fulfil his need to be alone with her, to take her home, to have her by him, to be inside her. It was not a sexual need he was experiencing, though he was certainly powerfully sexually attracted, it was a desire to ensure that she could *see* him. He was sure that if he were to take her home, and to make love to her, she would feel honour bound to see him at least once more. It was the essential key to the door that would lead to another meeting. And he had to have that.

He felt his energy beginning to slip away, even as his desire grew more compelling. He felt her beginning to slip away, even as he tilted uncomfortably towards her, until she offered him the chance to tell her his name. It seemed to be like a charm to her. She smiled so broadly on hearing it. That was odd. He liked his name, but had never before had reason to be grateful to it. And when she had told him her name, as though she were giving him a gift, he had understood better: she was a weaver of words, of incantations. He cursed his poor English. In German he could play such magical games that he need never lose her, never. He had to act.

Seeing her now, subdued in the kitchen, stirring the sauce she was insisting he would enjoy, he was almost angry with her, and angry and frustrated with himself. Angry with her because she seemed to think she needed to please him through this most ordinary of methods, when, to him, she was the most extraordinary of, of creatures. No wild creature ever stood, patient, bent in front of a stove, stirring. And now crying out because it would not go right.

'Please Zoë, can I help you?' he asked, not knowing that his voice was thick with patience, that it reminded her (oh, how could he know?) of James's voice when he spoke to Caroline about matters he was sure poor Caroline would never understand but that somehow, he, James, would be good enough to illuminate for her.

'No, you can't.'

'I think, excuse me, that perhaps the meat . . .?'

There was silence in the kitchen. It was only too obvious that, excuse me, the meat. Zoë should have laughed. Part of Zoë wanted to laugh. All of Zoë needed to laugh. But she couldn't. Her pride had dislodged and slipped into the thin thin sauce. Her dreams of Gabriel being thrilled and awed by her culinary feats were in a heap around her and still he wasn't leaving the kitchen but was speaking

119

again, in that godawful don't-kick-me-now voice, saying, 'Zoë, it doesn't matter.'

'It *does* matter,' she screamed. Believing it. Then watched, in horror, as her own hand lifted the pot from the stove, turned it over, and allowed the hot sticky mess to run all over the floor, the same floor she had seen Gabriel, down on his hands and knees no squeezy-easy mop for him, wash only hours before.

There was, again, silence in the kitchen. Why didn't he scream at her so she could scream back? She felt tight, suffocating almost. Why was he just standing there like some bloody statue? Did he have no feelings at all? And the mess! It was horrible, and spreading.

Zoë threw the saucepan into the sink and jumped, unsuccessfully, over the sauce. Her boots were covered in it and made sticky marks as she pushed roughly past Gabriel and ran through the flat to the front door and down the stairs and out into the street. Leaving Gabriel behind.

She ran towards Earls Court. It was early evening. She had no money with her but, with any luck, she might come across a friend who would buy her a much-needed drink.

After more than an hour of running and walking and heaving she had met only somewhat curious flickers from strangers.

During the hour she had begun to quieten down, to see how absurd the whole event was. Gabriel's patience with her would have to be gone, surely. He'd probably kick her out. Yes, Zoë was certain he'd do that. Anyone in their right mind would and, as she told herself, if anyone was ever in their right, thoroughly sharpened mind, it was Gabriel. Razor brain, she'd called him more than once to hide her awe and perhaps her envy behind an easy joke. But sharp as he was he couldn't know that she'd kept her temper along with a whole heap of other raw emotions locked up in the freezer for years. Nor that the door of that freezer was hanging open now and frightening her as Gabriel's warm breath blew on it again and again. To him she must surely seem like a barbarian. He'd not even asked her to live with him, after all. She'd pushed herself on him. Pushy, just as James and Caroline had always said to make her ashamed. Wild, uncontrollable, self-centred: just as James and Caroline had always said.

'Oh to hell with bloody James and Caroline,' Zoë muttered aloud.

She'd come thirteen thousand miles to escape their low opinion of her, not to have it hanging around her ears. It was Gabriel she wanted to impress, Gabriel she wanted.

Zoë was grateful for the clarity of this desire. She had revelled in the desire he showed for her, not just for her body it seemed. For her, whatever that meant. Wanting him, wanting to know him, wanting to move towards him, that was taking longer.

She wouldn't waste another minute. She'd go home now, risk his anger, clean up the mess, beg his forgiveness, promise never, never to attempt to cook again, never, never to lose her temper again, never . . . She puffed and ran and ran and puffed, repeating her resolutions until she almost believed every one of them.

With words of contrition ready to fall from her lips, falling even as she crashed through the front door left ajar into a spotless flat, she hit against the silence. Gabriel wasn't there.

She felt frantic. My God, she felt abandoned. Suppose he had gone forever? Suppose he had left her to give someone else that miraculous quality of love and devotion which she, Zoë, now knew she wanted? Suppose he'd run out into the street blinded by grief and had been run over? It would be all her fault. Suppose he was at this very minute bleeding his last in hospital, whispering her name? Suppose he was already dead, cooling in a mortuary, beyond the consolation of her passionate resolutions?

She looked at her watch. Mickey Mouse grinned up at her without a sliver of discrimination. She had been gone only an hour and a half. She returned to the scene of her crime and opened the oven door. A shrivelled, definitely dead piece of meat lay in congealed fat. She wrapped it in newspaper and put it into the bin. There was nothing else she could do in the kitchen. Even licking the floor by way of penance wouldn't make it any cleaner.

Zoë went into the bedroom ready to throw herself on the mattress, pictures of Gabriel's beautiful, under-appreciated body, dashed, maimed, dead, flashing before her eyes.

On the pillow, on what they had begun rather self-consciously to call 'her side', was a note. Around the edge of the words Gabriel had drawn in coloured chalks an unbroken chain of flowers. Zoë remembered the drawings with which Maria used to embellish her letters. She sniffed. Damn. And read: 'Forgive me. [Forgive *him*!

Shit.] I would always rather drink with you than with myself alone. At the Queen's Arms. Viele Küsse. Dein Gabriel.'

Zoë was elated, and desperate to get there, to see him, touch him, tell him it was he who must forgive her, not she him. But first she must change her clothes. She didn't want him to see her again in those clothes in which she'd stomped out with such loss of dignity.

She chose a white embroidered shirt and short red skirt which he had admired when helping her to unpack. She took out her best French sandals, bright scarlet and high heeled. She doused herself in perfume, made up her eyes, grabbed her handbag and ran somewhat uncomfortably down the stairs and into the street. In time to find Gabriel, no longer in the pub but walking home agonizing over his loss, transformed when he heard Zoë scream his name, oblivious to passers-by, and run towards him, clumsy on her high heels and almost bowling him over in her enthusiasm to hug him and to drag him, all the while talking talking so fast he cannot begin to comprehend but can only smile, back towards the flat, towards the room, towards the mattress, towards herself.

Three

Zoë would not have been able to say precisely, even to herself, if she enjoyed her hours in bed with Gabriel during their first days weeks months years together. She would have been embarrassed by the question and would have met it head on with an extravagantly coloured declaration of devotion and ecstasy.

She was always eager to lie down with Gabriel, to put her arms around him, to stroke him, to play with his hair, to sit on the edge of the bath waiting until she could dry him, to turn to him as she woke, to hold him as she went to sleep with her breath warm and slightly moist against his back.

She was both appalled and in awe of the level of attention he directed towards her. Some small-girl self almost lost inside her remembered Jane, took this attention as her due, and flourished. Grown-up, self-made, now-you-see-me-now-you-don't Zoë was way out of her depth. She knew greedy tendrils were growing out from her towards the light that was Gabriel, wanting his care, longing for his approval, revelling in his talents, lusting for his attention and almost every day, every hour, imagining herself without it, without him.

From the beginning came the dreams of his dying. Night after night she woke wet with sweat, trembling, overwhelmed with the agony of her loss, and he would be sleeping, still and silent, beside her. As still as a corpse, but warm and breathing.

Zoë would turn to him, putting her hand to his chest to measure its rise and fall, moving as close to him as she dared without waking him, burrowing towards him as a primitive creature might burrow in search of its lost, essential home.

When, in his sleep, he would stroke her, sometimes kiss her, she could feel herself soaking that in and could sleep again, sweet dreams now. Sometimes still almost asleep, certainly not awake, he

123

would become hard and fuck her, fast and deep, for several intense minutes. She would feel grateful and alive, much more alive though she couldn't understand this and pushed it from her thoughts, than during the hours of exquisitely choreographed love-making that took place when Gabriel was fully awake, looking at her, eyes wide open. When, despite the beauty and intensity of emotion, Zoë would feel herself coming adrift: becoming a small thing, a speckle almost, a princess-become-pea as the frog-become-prince looms over her, larger and larger, more and more magnificent as he grows, sweating, flowing and glowing into the damp cinder, the dying ember of her body.

Gabriel worked every day. He was oblivious to the notion of weekends. Zoë assumed he would stop this when she gave up her own job. But she was wrong.

She had been living with him for several weeks, daily more conscious of how absurdly little time they still had together, though scarcely able to believe he would really go. She wanted to order him to stay, to insist that he must stay. She wanted to tie gold ropes around his ankles and weight them down with her jewelled arguments as to why he must not speak, must not dream even, of going from her.

He was so hungry for her. He'd starve to death without her, wouldn't he? And if breakfast and supper were barely enough then she'd lay herself on a plate, garnished, at lunch time too. Perhaps only until – she is turning from the thought – he left.

Zoë liked the job which stood in the way of being available to Gabriel all day. It had been surprisingly difficult to get something challenging when she arrived in London wet from her colonial cocoon. Go dry out your wings on menial work, they seemed to be telling her. Though more usually they simply ceased to listen when they heard her give-away voice on the phone. Australians and New Zealanders are said to be unreliable, incredulous fellow-travellers muttered. Good only for waitressing or nannying. Or driving buses across the Sahara, if they were boys. But she was here to stay, she wanted to tell them. Words were her calling, not babies or plates. She wanted, not to call this England home, but to settle down far from that place she could call home. She needed something real, something big to write back about, to embroider for Rebecca and make her proud. To justify leaving Rebecca to that husband.

The answer to her prayers for work fell into her lap at a party. A very drunk girl, barely able to see from beneath her dark red fringe, had spilt wine over Zoë, reeling on her heels as she flirted with a hero, sober when she saw the mess she had made of Zoë's clothes. They had gone into the kitchen and as they hopelessly sponged they had giggled together, instant conspirators. When the hero had appeared at the door to ignore Zoë and demand the girl's attention they had both stared at him, laughed again, and then pushed past him to leave the party together. They met often after that, to talk and share secrets. Zoë had badly needed a friend like Rosamund. She'd had many girlfriends at home, from school and university and work. She loved them and showered them with attention though they and she understood that all girlfriends stepped aside when a knight rode into town. Even when he rode in on an ass.

Rosamund was irreverent and crazy, qualities Zoë had been missing in her English women friends. She was also passionate about Zoë and eager to settle her more securely into London. She introduced Zoë to her own famous boss who was, she declared, lousy in bed but who owned magazines and warships and ingots in the bank, as well as a chain of bookshops where Rosamund worked.

The boss had been pleased to flex his magnanimity for Rosamund's sake and to offer her eager young friend a chance on one of his less important ventures, a business magazine aimed at executives with the tenacity of Sisyphus. Zoë wrote lively reports on conferences she had not attended, occasionally interviewed the nearly successful, but most often added violet to the ink of agency press releases. She also had fun with her fellow workers who were bound together by their contempt for the magazine and their enthusiasm for each other, and for the drinks on which they floated their days.

Zoë knew *Business World* was only a stepping stone but she liked the union card that came with the job and could easily have stayed long enough to win herself the right references and contacts to journey forward. Now, in the world of After Gabriel, she found the days almost impossible to endure. The chatter and flirtations of the office were sickening her. She knew she was hurting her colleagues as she withdrew from their games, but she had been generous in her descriptions of her wonderful affair so they were inclined to forgive her and continued to cajole her.

Zoë was also having difficulty concentrating. She had always been punctilious about getting even the most tedious copy in on time, but spent all of one busy afternoon writing 'Zoë Bongiovanni' in her shorthand pad. Zoë did not want to marry Gabriel. Deep in her memory were impressions of Jane, apparently well-off without a husband. Clear in her memory were bitter pictures of married James and Caroline, trapped. Right at the front of her mind, too raw even to be glanced at, were pictures of Rebecca, married and numbed. No, it was not marriage she wanted. It was a link, a sure link between them, something she could trust beyond next week.

She seized the pages covered in her handwriting, tore them up, threw them into the waste-paper basket, pushed back her chair and went in, knocking as she pushed the door open, to the editor's office to tell him she was resigning. Today. No notice. Yes, she did understand it would mean no reference. She was, of course, sorry, but there was nothing else she could do.

'You see,' declared Zoë without any self-consciousness, 'I'm in love.' She gazed intently at the editor who had seen better days and did not regard this as news. With her hand literally on her heart and with no irony intended she said, simply because she meant it, 'I've got to be with him.'

The editor shrugged and turned away from her, discomforted by her frankness and furious that she'd let him down when he had hired her on the recommendation, no, on the insistence of the boss man himself. Furious, too, because she had actually turned out to be rather good.

Zoë left the editor's office, went to her own desk in the crowded open-plan room, tidied out of it her personal possessions, pushed her typewriter to one side, climbed on her chair then up onto her desk, waited until all typing had stopped and voices had quietened, and then until all eyes were turned towards her, and said, 'Well darlings, I'm about to leave you to rock this sinking ship without me.' She judged the pause. Grinned, and went on. 'You'll understand – I no longer want to get up in the mornings.' She winked and her audience roared suitably encouraging lustful noises, sad she was leaving, surprised at her timing, but gratified she was sliding out on a bright streak of the vulgarity they had all encouraged in her.

Zoë jumped down from the desk, and blowing kisses and shouting promises to see them all soon, ran out of the door and home to Gabriel who had never, in his whole life, heard of anyone leaving a good safe job on a Tuesday afternoon without notice, references or pay.

Zoë was herself beginning to feel a little disquiet about her action, and needed to prop it up with a blaze of conviction. She had arrived home with champagne and wanted to insist that Gabriel came to drink it with her now, in bed. Yet, there he was, obviously involved with his drawings, sweetly paying her attention but dragged back, she could see it, to his drawing paper. 'In just an hour or two, Zoë, I've nearly got this right.'

She went into the kitchen, opened the near-empty fridge, placed the bottle of champagne inside it, went into the sitting-room, sat down on a big cushion and picked up a book. It was 1970 and Zoë was reading Doris Lessing.

Gabriel had not always worked so hard. Nor had he always been a sculptor. He had, when first at university, studied law. A subject chosen if not at the insistence of, then certainly to please his parents.

Gabriel's father had been a foreman in an electronics factory, a clever man whose university career had been permanently curtailed by his conscription into the army of the Third Reich. His mother had done better. She was a lawyer by profession, but in more recent years had worked as a senior administrator for a state-funded housing project. Gabriel was their only child. He was conceived in the last moments when victory for the Third Reich seemed possible though not, for his parents, desirable, and was born when that possibility was real only in the voice of the propaganda machinists.

His early childhood was typical of children born in Prussia in the last years of the second world war: father missing, mother starving, child and mother frightened, child crying, mother desperate, mother begging, child starving, child confused, mother weeping. She had escaped to the West by imploring American soldiers to give her petrol. It had been unspeakably difficult for her to do this, and utterly necessary if they were to survive. They had finally reached a small village near Tübingen where the mother had relatives too timid actually to tell them they weren't welcome, that there wasn't enough to be shared two more ways. She had tried to get work there, tried too to get news of Gabriel's father's whereabouts, or even a clue as to whether he was alive or dead.

By the time Gabriel started school, thin, anxious, seven years old and wearing over-large *lederhosen*, his parents had been reunited so long they'd had time to drift apart. They had also moved, to Frankfurt, a city which, being in the American sector of divided Germany, they correctly considered likely to flourish to provide the necessary facilities for rebuilding a stable, meaningful life which would not include memories of starvation and begging and home-lessness and rejection, nor of being seen by the British of whom you were a prisoner of war as a vile Nazi *Schwein*.

Mother and father and no-longer-baby Bongiovanni lived in an apartment that had been quickly created out of two rooms in a graceful four-storey nineteenth-century house near the Palm Gardens. One of the rooms, used both as drawing-room for the family and as a study for his parents, had retained the high, light proportions, the elegance and style that had once distinguished the whole house, when it had been home to not eight families but one. The other room had been clumsily divided, paper-thin partitions making several cartoon rooms, of the one-dimensional kind drawn by little children: his parents' bedroom, Gabriel's room, a kitchen stacked high with cheap tinned food against the terrible moment when rationing might again be declared, or war. The Bongiovannis shared a bathroom, outside their flat in a corridor, with the other family on the floor. It smelled, always, of souring cleaning fluids, and disinfectant.

Those years in flight and in Frankfurt continued to shape Gabriel's life. He went on belonging to that time, even after his parents moved to the suburbs, to a neat quiet house with a garden, all their own. He ate much too fast, despite his ulcer, and could leave nothing on his plate, even food he didn't like or want. He could not bath slowly, nor use more than a pitiful minimum of water, always seeing the ghost of someone who might need to follow him. He cleaned behind himself in the kitchen and the bathroom as though he had the plague and must spare the evil spreading. His silent sleeping, involuntary though he claimed it to be when Zoë remarked on it, seemed on reflection to have been born from the repugnance he had felt at hearing his parents move, sniff and snore as they fell into exhausted sleep just beyond his wall. When he made love to Zoë he would whisper to her, speaking to her in German, something he never did at any other time, even when later she needed this. No sounds of involuntary pain or pleasure ever emerged from him. He never cried or screamed or shouted out to God as she did, nor laughed loudly nor wept. Except in silence.

Gabriel worked most diligently at school, did what he was told and what was expected. He was anxious to avoid bringing any more stress into the apartment than his parents carried home with them each day from work where they were hacking out, hands to the chisel, their share of German reconstruction, the German miracle of democracy and financial stability.

When he was nineteen, and about to begin the final harrowing year of preparation for his *Abitur* exam which would give him the right to go to university, his father had a stroke that left him paralysed, and Gabriel's first girlfriend, a schoolmate, became pregnant.

Gabriel was not religious, though he did sincerely believe in God and had been taught, as a necessary part of being good, the basic doctrine of the Lutheran faith. He prayed with great fervour to God at this time, desperate to understand why his father should be struck down now when the possibility of an easier life was a tiny but surely visible speck on the horizon. He prayed to God to help his mother, whose reaction to one more event beyond her apparent control was near to despair. He prayed to God to help him cope with Christa's pregnancy. But if help was to be seen, then Gabriel was blinking. No help came for him, for his father, his mother. Nor for Christa.

Gabriel and Christa had made love once. They had been kissing and touching and hugging and talking and wanting each other for more than a year but, terrified of the vivid spectre of pregnancy, had always stopped short of actual intercourse. They both intended to go to university. It was part of their parents' expectations for them, part of the reason their parents worked so hard and were always too

129

tired for any pleasure. Their sacrifices were to ensure that their children could do better, could enjoy the fruits of the miracle, could stroke with familiarity and pride the phoenix which had risen, trembling, from the ashes of the Third Reich.

It was Christa who had finally urged the plunge. She had discussed the matter with her best girlfriend, a doctor's daughter, who had assured her that if Christa and Gabriel were to make love only a day or two after Christa's period had ended, and if Gabriel withdrew before coming, then they would be quite safe. Christa passed on these tidings to Gabriel during recess at school. Gabriel was no less apprehensive, hearing Christa's earnest voice, but he was much more aroused than he had ever been and this was not appeased by increasing his silent hours of masturbation, an occupation he found utterly compulsive, and repelling.

Christa raised the matter with him again one Sunday afternoon. He had been invited by her mother, pressed by Christa, to coffee and cakes with the family, submitting, to be near Christa, to a tortured hour of polite conversation as cakes and thick whipped cream and sugar were passed up and down the beautifully laid table in a vain attempt to sweeten the proceedings. When her father had finally left the room and the table had been cleared, Christa asked Gabriel to come with her out to the terrace to admire the clematis, spread luxuriously over a large trestle, which was her mother's summer joy. As she held one of the deep pink blooms in her hand and turned it, this way and that, holding it too tight in her nervousness, bruising it, Christa suggested to Gabriel that they take a walk and, looking intently at him, she was asking him to understand that she was offering him something infinitely more delicate than the bruised bloom in her fingers.

Gabriel waited in a state of frozen anxiety while Christa went in to receive her mother's permission for their outing. They headed off, without needing to discuss it, towards an old graveyard, disused for many years, where the graves of Jews lay unkempt, no relatives surviving to care for them. Behind the graveyard was a hill, wooded and dark. Gabriel had hated this place as a child, had been afraid here. He was afraid now, not of the woods, but of Christa and her implacable determination.

When they had gone high into the woods, had found a clearing, had even heard birds sing, they lay down on the grass. Christa took off her pants, Gabriel undid his jeans and took them off, then folded them neatly to make a cushion for Christa's head. Neither of them removed their shirt. Christa pulled up her skirt so Gabriel could touch her. They were both rigid with nervousness. Even the kissing which usually calmed as well as excited them tasted strange. Gabriel's erection pressed against Christa. He pushed and strained as she spread herself wide for him, accepting the pain she had been warned by the doctor's daughter to expect. Gabriel felt aroused and eager and extremely uncomfortable. But he was also coming, coming almost at once, even before he had gone right into Christa, coming just inside her when he should have pulled out.

It was virtually impossible to get an abortion in West Germany in the early 1960s, not if you were a healthy schoolgirl from a good Frankfurt family. Christa and Gabriel got married. She had to leave school, already three months pregnant. Gabriel was permitted to stay until he had sat and passed the *Abitur*. Their child was a boy. They named him Stefan-Georg.

Gabriel couldn't seem to find the right moment to tell Zoë about Christa and Stefan. He wanted to. He knew his delay was increasing the danger of it becoming an issue between them. Zoë was eager to know about his past – his life 'pre-me' as she called it. But each of them approached the recounting of their history warily, stressing the absolutely immediate past that was their shared time, stressing the present, avoiding discussion of the future.

Gabriel had realized almost at once that he was unable to predict Zoë's reactions to events, statements, gestures, moods and soon wondered if she could predict this herself. He envied what he perceived as the breadth of her emotional range, her ability to flare up, or collapse in a heap weakened by excesses of laughter, to cry out his name or God's when they were making love uncaring who in all London might hear her. He had begun to notice that she didn't cry. He also noticed how quick she was to withdraw into herself, like a snail when it's touched, perhaps into that place she had been when she first turned to meet his voice at the party in Chelsea. He had seen again since that odd fudging in the colour of her eyes, the very slight dilation of her pupils, the tightening of her face and skin against him. He couldn't bear it. Couldn't bear the possibility that, when hearing about Christa, she might fly inwards to perch alone where he could never reach her.

The tightening came, he was able to observe, when he failed to adjust quickly enough to her changes of mood, to that wonderful enthusiasm which was like a foreign language to him, made up of symbols and pictures and delicate strokes, like a language of the East, forming a pattern still entirely mysterious to him.

He envied, perhaps most of all, that incandescent spontaneity which seemed to him to be drawn out of the near-empty new country she came from. That kind of spontaneity was surely crushed and buried long ago in Europe. It would have had no place to breathe in the country where he had been nurtured and moulded. He wanted to learn at least a pale version of that spontaneity from her, but was clumsy, even in his responses to it.

She had been badly hurt then quick to hide it when, home for the last time from her work, eager to celebrate her self-won freedom, a gift for him, she had offered champagne and a painful dilemma. The drawing that lay in front of him represented problems almost solved after hours of concentrated work, but the solution was sneaking away even as Zoë filled the room with her story of her clamber onto the desk, her colleagues' cheers and encouragement, her pleasure in now being able to be with him, here, all the time.

Gabriel knew Zoë had done this to please him. She had described to him how hard it had been for her, more subtly a foreigner in this country than he is but foreigner all the same, to get a job she liked. She had made this grand gesture out of love. But also out of ignorance of his need, his absolute compulsion to work, perhaps not stronger but certainly much older than his need for her. She didn't understand this; how could she, without knowing that it was born from all those years when he had tried and failed to be a good son husband father lawyer. The man whom his parents and Christa and Stefan-Georg needed him to be.

He had indeed tried. It was only when he finally rebelled, when his exam failure had given him the excuse he needed to be frank, to say that what *he* wanted was not to be a lawyer but to go to art school to study sculpture, that he realized how he creaked and ached from being confined so long within other people's dreams.

The energy he began to feel when he was accepted to study in Berlin had never left him. He knew he had been transformed. Even the guilt he continued intermittently and uselessly to feel about Christa and Stefan could not deflate him. He and Christa were still married. Between them existed a scarcely tended presumption that they were a family and would, one day, live as such again. Yet there were days on end when Gabriel seldom thought of them. It was not other women who filled his mind, though he was effortlessly attractive to women and enjoyed that. It was his work which was central, which challenged and expanded him, which *created* him. It had been, until he met Zoë, only through his work that he could feel he was experiencing himself as the person he was meant to be.

By his fourth year in Berlin Gabriel had been visiting Frankfurt increasingly less often. He and Christa told each other how sad it was that the expense of the journey kept them apart. He knew, because she had no reason to conceal it from him, that Christa had a lover, a man who was fond of Stefan and cared for her too. She also said, quite clearly, that for her it was only a comfort. Just until they could all be together again. Perhaps until she could free herself of her need for her parents' support and bring their son to Berlin.

Also in his fourth year, the head of the school of sculpture told Gabriel he had recommended him for a scholarship which would allow him to leave Germany and to study, with all expenses of living and tuition paid, in the Western European country of his choice. The prize money would be sufficient only for himself, a quasi-single man.

The prize, Gabriel had realized at once, would be magnificent. Except for a weekend with Christa in Paris, when tiny Stefan had been left with Christa's still-unforgiving mother, Gabriel had never left Germany. He was constantly poor, knocked bare even by the money needed for the long day-and-night journey from Berlin to Frankfurt.

More important even than the prospect of travel, Gabriel was stirred by the possibility that the prize might enable his family to see his decision to work as a sculptor as one of validity and honour, taken not to hurt them, but because anything else was a compromise that would cripple him.

When the award was his he chose London, discarding Paris only

133

at the last moment and with reluctance, not knowing quite why, but reminding himself that he had been praised for his English at school, that Karl Marx and Engels had spent years of great achievement there, and that it was an island, separated by water from the continent where he had spent all twenty-seven years of his life.

Four

It was that rare and therefore precious jewel: a hot clear summer Sunday in London.

The windows of their third-floor flat had not been cleaned outside for years. Perhaps not ever. Gabriel had been astonished to see them when he took over the flat from a retreating Belgian painter. Such flamboyant filth was unknown in Germany. But he had grown used to the streaks and smears that changed with the passing of wind and rain and sun against the windows. Through the windows, pushed up to be wide open, the sun was pouring in on Zoë and Gabriel who lay, slim bodies naked, on the mattress they had pulled over to the centre of the room to catch most warmth.

Zoë is reading to Gabriel from the Sunday papers she has been out to buy, first pulling over her body his jeans and T-shirt, sweat-stained and crumpled, discarded on the floor the evening before when they had dropped into bed, late, a little drunk, too tired to make love but content to nuzzle as they fell quickly asleep.

Gabriel is fully aware of Zoë's voice as she reads, and smiles when she laughs, but he cannot understand the words without moving his attention from her body and he prefers to concentrate on the just perceptible changes over the form of her body as the light shifts across it in snail-slow movement. He has been saying to himself daily, several times daily, as a private internal pinch of delight, that never in his life could he have imagined the physical pleasure he is discovering with Zoë. A pleasure which transcends the physical, which he can liken only to the moment at which a drawing begun on his page is transformed into a finished three-dimensional sculpture, shaped by his mind and hands and skill with his tools, born from a moment of meeting between his imagination and the paper, and now able to stand, alone, as he walks away from it. But his feeling for Zoë, or the feeling she elicits in him, exceeds even that. In some place inside himself he has sensed that hers is the body he was meant to love. He is profoundly uncomfortable with this insight. It smacks of a quasi-religious naïvety, a fundamentalist determinism that is not part of his usual intellectual vocabulary. If someone else were to say such a thing he would laugh, cough, roll a cigarette, feel something like pity. Yet, moving into her, sliding into her against the slight resistance her body continues to offer, he feels, as well as passion, such extraordinary relief, such an easing of self-consciousness, of consciousness of himself, such a rising up of abundant comfort as though he were – there is no other way for him to express it – coming home. It is not 'simply' or 'only' the look of her, the length the weight the shape of her, though he finds all those things, separately and in their wholeness, beautiful and touching. It's more than that. More than the way she touches him and stirs beneath or beside him. More than her own individual smell which floats towards him, defeating whichever of the perfumes she constantly wears: Je Reviens, Madame Rochas, Eau Sauvage. It's more than the hesitant, loving words she occasionally whispers into his ear, which he strains towards even when she's not speaking, which he wants to hear even when her mouth is open only to be pressed against his own. It's more even than those magical transforming leaps of energy, sometimes as small as the flicker of a match, sometimes so large she must move with them to dance or leap around the room, to throw him down, to wrestle with him, laughing and shrieking. The energy is there constantly inside her, catching him alight too, heating him up into an almost continuous state of excitement and anticipation.

One month has passed since Zoë arrived with her suitcases at his front door. In less than a month he should be gone, the scholarship over, the last precious freedom-giving cheque cashed, back to Frankfurt for some weeks with Christa and Stefan and his parents, then on to Berlin to a final semi-protected year at the art school before – before what? Not much, probably. The future for a sculptor has never been bright. On his own, alone, he could probably scrape together a life that would allow him to continue with his work. Doing odd jobs when he needed to, or taking unsociable night work to leave him free in daylight hours. Whatever extra he could make, above his minimal living needs, must go to Christa and Stefan, for far too long, all of Stefan's life – in fact, worse, all of Christa's life too – reluctantly and uncomfortably dependent on Christa's parents.

In Berlin with someone else, a foreigner, with Zoë, total stranger in that strange country of his, how would he survive?

As much as he loves his work, as much as he needs it and starves for it when parted from it, he knows he can work well only with clear stretches of time, without interruptions or even the anticipation of an interruption, without solicitous enquiries as to progress, no matter how lovingly meant; with the total concentration and absorption that crumple timetables, that make it nearly impossible to meet even the most reasonable demands of an intimate relationship.

He has seen it all before. And the anger when neither the work is done nor the love honoured. And both in ruins. Only accusation and recrimination flourishing. With Zoë in Berlin he would surely have to forget his work, take a job, any job, to look after her and keep her. Until a death did them part for having killed his dreams, no, having killed the fully alive part of himself, what possible good would he be to her? He would be bound to come to resent her, perhaps even to want to punish her. He would surely and quickly lose his great transforming love for her. They would both be desolate, marooned on a concrete island in the middle of an immutable land-sea called the German Democratic Republic, far from the waves which can wash and heal and carry, slapping or surging around the islands of New Zealand.

Zoë, who was breathing him in through her skin and reading with only a tiny part of herself, was aware that Gabriel was ebbing away from her. He had been lying on his side, his head supported on one hand, propped up to look at her as she lay face down and read. Now he slipped down to lie on his back and Zoë could see at once, from the most fleeting glance as she continued to read, that he was sad, that his hair-shirt brown eyes, as she'd named them, were sitting slow in his face. She put down the newspaper and tried to calm her breathing, to push away the panic that threatened to invade her suddenly hollow centre when she feared she might have done something wrong, or have caused pain to someone she loved.

137

She remembered the first night she had lain on this mattress with Gabriel, irritated by his determination to unbutton her dress, trying then to calm herself too, not because she had been fearful of some inadvertent transgression but because she had been confused by the apprehension rising in her faster and more convincingly than any sexual desire. In that now far-off first moment she had been sure only that here was no gentle stroker, no Craig, no home-grown bloke she could play with, charm, toss veils at, and be safe from.

Through these recent weeks she has been aware of Gabriel peeling her back, layer by delicate layer, to look inside. She has felt anxious, exposed, but curious too, looking in there with him, sneaking looks alone, and gratified and grateful that he cares to find not simply a confirmation of attitudes, or a reflection of himself, but Zoë, whoever she may be.

'You're so — what is it? — *unfixed*,' said a woman to Zoë once, to reprimand, to accuse, to diminish her.

'But who'd *want* to be fixed?' Zoë cried out in reply. Claustrophobic already at the image of a giant pin through her heart fixing her: but to which moment, to what attitude, to what point?

Now, though, she is lying still. It is Gabriel who is moving, even as he lies apparently motionless beside her. Gabriel who is slipping, out of touch. She reaches to take his hand and to guide it, to move it across her body until it will move alone. She turns to lie on her back putting, at the same time, her hand on his stomach, circling his stomach and chest with her fingers transformed into a small fleet of butterflies, then harder, butterflies flown, pressing into his skin, reminding them both of her strength as she kneads the firm flesh of his thighs, not touching his penis, not yet, knowing that it will rise and so will he to lean over her, to look down on her with all that longing which is what she is longing to see, which will fill her up with relief and gratitude but with room left for him as his body pushes to fill that space between her legs which opens out like a sea anemone when touched with love, opens out to take him in, to hold him safe, to hold her safe beneath him, rocked, anchored, harboured. She pulls her hand down his back, wanting to enter him too through the surface of his skin, to plunge or plunder more deeply than even this embrace can allow.

Yet even as she arches, pushes up towards him to prolong this precious contact, it's becoming a memory. She can see the moment rushing towards her when he will lie outside her, penis small and soft, spent inside her. Her open eyes will see him looking at her. She will smile, bound up from the wet spot where she has been lying to crack a joke, to crack open the moment so the intensity can drain out. Knowing, too, that time is running out, that somehow, though not from her, he will find the strength to leave her, to run out on her; that it is, indeed, the devoted Gabriel who is running and not time which is, now, standing still.

A wasp turns slowly in the air above her, threatening to land.

'What is it?' Her voice, to Zoë's ears, sounded normal enough. The wasp flies lower, daring her, menacing her. Her eyes follow its movements.

'I'm thinking of you, Zoë. Of how beautiful you are. Of how happy I feel here, beside you.' Gabriel's voice is not happy. It is reedy and misplaced. His hand waves absently at the wasp which retreats, but only just.

'Then why are you so sad?' And why are you going then? she doesn't yet ask.

'Oh Zoë.' The wasp is lower than ever now. Zoë knows that if it lands and stings her she will suffer but she can do nothing to make it leave her. She can only lie, scarcely breathing, hoping this inactivity will render her invulnerable.

His voice crosses space. 'We couldn't stay here, in this room, holding back time. Not even if we wanted to.'

But only one of us is leaving, she doesn't yet say.

He turned towards her, to hold her. She rested her head against his chest. His arm was across her ear, blocking out all sound. When, after some immobile moments, she stirred and moved up her head, she realized the sound of the wasp was gone, and not only the sound but also the wasp. She shook herself.

'Gabriel, why don't we call today a free day? A *Freitag* even though it's Sunday.' She smiled at her first German joke. 'We deserve that, don't we? A playday?'

Gabriel was smiling too, but awkwardly. He scarcely understood what she meant but was longing to please her. 'Tell me what you've got in mind?'

She sat up, legs crossed, her face animated as she raided her memory, her hands moving to suggest emotions larger than her words.

'When I was a child my sister Rebecca and my mother and I would make up stories together. I suppose they were fantasies we could all share somehow. One of us would begin, sometimes using an incident or character from a story or a fairy tale – you know, like the German Grimm tales – or sometimes taking something directly out of our own heads. Perhaps those were our wishful stories, our "if onlys", I'm not sure. But anyway, whoever began would have her story embroidered onto by the others. We could spin these stories out for days and weave one into the next. Sometimes we'd carry favourite characters over into lots of stories and repeated jokes until, I can't remember why, they'd fall away and other characters would have popped up to take their place.'

This was the most vivid picture yet that Zoë had offered of her childhood. Gabriel was eager to know more. 'It sounds lovely. Did your father play too, or was it just your mother?'

Zoë's features tightened. Her hand moved in front of her face as though to swat away a fly. 'No, no. He didn't live with my mother. I'm sure I'd told you that? He moved out before I was born. It was just us, Rebecca, my mother and me. And sometimes Maria. She was my mother's great friend.' There was a slight pause. 'James, my father, wouldn't have been able to play even if he'd wanted to. Even if *we'd* wanted him to which we didn't. The only fantasies he ever had were of buildings no one wanted. And even those hardly got a mention. Not by the time I really knew him anyway. But we could always do it, as far back as I can remember. Though I've not thought much about it for years. Not until now. I've been thinking quite a lot about that time in these last weeks. Funny little snippets which I'd forgotten years ago have sprung up for my attention. It's odd, isn't it? What do you make of that Herr Oracle?'

Before he had time to answer she was going on, 'Let's try the story-telling, shall we? It'll be fun! It doesn't matter if we're no good.'

'Fine, fine, of course we should try it. But please, you must forgive me if I'm *idiotisch*. We had no such games in our household. Stories, yes. All dutiful parents read to their children in bourgeois

German households. But the stories were of the outside. They told of other people's lives and were not of my life or from inside my head. I had only the drawings which I made then everywhere, even – but once only – on the walls of my parents' flat. In their best room. For this I got a rare beating but in a sense I still won because I'd made these drawings with waxy crayons and they could never entirely remove the marks. So always, before me, or until we moved anyway, I had the traces of my rebellion to admire!'

Zoë laughed and hugged him. She was delighted to have this hint of anarchy rippling the picture of an obedient, circumscribed life his bare references had suggested.

'Right then, I'll start.' She paused, closed her eyes, smiled, then opened her eyes and spoke again.

'You, my sweet, are the son of an armaments millionaire.' Gabriel lifted his eyebrows and flared his nostrils. 'Of course you're frightfully embarrassed by the source of that filthy wealth,' Zoë continued, 'which is why you take nothing from him and live as you do, in these humble rooms with bare light bulbs and only a pair and a half of jeans to your name. But now, as a result of falling, no, *tumbling* dizzily in love with me, you wish to make peace with your Big Daddy. In fact, you wish to forgive him his trespasses. Do you know what I mean? Like in the Lord's prayer: "Forgive us our trespasses as we forgive those who trespass against us . . ." '

'Ach ja. *"Vergib uns unsere Sünden wie wir vergeben unseren Gläubigern . . ."* That's it!'

'Well, having received your forgiveness Big Daddy absolutely *insists* that you permit him to give you enough to live on, which just happens to be enough to create all the sculptures you could ever dream of, with enough left over for me too. But here comes the best part. He's so moved by the obvious bliss and beauty of your love, of *our* love, that he can no longer continue to make instruments of death. So he turns his factories over to making butter dishes for the haute bourgeoisie. Or better still, into worker-run collectives making dishes for The People.' She grinned. 'No, maybe not. Anyway, whoever the butter dishes are intended for they are what the public has always wanted, so despite himself the Old Dad gets richer and richer and so do we. And as a mark of respect to my origins, in all his advertising, centred on that sparkling slab, is a fat pat of delicious creamy butter from the green paddocks of New Zealand.'

Gabriel laughed as he took her hand and kissed it. 'How can I follow this? You're crazy. And also wonderful and I love you. You're right. We should play together. In the park maybe?' Zoë nodded eagerly. 'We could stroll, I like this English word *stroll*, through Kensington Gardens, licking on ice-creams and when we have strolled enough we should sink, slowly down onto the grass where we'll hum in harmony to worms who will emerge to sit in a circle about us, grateful for this interruption in their dark, dirt-filled lives.'

'You have it exactly, that was exactly right. You're one of us! That was told in the manner born. Humming to worms, I love it. Have I ever told you that you're quite the most intelligent, sensitive and gorgeous man I've ever known?'

She had indeed told him.

Zoë leapt to her feet and bounced up and down. 'Let's go. Who knows, after humming to worms we could sing arias to birds, choruses to the caterpillars, recite verses to the ducks. There's no time to waste.'

'But first,' Gabriel stood up too, then touched her face lightly with the tips of his lovely fingers, 'the son of the newly reformed armaments chief would like to undertake a small item of market research towards his father's new enterprise. I believe that it's my duty, my *solemn* duty – is this correct?' Zoë nodded. Gabriel went on, 'My solemn duty to lick this woman of New Zealand over every inch of her body in order to be able to report to Herr *Butterchef*, in triplicate of course and with graphs and diagrams as I am a most serious person, as to which part of the said New Zealand woman's body has benefited most by the eating of much of that butter.'

Zoë lay back giggling and sighing as she welcomed the enveloping embrace of the sun on her body, knowing they had yet to face the discussions that lay before them, but relieved to be able to lie here today in a safe-place valley where, with her eyes shut, she can imagine that there is a sky outside higher and bluer than any England has ever lain beneath, that she is brown under South Pacific heat, taking such a day for granted, though not taking for granted the pleasure, the utterly specific pleasure she is feeling as Gabriel's tongue moves up from her inner arm to her armpit, down past her breast, downward, tickling her, tricking her into tender melting absolute happiness.

They walked through Sunday-quiet streets from Chelsea up through the immodest splendours of South Kensington to Kensington Gardens, entering the Gardens through Queen's Gate and heading by unspoken consent to the tiered, visually flamboyant Albert Memorial, glorious tribute from mourning Victoria to dead Albert, as excessive a creation as that love itself.

From a distance they were a dark two-headed creature dressed in white. Zoë's long legs extended beneath a dress which entirely covered her arms in loose full sleeves but barely reached the top of her thighs. Closer to, an observer would have been able to see that Gabriel was slightly older, leaner, taller and perceptibly more 'foreign' looking. Closely observed, Zoë's apparently all-white dress could be seen to have sprigs on it of palest pink flowers edged in a trace of soft green leaf. On her bare feet were white, long-laced espadrilles. Gabriel's clothes had been hunted out for him by Zoë at Portobello Market: white sailor trousers with buttons marching shipshape up each hip, wide flares, and topped with a plain white T-shirt which showed off his dark looks in a way he himself could modestly but accurately measure.

They were both aware of the effect they created, individually and now, better still, together. They were aware of the striking similarity of their mops of dark hair, the beauty of their health and height, the extravagance of some of their gestures of love which raised approval or amusement in some onlookers and unwittingly caused others – the undemonstrative, the unloved, the bereft – to turn away in shame, pain or envy.

Zoë sometimes left Gabriel to run ahead as a child might, to whirl and twirl in front of him and then to run back to throw her arms around him, or seize a hand, attempting to make him run with her, or to slow him down until they were almost standing still so she could cup her hand behind his head and draw his mouth down to her own.

Showing off. Unforgivable showing off, Caroline would have called it.

They took photographs of each other at the Memorial, memorializing their own love, their own moment, in the way most appropriate to the seventh decade of the twentieth century.

Gabriel directed each shot with precision and innocent, complete disregard for Zoë's suggestions. Whichever of them was the subject of the picture, he told Zoë exactly where she should stand, how she should look, or what she should look for, when she should shoot. She took his instructions in good part, expressing her — was it surprise, rebellion? — only by offering an exaggerated click of her heels and a mock lop-sided salute at the end of each new round of orders. An American boy, short-haired, gawky, very tall, standing nearby, unashamedly watching as they moved around the Memorial exhausting poses and backgrounds, called to ask if they'd like some pictures shot of the two of them together. Zoë handed him the camera at once, touched his arm briefly to thank him then ran towards Gabriel as the American moved in close, transformed out of his shyness by his familiarity with a camera, at once confident and intimate, shooting a series of pictures in quick succession, moving closer and closer to their faces, moving their faces closer and closer together until they were kissing for him, faces merged, Gabriel's hand sliding up Zoë's neck to hold her hair back in a knot.

When the kiss was finished the film was too. They parted, self-conscious for a moment, blinking slightly as they turned to face the American boy who, without his part to play, could only grin at them, pass the camera back to Zoë, wordless, and disappear, a magic genie, slid back into Aladdin's lamp.

The pictures when developed were exceptionally successful, especially those the American took. Gabriel and Zoë's matching intensity was magical and the subtle changes as their heads moved closer together until they dominated the entire frame were shown to maximum advantage when Gabriel blew up that section of the contact sheet, creating a huge succession of Gabriels and Zoës, moving across the wall above their bed like a backcloth to an altar.

Standing by the Albert Memorial, the awkwardness between Gabriel and Zoë exploded with his proposition to race her until one of them collapsed.

'But I can't run properly in these,' Zoë pointed down to her canvas espadrilles.

'Then take them off and I'll take my shoes off too.'

144

Zoë crouched down and unlaced the ribbons, tied them in a knot around her neck and with a shoe bouncing clumsily over each breast ran, head high and breath soon burning in her chest, though not as fast as Gabriel who astonished her by speeding ahead across the bright green weedless grass, weaving around people, flower beds, trees, prams, balls and ball throwers, then waiting for her, grinning with self-satisfaction, arms out to embrace her as she puffed up to him, half walking at the end then, reaching him, ignoring his arms and throwing herself down onto the grass.

Zoë's world had tightened to her chest which was moving up and down in great heaves as she fought to recover her breath. Only gradually did it expand to include her awareness of Gabriel, lying beside her, then aware too of her own hot sweaty smell mingling with the faint welcome smell still on her body from their love-making and over this, like a delicately embroidered teacloth thrown over a pile of dirty dishes, the murmur of Je Reviens, the perfume she had been given and had begun to wear just before she left New Zealand though knowing, even then, before even her toe had entered the pool to test the temperature of the world outside, that she wasn't coming back. Not to stay. Not ever.

Her hand moved across the grass until it found Gabriel's. She lay with two armslengths between their bodies, content to have their fingertips touching, thinking, why now she wasn't sure, about Rebecca, how much she continued to miss her sister and how lopsided her life was without her.

For a year before Rebecca married they had shared a flat, not on their own, with several other girls, Rebecca's friends from when she was at university. But they made time almost every day to be on their own. They would sit in Rebecca's room, the best in the flat as she'd been there longest, looking out to the ocean and talking. Their direct exchanges were minimal but they managed to convey to each other most of the important details of their lives and to bring into bearable proportion some of the deep-buried pain and fears they shared.

Zoë occasionally wondered if it was the nearing reality of her dreams of travelling that pushed Rebecca into premature marriage. But Rebecca could have come too, couldn't she? Zoë had intended to entice her with stories of what was possible, over there in what they only half jokingly referred to as 'the world'. But somehow she had succeeded in creating a scenario in Rebecca's lively imagination that daring Zoë would do better alone. Zoë had teased and protested and was sure she would win. Until Rebecca came home one morning after she'd been out all night to tell Zoë she had decided to get married. It was exactly what she wanted, and children too, she insisted, silencing Zoë who was bursting to protest that this emotionally atrophied boy-man was no solution, that he was a hopelessly drab version of the gallant hero who had starred in Rebecca's plays and dreams since they both could remember.

They had understood that each of them wanted a lover who could offer some renewal or at least a reminder of the quality of love that Jane had taught them could be theirs. But they couldn't speak of this and Zoë kept her pain to herself at Rebecca's early resignation from this dream, hiding it behind jokes about perfect wife-mothers and gallant world travellers on the increasingly infrequent occasions they were alone together.

Rebecca had kept silent too, about the compromise she refused to acknowledge she was making, and her fears that Zoë might be the lemming right behind her.

Zoë's breath had grown quiet in her body and she was lulled almost to sleep when she was knocked on the head by a ball. Her head jerked up and her eyes flew open. She was ready to swear but was immediately forgiving when she looked up to see the dismayed face of a small girl dressed in the 1930s-style smocked Viyella dress which uniformed her as of the English upper-middle class.

Zoë was on her feet at once to toss the ball back to the child who had been bracing herself for a rebuke and was astonished when instead this tall woman laughed and seemed eager to play. They threw the ball back and forth and Zoë called to the girl, 'I'm Zoë Delighty, who are you?'

'I'm Camilla,' the girl replied. 'I'm Joshua's big sister.'

'Oh really!' Zoë grinned. 'I'm Rebecca's little sister.' She laughed and so did Camilla who found it hard to believe that anyone as tall as Zoë could really be a little sister. Zoë held onto the ball for a moment. 'Where is Joshua?'

Camilla looked around. 'Over there, with Mummy.' Zoë looked

to where she was pointing and saw a woman and a very small child walk out of the distance towards them. Camilla seemed less keen to throw now and when her mother drew near she ran to the woman, clinging to her as she whispered and the woman nodded, with some embarrassment, at Zoë who stood for some seconds, feeling foolish and oddly disappointed, before turning away with a quick wave to Camilla and walking back to where Gabriel was lying, propped up on his elbow to watch Zoë's small drama.

'That was fun.' Zoë hesitated. 'At least until mama turned up. The child positively withered. God keep me from the cold-blooded uptight English for ever and ever Amen.' She laughed. 'Just wait till I have a child. No bloody Miss Prim smocks for my kids. Especially not if they're boys.' She laughed again, enjoying the Technicolor image that danced across her mind of a small boy with almost-black curls and hair-shirt brown eyes. 'I'd love to have a child, perhaps a whole tribe.' She glanced at Gabriel and coloured slightly. Was he listening? 'Oh not now, please don't think I think . . .' she trailed off.

Zoë plucked a piece of grass the mower had missed. A question was turning over in her mind, then growing and multiplying. Gabriel hadn't spoken. The question burst free. 'What do you think about them, Gabriel? Kids I mean. Do you want some of your own? Have you even thought about it?'

Gabriel didn't move. From where he lay he could see that there was a hole in his white tennis shoe where the material had worn through. His mind refocused. Where was their playday, their *Freitag*, free of problems, mishaps, disasters? This was to have been a day to celebrate their love. But now he was high above a crevasse, about to plunge without pick or rope or hand to save him. There was little breath left in his body as he sat up, slowly. He heard a voice, his own, say, 'I have a child already. A boy. A son.'

He has jumped. Down, down. Was there a ledge, anywhere, on which he could land, which could save him from calamity? The calamity of calumny.

'Is this true, Gabriel?' Zoë's voice came out of her body stretched along a thin wire of incredulity. 'Is this some kind of *joke*?' Her voice box was shutting down fast, allowing only that strange narrow thread of sound to escape. 'Why on earth didn't you tell me?'

His gaze was fixed on the ground. The very ground out of which worms were to emerge at the sound of their humming. The ground that he now wished would tear apart so he might bury himself in it, seeking the company only of those worms. He remembered a strange child's verse that Zoë liked to chant: *I'm going down the garden to eat worms. Long thin slimy ones, short fat fuzzy ones* . . . He couldn't look at her, but heard her when she spoke again.

'Don't you love him, is that it? Don't you care about him? Shit, Gabriel, all this time we've been close and not a single word about your own child! I know lots of men don't care about their kids, don't give a stuff about anything but themselves – my own father doesn't care about me and that's for bloody sure – but you, you're . . . oh Mother of God, I thought you were . . . well, it's obviously pathetic and says a great deal about how stupid I am, but I thought that you were different.'

This is, Gabriel could not avoid noting, the second time today that Zoë has spoken of her father, and also only the second time since he has known her. She has spoken tenderly, reverentially almost, if very rarely, of the perfect sister and the perfect mother, but of the father, not at all. Still, this was certainly not the time to pursue that. He must force himself to look at her. To face her. *Face en face*. His mind was full of useless words and images, juxtapositions of astonishing apparent incongruity. He saw Artemesia Gentileschi's Judith, mysteriously upright and walking, in black and white, towards him with the severed head of Holofernes held high before her. There was blood everywhere. A single spreading colour: red. The mouth of Holofernes was opening and shutting and apparently pleading, but no sound broke the silence.

Gabriel forced himself to raise his eyes, to look at Zoë, to reach out to touch her arm, but she shook herself free of him at once.

'Come on. Spit it out. Tell me.' Her voice was higher than he had ever heard it. She was looking at him with the contempt she might have bottled up and saved for a childbeater, a murderer even. It did not occur to him that what she was experiencing was the death of her trust.

'It's not that.' A clear picture arose in Gabriel's mind of the child laughing and calling to him, 'Papa, Papa,' newly woken from sleep, pink and soft and eager to play. 'It's not that I don't love him. I do. I love him very much.'

'Then where is he and why the secrecy? I mean, it's important whether or not one has a child! It wasn't some pet you simply "failed" to mention.'

'No, he's not a pet.' Gabriel looked down again to give himself momentary rest from Zoë's apparently unblinking gaze and her need for the truth and immediate explanation. 'He lives with his mother.'

He paused to hunt for words before he must explain about Christa. But Zoë seized the pause and filled it. 'Who is his mother? Where is she? You never even mentioned . . . and I thought. Oh God no. Are you *married* Gabriel?'

Gabriel still didn't speak. His hesitation was entirely too much for Zoë who was fighting to banish from her mind sordid, cliché-packed headlines: 'other woman', 'love triangle', 'duped lover drowns in swamp'. Quite unexpectedly she heard James's voice singing a nonsense song to her: *Be kind to your four-footed friends, 'cos the poor little sods ain't got no mothers, they live all alone in the swamp, where it's very cold and damp-to-rhyme-with-swamp . . .* She shook her head, buried it in her hands, and tried to hide from the avalanche of betrayal that had begun to descend on her. Gabriel married. And not to have told her. It was unbelievable. She had to believe it.

'Please Zoë, could you take your hands away from your face and look at me?'

'No. I mean, you can talk to me and I think you damn well should. But I'm not going to look at you.'

He didn't speak. The world seemed silent.

Zoë examined herself. She begun to open herself up to this man. She had dared to begin to trust him because of the marvellous care and love he'd shown her, the first person to do so. Her thought stopped. They had made jokes together, she and Gabriel, about what a good mummy he was, but not until the pain of this moment had she allowed herself to recognize that truth: he was more than a lover to her, he was caretaker of the child in her who had been abruptly left.

And yet all the time this man she believed she could trust had been lying to her. She had begun to open herself up, only to make of herself a vessel into which he could pour the poison of his betrayal. How could he? Gabriel.

'All right. I'll look at you but wait a moment.' At least to her own ears Zoë's voice sounded brave. Gabriel's hand touched her head in reply, as fleetingly as the wing of a bird might skim a surface as, too close, it flies by.

Zoë knew she must calm herself. She must attempt to concentrate on the present. This was no time to get stirred up about Jane. Or Rebecca. Left by her, Zoë.

A fearsome litany formed in Zoë's mind. One: Gabriel is returning to Germany. Two: He has a wife and child. Three: I am not the single, transforming love I thought I was. That he did, surely, tell me I am? Four: I will be alone again, but this time I'll be lonely.

'Oh Gabriel, why didn't you tell me? Why didn't you trust me enough to tell me?' It wasn't anger he could hear in her voice. It was the peculiar pitch of betrayal, the shriek of abandonment conveyed in a near-whisper. Her neat teeth were still sitting in their even rows, but he and she both knew that with a softly cushioned foot he'd laid a blow to his beloved's mouth.

She spoke again. 'I suppose that's why you've never asked me to go back to Germany with you. God help me, I'm such a fool. Such a bloody smart-arse and such a fool. This antipodean primitive took you at your word, Gabriel. Or your lack of words rather. So what else is there you should tell me?' Her voice had grown hard. It was building up a jagged-edged wall behind which she could crouch to hold down her pain. 'Come on then, what else have I omitted to ask?'

It couldn't be worse. She was extremely angry. Gabriel had to speak.

'Christa – she's my wife – became pregnant when we were pupils together, still at school.' Gabriel dared to glance at Zoë but her gaze was fixed at some point far from him. She would throw him no line, unravel no safety net. If he fell she'd not reach out to save him. Why should she? He finished rolling two cigarettes, replacing the lid on his Old Holborn tobacco tin with neat, firm gestures. He lit both cigarettes, handed one to Zoë who rarely smoked, and continued.

'Zoë, can you understand?'

'Probably not. I'm almost certainly too dumb. Not *European* enough to handle sophisticated deception.'

He pushed aside the weight of her painful irony.

'It was absolutely necessary to marry her. There was no other way. I couldn't have abandoned her.'

You're abandoning me, Zoë thought.

'It would have been unthinkable. Christa's a fine person. In many ways a wonderful girl. I've even thought how much you'd like her. But please, you may believe me Zoë, I have loved no one, not Christa, not no one . . .'

'Not anyone,' Zoë automatically corrected him.

'Not anyone,' he echoed. 'I have loved not anyone as I now love you.'

Zoë was taking long drags on the roll-up. Puffs of peace? He could only hope.

'I did love Christa; I do yet love her but I loved her then as a boy loves a girl for the first time. And I love her now, well, I suppose as an old comrade with whom one's been through a great deal. But we were at school when this started. Two innocents. She was my first friend – my first girlfriend as you'd say it.'

Zoë discarded the damp end of the roll-up, burying it fiercely in the grass, then turned to face him, her face so transformed by pain it was almost unfamiliar to Gabriel.

'But what good does this "special love" do me if you're already married, committed to someone else, to two other people in fact? And not to tell me! That's what I can't bear. That you would have kept something from me which is essential to your life and to who you are is simply insupportable. Unendurable. I can't endure it. How would I ever trust you again? Tell me that. Even if we had a future, which clearly we do not.'

He took her hand, pressed it hard and stared at her, his eyes crossing her face begging it for some sign of forgiveness. 'You may trust me, Zoë. I've been cowardly. That's my worst sin. I was afraid to tell you. Terribly afraid and of course it grew worse. I didn't tell you at once and then it magnified until it came to be nearly impossible and so . . .' he paused to flick through the lexicon in his mind. 'And also it was, in fact, perhaps partial with the other issues of why or why not you should come with me to Berlin. And there was my duty too. I am a German.' He made a wry, self-deprecating gesture. 'There's my son. I have my duties to him and my love for him also.'

Zoe's voice again emerged from that squeezed-out place, distorted with longing. 'What's his name, your son? How old is he? Where are they now?'

'Stefan-Georg, for my father and Christa's. He's now seven. They live in Frankfurt, not in Berlin. Still in Frankfurt, quite near the house of my parents at the home of the parents of Christa.'

'Seven! Oh God.'

'Zoë, as I told you already it's from the time we were at school. I was nineteen when Christa became pregnant and twenty when Stefan was born. She was the same age. Well, a month or so younger. She has the sign of Leo.'

Zoë allowed herself a brief smile. She knew Gabriel had offered this last information in an attempt to please her.

'And all this was going on,' he continued, encouraged by that flicker, 'while you were what, fourteen or fifteen, safe in your tropical paradise.'

Safe! Tropical paradise! Zoë shuddered. Dream on, Gabriel. She knew some hope was fighting for resurrection but she pushed it down hard. So what of the past. Where was the future? What was its shape and colour?

The colours now inside her head were all dark: dirty browns, purples and greys. A headache pierced the right side of her head and pulled her teeth tight in a brace of pain. Gabriel's hand was moving towards her, taking hold of her chin and turning her fully to face him. He spoke again only when she reluctantly met his eyes.

'I ask myself again and again, are Christa and Stefan really the issue? Are they reason enough why it seems sometimes impossible for you to come with me to Berlin? Or for me to discuss this with you. I know you'd come. I know how much it causes you pain . . . excuse me, I know how much *I* cause you pain that I don't speak of your coming. *Scheisse*. It seems too complicated. There are Christa and Stefan. There's you. There's my need for you and my love for you.'

'And my need for you too.' Zoë's interruption was bitter.

'Yes, of course, your needs too.' But he was speaking too quickly.

'Though you Zoë are – how can I say it afresh – you are so *free*. I envy you that. More than anything I envy you that freedom.'

There was nothing Zoë could say.

Oh freedom.

'Christa and Stefan, they are my responsibilities. My neglects are already very great. I must think of them and give them whatever small money I can earn. Christa hasn't been able to study or work since Stefan was born. She must live still with her parents and on their support. That's hard for her. At first it was acceptable to her and to her parents – and to me too – because I was going to be a lawyer and could repay them. I don't mean only the money, I mean by being the kind of person Christa expected in a husband and her parents were expecting in a possible son by marriage. But when I gave it all up and went alone to Berlin to study sculpture which is nothing they can get comfort from, well, since that time it's been even more uncomfortable for Christa. They nourish her anxieties and agitate her about my political activities which God knows are insufficient enough. I believe her parents feel pity for her. And they seem to believe they can interfere in her life because they pay for that privilege.'

Gabriel trailed off, looking bleak. This time it was Zoë who applied the pressure to their still-joined hands.

When he began to speak again his voice was low and Zoë had to strain forward to hear him.

'I feel almost helpless. I don't want to live with Christa again. Even before I became involved with you I don't think I wanted that. It was not by chance of course that I chose Berlin. One could get away no further . . . But I *owe* her something. Her chance maybe? I cannot give her money and stability as she wants, or I believe she wants. So perhaps I think I must give her my success as a sculptor to repay her. To make reparations: an old German custom you know.'

Again that painful irony crossed his face. 'That's the point, *Punkt*, *point*.' He beat out the word as if to give it the force no single language could convey. Zoë waited, silent, as he raided the Old Holborn tin again, drawing onto the paper a tidy line of weedy tobacco, then rolling it, neat and thin.

'You see I want also, more than anything else in the world –

except perhaps you, Zoë—' self-absorbed, he failed to notice that his 'perhaps' leapt from his sentence like a whip towards her wounded self, 'to be able to work. Not just to work, but to work in the way *I* need to. It's too much really, to ask another to bear this. And with no money. And in a country not your own. It is too much.'

Gabriel pulled a clean, pale grey handkerchief from the waistband of his white sailor trousers, wiped his face, folded the handkerchief with care, and replaced it.

'It's all something of a mess. You'd be correct to say so.'

'But I didn't say so. You said so and naïve I may be, but I don't yet need someone to speak for me.' Zoë frowned.

When she spoke again her voice was easier.

'Though I could have said so, that it's all a mess I mean. But there's still a whole lot I don't understand. If you're not living with Christa and Stefan anyway, what's the problem about living with me? No. I don't understand. You mention your work, but I wouldn't interfere with that. I promise you.'

Her face brightened. 'Is it money?' She paused. 'If it is money then please don't worry. I'd work. I've always worked. Even when I was an idiotic sixteen-year-old I was able to find someone silly enough to give me work. I've supported myself totally since then. That's terribly important to me. So I could help *you*, Gabriel! I'd not be a burden. We may be primitives in New Zealand, inarticulate barbarians in contrast to you European effetes,' her smile reduced the sting of her self-mockery, 'but the one thing we can all do is roll up our sleeves and get on with things. If we were born clothed the sleeves would already be rolled up ready for the first task. "Getting on with things" is bloody nearly a national characteristic. It comes from our pioneering genes pushing us to chop through virgin bush and build a log hut with our bare, callused hands. It was the most adventurous of Brits who made it to the colonies, you know. And the other kind who stayed behind.'

'Well there are few enough opportunities to chop through bush, virgin or not, in Berlin, and as for log huts, they fell down long ago. However, there are many beautiful trees in the city so perhaps you could lead a new trend.' Gabriel smiled and noticed that for the first time he was breathing from his chest rather than from a tiny pocket of exhausted air near his throat.

154

'I'd hardly have expected that, idiot. No need to be literal! It's the *principle* of self-reliance that's important. I'd never have perceived this without leaving New Zealand but now it's one of the things I value most. It's one of the reasons I'm constantly grateful I grew up there and not here.' She threw her arm around in a gesture expansive enough to take in Kensington Gardens and the land beyond.

'You can't know how hard it would be for you, Zoë. You speak no German and you love to talk. You'd have no friends, no one but me, and you'd soon tire of that.'

Zoë saw a crack in the dam of his resolve and pushed, ignorant of the panic rising in Gabriel again as he envisaged Zoë alone in Berlin, dependent entirely on him, perhaps not dependent financially, but waiting for him, needing him, wanting to be with him. His pocket of air shrank once more.

'I'd learn German, in no time at all – you'd see. You'd be amazed at my skills.' She was crouching up now, bouncing on her haunches, determined to convince him. 'And I'd find friends. I came here knowing no one and it's been just fine. But I can't stay here without you. Not now. You must see that?'

She raised his hand to her lips and kissed his fingers. 'Without you it's all too pale. *You* are in colour. I need that colour that is you. I need the colour who is me when she's with you. Things weren't pale before I met you. I could colour them then all on my own. But now you've shown me more intensity than I had guessed at. You can't take that away! I know you understand, Gabriel, because you feel it yourself.'

He didn't reply. A battle was waging between his head which was warning him to be cautious and his heart which pounded with fresh optimism.

'Write to Christa at once about me. Tell her that I'll help her. That we'll both help her. She and Stefan could come to Berlin too. Maybe we should all live together and I'll help with the child?'

'Zoë!' Gabriel was laughing. 'I think this may not be the best idea you've ever had. You and me and Christa and Stefan-Georg! But you're sweet to think of it. I adore you for that. I *thank* you for that. We must both give more thought to the whole situation and discuss it more fully when we're cool. I'm sorry, really deeply sorry, that I didn't tell you before.' His face became grave again. 'It was quite evidently a ridiculous failing on my part, but the thought of losing you any sooner than I had to, that was insupportable.'

The poisonous distress was diluting in Zoë's body. Her face muscles were falling back into place. She hated the continuing lack of resolution and her unwilling dependence on what was apparently to be Gabriel's unilateral power of decision over her life. Yet she was gradually aware she also felt something approaching contentment. Gabriel had stepped out of a history quite different from the many she had imagined for him. Perhaps they could have a future together too, quite different from the loneliness she had evidently been bracing herself for.

He couldn't fail to agree to her going now, Zoë reassured herself. There simply was no other way. His hesitations had been shown to be ridiculous. And she knew, she absolutely *knew* how essential she was to any happiness in his life.

She could see them vividly: busy, fulfilled, radiant. Their days would be filled with work. Zoë's with some still-vague but honest and enriching labour which would allow her enough time to decorate their rooms with flowers and arrange perfect surprises for Gabriel when he returned each evening, weary but happy, from his studio. He'd be inspired by the consistency of her presence and would reach new heights of creativity. She'd soon have around her a coterie of witty, original people of different nationalities and tormented histories who would adore her grammatically admirable but charmingly accented German, and would be half in love with her too. Though she would be entirely faithful, of course, and everyone would remark on what a truly exceptional and enviable life she and Gabriel had created together, charged as it was with the splendour and generosity of love in its fullest expression.

Zoë turned to her lover, lying eyes closed on the grass beside her. 'Let's go home, Gabriel. Though first,' the future faded from rosy to the cool greens and blues of the world around her, more appropriate to the day's continuing indecision, 'maybe you should examine your conscience to see if there's anything else you should tell me.'

'Thank you, Mother Superior!' He grew more serious. 'Only that I love you. More than ever since you constantly surprise me.'

She coloured with pleasure. 'Not *that* again!' Her heart was thumping. She had to hide. She buried her face in his chest and began to nuzzle him, then to wrestle with him, two long dark white-dressed adults rolling over and over again on bright green grass, tumbling so fast that two, again, looked at from a slowly increasing distance, might seem like one.

Five

I am lying on my side. The shifting black tent of night is above and all around me. My knees are drawn up, as a foetus might draw up her own, to tuck myself into myself, to avoid treading down where it might cause pain. I have been in this dark place for a long time. Longer than memory, before 'Who am I?' was taking shape in my mind like a smoke signal, a slow curling sign moving to form a question mark. Then fading again.

There have been visitors into this darkness. Not guests, called-for, but not unwelcome either. I am here to receive them because I can be nowhere else. I cannot move. They are small snatches of people: a pair of eyes, a lock of hair falling, a mouth moving into the shape of a smile or downturning in pity, pain or anger.

There have been gestures: a hand coming towards me but before I can feel if it moves forward to comfort or to strike, it passes away again. Am I unreachable?

There have been sounds: old, old sounds of a woman crying, her grief emerging in terrible wails then returning to emerge and to return again, binding her in a circle of grief. More sounds: a door banging, a man shouting as the door bangs, then the sound of silence, filled still with the woman's pain, made big, puffed out by it, helium without helios, air without sun.

The pain belongs to me. It is mine, mine and no one else's. Yet I am not alone with it. In it. That woman wailing, grieving, may not be me. Then, further into the silence, I can hear the pain as my heart beats or breaks, as my pulse beats, as my blood moves through me carrying that sound in its stream, soundless sound (is it only a feeling?) but it shrieks at me, clutches at me so that I want to turn from it, so that I fling my head from side to side, and again, and again. But I can't escape it and it laughs at me. Can laughter have no sound? Can silence laugh?

I remember the wisdom. *Go into it, Zoë. Don't fight it, Zoë. Go deep down inside it. Become it, Zoë.*

Become that pain? That shrieking? I can't. I shrink. It shrieks. I shrink. I will die of it. I will die inside it. But, as I am already dying, I will try. There is nothing left to lose. I know, but don't know how I know, that I won't be alone inside that pain. I breathe, take in my breath as slowly as I can and see, or imagine that I can see, a gate around my solar plexus. I stretch my legs so that I can lie on my back to give this gate most room. I breathe more deeply, so deeply that I want to ask (but there is no one to ask) if I am taking in more than my share of air, if I am a monster, sucking the whole world dry of air. And I want to ask: Where is it coming from? and, What am I returning to it?

Then, gradually, the gates move open. They are tall and wide, curved at the dark corners where they belong to the hinges, made of iron, moulded in fire, crafted with skill into shapes that are strong and plain and beautiful. They are old gates and I admire them as they move, at their own pace and not easily at all, open.

But I am confused. The gates are not only opening out from me so that I can take in all the air I need, they are also opening out so that, more buoyant now, I can leave myself and enter that sound which has been crouching, waiting for me until the gates were fully open but which moves up now from its crouching position to take me in, to surround me, to welcome me as part of itself, nothing left behind. I exist, this is clear, only as part of those contradictions: shrieking in silence, silent shrieking. It is easier to be here, inside it, to have ceased to resist. I was too tired to go on struggling.

I can lie on it now, lie in it, drift on it filled up with it, and as I drift I feel it change its shape, transform into more differentiated lines with higher notes, and lower ones, and, listening with care inside and out, I can hear three voices, though none of them is making a single sound, and then I hear the sound which is like a rope tying those three silent voices together, joining them, braiding them. Then out of those voices come the shapes which I wanted, surely not, to push away. I can see them clearly now, and can hear them too. I am reaching: up or down or out, I'm not sure. They are all around me and deep down inside me. I want them so badly that it is this longing which might kill me. It is not the sound that I will die of. (I have been hearing that always.) But they elude me. I stretch out, further, further, but never far enough. I am one of them, and cannot reach even myself. We are joined forever, and yet the pain I hear and feel and exist is as the pain of being alone. I am alone. She is alone. She is also alone. We three are alone.

The crying began when she had to leave us. (*Chose* to, Zoë, chose to.)

In silence, in silence. The crying began in silence.

Don't push the river. You are not the stone.

Don't push the river. You *are* the river.

Stay inside the sound. (I can do nothing else. It is all that I am.)

You are not the stone over which the river flows. You are the river.

(Take me with you. Take me with you.)

Don't push me. I am not breathing. Let me be, let me be here in the pain with my mother and my sister. Outside this pain is life without them. Let me taste the salt of their tears making the world wet as they fall and fall, mixing with my own salty sea-water waterfall, falling and falling away from the sound, the rope which is tugging, unravelling, loosening its hold on me. I cannot hold onto it, for how can I touch sound? I am floating, drifting, carried by air I have sucked from the world, carried into that high place: where no one can reach me, where there is no place to rest, where I am dizzily circling and there is no one to lean on: from where I can look down and feel quite unsure – as to whether I have abandoned the world, or the world has abandoned me.

Six

I caught this morning morning's minion, kingdom of
  daylight's dauphin, dapple-dawn-drawn Falcon, in his riding
  Of the rolling level underneath him steady air, and striding
High there, how he rung upon the rein of a wimpling wing
In his ecstasy! then off, off forth on swing . . .
            . . . . My heart in hiding
Stirred for a bird, — the achieve of, the mastery of the thing!

Beneath Zoë was the comfortable leather of an old train seat, set in
a long train carrying her fast from Paris to Berlin. Her head and
heart were already with Gabriel, connected to him by the pictures
she was seeing and feelings she was re-experiencing of their time
past together, and with visions of their time ahead.

The rhythm of Gerard Manley Hopkins' poem suited the thrill of
her expectation, her leaning towards the moment when. When the
train would pull into Berlin Zoo station. When Gabriel would help
her down from the carriage and into his arms. When he would
know, seeing her, how foolish it had been to imagine leaving her
behind. When he would open the front door to their new shared life
together. When, in his arms, she would feel, in a new country, on
a new continent, at home.

The music of 'Windhover' felt just right as punctuation between
the life she had led up until the moment when she had stepped onto
this train and the new life to begin when she alighted: off, off forth
on swing. She smiled as the words, miraculously juxtaposed for new
meaning and vigour, rolled through her carrying her back to see
again the colour rising in Sister Veronica's face as she had moved to
the beat, the excitement, the building magic of the imagery, as she
had told them, neat girls in neat rows, that the poet was 'one of us',
a Catholic priest, a Jesuit, that this very poem which Zoë was riding
now, travelling over it as a surfer might ride a wave, soaring with it,

cresting it, then down but with exhilaration still rising, that this 'Windhover' was dedicated 'to Christ Our Lord' but oh, so much life in it, such turning up of the face with joy towards the sky as a sun-worshipper might, so little in it of death: the shame, the guilt, the agony of Christ crucified.

How different the Catholic world would be, Zoë reflected – the entire Western world come to that – if the central celebration of the Church was not nominally but truly and exuberantly that of the resurrection, of the returning to life, of choosing life over death, accepting the complexity of life with all its mysteries and abundance. How different if, in the mind of all those touched by Christianity, there was memory of the celebration of this delight in life. If the parishioners of every church or chapel in each succeeding generation created anew a gigantic celebratory unfolding of their individual and collective experience of choosing to be alive, of choosing their connection to all manifestations of life, and that this is what the seeker after meaning found – looking up from the pew at the back of the church, uncovering a weary face to meet an affirmation of eternal potential instead of the dying Christ, hanging on dead wood hacked down from the tree of life. A sombre, dying Christ with His weeping, helpless mother, and the friends gathering, inconsolable.

It had not taken Zoë long to say goodbye to England. The over-used soil of that island had offered little invitation to put down roots. She was, she decided, definitely above ground.

Saying goodbye to Rosamund reawoke the pain of saying goodbye to her friends in New Zealand. Just as they had done, Rosamund made it easier for her by entering with enthusiasm into the spirit of adventure, as pleased and excited for her as Zoë could have hoped. Rosamund thought Gabriel was wildly attractive and delighted Zoë with the frequency with which she repeated this opinion, distin-guishing each repetition with an extravagant adjective for some singled-out part of the wildly attractive whole. 'The most *memorable* mouth,' she would say, or, 'such a *thrilling* voice', or, 'a totally *delectable* little bottom'.

Rosamund also found Gabriel strange, unplaceable, though this did not form any part of her litany. She kept the opinion entirely to herself, even during the wretched conversations as they sat at her kitchen table and Zoë uncovered glimpses of her agony that Gabriel might return to Germany and leave her behind.

Gabriel rarely spoke to Rosamund when she visited Zoë at the Chelsea flat. He would acknowledge her arrival with what looked suspiciously like a curtailed bow, then would bring in tea or coffee, with cakes or biscuits making an additional pattern on an old decorated plate. He would leave these offerings with the two women, perhaps staying long enough to pour. Rosamund had not met such apparent self-effacement in a man. Neither had Zoë, but she was quick to adapt.

Rosamund couldn't stifle her curiosity as to what the pay-off might be. Could a man actually *like* waiting on girls and if he did, what could that mean? She could find no answer but knew that it felt, well, *weird*. As was the way Gabriel loitered at the door while she and Zoë took their time to say goodbye. He would stand and stare at her, and at Zoë, always more at Zoë, as though they were freaky creatures in a zoo or astonishing exhibits in a gallery. Zoë had told Rosamund that Gabriel didn't enjoy socializing, that he did it, and then only rarely, to please her. He said how different it was for him in Berlin where, at home in his adopted city, he welcomed the chance to go to bars or restaurants, knowing who he'd find where and when, but that here in London with his poor English, he found it unrewarding.

Rosamund's loyalty to Zoë kept her from saying she believed the reason for this was that Gabriel was jealous. Zoë had impressed on her friend Gabriel's low opinion of monogamy, but it was Rosamund's opinion he wanted Zoë entirely to himself, at least while he was in London and that suited him. In her view he couldn't bear to see other men seek Zoë's attention; nor could he bear to see Zoë flirt with them, almost unaware of what she was doing even while finely balancing the effect, operating on the automatic pilot she had set as she entered puberty and which she had not yet seen reason to turn off.

Zoë promised as she pressed Rosamund's face deep into the lapels of her huge black overcoat that she would write, often, though even as she said it and wanted to mean it she wondered if it would be true. The entries in her journals, unmentioned even to Gabriel, were growing longer. Her letters to New Zealand were increasingly brief. Most bleak of all, there were now gaps on both sides in her once weekly correspondence with Rebecca.

Gabriel had left England a month before Zoë was to meet him in Berlin and three weeks before she herself left for a week in Paris, en route to Berlin.

She had slept badly in the shabby flat without him, waking, night after night, out of painful and immediately lost dreams, her throat often completely dry as though she had been gasping for an unreachable breath. She moved into wakefulness by sliding down a chute, entering the daytime world with a jarring bump from which she might never recover, leaving behind all that was familiar to her and which was leaving her even as her hand moved across the mattress to the empty place where Gabriel was not sleeping.

He had gone before her: beacon carrier, paver of the way. He needed time alone in Frankfurt, he'd told her, not unreasonably; time to see Christa and Stefan-Georg, to explain to them about Zoë, and to break the news to his parents.

The period that preceded his leaving had been wretched. It was not until days after his revelations in Kensington Gardens that Gabriel had finally relented and told Zoë she could join him in Berlin. He had whispered to her after making love one night when they had made love all day that he could not, of course she was right, live without her. But there had been so much tension and so little joy in his voice that Zoë had continued to lie in silence next to him, speechless, wordsmith lost for words, relief and continuing anxiety fighting for mastery over her.

The day had been increasingly uncomfortable for Zoë. They had made love so often she was sore. Her vagina burned as though it had lost an essential layer of skin, but Gabriel had seemed frantic, in pursuit of something that was clearly still eluding him, and she had been unable to bring herself to say stop, knowing that he would at once, that he would apologize and want to appease her, and that it wouldn't be enough. She was desperate for him to be close to her but could feel herself losing him each time he entered her body. He sensed her distress and tried harder to please her. He succeeded only in increasing her self-consciousness and her loss. She felt she could, if she stopped caring for one moment or stopped guarding for an instant, lose herself, could disappear forever leaving just a faint, damp patch, and that quickly drying, where she had once been.

She had known she should get up, that lying beneath Gabriel then beside him then beneath him again was increasing this terrifying sense of helplessness, this imminent loss of self. She should get up and run she told herself, feeling the hard pavement beneath her feet as her long legs took her fast along the embankment, past the bridges, the almost-still Thames, the line of slow-moving cars. But she had continued to lie, to sag, almost to disappear. She had continued to allow Gabriel to touch her, to whisper to her, to enter her as she lay, almost the only movement in her body the pictures passing across her mind like an interminable slide show: of Gabriel leaving her, of herself staying; of Gabriel saying goodbye, of herself alone without him.

She had left childhood and entered adulthood scrupulous about guarding her exits, noting where her back was, and keeping it far from the wall. It was Gabriel's tenderness that had ruined her strategy; or perhaps it was that his unappeasable interest in her could, apparently, co-exist with the possibility of leaving her behind when he returned to what Zoë was increasingly perceiving as his 'real world'.

The words that conveyed his message were, when she heard them, oddly muffled, as though they must reach around to her through a hearing trumpet blocked with dust, or must escalate over the cacophony of voices that had ranged up in permanent positions inside her skull to shout: yes he will, no he won't, yes he will, no he won't, until she could have screamed and wept for loss of silence.

'You're right,' Gabriel had said. 'It's impossible and quite intolerable to imagine living without you.' He had paused, testing the weight of his utterance. Then continued, 'Somehow we'll manage. We'll have to. I'll discuss everything with Christa, not write to her. I'll go to Frankfurt and do that. Then you could meet me in Berlin, Zoë. We'd be apart for only a couple of weeks, two or three at the most. It's not much when I thought I might lose you forever.'

She had wondered then at her anger, a quick clean flare which went nowhere but burned, en route, the dust from her hearing trumpet and made ashes of the voices.

'*Ask* me Gabriel,' she had said. 'Ask me nicely. You mustn't assume . . .'

He had looked at her. 'Of course not. I'm very crass. Please forgive me.' With a sudden movement he left the room and returned wearing an ancient dark-green velvet cloak that belonged to Zoë draped over his naked body. He had knelt down beside where she lay on the edge of the mattress, had flung the cloak back over one shoulder in a mock-heroic gesture, had taken her hand, kissed it, and said, 'Please Mademoiselle Delighty, may I beg you to consider coming to Berlin with me, despite that it's full of Germans, despite all you know of this German, of my many failings and enduring insensitivities?'

'And despite your thin pocket.'

'And despite my thick accent.'

They had laughed then and hugged with genuine pleasure and would have made love except that now Zoë could tell Gabriel that no, she was sore, and it wouldn't do. Gabriel had kissed her gently. Then, still wearing the green cloak, he had lain down beside her and spread the cloak over them both. Neither of them spoke again. Soon they were asleep.

Zoë knew because Gabriel had told her so that German trains ran on time. An hour before this train was due to arrive in Berlin she went to the cramped toilet cubicle to make up her face, renew her perfume, check her smile for the absence of food particles, and to insert the new diaphragm that had released her from taking the pill.

Everything depended on the success of this reunion. She had to show Gabriel that it was, that *she* was, worth all the disruption she was causing in his life. He had called her only once since leaving for Frankfurt and not his words but his pinched anxious tone had told her what stress he was under. But that was Frankfurt. While she had been in Paris he had returned to Berlin, the city of his own choice. Things would surely be better?

He was, of course, on the platform to meet her. She saw him first, catching sight of the brilliant multi-coloured sweater she had finished for him the day he left England. He was running up the platform and back again, searching for her through the filthy windows of the train. She pushed down her window and yelled, 'Gabriel, here! Hey, Gabriel, here I am!' But in the noise of many arrivals and departures he couldn't hear her. She dragged her cases to the train door, heaved them off, then stood for a few seconds on the platform until, at last, he glimpsed her and edged rapidly through the crowd towards her, hugged her and tried to pick her up while she wriggled and laughed and wanted to cry though to do so would be to sacrifice the efforts she had made in the train's tiny lavatory.

'Na Zoë, and here you are! Welcome to Berlin.'

'Thank you I'm sure.' She stepped back from him slightly to execute a mock curtsey, then forward again to hug him, to kiss his neck his face then finally his mouth, though he pulled back from her, embarrassed perhaps, picked up her cumbersome cases and went on ahead.

There wasn't much chance to talk on the U-Bahn. It was crowded with people making their way home from work but Zoë was relieved to note how much cleaner, quieter and less claustrophobic it was than the London tubes which she had to force herself to take when no other choice remained.

Gabriel and Zoë stood close together, occasionally looking into each other's eyes then looking away, disconcerted by the unexpected awkwardness lacing their reunion excitement.

After a short ride Gabriel indicated that they should get off. They travelled in silence up the long escalator and into the street where he told her it would be only a short walk and then she'd be at home. He had hesitated then, as if he wanted to say more, but again in silence, he picked up her cases and she again followed close behind until they reached a tall, early nineteenth-century building, grey and somewhat run down but with marvellous plaster relief work intact under its rolling, curved roof top showing ancient heroic figures stretching across the width of the building to pass garlands and good wishes.

Zoë stopped at the high impressive doorway (could this be home?), then stepped back to take in the rows of curved bay windows that ran up and down either side of five storeys with more sober rectangular windows in a contrasting line between. Immediately outside the building was a massive tree, its lowest branches beginning their great stretch way above her head. When Zoë looked back and forth along the considerable length of the street she could see many such trees at the edge of a pavement as wide as many London streets. She had been forewarned of the claustrophobia of Berlin but there was a lovely unexpected sense of space here. She was sure she was going to like it.

Gabriel opened the wooden front door with a long key such as a nineteenth-century gaoler might have used, pushed back its weight, then went inside. Zoë followed him up stairs which were wooden, uncovered and worn down in the centre from decades of human traffic. They passed three doors on each floor, each with a bell beside a name plate. Through a few of the doors muffled sounds could be heard or smells of cooking caught as occupants made preparations for their evening meal. But they passed no one on the stairs and at the fourth floor, when even Gabriel was puffing and weary, they stopped. Gabriel took out a set of smaller keys, undid two locks, and they stepped inside.

The room they stepped directly into was quite the most perfect backdrop Zoë could possibly have imagined for the grand opera of Berlin life in which she and Gabriel were to star. She had never seen anything like it, not through lit-up windows in expensive London and certainly not in New Zealand when at the time this building had been erected almost no Europeans had yet arrived and those who had made do with tents or roughly erected wooden shelters. Comfort and elegance came later, of course, but it was never inspired by the excesses of the Prussian Empire. This room was vast, not only in its floor space but because the ceiling soared far above Zoë's head, too far quite obviously for a decorator's brush to reach. It was dingy in colour but she didn't mind that, not with such height and the marvellous window, one of the bays, a perfect half oval relieving straight lines. From the window, even in the little remaining light, she could look down onto the street below and almost touch the tree outside. She saw in her mind's eye lines from Ezra Pound's 'The Girl': 'The tree has entered my hands/The sap has ascended my arms.'

It was perfect that there should be such a survivor right outside their window, she thought, quite perfect.

168

At the end of the room opposite the window was a curtained-off area. Gabriel was pulling the curtain back along its rail to show her a makeshift kitchen with a tiny fridge, a stove of sorts with two gas burners, a cupboard neatly stacked with plates, glasses, cutlery and a few cooking tools and pans. What more would they want when neither of them was a cook?

In the main part of the room was a big, very low bed, already made up, a rickety commodious chest of drawers and next to it a severe, unornamented wooden wardrobe with elaborately carved low legs which suggested the feet of a wild beast caught forever under the weight of dead mahogany. There was a table too, over by the window, covered in a cloth of heavy greyish-blue chenille, and beside it were several straight-backed wooden chairs. A big old grey armchair faced the bed. The floor was polished wood which squeaked slightly and reminded Zoë of the floors at school and the efforts rows of girls had made, down on their knees with fat dusters, to rub in wax and keep them perfect. There was one small rug. It was beside the bed and was oddly colourless.

Through a door parallel to the kitchen Zoë could see a tiny trace of a room with a grand old-fashioned lavatory which had a long chain and a comfortable wooden seat, a handbasin as big as a baby's bath and a shower as makeshift as the kitchen, guarded by a fierce gas burner.

They still hadn't spoken but when the inspection was completed Zoë allowed herself to realize what was worrying her. It was a wonderful flat – magnificent even – and far better than she'd have thought they could afford, but where were Gabriel's things: his clothes, books, tools, drawings? This flat was empty except for the ghosts of those who had already made scratches, stains and burns, had worn down floorboards and probably bedsprings.

'Where are your things Gabriel?' She gazed at him, touched to notice how elegant he looked standing by the big grey chair. 'I thought you'd have moved in already. Where have you been living if not here?'

'Let's have a drink and then I'll tell you.'

From his own bag Gabriel took out a bottle of sekt. From the kitchen cupboard he fetched two tumblers, then unwrapped the foil and wire from the cork, pulled the cork and quickly poured them each a drink, toasting as he did so, 'To Zoë! May she take Berlin by storm and be taken to its heart.'

He kissed her then, before she had even tasted the bubbling liquid. She laughed into his mouth and began to relax and to kiss him too and to push him back towards the bed where they rested for a moment, she noticing the smell of past encounters which a strange bed always yields up, he noticing only the wonderful familiar smell of her, Zoë. They made love, taking off just essential clothes, avid for each other, greedy, graceless, fierce. When it was soon over they lay on their backs, then rescued their glasses from either side of the bed, lying together, still half dressed or undressed, jeans pulled down, shirts pulled up, only their hands touching across the space of the bed as their eyes explored the distant ceiling.

Into Gabriel's mind came an image of Zoë standing at his door when she arrived to live in the flat in Chelsea. He shook his head. The image remained. He remembered the surge of flattery he had felt because, after all, she too wanted him badly. He remembered his anxiety because his departure was already looming. He felt, more than remembered, that he had sensed danger. Was it then, or had the suspicion come later, that his life would never again be the same? This free spirit he was inordinately attracted to and was desperate to emulate but not, oh not to tame, was eagerly smoothing down her colourful feathers to make herself a tidy fit for his nest. Had he already sensed that somehow – and this confused him – in reaching towards her free spirit he could be endangering the beginnings of freedom he had managed on his own?

Zoë seemed so ripe and trusting, malleable almost. Sometimes he saw himself as an animator from an old fairy tale who could have her become wholly plastic and shape her as he did his sculptures but, unlike his sculptures, breathing thoughts into her, and opinions, and only when he was completely satisfied need he embrace her, watch her spring up before him to gaze at him with all the love he had seen so often in her eyes, and then she would wait – for whatever next he was to do with her.

Again he shook himself. It was too fantastic. The strain of the last weeks had affected his imagination. If anyone was their own creation, it was Zoë. She was self-made in a way he hadn't met before and was only beginning to understand. Really, he was being ridiculous. He was overtired, that was the matter. The weeks in Frankfurt had been harrowing. He had wanted to make a clean break with Christa, create a definite divide between the time past when they had seen each other – albeit tenuously – as husband and wife, and the present when their appreciation of each other must be as friends, and shared parents of Stefan-Georg too, of course. But Christa was unexpectedly bitter, devastated in her loss of hopes he'd had little idea she continued to nourish. She believed, and repeatedly told him, that he had taken the love and future which were rightfully hers and had given them to another. Gabriel had been confused by this. It suggested much more choice and detachment than he sensed he had. The depth of passion and tenderness Zoë stirred in him was something which had never been touched by Christa. And with Zoë too he felt envy for the first time in his life. He was not yet sure what he envied, but there was something and he was curious to discover it, perhaps to have some of it. Yet how was he to explain any of this to Christa? How could he make sense of something that made little sense to himself? He hadn't even tried, and his apparent lack of comprehension as to why he 'preferred' this new woman to herself had infuriated Christa and driven her to denounce his weakness, his lack of loyalty to her and to their son and it was, finally, their son whom Christa, made desperate by Gabriel's increasing silence and withdrawal, had used as her effective weapon.

But when he had succumbed to her pleas and then threats that if he were to live with Zoë he would not see Stefan again, when Christa had allowed her voice to rise above the whispers in which for weeks they had conducted their battles, knowing that her parents could now hear them, had he not also felt a small if quickly buried flutter of relief? He could never, without the armour of such a reason, have made this proposal to Zoë. She'd given up everything to come to Berlin to be with him (but did he want that, did he want that?). It would have been churlish to respond to this with anything less than complete enthusiasm, once his commitment had eventually been made. Christa believed that by this agreement she was winning a chance for herself. Gabriel knew that she was giving him a chance: not only to be with Zoë as he did, surely, want to be, but also, sometimes, to be alone. As he did, surely, have to be.

From the corner of the room came the rumbling of the big

radiator, like the stomach of a dyspeptic. This made them both laugh and sit up and pull up their jeans and pull down their shirts and prop themselves up on elbows to drink and to kiss and stare, wanting to understand from this reading of the face of the other all the meaning of the absence just passed.

'It's a heavenly room Gabriel. I hadn't for one moment imagined us living anywhere half as grand.' She surveyed it again with satisfaction. 'Is this grand for Berlin?'

'Well, yes and no. We've been lucky. Two friends – you'll meet them, Klaus and Ingrid – they were moving out. They'd been living here and also in Ingrid's flat but finally decided to live there only as Ingrid expects a child in some months. They sold me, well, almost gave me the furniture you see here, even the plates and other kitchen things. I made a deal with the landlord immediately. These old Berlin flats almost never come onto the market. One must be the cat waiting to pounce when the mouse appears. Most of them are much bigger than this with lots of rooms and much more expensive so, really, we were in great luck.' He kissed her again.

After some moments Gabriel got up off the bed, walked across to the table, picked up one of the wooden chairs and carried it across to place it neatly on the rug beside the bed. He sat down on the chair with unusual care; the back of the chair was facing forward and he had to spread his legs rather awkwardly, one to each side, before leaning his chin on his hands which he'd crossed on the wooden top.

'But you're to live here alone Zoë. I'll be near and will see you all the time of course, but this is to be your home, yours to do with whatever you want.'

The colour disappeared from Zoë's face. Her eyes moved unnaturally quickly.

'Why?' She appeared to be swallowing. 'We've never discussed this as a possibility, my living alone. Christ, Gabriel, you're like a seedy magician, always pulling some new, foul rabbit out of your inflatable hideaway hat. First you keep me interminably waiting: will you won't you, will you won't you graciously assent to my coming to Berlin. And now that I'm finally *allowed* to be here, you spring this.'

She was more angry than sad, but still she could feel disappointment draining away her pleasure and anticipation. It had taken her such effort to restore some belief that his hesitations were truly contained within his descriptions of them. In just seconds Gabriel had robbed her of that, leaving her empty, even of words.

He took a cigarette, already rolled, from his tin and lit it.

'It's because of Christa. I know that sounds weak but it was all much worse than I ever imagined. She seemed to have kept such hopes in me and that was such a surprise I didn't know how best to deal with them. Finally I did promise her that I'd not live with you. I said I'd live where she could also come and bring the boy though I did tell her, I promise you this Zoë, that you are the one I love and there is not and cannot be competition between you two. But Christa said she would keep Stefan-Georg entirely from me if I didn't agree and while I find this hard to believe of her I was defeated by the pain that made her say this most uncharacteristic thing. Can you understand Zoë? I had no choice.'

'Dear God, Gabriel, we always have a choice!' Zoë hadn't believed in the Catholic God for years, but in times of anguish, irritation or pleasure she could not contain the reflex which drove her to call on God or one of the panopoly of saints with all the passion and imploring of a true believer.

She was confused. Gabriel had behaved appallingly. She ought to make a stand. Now. She should protest, insist. But on what? She should leave while her bags were still packed. But to go where? And then she would be without him entirely, returned to the misery of these last four weeks without the alleviating anticipation. Perhaps, she thought, Christa and Stefan did have some rights?

Compassion for them all was weakening the thrust of her anger. She got up off the bed and perched on the tiny chair space left behind him, leaning her head against the back of his neck, mixing the top of her dark curls with the bottom of his own, holding her arm around his slim waist until he took her hand and rubbed it, as a person might rub to comfort a cat.

'I'm living just fifteen minutes from here by foot and it's much less by U-Bahn. We can see each other every day, have two homes really, and we can sleep with each other whenever we both want that.'

'Except when Christa's here and she's the wife and I'm the bit on the side.'

173

'Zoë. You know it's not like that. You know it. I'll maybe sleep with you then also. We'll have to wait and see. I mean, with all our money worries and it being very far from Frankfurt to Berlin, that would anyway be rare enough. We all know that.'

'Speaking of which, since the cruder facts of real life seem insistent on intruding,' Zoë got up and moved around to sit on the bed in front of him, pulled a face, then relented and smiled, 'I've got to find a job quickly, and a language course, and my way round town, and some friends of my own, and maybe a little lover to be tucked away, just in case.'

'I have a map for you already. But for all the rest and especially for the little lover, tomorrow must be soon enough. Tonight your old lover, your devoted Gabriel . . .' he trailed off as she interrupted him.

'My devoted Archangel Gabriel with *extremely* tarnished wings . . .'

He went on, 'Tonight I wrap my tarnished wings around you here. But now, do you want to unpack first, go out to eat first, go back to bed at once? You name it.'

'Ah ha. Some choice for me at last.' She smoothed the irony out of her voice. 'To hell with the unpacking. That can wait until tomorrow. Let's go and eat and see something of my new city. Then we'll hurry home and christen this bed with real ceremony. What do you say?'

'Fine. I say fine. Your sense of priorities is always quite excellent. So let me invite you to the finest *Kneipe* this quarter of town has to offer. A *Kneipe*, by the way, is better than a bar and different from a restaurant. You'll see. It's a place to eat or drink or play chess or read newspapers and with all those activities to talk and stare and stay for hours or pass by for minutes.'

'Sounds fun. Give me five minutes to change and I'll be ready to face it. Since it's now my turn to be the complete foreigner I want at least to look my best so heads will turn and people will ask each other in those rolling German sentences: who is that *gorgeous* stranger? And they'll pass you notes begging to know where I've come from, which you'll use to light your cigarettes.'

Zoë laughed. She enjoyed her own jokes. Then she dived into one of her cases, pulled out most of the contents and strewed them across the floor before selecting and shaking out a pair of loose crepe trousers printed with small blue flowers on a black background, a blue shirt and a striped flannel schoolboy's jacket. She brushed her hair, briefly repaired her make-up in a small plastic mirror, pulled on black boots and clattered noisily down the wooden stairs, this time with Gabriel following.

Seven

Symbols for a new beginning were there, in Gabriel's notebook: an egg, a sun rising, a branch coming in to bud.

Yet it was that first beginning to which he kept returning. The instant between never having seen Zoë at all and her being there, indelibly sprung into his life, in that Chelsea doorway.

Gabriel looked around the partially screened-off space which was his own in the large studio he shared with other students. He examined slowly and with a strenuous attempt at freshness the familiar pieces he had created over the last few years and which were, for fairly arbitrary reasons, with him here in the studio rather than loaned out to willing friends or in the dark of the cluttered storeroom below. He stared at their shapes.

It was a curious quest he was on, to create something which would sit or stand, apparently capturing a moment but which must also evoke or celebrate the power of movement which would have begun its journey long before the moment caught and would continue in its flow long afterwards. Gabriel wanted to see in his sculptures that essence of elevation, of drama through motion which Zoë had, standing still in that doorway and often since, perfectly expressed. Even when she was motionless, geyser stilled, the careful spectator could experience incipient movement, could sense and be exhilarated by the energy which was what he craved to reproduce for the spectator of his own creations; even a suggestion would satisfy him of that genuine spontaneity suggesting such limitless possibility. It was that he must capture but not subdue within the limitations of his work.

He looked away from his pieces and back to the drawings in his notebook, wondering at these doodled messages from his unconscious and their apparent relationship to each other. New optimism was stirring in him and he wanted to share this with Zoë, but it was late already. The building he was in was quiet, almost desolate. He was

176

probably among the last here. Zoë was lying in her bed not far from this studio but he knew she was not alone, though he didn't know with whom she was sleeping, or even quite why.

The first time he had gone there, rung her bell, heard the faint sounds of her radio emerging but saw no sign of Zoë, he had been confused, banging on the door, hesitant to use his keys, and calling out, 'Zoë are you there? It's me, Gabriel. Are you all right?'

The door had eventually opened not to let him in but to let Zoë out. It was late afternoon but Zoë was wearing her pale pink Chinese silk dressing gown with lavishly embroidered dragons which crossed at the back and ended their journey with a somewhat ignominious dive into each large loose front pocket. They had discovered this garment together in a small fantastical shop called Par Hazard selling old clothes and objects, rubbish mostly, but with an occasional find like this one.

Zoë had become quite friendly with the woman who owned the shop, a Czech refugee called Kristina who spoke some English and a little French and was usually doped up enough to enjoy their bizarre multi-lingual conversations with exaggerated mime to fill in the vocabulary gaps on either side. Kristina bored Gabriel. He saw her as a type who made him uncomfortable, rather than as the possessor of any real individuality, but Zoë could stay entranced in her shop for hours. She said she had always loved those shops where customers had to forage as though on a treasure hunt and had related to him a long story about such a shop in the town of her childhood. It had sounded to him like a heightened mixture between the place where Alice emerged when she passed through the looking-glass and the land to which the magic carpet would carry the sufficiently credulous child.

Zoë looked pale in her dressing gown which was pulled tightly across her body and tied with a hastily chosen and ill-matching scarf. But on top of her paleness, as though put there by a clumsy make-up artist, were two spots of high red colour, one on each cheek.

'You didn't tell me you were coming,' she had said, without greeting or touching him.

He was taken aback, still more confused. 'Well, no, but as I hadn't seen you for a day or so.'

177

'Three days, Gabriel. You've not seen me for three days.'

He was beginning to feel less confused but also defensive and even a little angry, though he knew he had no right to be. 'It's true. Three days. But can we talk about that? Could you let me in and we can discuss it?'

Zoë was gazing steadily at him, as if from a distance. Gabriel felt the beginnings of his anger curdle into dismay. She seemed a great deal taller than he and growing taller even while he shrank. She finally spoke.

'No, you can't come in. I'm not alone. There's someone here. A man, actually.'

Now she appeared to shrink a little, though only briefly. She held his gaze then turned her own to study her name on the plate by the door: Zoë Delighty.

'I'm not working tonight so let's meet later, shall we? Perhaps at Le Monde Rouge?' She named a bistro they both liked. 'I tell you what, I'll invite you.'

'Okay.' The Americanism sounded less than adequate. 'Yes, fine Zoë, that'd be fine. What time then?'

'Eight, quarter to eight?'

He nodded, hesitated, shy perhaps, anyway unsure as to whether he should kiss her, but she had touched his arm briefly and slid back through the door while he stood, still hesitating, on the landing.

When they met that evening he waited for her to talk but although she had indeed talked, had been as funny and as fluid as he had ever heard her, she did not again refer to his neglect, nor to the person in her room. As they left the bistro to go home she had merely said, 'Let's go to your place for a change, shall we?' They had taken their time to get there, stopping in a bar on the way, ordering a cognac each and holding hands while they sipped their expensive treat. But once at Gabriel's room they were silent while they undressed and when they lay down on his bed where they rarely both slept, it was as though they were long-married people, side by side but nowhere touching.

Throughout that long night of uncomfortable wakefulness, the questions in Gabriel's mind multiplied. Who had Zoë been with? Someone he knew perhaps? How often had she seen this person?

178

Did he matter to her? Did *it* matter to her, this event she'd not discussed with him? Why would she have taken this step? (His mind recoiled from that as he heard again the tone of her voice saying, *Three days, Gabriel* . . . and knew it wasn't the first time she'd endured such neglect.) But she had seemed busy and happy enough of late, hadn't she? He was unsure.

He cleared his throat repeatedly in preparation to breach the silence but always came up hard against the power of his own rhetoric. Phrases in praise of sexual freedom had fallen glibly from his tongue, despite Zoë's occasional protests. They returned now to thwart his needy curiosity.

Pictures slipped into his mind of Zoë's naked body, spread somewhat obscenely by the side of an unknown man. These pictures were repugnant to him, but also titillating. He wanted to talk about that to Zoë, to seek her reassurance perhaps, but was ashamed, and ashamed too that the anger which might have hurt them both but might also clear the way towards some necessary discussion wasn't in him. Directing his thoughts away from Zoë and onto himself he could recognize, as a disinterested onlooker might, that he was somewhat numb and around the edges of that numbness was a petty kind of caution which also kept him silent.

After that night, and the sparse breakfast they rushed to end, Zoë seemed to have adopted a new policy. Or perhaps it was no policy but a strategy, or perhaps not a strategy at all but simply the only way she figured she had left to behave. Whatever it was, Gabriel felt outside it and her.

She would say, brightly, 'I'm free . . .', and name some days and times, and he would respond, '. . . is fine with me'. They had shrunk to become appointments in each other's diaries, Gabriel fretted, and when she wrote his name down she would keep the book tipped close to her body so he couldn't see what other days were filled, or nights.

Gabriel looked back to the symbols and chose one from among them: the egg, took a large piece of thick white paper from the folder tied together with a ribbon and drew that symbol again, carefully this time with minute attention to detail and to the placing of the egg on the page. When he had finished drawing it he could see it wasn't enough, on its own, to suggest what the combination of elements had shown him, so he re-drew, alongside the egg, the branch coming into bud and the sun rising and when he had finished he wrote beneath the composition in his tiny, almost impossibly modest handwriting: *Life is never still. In love with you Zoë, your Gabriel.*

He took the sheet and placed it with care inside a heavy brown envelope. Tomorrow he would deliver it, by hand.

Eight

Zoë sat alone at the window table in a coffee shop, a tiny place
tucked neatly into the ground floor of a large, relatively modern
apartment block, and abutting a flower shop whose colourful wares
spilled brightly across the broad pavement outside. The generous
slice of cake on the plate in front of her was excellent, the hot
chocolate burdened with thick whipped cream was equally delicious. She was ignoring both. Outside in the street a small child,
aged two or three perhaps, pulled a bundle of dripping flowers
from a bucket to crush and hand to his embarrassed, apologetic
mother.

In less than an hour she had to be at work, brisk and smiling
and eager while she served and cleared and washed and dried and
fetched and carried, all the time struggling to understand more
than the words of direction and request which unfailingly seemed
to reach her. She looked with sympathy at the waitress in this
shop, leaning back against the big glass counter that housed the
cakes to take some of the weight off her poor feet which must carry
her all day. The woman was dressed in typical waitress-maid's
uniform: black dress, frilly white apron, absurd hat perched on top
of neglected hair. She was wearing high, thin-heeled shoes over
the edges of which her feet slightly bulged. Zoë shuddered. She
had been a waitress herself for six months now. The novelty had
quickly worn off. To compensate for that, she knew the short cuts
and the best route to a more generous tip. She had her own effective
methods for cutting up time into neat sections behind and ahead
of her and for cutting her own self in two so that while the outer
Zoë smiled and hurried and played waitress well enough, the inner
Zoë could remain detached, waiting for the game to be over.

She also knew some of the customers now, on her own, not just
those who were Gabriel's friends. Or she knew them as well as

anyone who is busy until the doors have closed can know people free to sit or to leave when they choose.

Gabriel had taken her to the *Kneipe* where she now worked on her first evening in Berlin. She had loved the crowded room with its large central bar behind which the staff stood or ran. Papers and magazines hung from wooden bars on the poster-covered walls. A few people were playing chess. Most were drinking, eating and talking, standing near the bar or sitting close together around too-small tables. This room, these people, had matched her expectations. Zoë had been preparing herself for Berlin, or trying to, and had hardly dared hope she would actually find this roomful of apparently casual, inclusive relationships, people drawn together in play by their common political assumptions.

She had been excited by the nods and shouts across the room, the shifts of energy as people arrived or left or moved from one table or group to another. Beer appeared as if by magic to be noted down with a swift stroke on the edge of a cork coaster so it wasn't until the end of the evening when sufficiently anaesthetized you'd mind much less, that your moment of financial reckoning came. It had seemed like a splendid party which might continue into infinity, played out by attractive, intense people who were, Zoë realized, taking themselves and each other seriously. Giggles rose to her throat, but she was also stirred and challenged, and impatient to take part.

Christopher Isherwood and the young Katherine Mansfield had come with her as companions to this complex new territory. It was Isherwood's Sally Bowles she felt close by that first evening, sensing drama, mystery and tremendous potential even in the most ordinary words, embraces, gestures. She also, less willingly, carried fears and warnings about German people which had sifted through her brain since she was a small child, which had been fostered during the period she and Rebecca had been Israel devotees, and which had risen with unwelcome force to the surface of her consciousness since she had fallen in love with one of them. Zoë knew that 'the only good German is a dead German' was the conclusion of a blistered mind, big with unease and ready to pop. But they were, after all, these Germans, some of them, capable of deeds beyond imagination, and if not these young people then their parents

182

perhaps, or parents' friends, protected neighbours, or relatives. Someone must have known. Done it. But Gabriel's commitment to the contemporary fight against fascism was fundamental to him, and he shared this commitment with thousands, perhaps millions of his countrypeople. She needed to know more about Germany's history of resistance to fascism. It had been no part of the one-dimensional portrait of the twice-vanquished nation which the victors continued to hold aloft, despite current and expedient sophistries.

As Zoë looked around her she recognized that she had come to somewhere much stranger than the England she had been culturally prepared for since birth. Her supposition was confirmed that she could never really know Gabriel until she understood the country which had produced him. She saw the focused intensity she had assumed to be unique to him reflected on a number of the faces which came up to them in an apparently unending parade. She had never envisaged Gabriel would be so popular, nor that there'd be other people remotely like him. He was completely at home in the *Kneipe*, opened out in a way she had never witnessed in London. People called to him, newcomers to the increasingly crowded, smoky room came to where he sat to shake him by the hand or playfully punch his arm in greeting. He was punctilious about introducing her, explaining, in English, that Zoë had just arrived, that she'd come to Berlin from London but that no, she wasn't English, she was from *Neuseeland*.

This last was apparently striking. His listener's eyes would widen, the exotic name would be relished and repeated. 'It must be very beautiful, no? And so far away, yes?'

'Very beautiful, very far away. Near the Antarctic, actually. No. Not part of Australia. As far from Australia as Britain is from Greece. No, not the same as England, really quite different,' she informed, eager to suggest with just a moment's chance how it was different and what that meant.

But through the elation of that evening, real though that was, Zoë was also aware of a growing sense of isolation. She was far away, not just from New Zealand but from anywhere she could, simply by assuming it, belong. She touched her skin. There was only who she was – and she was uncertain of that – and Gabriel.

She needed Gabriel badly. She needed him to look at her and see someone there. To touch her and find her familiar so she could, in his embrace, be familiar also to herself.

Where were her friends now? Where were James and Caroline, Ian and Brendan? Where was Rebecca?

It would be early morning, tomorrow's early morning, in New Zealand. The people she had known and lived among would be rising to a day quite different from anything she could contemplate here. The light would have all the expectancy of spring, and none of the used-up quality of this autumn.

Was she, in beginning this new German life, making of herself someone they could no longer touch, or would even recognize?

Beyond that evening as the introductions continued Zoë would go on to say of her homeland, 'Only three million people and yes, many sheep, indeed, many more sheep than people.' Sometimes the temptation to add an authentic 'baa baa' at the close of this inanely inadequate recital was almost too great to resist, but she would keep her face relatively controlled and drown the sheep calls in her beer.

In the face of the giants of European history it was hard to offer, as implausible balance, sheep. The moment never seemed to come when she could begin to explain the liberating experience of space which such a tiny population allowed, or the immensity of South Pacific sky to which her mind returned her night after night as she lay trying to sleep, or the rapid movement of hard and soft lines as startlingly different landscapes took their place within the patchwork of that small land-sea-and-air quilt. Impossible too to explain the brief span of history in its more positive sense: no weighing down with past generations' deeds so great as to seem unrepeatable, but instead a sense that almost anything could still lie ahead.

And no indelible stain of fascism either, she'd sometimes mutter to herself, deflecting her knowledge that in their efforts to 'civilize' her beautiful country the English from whom she was descended had killed, raped, stolen and destroyed. Not just at a material level either. Perhaps worst of all they had been capable, those proud early settlers, of standing before a cultural history made rich by people who knew the land of which they sang and who could read the sky and the sea, and could declare to each other that the history of New Zealand was about to begin.

When the geographical exchanges with Zoë were over the real talk of the evening would begin. In German. Occasionally some kind soul would say, 'Excuse me, my English . . .' and with a shrug to show how poor their English was would launch into their very fast and presumably excellent German to which Gabriel would, of course, reply in his own fast and likewise excellent German.

Of course she didn't mind. What else had she expected? It was something new to be unravelled, this German. She liked the sounds and was struck by how different they were from the bastardizations that passed for German in English and American war films. Then it was shouted or screamed from a tight, stiff head, detached from body and perhaps from soul. Zoë liked the pitch she heard now, pulled up from deep within the speaker's being. It made everything sound full of thought and weighty meaning. She felt quite confident then that soon her own deep voice would find new depth and roll clever German sentences to eager targets across crowded tables.

At the end of that first evening, Zoë and Gabriel had walked towards her room, relishing their pleasure at the hours still ahead. Zoë asked Gabriel to tell her what had been said. He had been visibly enlivened by the talk; there must be lots for him to share. But he had stopped, kissed her slowly and tenderly and had said, 'Oh that? It was nothing Zoë. Really there was nothing of any real interest. Nothing new, except you.'

She had not dared to pursue it, to take any risk of further disruption on this precious evening of reunion, but she was surprised and hurt that 'nothing' had been quite so compelling.

They had not returned to the first *Kneipe* for some days though in the meantime went to others very like it: one distinguished by 1950s Hollywood posters, another by a complete wallpapering with stylish *Rothändle* ads, giant cigarettes making a warm pink and black cave. Wherever they were the routine was much the same. Zoë was curious that Gabriel seemed not to tire of it. She also began to wonder whether he knew everyone on the left in Berlin, and why this thought should trouble her.

Too soon they were seeing people for a second or third time. Even the brief introductory exchange became unnecessary. Zoë's participation dwindled to being gripped within a firm handshake and having her name repeated to her as though she might have lost this precious piece of information on her way to the rendez-vous. Then she, too, would repeat the speaker's name: Lothar, she would say, or Franz, or Ulrike, Astrid or Dietmar. She would hold the speaker's gaze while names were exchanged for several long seconds, just as Gabriel had instructed, and just as she must do with each person in turn around a table whenever a toast was made.

Gabriel was eager to help with these new customs. She couldn't complain. He was eager, too, to have her look her best each night and to smile and smile even when it was hours since she had understood a single word to stimulate such a smile. She was grateful for his coaching. She had no wish to appear crass and to shame him. But when it came to language – nothing less than her trade, her talent, her lifeline to the world and safety net within it – Gabriel seemed much less willing to help her.

'Go to a school, Zoë, it's the only way,' he repeatedly insisted. 'The conversations I want to have with you, they'd be so boring in German. Once you've mastered the language then of course it will be different. But now I want to be able to talk to you, really talk to you, not just stumble through baby phrases together. Our time together is too precious for that,' he would say, unbuttoning her shirt. 'When we're together I love to speak English with you,' he would say, caressing her pale nipples. 'It feels like *our* language, the language we began with, something private and lovely between us,' he would say, unzipping her jeans. 'I can speak German with all those people out there, but I speak English only with you,' he would say, his hand moving between her thighs. 'You'll learn German in no time once you go to a class,' he would say, his fingers finding her clitoris, 'and in the meantime, why waste a precious second? You wouldn't want that either. Would you?'

'Perhaps we should both learn Italian,' he began on another occasion, as they sat in an Italian restaurant so excessive in its national display it seemed entirely fake. They were replete with

186

excellent spaghetti cabonara and a great deal of rough chianti. A waiter with a very loud voice and absolutely no neck was rendering a song which would scarcely have been bearable from a Venetian gondolier as you sat under the night sky to star in your own cliché.

'It'd be a language new to us both, Zoë.' Gabriel was shouting to make himself heard. 'Despite my Italian name you like so much it's never been a language in my home. I believe my father has just a few words. We could learn it together and then neither one of us would have the advantage of speaking in a mother tongue.' He sat back, waiting for her to admire his clever solution.

Zoë was silent until the waiter's due round of applause had followed the last, interminable chorus. Then, playing with her napkin in a somewhat distracted way, she said, 'Gabriel, I haven't learned *German* yet, the language of the country I'm living in. It's not just what I speak with you, or don't. It's what I hear or don't hear all around me. It's what I can or cannot read, or understand. It's what I can or can't follow on television or at the movies. It's being part of things, or separate from them. And let's face facts, I won't learn German or even stay here unless I can make some money soon, to pay the rent, let alone to pay for classes. You *must* teach me until I can afford the Institute. Please do that for me Gabriel. Even a few words or a single construction a day would help. It could be fun, really it could. I'll address you as Herr Professor and you'll be obliged to keep your face serious at all times and to excuse any blots on my copybook.'

He laughed then and her hopes rekindled. She had, after all, tried repeatedly to explain to him what it meant to sit as though on a rock far out at sea while the tide of conversation rose all around her and how agonizing it was to hear nothing but the crashing of sounds, their individual nuance and meaning lost. She had begged him to pause occasionally to explain a little of what was happening so she could try to make guesses between the few words she recognized from her books. But he always told her, 'Later, Zoë, I'll tell you later,' and when later came would repeat that nothing had been said that would interest her, or was worth their shared time to translate.

Zoë knew it was her own fault. Gabriel had increasingly to remind her she was frowning or looking bored. If only she could

187

be more open and relaxed, rather than tight and defensive, then the sounds would surely come to make some sense? She had always blithely assumed herself capable of picking up any new language through a process somewhat like osmosis, soaking up meaning through her pores to hear it emerge as beautiful, pertinent sounds through her correctly adjusted mouth. Why didn't this happen? The books she bought and gazed at dismayed her. Such a complicated structure to master even before she could distinguish one part of speech from another. And their games: the clever winding deceptive journey a German sentence could take to flatter the speaker and delight the listener and to confuse, utterly, the language's neophytes. All Gabriel's friends spoke quickly, except when they spoke in English. Then, it seemed to Zoë, they addressed her as though she were the foreigner in that tongue, or the idiot she increasingly felt.

It was one of the women in Gabriel's closest circle who suggested to Gabriel that Zoë might try for a job at the *Kneipe* she worked at now, the Humphrey Bogart. The woman had never taken any overt interest in Zoë, had never interrupted her rapid intense conversations for more than the most cursory of greetings which might pass as polite. She was exceptionally clever, Gabriel had said with some pride, as though this reflected well on him too, and certainly observing the manner in which she spoke, even if the words themselves were unintelligible, and watching the attention she commanded at the table, Zoë thought this must be true. The men vied to feed her lines, to have her attention, or to challenge her to the poorly disguised admiration of the others. The woman's name was said to be Sibylla Kreuzberg. It was rumoured though never confirmed, or indeed denied, by Sibylla that she had adopted this surname to declare sympathy with one of the poorest sections of Berlin where many of the ludicrously designated Turkish 'guest workers' lived.

Zoë found Sibylla fascinating to observe, noticing that it was with her wit and intellectual skills that she both attracted and held off the men. She was verbally aggressive in a way new even to Zoë, and this aroused in her a sense of increased possibilities in her own behaviour, if the cat ever returned her numb tongue. At first Zoë tried to disguise her concentration on Sibylla, nervous that the woman would notice her staring and find it offensive. But they all seemed to stare, these people, taking it for granted that if you were interested what would you do but stare, so Zoë stared too, at all of them, but most of all at Sibylla, and the evenings when she was present at whichever table they sat became easier for Zoë to bear.

Gabriel did not immediately pass on to Zoë Sibylla's suggestion. He waited until they were walking home, arms around each other's waist, enjoying gazing in through the lit-up, uncovered windows of those Berliners still awake at this soft hour of early morning. She was grateful for his consideration as it meant she did not have to react with gratitude to Sibylla right away, nor in front of the others. She was touched and surprised that Sibylla had thought of her and thought her suitable for work, even for something as ordinary as waitressing. It made her feel that perhaps she was visible through the silence. She'd had so much time during her long, observing evenings to conclude that if she were to disappear from the table it would make no difference at all. People would, for a moment, notice they were slightly less crushed. Their arms might spread a little to take up the space, but shortly a newcomer would join them and they would be as close as ever before. She felt as a flying fish might who leaps in joy and adventure from the water only to land on the hard, dry deck of a foreign vessel instead of back in the sea as she'd planned.

Zoë wanted to find the right words to thank Sibylla. She knew the woman could speak some English. They all could. Their cultivated, rigorous education had seen to that. But Zoë sensed these particular people chose not to, almost always, disliking intensely the American presence in their city and the cheap American culture which had permeated all their lives, but particularly the lives of the working class in whom they needed to believe. America was the fascist country now, fighting a war in Vietnam which they spent much of their time protesting. English had become the language of contemporary imperialism. They had all heard the naïve fudge that oozed through the radio each day from the American Forces Network and the Voice of Free Europe. They had read the American newspaper reports and laughed at the apologia of US political scientists whitewashing for their country.

They had experienced a lifetime of contempt from Americans for themselves as Germans. They had seen the war films, they had heard the jokes, and they believed the Americans understood nothing.

It hurt Zoë that what she perceived as their resistance to the language of the imperialists could extend to her also. Though perhaps it occurred to none of them she might be interested in what they were saying?

When she next saw Sibylla, Zoë tried to thank her in German for her help, using words she had pieced together, practised and memorized. Zoë had her back to Gabriel as she spoke, desperate that he'd not witness her awkward attempts. Sibylla replied to her in English, 'Really, it's nothing, Zoë. How about you just ask there and see what happens? I heard of it only because my girlfriend Monika used to work there herself. She knows the boss and found it not such a bad place.'

Zoë went alone the next afternoon to the Bogart and asked for Peter the boss, again in rehearsed German. But when Peter appeared – each recognizing the other at once – she became hot and embarrassed and blurted out in English her request for work. Peter had noticed Zoë sitting silent by Gabriel's side. She had seemed to him an unlikely choice for Gabriel, pretty enough for sure and always well turned out, but why would Gabriel want a regular girl at all when he never had before, why would he want a foreigner, and someone outside the political scene at that? But if she was happy to carry his dishes, as she was insisting now she was eager to do, then what did he care for her politics or sex life? He would lose nothing by giving her a try.

Zoë finished off the last crumbs of the cake and swallowed down the cooled hot chocolate as a voice echoed 'Waste not, want not' from the depths of some New Zealand kitchen. Her mind focused, but brought her little consolation. She was changing fast. She knew it but could discern no pattern to bring her comfort or help her to maintain the fiction that these were changes she was controlling. She wanted to talk to Gabriel and find out if the changes were noticeable to him too. She needed to ask – no, not to ask, to *know* – what place she now had in that busy, fulfilling life of his. More even than his sense of being at home in Berlin she envied Gabriel his work, longing to be absorbed as he was. She grew hot then cold as she recalled asking him, though really she hadn't wanted to, had longed to swallow the words and hide them in her clenching stomach, 'Do you care for me now Gabriel? Do you still really care for me?'

She had tried to keep her escaping voice light to convince him this was just a tasteless game she was playing when she'd forced him so often to tell her that yes he does, deeply, deeply care for her.

Why had she asked him yet again? Why had she exposed herself to the torment of seeing him force himself from his work to pay attention to her, moving his head up slowly so that when he meets her gaze he has successfully erased the irritation which of course he must feel?

For years she's felt neat inside herself, tidied up into a self-made order, willing, even eager to offer a strand of herself to this person, a mask to that one, a real glimpse to someone special, but never her whole self who was now in revealed state exposed as nothing but a scooped-out space.

It was the irony of contradiction she minded most. Gabriel was willing to accept her, accept who she was, at least in private, and who she was interested him, she could almost say obsessed him. But the more accepting he showed himself to be, the less acceptable she found herself, and the less she could locate of herself.

The reassurances Gabriel went on giving her disappeared even as they left his mouth. They became as insubstantial as bubbles blown by children through a thin circle of wire which make a colourful pact with the light and air then disappear, leaving no trace. How could she reach forward to bring his words inside her, to use them to build herself up again until she is, once more, solid? Sometimes the hollow feelings were so bad she found it hard to believe the evidence of her eyes that there really was a body surrounding them. It seemed much more credible that she – whoever she was – existed inside that hollowness: rootless, weightless, worthless, diminishing.

As she left the coffee shop, half-running towards the *Kneipe* as she had lingered too long, Zoë resolved to confront Gabriel, to clarify who each of them now was for the other and to evaluate, as calmly as she could, whether that was still enough to keep her here, balanced precariously not only on the edge of any real sense of Berlin, but at an increasingly dangerous and mysterious edge of any real sense of herself.

The evening moved slowly. When Sibylla appeared, alone, Zoë's spirits lifted from a very low place. None of Sibylla's usual friends were in the *Kneipe* and although she nodded to a few people and spoke briefly to those who sought her out at the big bar, she appeared to Zoë to be preoccupied, sad perhaps; or was this just Zoë, sad herself and seeing it mirrored? Without being asked to, Zoë took Sibylla a bowl of the rich 'one pot' soup for which the kitchen staff were generally praised. She also carried some of the slices of dark sour bread which she'd noticed Sibylla usually stole from whoever was eating to tear into pieces and chew between vigorous puffs on her rough, untipped cigarettes. There was no conscious intention on Zoë's part. She was moved by Sibylla's apparent preoccupation and was perhaps a little curious to have some conversation with Sibylla while she was alone.

The German woman looked up with surprise when Zoë appeared beside her with the food. She thanked Zoë profusely and before she began to eat asked her, with real warmth and in careful, just-slowed-down German, how she was and whether she was now settled in their strange city, Berlin. Zoë hesitated: it was not only Gabriel but also his friends that she spared her German. Yet to reply in English would betray her as nervous as she was. She took a piece of the bread she'd brought for Sibylla, put it into her mouth, chewed, swallowed, and blurted out, 'I like it a lot but in no way I could have predicted. I feel very alone here and this confuses me as with Gabriel I'm more loved and in love than I've ever been in my life. In my adult life I mean.'

If this answer was more than Sibylla had bargained for she didn't show this. She had, in a flash, a picture of the woman who stood before her now and the vivid pretty girl, so like himself in physical appearance, Gabriel had introduced to them. Zoë looked dimmed.

'I think I know what you mean. Would you like to talk about it some more?'

Zoë grinned, almost flirtatiously. The change Sibylla observed was remarkable. And then she said, looking aside, 'Oh maybe, maybe not. I'd like to try if it's not too boring. But only if we can also speak in English. My German . . .'

'Your German is much better than you fear. Why not lunch then, tomorrow at my house? Perhaps before you come here to work? My afternoon's quite free.'

Zoë nodded, more pleased than she could immediately find words for, grateful that she could hide her pleasure in a rapid movement back to her waitress role. Sibylla held her back and spoke again, 'Until tomorrow then. Here, I'll give you the address.' She dipped into her large canvas bag, pulled out a notebook from which she tore a sheet of paper and using a heavy, expensive pen wrote on it, in startlingly attractive handwriting, her address and phone number.

The house in which Sibylla lived was of a similar period to Zoë's but had been cut up much less finely so that the floorspace of each individual apartment was massive. Sibylla lived there, Zoë judged from the names by the bell, with a large group of people. Off the end of a long, uncarpeted passageway was Sibylla's own room, a luxurious cave draped with pieces of what looked like old Persian weavings, overlapping until no single inch of wall showed through. On the floor were a couple of mattresses side by side, covered with the same exotic fabrics, also in dark reds, orange, purples, browns, with a pile of cushions set to one side and indented where Sibylla had apparently been leaning. There was a plain wooden office desk in one corner beside a well-filled bookcase. On the desk were piles of books, papers and folders neatly ordered in wire baskets of different colours. Set before the desk was a plain wooden chair. At the end of the mattresses stood a cane coffee table with an overflowing ashtray and pretty china cups and a matching teapot set on it. There was the long, elegant window which Zoë had come to expect in apartments such as these and the wind which blew faintly through it caught the row of windchimes Sibylla had strung in front of it. Their persistent tinkling was tranquil and reassuring as she looked around. Beside the desk she noticed a cork noticeboard propped up against a section of the drapes. Various pieces of paper were tacked onto it, encroaching on a large poster of women looking happy and emboldened beyond Zoë's present sense of reality.

Sibylla enjoyed watching Zoë's careful appraisal of her room and when Zoë turned to her with words of admiration Sibylla's somewhat severe dark face burst into life as she began to explain the history of the Near-Eastern cloths and how impatient she sometimes became with herself that she'd begun this fetish of collecting, but having begun she seemed unable to stop, although she could not afford to go on buying sufficiently fine pieces to satisfy her increasingly sensitive taste. And anyway, as Zoë could see, she didn't have an inch more space to display new-found treasures.

Part way through this fascinating recital – fascinating because it revealed a Sibylla very different from the political aesthete Zoë was pretty sure she passed herself off as being – Zoë realized she was understanding almost all of Sibylla's German without making a blackboard translation of the words in her mind. This had happened before, though never in Gabriel's presence, and if he came into a room where she was speaking or listening to German the words would instantly disappear, no matter how desperately she tried to hold them back. Gabriel knew that she had acquired some words and praised her extravagantly for her success. She hated this. His applause felt to her as though it came from profound surprise that she could learn at all, or belonged to the category of excitement a dancing chicken might provoke.

Sibylla stopped speaking and moved to the coffee table to pour tea into delicate cups which she had, she told Zoë, inherited from her grandmother. This woman had been a young fighter for women's rights in the socialist movement of sixty years before. 'My own mother repudiates her efforts.' Sibylla shrugged. 'And mine too, I expect.' She laughed. 'Perhaps there's some awful cosmic game of "jump the generations" going on which means that at best every other generation is engaged in pulling forward from the place where intermediate generations would try to mire us.'

Sibylla's hands began to move in a way Zoë found familiar. 'Our most famous example here in Germany is Hedwig Dohm. She was the mother of Katia Mann – do you know of her?' Zoë shook her head. 'She was a shy woman but determined enough for justice to overcome this and fight for women's rights as well as for the right of her own daughter to be educated. Yet the greatest use this daughter could think of for her education was to offer it to the service of her husband, the writer Thomas Mann, and to belittle her mother's heroic courage in private and also in public, as a neurotic deviation.'

Sibylla's face was flushed. There was none of the caution or irony Zoë was accustomed to seeing in her manner. There had been times when Zoë had questioned how much warm heart balanced Sibylla's cool head, but she had no doubt of that heart now. Zoë was moved to tell her that New Zealand had been the first country in the world to enfranchise women and had also been the setting for a number of at least temporarily successful utopian settlements incorporating the kind of principles she thought Sibylla was fighting for.

As soon as she had hung this information in the air between them, she regretted it. Sibylla would want details, analysis, opinions. Each time she had blazoned such a remark before Gabriel she had realized her mistake when she couldn't contextualize it, or even pretend fully to understand what she'd just said.

But apparently Sibylla didn't need to know more and if she was patronizing Zoë who knew that her reputation as a political naïf went everywhere before her, then too bad. She could stand a little patronizing when it made her feel this good.

Sibylla excused herself then returned to the room with a tray of goodies arranged almost as beautifully as Gabriel could have done, with cheeses, cold meats, a small bowl of salad each and an assortment of dark breads. They continued to sit on the floor, legs crossed, tailor fashion. Zoë spoke English sometimes and German sometimes and only occasionally paused to consider which was which. This was the liveliest conversation she'd had for months and if she wasn't mentioning the dilemma that had yesterday wholly occupied her, then she was grateful enough it should have subsided.

When she really did have to go, Zoë kissed Sibylla warmly, first on one cheek and then on the other, remembering as she did so the starched, scratchy veils of the nuns as they had kissed her in this way at school. Sibylla accepted her kisses, turning her head in an exaggerated way, but when she had helped Zoë into her old leather jacket she pulled her quickly towards her and kissed her on the mouth.

Zoë was startled, but laughed to cover this, and called out as she went down the stairs her thanks and pleasure and wish to see Sibylla again, soon.

At the end of that long evening's work Zoë realized she was again eager to see Gabriel. The need she had acknowledged to herself the previous day, to discover their place in the other's universe, had come back with renewed force. The comforting intimacy of her lunch with Sibylla told Zoë how lonely she had become, much more lonely than she had admitted even in her daily writings. She was also stirred up, and she found this strange, by Sibylla's kiss, though she knew, of course she knew, that it was nothing more significant than the gesture of a politically sophisticated woman to someone she was treating as an equal. Zoë wondered if what she felt was aroused, or if she was simply flattered, by the ease of the afternoon as much as by the kiss?

But her impatience to see Gabriel would have to be set aside. She was already committed for the rest of the night.

The man's name was Frank Gapes. He was an American, a Californian who had grown up on the other side of the great Pacific ocean which rolled between his country and her own. He was also an officer in the loathed, despised, reviled US army. He seemed to have no shame about this, nor about the journey that had taken him to peace-time Germany instead of to Vietnam. He had boasted to Zoë of his daddy's silken strings and how wonderful it was that a short tug between daddy's Stanford headquarters and decision-makers in Washington had landed him here, alive beside her, rather than dead with the gooks in the jungle.

Yet Frank hated his job in Berlin and frequently repeated his reasons why. One: it was keeping him from the escalation he would otherwise be making up daddy's golden ladder. Two: the Germans were ungrateful for the fact that but for the miserably bored American troops (with a minimal amount of help, perhaps, from the French and British forces), the Russians would crash through the Wall and take over Western Europe.

Frank knew that Europe was a sadly pathetic place in comparison to the United States which was, and he liked to repeat this also, possessed of all the virtues God had come to realize were lacking elsewhere. Frank also knew that everyone who was not American wished to be so and after their second date but before they went to bed he had solemnly and quite unnecessarily informed Zoë, to be absolutely fair as he put it, that he could never marry a girl who wasn't American, even though he did appreciate that many believed this was the only route they could take to enter his country on a permanent basis.

It was obvious to Frank how phony that veneer of sophistication was which made some Europeans claim preference for their ancient piles of shit, but he was prepared to be tolerant, well, up to a point, and as the final refrains in his litany went: this wasn't Vietnam, wasn't for ever, and wasn't even for long.

It took a little more skill for Zoë to prise out from Frank his unsurprising views on women. They came in two kinds: wives, whose fathers ought to have money and whose mothers will have brought them up right, and whores, who were better or worse in bed and stayed for longer or shorter times accordingly.

There was little doubt in Zoë's mind as to which category she must belong. After all, her mother was dead and poor James's fortune wasn't. She didn't mind. Frank probably quite liked whores, and she quite liked Frank. It would have been difficult for her to defend this judgement. He was obnoxious in almost every way she could have imagined and gave her constant stimulation to imagine new ways, but self-absorbed, astoundingly ignorant, prejudiced and complacent as he was, he could also be fun in a bounding, childlike way which part of Zoë hankered for. It was entirely in Frank's interests that they should have fun together. He was amazed to have found her. After all, she was not a German (all fucking Nazis underneath), nor one of the few unmarried American women in town, types he viewed with mistrust, being quite unable to fathom why they would be here when they surely didn't have to. Also she wasn't stuck up like the damned English and she was, he had to face it, a great, no, a fan-fucking-tastic lay.

During the time they had been seeing each other they had developed simple, satisfying routines. Frank's salary as an officer, plus the dollar-baubles daddy sent, meant they could eat and drink anywhere, anything. Because Zoë's evenings were mostly taken up with work, Frank usually bought a picnic spread of delicacies for them and after a short time, in response to Zoë's enthusiasm, he began to scour the duty-free shops of the Frenchies as well as his own comissary and PX, for treats to please them both.

He had deposited in her room a tall jar embellished with a winking, somewhat overwrought Uncle Sam which contained the best grass the US army had on offer. Whenever the supply was even slightly depleted he would top it up generously, protection against the terrible day when supplies might run out and he'd have to face this mother of a city entirely straight.

Zoë and Frank did not discuss their personal histories, their views on politics or on the meaning of life. When together they existed in a little cocoon sealed with food, drink, dope and sex and always strictly in the present tense. They went out when they could, once in a while with fellow officers and their German girlfriends who spoke awkward, Hollywood-inspired English (the men spoke no German) and seemed pathetically keen to nurture these army men's notions of the rights they could expect abroad. Zoë and Frank danced, joked, and played silly made-up games. Occasionally Frank would massage Zoë and through his hands would come a rush of the kindness his head sometimes forbade him from expressing. They always parted tenderly and forgot each other almost entirely until their next meeting was due.

Frank had a wonderful American body: tall, supremely muscular, a hairless torso, broad on the shoulders with narrow hips above long, strong legs. He had played sports all his life and football for his college. This stupendously aggressive and competitive game, with huge players caged and padded, was described by Frank to Zoë in terms as mystical and lyrical as his vocabulary would allow. She sensed that for him it symbolized much that was uniquely American. It was rough and tough; it was played by men for high stakes in front of vast audiences, and all the pleasure was in the winning. It may have affected his brain.

He moved beautifully when clothed but was unexpectedly clumsy and naïve when naked and was touchingly grateful when Zoë, more smashed than usual one evening and willing to show off, put his cock in her mouth and sucked it. He could never bring himself to mention this activity precisely, and never liked to think about how much he liked it in case, as he suspected, that was queer, but when he was desperate for her to repeat the gesture he would point, or say, 'Could you, honey, you know . . .'. She knew. And occasionally she would.

The sense of control, of power almost, which Zoë had been used to feeling and which was now no part of her daily life, came flooding back to her when she was with Frank. Their expectations of each other were slight but she knew herself to be entirely capable within that range. She could trust herself, almost like herself, even when she was doing things which a voice from above her head told her were ridiculous. There was a most particular satisfaction for her in feeling Frank's excitement rise, rise, then crash into climax as she tendered him tenderly, and kept herself apart.

Zoë found sex with Frank a repeat, almost to the shudder, of sex with all the men she had known before Gabriel. Perhaps they were all the same man who ran behind a screen of time and re-emerged with a new face, name or nationality, but the same cock, urges and attitudes.

She had despised this predictability in the past. The hero of her imagination would be resourceful, wise and patient. And so her hero was, she told herself. But it was he and not Frank Everyman who could produce a banana skin to place beneath her heel.

At half-past midnight Zoë found Frank waiting for her in a bar a block from her work. It was the kind of place she usually avoided, just an anonymous spot for strangers to sit and drink under a shared roof.

Frank was standing by the long bar looking out towards the door, anticipating her arrival. His lithe, handsome looks were shown off to excellent effect by the expensive honey-coloured Californian college-boy clothes he always wore when not in uniform. He glowed with the patina of good health and a life-long history of plenty, enhanced by the scrubbing his skin would recently have received in the second of his twice-daily showers. As he leant towards Zoë to kiss her in greeting she caught a faint odour of his manly aftershave mingling with toothpaste and soap. He was the man for whom the phrase 'clean sex' might specifically have been invented, she giggled to herself, knowing he would take a third shower after they had made love.

Zoë could feel herself beginning to relax. Frank's faults were many but so irredeemable they weren't her concern. Alongside the increasing uncertainty in the rest of her life her times with Frank were forming up very nicely into patterns of comforting familiarity. She noticed too, and was more surprised by this, that she felt stirrings of genuine pleasure when she imagined lying down with him later. In that best post-coital time when they lay drinking, smoking dope and talking, she often played with the dog-tags he wore on a heavy chain around his neck which identified him as a serving member of the US Army. He refused even to contemplate removing them, though Zoë had tried to persuade him, made uneasy by the suspicions which hovered in her mind that somehow she enjoyed this brash display of military allegiance in the bed she usually shared with Gabriel the Good.

Frank had told Zoë it was against the rules to remove the tags. But it was also against the rules to smoke dope, snort cocaine, discuss the intricacies of his work, or to reveal to a hostile civilian the extent of boredom, vice and crime among the US defenders of freedom. Zoë concluded that Frank needed the tags to remind him with just a brief touch of metal to his skin that he was part of a mighty institution, and not a solitary foreigner, castaway on uncharted land.

She imagined removing the tags while Frank slept, watching him go off unknowingly without them, then leaving them under her pillow to be discovered by Gabriel.

It would be too awful.

She enjoyed, no, *savoured* the thought.

How mystified Gabriel would be by her behaviour. She considered that through a haze of dope when going to bed with Frank for the first time. But Gabriel's mystification or even his disappointment seemed a risk she would dare take to win back the pleasure of acting a role she knew well and believed she could still enjoy.

She knew, oh how well she knew, that if she groaned, called out his name, if she pushed her hands forcefully up and down his back and thighs as though to have wonderfully more of him, if she heaved sometimes with her strong body and moaned a little, if she bit his ear, ran her tongue around it and whispered into it, he would come more quickly. She liked to move around the room, slowly, while Frank lay on the bed, already naked and impatient, knowing that he was admiring her firm immodest body and giving not a single thought to her mind. She also liked to kiss, tenderly and with the skill of practice, wanting at least that for herself, though sometimes he would destroy that moment of sweet connection by mistaking force for passion, as though her mouth were not something that was individual, expressive, and subtle.

If Zoë were to talk to Gabriel about Frank she was sure he'd want to understand. He was inevitably rational, even liberal in his responses. But an army officer, and an American army officer at that, would really push his limits.

It had clearly been difficult for him to refrain from asking Zoë who her mystery lover was. She had intended to tell him. Had wanted to do so before that awful afternoon when he had turned up unexpectedly at her door. She was willing, even eager to tell him as soon as he asked. And when he didn't ask she admired the self-control she could never have emulated and, in a curious way, despised it, wondering just what would jolt him into anger, or at least into the display of some curiosity she could feel kin to.

Because she loved him she eventually told Gabriel the man was English speaking. Though she could see that his gaze continued to linger when someone outside the far-reaching boundaries of his circle was talking to her more than was usual in the *Kneipe*, or seemed persistently to be seeking her attention.

Frank ordered a drink for Zoë and another for himself. Then he turned to face her, looking shifty somehow as though uncertain how best to arrange his pleasant unlined face. He obviously wished to postpone or avoid any discussion of his own state as he ignored her genuinely curious question as to how he was, expunged his frown and pressed her for details of her activities in the days since he had last seen her. Zoë recounted with what she hoped was the right mixture of discretion and pleasure her lunch with Sibylla, then went on to supply various amusing anecdotes gleaned from her working evenings.

He was a gratifying audience, laughing, admiring, interjecting with questions to make more of each story. But finally she stopped and asked him what was wrong. It was over a week since she had seen him for a brief lunch. It was at least a couple of weeks since they had spent a night together. She was impatient to feel closer to him again. She was suddenly grateful to him, grateful that he should be as transparent as Gabriel was opaque.

'Let's drink up and get out of here, do you mind?' Frank was looking at Zoë cautiously.

'Not at all. I'm tired of bars.'

They went into the street. Frank had his arm around Zoë's shoulders but she wriggled free. She had to run, to take in gulps of air and leap ahead. She ran just a few steps before he began to run too, laughing now and shouting that he'd race her to the end of the block. In just seconds he was there, still laughing as she panted up behind. Not for the first time. 'You should run more often. You're way out of practice, Zoë. I do believe I'll take you in hand and get you going on a fitness programme. How about it, eh? You'll feel like a new woman in no time.' His face fell. He hesitated.

Zoë poked him in the ribs. He looked like a kid, crestfallen, about to confess to having spent all his pocket money or to having lost his brand new bike. 'Come on, Frankaloon. Spill the beans. What is it?'

'I've gotten the clap.'

The expression on Frank's face had descended to woeful. He could have been telling her that the Russians were at long last coming or that a woman had been appointed US Secretary of Defense. She had to laugh. 'Is that all?'

Now he was bewildered. 'Is that all? Honey, do you know what this means? I can't sleep with you now and I guess that,' he paused, 'I mean to say, I guess I thought that'd be curtains for us. Well hell, if we can't make love and it'll be a couple of weeks at least until I get the green light, I'd have thought you'd have no interest in seeing me any more? And there's the moral question too.' He was fully serious now as his mind sought words sufficiently weighty to express his feelings about this moral question. 'Shit, Zoë, pardon me, but you'd be quite within your rights with no hard feelings on my side at all if you were to say to me, "Frank

Gapes that's just disgusting and I never want to see you again." I
mean, I could really understand that. I'd probably say it myself.'

'Do I have it? I mean, could I possibly have it?' Zoë interrupted,
suddenly fearful not only for herself but for her relationship with
Gabriel. Would his liberality extend to the clap?

Frank rushed to reassure her. 'No way. It was a German girl
and it all happened since I saw you last. Well anyway since I
stayed with you last. You remember Doug's girl, the little one
from Hamburg? Called herself a dancer or something.' Zoë did
remember. 'Doug's girl' was tiny with close-cropped dark hair and
clever, rather theatrical make-up. She had initially seemed likely
to be a more lively companion than most of the German girlfriends,
but soon revealed herself to be another simpering limpet clinging
to a khaki shore.

'The three of us had this scene. You know how it is? We were
smashed out of our heads. Not only dope, coke too. The girl was
real willing. Doug only had to ask her the once.'

Poor limpet, thought Zoë. Still, she'd left her mighty mark.
And paid for it too, no doubt.

Zoë caressed Frank's upper arm. 'Actually, Frank, I don't mind
at all not making love. Honestly, it's not all that important to me.
And as for your having the clap, well neither of us promised fidelity
to the other, did we? It's bad luck for you, but that's all. It's
nothing awful for me.'

Frank's face was transformed by surprise and gratitude. He
assumed Zoë was willing to make a great sacrifice to maintain their
friendship and was moved near to tears, dammit, by her broad-
minded generosity. Zoë herself was suddenly aware of her mam-
moth relief. She had the perfect excuse to play with Frank, to have
her secure, comprehensible times with him, to have his attention
and gratitude, and not have to fuck him. Maybe he could have the
clap chronically?

They went on to Zoë's room in a mood of new tenderness, lay
down on her bed, kissed a little, cuddled and fell asleep, curled
together like forks in a drawer. Zoë slept throughout the night
without any of the dreams that usually shook and coursed through
the darkness. She woke refreshed, as though she had slept in the
open air, as though that air had been in New Zealand, out under

the stars of the Southern Cross, close to the trunk of a big pohutakawa tree, sheltered by its giant branches, cushioned by long grass on a bushy verge abutting golden sand running down to the fresh morning ocean she missed persistently and profoundly. She felt she had survived a storm, dark and tumultuous, strong enough to threaten her but also to carry away in its wake clouds, mist and débris, leaving behind an horizon wiped clean and ready for new impressions.

Nine

The great tree outside Zoë's room was fully green. In just a few weeks its leaves would begin to change colour, and then to fall. But now the sky above was a huge blue basin and from the pavements heat rose in the final sweltering weeks of a continental summer.

Summer heat had apparently gathered into the upper reaches of Zoë's high room to hang there with such authority that the occasional breeze which came in through the window was mocked and quickly disappeared in shame.

Zoë had filled the room with plants. Dark green plants stood in big pots made out of clay and decorated with Zoë's rough brushwork. Smaller, lighter green plants sat on shelves or hung from hooks. She sprayed them daily and coaxed them as best she could so that in the room there was now a smell evocative of a hot-house with its warm damp soil in which unseasonal flora could grow. Despite her efforts the plants seemed to be wilting and Zoë felt at one with them, lying on her bed, languid, wasting precious free time when there was much she should be doing.

Gabriel had been away from Berlin for a week. His last semester at the art school had come to a close earlier in the summer. He was still searching for a suitable new studio and meantime his tidy flat, barely large enough to accommodate the living needs of someone rarely at home, was packed to the walls with his work, his tools, his materials. He had found a light industrial job which he could do for three weeks out of every four. He considered himself lucky, saved by the mercy of a sympathetic foreman who understood his need for balance between the money earned by work, and time for his sculptures, but each three-week period would be grindingly dull. Gabriel swore it was what he wanted, that to be free in his mind was worth more to him than the spurious prestige and stimulation of a white-collar job, but Zoë was nervous. In his enthusiasm to make a success of this new arrangement he probably underestimated how dull work could dull you so that only with the most persistent effort of will could you sustain the creativity the dull work was intended to support.

She knew she could not continue with her own dull work for much longer and was increasingly afraid that the additional strain of Gabriel's work would cast a shadow on their relationship too long to escape.

Another shadow. Yet they loved each other so much.

She looked around the walls of her room, decorated with a mass of Gabriel's drawings, many of them of herself. Her eyes stopped moving at the still-life, set apart by its subject matter from the others which were all figures, or parts of figures. She couldn't read the tiny words but could immediately recall them: *Life is never still.* She sighed. Nor predictable. She looked at the sculptures which Gabriel had carried one by one to her room. There were some early pieces, including one of the first he ever made. His work had been much rougher in finish and more abstract in shape then. Only with increased confidence had he been able to turn his back on what the teachers and other students were doing and stubbornly follow his own urge to concentrate on apparently representational work which transcended any single vision. Zoë knew that despite his persistent refusals of her offers to model for him she was nevertheless constantly in his mind while he worked, or not *herself* perhaps, but that almost-stranger, that past-ghost whom Gabriel had met and fallen in love with. That 'free spirit', as he insistently named her. The free spirit seemed increasingly to be leaving her and passing into Gabriel's pieces which were, her untrained eye could see, growing in grace and fluidity and something quite indefinable which caught the breath and moved the heart. Strikingly unfashionable.

Zoë pinched her nearly flat stomach then turned over onto her stomach and pinched the flesh of her bum. There wasn't much to grab, but she felt like lard anyway, white, pasty, excessive in what could be trimmed and discarded and near-empty and still emptying of tasty, rich filling. She licked her arm and tasted sweat, then watched as the hairs slowly dried, paled and stood up again.

Without moving off the bed Zoë stretched beneath it to pull one of her suitcases into the room. It was unlocked and once the lid was thrown back it didn't take her long to find the bundles of photographs she'd been promising herself for months to sort through and order.

With her eyes tightly closed she chose a first group of pictures at random, delighted to find they were fairly recent pictures a friend had taken of Gabriel and herself in the formal gardens of the Schloss Charlottenburg during freezing winter. Their faces glowed in the photographs and she remembered the pain from staying out in the cold too long while Gabriel arranged and directed to achieve the effects he had visualized. Even with their red noses and frozen tears, she thought they looked marvellous together, set far apart from the ordinary, a fantasist's dream. She no longer had much confidence in her own looks. When she gazed at herself in the mirror, at her representations in Gabriel's drawings, or even in photographs, she found her image elusive, almost as though it were always slightly out of focus, or slyly disappearing like a polaroid picture gradually reversing out of view.

But at Gabriel's side, in his presence, *built up* by him, she knew they were exceptionally striking. Memories of that freezing day cooled and enlivened her, and heartened her emotionally. Everyone had their troubles. She tentatively nursed the cliché. She and Gabriel had every means to work through theirs: youth, determination, optimism, insight, love. Even yet they could do much better than survive.

She got up off the bed and went to Frank's jar, winked companionably at Uncle Sam, took out one of the small joints Frank had thoughtfully rolled to see her through his vacation absence, then lit it. Frank was in Southern California with his family, riding the waves that landed in La Jolla. Sibylla was on a camping tour of Provence with a group of friends. Gabriel was in Frankfurt with his parents, his wife and his child. The three essential points of the triangle of her Berlin life had all flown. She was alone in the city for the first time. She could have gone to England to stay with Rosamund, but that had seemed dangerous. The possibility of feeling even stranger, fitted in however cheerfully to a life which would have shifted across the spot she had briefly occupied, daunted her. Here at least were the streets she knew, her job, and her own wonderful room in which she could be wholly unobserved.

*

When Gabriel returned to Berlin it was Zoë who was at Berlin Zoo station waiting for the train to pull in, Zoë who led the way to the U-Bahn, Zoë who let him in with her key to his flat where she had prepared, for his return, a small feast made up mainly of goodies liberated out of tins and bottles donated by Father Frank Christmas. She had also decorated his sculptures with flowers, patiently weaving tiny garlands to sit on heads, across chests, or leaving single flowers to lie at feet or be cradled by small arms. The room looked and smelled beautiful and Zoë glowed with satisfaction at the sight of her own work.

She had intended to make much better use of the time that Gabriel was away. She knew she needed to think seriously about her life. She was aware she urgently needed to write more, to read libraries-full of beneficial books, to spend concentrated hours in the great Berlin art galleries of East and West. But time had, eventually, passed quickly or if not quickly then with very little to show for its passing. She had been forced reluctantly to acknowledge the existence of a most curious kind of fog which filled her brain whenever she tried to contemplate her life in a usefully dispassionate way, a fog which was damp, grey, clinging, which not only filled up her brain in seconds but threatened her throat and nostrils too until she was deeply, frighteningly claustrophobic. The only way to save herself from its clutches was to turn her mind to manageable activities, like reading a novel, taking a long shower to loud musical accompaniment, or writing amusing postcards to friends eulogizing her marvellous life.

As far as she could work out, the fog had first shown its misty tendrils whenever Gabriel said it was *time they should really talk*. The voices in her ears would at once begin to shout, in glee it seemed: *He's going to leave you, he's going to leave you.* At least until the fog enfolded them.

Until these last weeks of Gabriel's absence the fog had never descended when she was alone. It worried her greatly, not only because she understood neither its source nor its horrible, lingering presence, but also because she experienced it as a barrier between herself and the Land of Clear Thinking which surely all sensible people had access to at will? If that Land was out of reach then how was she to make any decisions of her own, or support Gabriel by taking her fair part in the discussions they were constantly proposing to the other they needed to have, yet she – or her fog – was as constantly sabotaging.

Now Gabriel was back in Berlin, in the room beside her and she suspected – no, she knew – that again she was waiting, passively waiting with nothing to propose, sitting on the edge of his uncomfortable bed doing a fine imitation of a Raggedy-Ann doll, feeling nothing but wariness – of the inevitable questions to which she would have no answers, but fully expecting that eventually and without too much display of resignation Gabriel would tell her what the next stage of their life together should be.

Zoë wondered if she should suggest they make love. She glanced at Gabriel. It wasn't the moment. He was clearly preoccupied. The voices in her ears began but she silenced them, turning over with some excitement the possibility of attempting to describe the fog to Gabriel. It would be such a relief to name it, share it, perhaps go some way to understanding it? She looked at Gabriel again. He was taking books from a bag. She feared he would be impatient. Who wouldn't? It sounded utterly implausible but when experienced it was more powerful even than her passionate desire to be the clear-thinking, quick-witted woman she had once fancied herself to be, whom she still glimpsed in the mirror of Frank's eyes, and who she knew she must again become. For Gabriel surely had little tolerance left for the numb-brain he was seeing?

He had straightened up. The books were on the floor. 'I've been wondering, Zoë, if you should see a psychotherapist?'

These were not his first words. Those had been fulsome praise for the floral tributes adorning his work. He'd been really delighted, she could see it. His smile had been wide and without doubt or hesitation. He had thanked her, kissed her, and declared what a shame it was that the flowers, unlike the sculptures, couldn't live for ever.

'Me? A therapist? What the hell do you mean? Am I now someone who's crazy?'

Gabriel's face was kind and his voice was reasonable. It was hitting the tone she found least bearable: rational man to imminently hysterical woman. It reminded her of James, and of the priests of her childhood. The voice was going on. 'No one's saying you're crazy, Zoë, or that anyone's crazy. But before Sibylla left for France she and I . . .'

'You've been talking about me with *Sibylla?*'

Oh God, let it not be true. Zoë felt shrunk to nothing and at the same time inflated to some likeness of a grotesque plastic blow-up person, a grinning idiot wobbling on a rounded, leg-less base. What was Gabriel on about? Had she revealed the fog to him in her sleep? Could this be her, whom he professed to admire, that he was talking to? And about?

'To talk about me behind my back, as though I were some kind of problem, as though I couldn't take care of myself just as I always have: how could you? It's unbelievably disloyal. And for Sibylla to talk to you about me! So much for women's bloody solidarity. What has she been telling you? That I cry sometimes all over her oriental cushions? That I confessed to her how I envy her her horrible, narrow-minded mother simply because she goes on being alive? That I feel out of my depth with you but am incapable of leaving because I feel lost inside myself? Did she tell you that, Gabriel? Did she? Did she? And did you squirm and beat your breast and wonder why *I* hadn't told you? And did she say that I am obsessed with fears of your death? That I would rather die than survive your dying? Did she tell you that little gem Gabriel? And then did you ache, finally, with curiosity, wondering what else I've managed to keep from you? Did you Gabriel? Well, did you?'

Gabriel had shocked Zoë into an explosion of words and he was, in turn, shocked himself. And silenced. Sibylla had told him none of those things. Their discussion had been cautiously general and almost uselessly discreet.

Gabriel had arrived late at a meeting and had taken a seat at the back of a crowded room. Sibylla had come in some minutes later and had settled into the last spare chair, just behind him. After the final speaker had sat down she had tapped him on the shoulder and suggested they might have a beer together. He had shaken his head and heard himself ask her, without premeditation, if he could meet her, tomorrow, for coffee.

If Sibylla was surprised she masked this in her search through her big bag for her battered diary which she quickly checked even while saying, 'Tomorrow afternoon's fine if you can come to me. About four then?'

During the years he had been living in Berlin Gabriel had come to accept as a matter of fact rather than pride that he was a catalyst in many people's lives. He was a gifted listener, in part because he was always genuinely interested in what lay behind a speaker's initial presentation, but also – and he shared this with Zoë – because being a skilful listener enabled him to give the appearance of intimacy with many people without revealing more of himself than he wished. It kept him, in some sense at least, powerful, but also somewhat isolated.

To make good use of this meeting with Sibylla, Gabriel would have to confront this pattern, expose his vulnerabilities, and the anxieties he was reluctant to continue to carry alone. It was not something he could easily do with his men friends. He was close to many men, bound to them by political conviction and mutual respect. There was an implicit sub-text to some of their conversations which told them all they believed they needed to know about their personal lives. But what was actually spoken of was practical, or theoretical; it concerned the real world, outside the bedroom and the heart.

When Gabriel had begun, with awkward hesitations, to speak of Zoë, to state his concern that he sensed some crucial distress within her which he couldn't get her to discuss, Sibylla had interrupted him.

'It could be more helpful if you were to speak of yourself, Gabriel.'

'But I'm fine.'

She had been quick to make her face impassive but not before he had caught a whiff of disbelief which had further discomforted him.

With some effort he began again, trying to make a joke of the irony that he was apparently the Desired Ear to many on the left and that, indeed, Zoë frequently told him she was revealing to him things she'd never revealed before. And yet he could not shake his conviction that for all his efforts to draw her out there was more she didn't trust him with.

'There seems to be,' he said, looking at Sibylla's noticeboard, 'a gap between the funny, bright facade Zoë's able to present, and who she is, or what she feels and fears behind that. But when I ask her to speak of it she most cleverly diverts me without realizing, I think, what frustration that causes me. Not only because she is shutting me out but also because of my sense that this unhappiness is something she can less and less easily control.'

Only after some moments did Sibylla respond. 'I think I know what you mean about the hidden uncertainty. But whenever I've tried to approach it, and that's only been a couple of times, I've got back from her a eulogy about your place in her life and her place in yours. She admires your talents extravagantly and is almost embarrassingly touched by the attentions you give her. She must have been parched when you met her? Good God, Gabriel, the way she talks you seem to be sun and moon to her, mother and father even, as well as lover. And worst of all, she sees herself in terms of such inequality with you. Though hopefully that won't last!'

Gabriel held out his cup as Sibylla offered more coffee. She went on. 'You should be more patient with her, if I may say so. She's in a strange country with people whose background and mode of expression is very different from what she's used to. And this at a time when – in my view mistakenly – she feels she's got much to learn and nothing to teach. All this is at its most exaggerated in relation to you of course. Yet it's obvious to me what she's taught you.'

It wasn't until he was walking down the steps to the U-Bahn that this last remark reached Gabriel. By then Sibylla was not there to explain.

'Throughout the time I've known her she's had terrifying dreams. She wakes out of them sweating and shaking. I believe they're centred on her childhood but that's a taboo area also. At least, in unhappy memory it is.'

'How do those dreams make you feel?'

'I think she's suffering. I think that if only she'd talk about them, exorcise them by talking . . .'

'Is that what you'd do?'

'She's so stubborn and somehow . . . I don't know, maybe it's elusive? That's part of her charm of course.'

He lit a cigarette for each of them. 'Her charm continues to work on me. I could even say I feel trapped in it.' He laughed. 'But that's ridiculous.' Sibylla looked away from him. 'I sometimes believe I can't get enough of her and perhaps that's why I mind so much about this hidden central core, if that's what it is. How could she hide anything from me which is that important?' His mind flashed to the days when Zoë was not available. And then he went on, 'I believe I make myself entirely available to her.'

Sibylla did not comment.

'Surely it would be better if she were studying, or at least working at something more appropriate to her talents than waitressing? I urge her to try. I encourage her in every way I can.'

Again Sibylla didn't speak. Gabriel put down his cup. He went to the window and looked out. It was raining. He had come without a coat. He felt irritation creeping across his afternoon. He had tried. Nothing had been gained.

Sibylla watched him. He did have a beauty and grace quite his own, Zoë was right. And there was a need in him to care which was special too. If Zoë had to love a man, she could pretty well understand her choice, though she wished she could see more pleasure in it.

As Gabriel was about to leave, Sibylla held him back. 'Be patient, Gabriel. And also with yourself. I break no confidence by saying that Zoë's elevated you and that until you and she work out some way to look at each other eye to eye you'll always have problems. But these problems are not only Zoë's.'

Zoë was crying, lying face down on the bed weeping loudly and without restraint. Gabriel took his eyes away from his decorated sculptures, and looked at her. The wholeheartedness of this at least was familiar Zoë behaviour, but Gabriel had never heard anyone cry with such anguish, and for Zoë to do so — who never cried. He was struck by the contradiction between this thought and what she'd just said. He tried to recall her words: 'Crying with Sibylla . . . envying her her mother . . . lost inside herself and out of her depth with me.' Oh Zoë. What have I done? thought Gabriel. And almost as quickly, What am I to do? What could anyone do?

He touched her shoulder softly but she shook his hand off. He tried to comfort her with words. 'Zoë, I did never intend to insult or blame you, just to help you.'

She was a Christian martyr whose life was being crushed out of her between the doors of humiliation and still the man was piling on stones.

At some point during her crying Zoë became aware of what she was doing and although her stream of tears and the great heaves continued from somewhere beyond her control, she was also able to observe the spectacle, to feel curious and in some uncensored way relieved and oddly satisfied that it should have occurred, though this feeling was certainly much less strong than her anger and acute embarrassment that somehow she'd been designated as the case who needed putting in the basket.

She suddenly remembered the year she turned twelve. 1959. Pius XII of hiccups fame was shepherding the Catholic flocks. It was her last year at primary school and there was a girl in her class, not a particular friend but a girl who was also good at English so someone she knew quite well, whose mother disappeared for long intervals and was never comfortably spoken of. Zoë had unwillingly become sensitive to this, but tried to stem her own feelings and ignore the odd looks, intensely grateful that they were directed at a girl other than herself, but also fearful, as though this girl's troubles with her mother – whatever they were – might remind people of Zoë's own differences which she wanted them to forget.

One Sunday at Mass she saw the girl with her mother. The girl's name was Lorraine. That came back to her now. The father had been there too, a much older man who was stooped and grey, and there were also a couple of adolescent brothers. But it was the mother Zoë's eyes had fixed on because even from behind and with just occasional glimpses of her face as she turned to her husband for guidance, she was like a person whose spirit has been scooped out and excised. With little nudges and whispered coaching she had stood, kneeled and sat more or less in rhythm with the rest of the congregation, but her mouth had not moved to utter any of the responses and when she looked up to find her way back from the communion rail to her pew, her eyes had looked dead in her parchment face. Zoë couldn't work out what could have happened to this woman, but she knew that whatever it was it would be better to be dead, like Jane, than dead inside a body still moving in the world.

When Mass was over and they had left the church, Zoë had held

James back and asked him what was wrong with Lorraine's mother. He had told her that the woman had been depressed, 'Sad, Zoë, for a very long time. So they took her to a mental hospital and gave her what are called electric shocks. Of course these are not the same as the crude electric shocks one might get by accident. They're carefully directed to jolt the brain to make it alert and break that pattern of sadness.'

'Then why does she look dead?' Zoë had asked in horror.

James had had no answer.

The image of Lorraine's mother entered Zoë's mind with such force that she was never again able to look fully at Lorraine for fear of enlarging it. She'd been immensely relieved when the girl went to boarding school the following year, or perhaps the whole family moved away as she hadn't seen them at Mass again.

Zoë knew why Lorraine's mother had returned to haunt her now. The tears soaking Gabriel's pillow had flowed out of the fog and cleared a path towards understanding it. The fog was no simple barrier between herself and some probably illusory notion of clear thinking. It was an accumulation of unshed tears. That fog was grief. And that awful hollowness growing inside and around her was not 'nothingness' but an echo-chamber for grief. Grief which could gnaw at her guts and her confidence, which could weaken her and drive her mad, into bins, into the arms of electric shock tormentors, into rivers, water to water, where she might float like Ophelia, draped in flowers as she had draped Gabriel's sculptures, catching weeds as she drifted: wet, bloating, dying, dead.

She stopped crying, sat up, blew her nose and asked, 'So what makes you think I need a therapist?'

Gabriel scarcely drew breath before replying.

'Perhaps I'm quite wrong Zoë. I know very little about psychoanalytic theory but I think in some curious way you are *wasting*, wasting yourself, wasting away — I'm not sure what it is. There has been some fundamental change in you since you came here to Berlin. I know I have some part in this but I don't know what that part is.'

She blew her nose again, and smiled at him. He continued, moving around the small room as he spoke, 'Sometimes I experience myself almost as a vampire.' He wanted to laugh but couldn't. 'It's as though I've taken something essentially optimistic from you because having seen it I wanted it for myself, or for my work. Anyway, what's the difference? Perhaps I've mythologized your New Zealand spirit as I called it until I have sucked it out of you, without offering you any safety in return.' He stood still, picked up one of the small sculptures and played with it nervously. 'I sense you're waiting, expecting something from me, but what it is I've got no idea. And when I ask you, when I beg you, Zoë, to tell me what's happening to you, you can say nothing, or will say nothing, or you avoid me by changing the subject to tell me a joke or a story or to have me make love with you.'

His voice was raw with impatience. 'But clearly whatever's happening is a great deal more than nothing. I thought it might help you, might even help us both if you were to talk about this, that's why I suggested . . . yet it's not that I think you're crazy. And it's not that I don't love you and want to help you myself. I do.'

Zoë avoided Gabriel's eyes as she began to speak.

'I need a new job. That's all that's wrong. I'm bored near to death at the Bogart and have grown to resemble the dying. But good God, Gabriel, I'm much tougher than you obviously think.' She grinned. Oh Zoë, what lies, what hopeless lack of trust. Trust him and tell him about the grief. Tell him now about the fog, that store-house of tears. Trust him and tell him about your dreams of his dying, of her dying. Trust him and tell him. What do you have to lose? Tell him you cannot think of love without fearing death. Tell him that. *Help him.*

The words were in her mind, pressing on her, perfectly formed. She spoke.

'Look, this is all terribly boring. Enough is enough. Once I get myself a new job I'll be fine. You'll see. And if you think I'm being a miserable drag just tell me. I'll glide off. Either back to my room to chastise myself with barbed rosary beads or even off to wherever. The great big world beyond Berlin is not an entire mystery to me remember. Don't worry about me! We should be having a good time.' She stood up to kiss him. 'Well that made a change, didn't it? Zoë the Stony-Faced turning into a fountain. Maybe you should toss coins into my apron for good luck!'

Gabriel smiled, but with effort, knowing she was deceiving him and pushing him away but unable to contemplate immediately probing the pain he had glimpsed. He pulled her towards him and held her close but he was recoiling, longing for the wild girl who perhaps she'd once been; looking over her shoulder with fierce lust towards the pieces he himself had created which were, at last, beginning to embody the spirit she had revealed to him.

Zoë buried their conversation beneath a mass of activity. Even at work she threw herself into the life of the *Kneipe* with a vigour that stunned her fellow-workers. They teased her, telling her summer was too hot for such excesses, but she worked and talked and laughed and flirted as though life were a mountain and she had glimpsed the peak.

She was sleeping with Gabriel almost every night, asking him as he left her room in the morning whether she should expect him back that evening and controlling, utterly, any sign of relief until he smiled, or nodded yes. She couldn't, it seemed, get enough of him. She cajoled him to meet his friends at the Bogart so that between her flurries of work she could sit briefly beside him, an arm around him, or could kiss him quickly as she passed by, or wink at him or smile as she caught his eye from across the room. He could not always be there. Some evenings he said it was necessary for him to be in another bar or restaurant and sometimes he didn't want to go out at all but stayed in his room to work as best he could in that confined space until it was time to meet Zoë. If he came for her at the *Kneipe*, or met her at her room when she walked home alone, she would always seize him to hold him tight until he would laugh, awkwardly, and ease himself away.

When they were in bed it was now Zoë who took the initiative, arousing him persistently even when they had already made love more than once that day. He suspected that she wasn't wholly enjoying their excesses of love-making though repeatedly she told him how she longed for these embraces, for this closeness, for him. He did not suspect that occasionally as she moved her body against his own it was of Sibylla she was involuntarily thinking, and it was Sibylla's face she was banishing from her mind.

There was something disquietingly hectic about her, yet the elongated silences and unpredictable moments of frightening passivity had disappeared. But all this new activity, and obsessive

217

attention to what she was apparently perceiving as his needs, was nothing which Gabriel could trust, or be comforted by.

Sometimes when Zoë lay sleeping beside Gabriel, violently twitching from time to time as though falling by stages down some bottomless pit, he would recognize his own pain and confusion. He would stroke Zoë gently so as not to awaken her, or would simply gaze at her through the darkness, wishing her tiny and himself full-breasted, wishing he could take her into his arms to feed her, and to rock her into a state of innocent trust.

With increasing force he was sensing how great was her need to be mothered, how she joked and mocked to hide her pleasure when he tended to her as a mother might: tucking her into bed, patting her, teasing her, bringing her treats on a tray. He was saddened at how self-consciously she received these small attentions, as if they were exotic, and transitory.

One afternoon as they sat together in one of Berlin's many parks, Zoë began to talk to Gabriel about Katherine Mansfield, sun and moon in her country's literary firmament. She urged him to read the stories, or let her read them to him. She recounted the outlines of Katherine's life making a vivid picture of her fiercely, perhaps defensively provocative behaviour; of her years in Europe, England mostly, at the edge of the snobbish Edwardian literary circles whose members envied her talent which was impossible to deny, but exiled her from any sense of belonging by privately scorning her as unacceptably colonial.

Zoë described and illustrated from memory those brilliant, tender evocations of New Zealand, the land Katherine could neither return to nor forget, and told of her slow, profoundly resisted dying from tuberculosis, of her obsessive love or at least need for the unscrupulous, unworthy husband John Middleton Murry, and the coughing spasm which occurred through excitement at his reappearance and brought her life to a close at the age of thirty-four.

It was not clear to Gabriel, listening intently, whether Zoë was at any level aware of the extent to which she identified with Katherine Mansfield. He wanted to provoke her, to suggest there wasn't any need for her to imagine a death as imminent or as painful as that moment of departure at Fontainebleau. But the words to say this didn't pass his lips. Perhaps if Zoë had been born in 1882 she too would have been eaten up, wasted by consumption. It wasn't only that this illness could now be cured, but it seemed to him also that the human body had shifted so that when it was sufficiently overcome with pain overspilling from the recesses of the soul it would consume itself by other still-uncontrollable means. Cancer. He felt his penis grow hard as his desire for life asserted itself. This time it was he who nuzzled in Zoë's neck, who whispered promises into her ear, who seized her by the hand to hurry her to the U-Bahn and back home.

Sibylla's name was rarely spoken of between them, but Zoë and Gabriel were both greatly relieved she would soon be back in Berlin. Gabriel knew he would risk Zoë's anger to discuss her with Sibylla again. Zoë concentrated only on her anticipation of the acceptance and expansion she had learned to associate with Sibylla.

Zoë and Gabriel were now most comfortable when they had a focus outside themselves and their nervous, almost wholly internalized questions. In her determination for self-improvement, and to meet her relentless need for activity, Zoë had at last become an habituée of the museums and galleries. She spent hours with Gabriel preparing for her visits or discussing what she had seen. These 'lessons' were not only about art history, but also about history, philosophy and politics. Gabriel's intelligence and curiosity were unconfined to any few subjects. He had read widely and retentively and thought most carefully about what he had read. He was a gifted teacher; Zoë was an avid pupil. The peculiarities and gaps in Zoë's parochial education amused and amazed him, but he was impressed by how directed she was in her search for connecting threads. He was also startled at how quickly she was challenging his point of view, and pulling him up when he was vague or unsure. He had already become aware she had a sharp eye for the fake, and a strong response to what was original or deeply felt, but he had not anticipated the pleasure he was getting from their discussions and chastized himself that they'd not begun this work together earlier, while he was still a student and could have gone with her to the galleries. As it was, she had to go alone. The days he wasn't at the factory could not be sacrificed, even for Zoë, though he was eased in his conscience when Zoë truthfully insisted she had always preferred to go to galleries alone: free to wander or sit entirely at her own pace, to formulate her opinions without influence or observation.

Gabriel began more insistently to suggest to Zoë she might study, at the Free University perhaps. She hated his urgings and was quick to deflect them. She had no wish to admit to her fears that he might think her ill-educated and possibly shameful. On those rare occasions when she offered an opinion to his friends he hovered nervously, frequently explaining what she had just said when she believed there really was no need. And as keenly as she soaked up his lessons, seeing herself as blotting paper to the ink of his knowledge, she also took what she perceived as a dangerous risk in exposing to him the extent of her ignorance.

The evening before Sibylla was to return – though this was referred to by neither of them – Zoë was free from work. She had proposed to Gabriel that morning to treat him to dinner at a nearby Greek restaurant. She wanted them to be alone for a simple night out. They spent few evenings without a backdrop of Gabriel's friends, and Zoë was delighted when Gabriel readily agreed.

As they entered the restaurant Gabriel was telling Zoë an amusing story from his factory day so it wasn't until some moments had passed that she realized Gabriel's name was being called, and also her own. Her heart sank. At a long, central table was a hearty group of Gabriel's friends calling to them to join in.

Gabriel turned to Zoë to pull an apologetic face. So much for their evening alone. Zoë shrugged. What else could she do but smile to cover her disappointment and wriggle into the small space made ready for them as people moved closer together and cheerful waiters brought additional chairs.

The group had not yet begun to eat but were pouring frequent toasts from bottles of ouzo. One of them had just been fired from his job as an undesirable subversive. It was around this event that the group was celebrating, or planning effective revenge.

After a couple of toasts Zoë began to relax, determined for Gabriel's sake to make the best of the evening. She wanted to show willing and talk to her neighbours but they seemed already engaged in intense conversations so she allowed her thoughts to turn inward, to drift on faintly aniseed waves and it wasn't until Gabriel nudged her that she realized plates of food had reached the centre of the table and people were beginning to dish it out. The bottles of ouzo disappeared. In their place came bottles of retsina. One bottle was apparently lodged by Zoë's elbow. As she was spending almost no time talking she had rather more opportunity than her neighbours to keep filling her glass and drinking.

It was rare for Zoë to drink with such persistence. Her enjoyment of drink was determined almost entirely by taste. Her fine sense of imminent oblivion seemed not to need the bottom of a glass to reflect or enlarge it. Working at the Bogart had increased her distaste for those who drank excessively, and she had become aware she was drinking ever less herself. Except this evening.

Sitting opposite Zoë was the brother of Klaus, the man who had lived in her wonderful room before her. Klaus was an ironic, gentle person, someone she had grown to admire, though her shyness with Gabriel's friends and perhaps some diffidence of his own had meant that their communication had not gone beyond nods and oddly supportive glances. His brother Thomas was a different matter, a compulsively competitive man, admired generally but clearly unable to internalize this as he constantly pushed for domination and attention.

Thomas had once left the Bogart late, when the staff were leaving and Zoë was about to begin her walk home. He had offered to accompany her and she had refused. He had been immediately abusive, asking her if she was afraid, if she was such a timid bourgeoise that she could think of nothing but rape when a walk home was suggested. Zoë had been tired at the end of her working evening and was in no mood to bear this man's drunken, misplaced abuse. She had hit him, quickly, her bare palm leaving livid red marks across his face. It was as shocking and surprising for herself as it had been for Thomas. They had both stood still on the footpath, looking and feeling rather foolish. He had apologized, and so had she. He had walked off and she had not mentioned the incident to anyone, nor spoken to Thomas since.

Now, staring at Thomas, Zoë was startled and uncomfortable to discover in his appearance some superficial similarities to Gabriel. Thomas too had long dark curly hair, strong chiselled intense features, small dark eyes, a slim active body. But there was an arrogance in his face that was never present in Gabriel's. His hungry need to dominate, to be right, meant that he looked almost painfully alert. Zoë knew Gabriel admired Thomas, in part because he was, apparently, an acute and uninhibited critic whose opinion of his work Gabriel claimed he valued and needed, but even more because Thomas had turned his back on his own art career to devote himself full-time to political work. Gabriel was nagged constantly by fears that there was some eroding immorality in a life devoted to art. That self-chastising part of his personality was impressed by, almost envious of Thomas's choice to renege on the talent that had been widely praised and admired, not only at the academy but by outside critics also. Gabriel had explained to Zoë in a somewhat holy voice that after the explosions of May '68 (a month in which Zoë's own most significant act had been to drop a good deal of acid) Thomas had realized he could no longer continue with his pursuit of what was, essentially, a 'bourgeois individualistic practice'. Revolution was imminent and he meant not only to be part of it, but also to shape it.

Zoë had pointed out to Gabriel the historic precedents for Thomas's 'conversion', beginning with Paul on the road to Damascus and taking in such luminaries as Francis of Assisi and Ignatius Loyola, founder of that great boys' band: The Jesuits. Gabriel had not found her analogies as amusing as she intended. In fact, he had been perturbed by what he described as her flippancy, which had only caused her to giggle in that awful, uncontrollable manner which had enraged James when she and Rebecca were children.

Continuing to stare, Zoë noticed how awkwardly Thomas's hands rested on the table. There was an odd lack of symmetry to his fingers. They looked as though they'd been through a season or two of arthritis, or had been broken or smashed and had mended badly.

The man might have sensed Zoë's staring for he moved his hands off the table, crossing his arms and turning his attention towards her. He spoke, in rapid, confusingly elided German. 'Well, Zoë, we've not heard much from you. What've you been doing?'

By some frightful mischance his question fell into a momentary silence and everyone at the long table turned to look at Zoë, waiting

for her to answer Thomas's question, the silence giving it support
and meaning out of any proportion to which she could possibly
respond. She squirmed inwardly, and smiled. She had to speak or
she knew Gabriel would speak for her. Which would be worse.

'I've been studying a little art history,' she began. Then realized
at once her dreadful mistake. He, and probably everyone else at the
table, would think her pretentious and would question her to show
her the error of her ways. That wouldn't take long. How could she
have trapped herself like this? Gabriel was tense, oozing insecurity.
She would shame him, not meaning to, not wanting to. She would
have to be bold and joke her way out.

'Well, nothing serious you understand.'

'And why not *serious*? Princes and scholars have taken the study
of art history seriously for hundreds of years. Why not you, Zoë?'

She hated the way he pronounced her name, stressing the 'Z'
beyond the requirements of the German 'tz' pronunciation, making
a foolish name of it, trivializing her prize, her gift from her mother.
She hated the arrogant bastard and knew he was mocking her.
Princes and scholars were the beasts in his field. He would honour
only those subjects his idealized working people might study:
history, economics, politics, and all seen through a view-finder Zoë
could only call dogmatic. He would want to spit on her world and
see it wither: art, literature, fantasies, dreams. These had no place
in Thomas's utopia.

'I've been following up an old interest in art history.' She began
again.

'Very good, very good. And who, in particular, *interests* you?' He
was pursuing her now as a bull fighter might pursue a frightened
bull, teasing her forward with his red blanket of words. There could
be no genuine reward for him in knowing what artists interested
her. He wanted only to expose her to this table of listeners, to
expose her and then dismiss her as the fool she undoubtedly was. He
was waiting for her to mention van Gogh and to speak of sunflowers,
or Bruegel and to discuss crowd scenes.

'Frida Kahlo.'

'Who?'

There was no modesty in his question. The fault was hers for
naming an unknown, not his for ignorance of the knowable.

223

'A Mexican painter. She died in 1945. She was married to Diego Rivera.'

'Ah ha, the wife of the Stalinist muralist.'

'He wasn't . . .' Zoë tried, then fell silent. She had no interest in defending Rivera. It was Frida, never Diego, who had captured her imagination and then her affection. It was Frida's life she had begun to trace and after some time tentatively to explore in her journal, encouraged by links she sensed but didn't yet understand with her own life, not as it was lived in the present, in the material world, but as it was unfolding to her in dreams, or moments of rare inspiration, or in the occasional experience of surrendered intimacy with Gabriel which allowed her to feel at one not only with him but with all those people living and dead who had plunged into life's experiences not knowing whether they would sink, or return to the surface armoured with new insight.

Gabriel spoke, no longer able to resist intervening. He was appealing to Thomas in his most man-to-man tone. 'She was taken up by the Surrealists but has something of the naïve painter also. A daughter of Paula Modersohn-Becker perhaps? Yet gifted and original, no doubt of that. Not one of the greats but she certainly had something. Her father was a German Jew, a photographer. Her mother was Mexican Indian. There's an authentic element of the exotic in everything she did. In fact her sophisticated primitivism displays a quite compelling contradiction. Perhaps that's why she appeals to Zoë.'

The alcohol in Zoë's veins was swimming high, oil on top of water refusing to sink. She turned to Gabriel and although he was only inches away from her she shouted, 'You, *lieber* Gabriel, may regard me as one of Rousseau's natural descendants and it could indeed be that the "authentic element of the exotic" *is* part of why she interests me. But there are many other so-called exotic or primitive painters who utterly bore me with their reductionist flights from reality. In Frida Kahlo's work there's the incredible power she achieves through her subject matter, her broadening of any conception of reality . . .'

Gabriel spoke over the top of Zoë's voice, directing his remark to Thomas. 'Her subject matter was herself.' He smiled, the placator, the traitor. 'Countless self-portraits.'

Now Zoë was wholly on the attack. Her need for defence was

224

forgotten. 'Countless self-portraits! What about your bloody Rembrandt! She was laying her whole body bare, her being, and her soul! And at least she was looking into her own self for understanding and not living like a lice off the self of another, Gabriel Bongiovanni. Her work was much more than "self-portraits". She was pursuing the relationship between individuality and universality. I mean,' Zoë paused, just for a second but this was really important to her, 'my reading of her work is that she was pushing her exploration of her self as a woman to an absolute extreme, and by doing that was making it universal.'

'You've been listening to Sibylla, Zoë. You're even sounding like her.'

'How can you say that Gabriel? I have opinions of my own too you know, just like you do, just like Thomas does.'

Zoë and Gabriel were saved from total public rupture by a man's voice from the end of the table calling, 'The woman you're discussing, Rivera's wife, is said to have also been Trotsky's lover. Rivera took him in as his guest in Mexico and Trotsky went off with his gracious host's gorgeous young wife!' There was vigorous male laughter all along the table.

'You've got it wrong,' Zoë started to protest, searching for the words to explain. She knew the words in English. She had worried at this incident in her writing, seeing it first as Frida Kahlo and Leon Trotsky's story, and then after some time experiencing the focus shift until it became Frida Kahlo and Natalya Trotsky's story, or the story of any woman in love with a man apparently more gifted, more worldly wise, more self-confident and less self-questioning than she. It had moved, like one of Frida's own paintings, from an exploration of the specific to an understanding of the general, in which world Zoë knew herself to be centrally placed.

Thomas's voice began again, denying her the possibility to speak. 'We're wasting time discussing trivial events.' The corners of his mouth moved downwards. 'They might be amusing enough but we can learn nothing from the antics of a few essentially bourgeois individuals. The only way we can learn is by immersion in the historic antagonistic conflict of social classes. Even Marcuse . . .'

Rage again freed Zoë to find the necessary words. 'But we *are* all individuals, each with our own story but a story which is reflected

225

in and influenced by a much greater whole. We need to learn from those stories which at first glance are the stories of individuals *precisely* because there we can find echoes for our own lives. Those feelings and experiences which Frida Kahlo portrayed tell me things I'd otherwise not know about myself and other women. They tell me about her, of course, but also about *my* place in the world, in history . . .'

Thomas swooped down once more. 'Zoë, Zoë don't you understand? It's not *feelings* we must examine, it's thought and action. Feelings are always individually experienced and are therefore without significance.' These were clearly the opening lines of a practised speech. Gabriel interrupted this time, apparently directing his remarks at Zoë but intending them at least as much for Thomas.

'You can't poeticize history, Zoë, in order to understand it. In a sense Thomas is quite right. If we were all to spend our time examining our individual feelings – even with some nods to the universal . . .' a smirk danced across his face, 'then mass movements for change could never succeed. Besides which, the examination of feelings is a luxury accessible to very few.'

'You hypocrite Gabriel! How can you sit there and say that? You spend most of your life devouring me and my feelings and then creating sculptures from what you've learned!'

Gabriel's tone was marginally chastened. 'Perhaps that's so. But this isn't the place to discuss it. What I want you to understand is that what we can learn from Trotsky has nothing to do with his *feelings*, and for analysis of the rape of central America by the US imperialists we don't turn to look at self-portraits of Frida Kahlo.'

'Then that's your loss Gabriel. And I severely mistrust what you're saying.'

Thomas looked across the table directly at Zoë. A veil of compassion was drawn across his excited face. His voice was low but pitched to carry. 'Your passion is admirable Zoë, and your ignorance is almost enviable. But we are right. There can be no doubt of it. You'll come to know that.'

He raised his voice and his gaze to take in everyone at the table, master of ceremonies he would limit and control. 'You're a dreamer Zoë. You're the dreamer among us. But history is shaped by the realization of ideals, not of dreams. Events occur in the harsh daylight and that's how we must study them: harshly. Facts, Zoë, facts. Not dreams or stories. Look to facts, that's where you'll learn.'

He leant forward towards a bottle of retsina. 'And now, more to drink for everyone?

Zoë turned inward. Her mind left that table and returned to her journal.

Ten

The night before she was to go on behalf of her husband, Diego Rivera, to the port at Tampico to meet Leon Trotsky and his wife Natalya on their arrival to take refuge in Mexico, Frida Kahlo had a strange dream.

She was in a large wooden summer house, high on sturdy stilts and edged all round with deep verandahs, where she had never been before. She was alone there, not even a servant with her, yet the house was quite beautifully kept and she knew that no personal effort of hers had made it so. Beyond the house, glimpsed through partially shuttered windows, stretched all conceivable shades of green, in jungle form. Inside, the rooms were large, perfectly proportioned, and cooler than would be possible in the heat of a Mexican summer although no fans were turning nor even hanging from the ceilings, and the summer song of the cicadas was silent.

In the darker corners of the room where she found herself standing were small tables, and piled onto these tables, threatening their delicate European legs, were voluptuous arrangements of tropical fruit, colour piled onto colour, a seventeenth-century still-life by Louise Maillon brought into dizzying twentieth-century relief by the addition of the colours and textures of Frida's own work. Behind the fruit were pale vases in which stood magnificent tall flowers, like majestic gladioli but in a mix of colours which suggested wild orchids, or hibiscus, and the perfume they emitted was as alluring as that of frangipani.

In the centre of the room, nearer to the point at which she stood, was an old rug, oriental perhaps, on which was, she could now see, woven a story. When she focused on it, her eyes drawn towards it as though magnetized, she could see that only parts of the story were still visible. It was a story to be understood through symbols: birds of paradise passed messages to lions and weary travellers fell from

228

the backs of camels to land beside deep pools which would, in their own time, ripple to reveal their secrets. Trees occurred and recurred, all sizes and manner of trees, and it was their branches which took the eye upward or onward or far down into the reaches of the soul. Those branches were the fingers she needed to hold onto, to guide her while she made sense of what was happening. She experienced an almost overwhelming longing to lie down on the rug, to curl into herself on it as a cat might, but she feared for its fragility. Could it bear the weight of her body, of her sorrows, of her fears for what was coming?

To the side of the rug she noticed a small worn-down wooden stool such as a young child might sit on beside a fire. Crouching down, her legs – even her withered leg – tucked up beneath her chin, her brightly coloured skirts sweeping the dark polished wood around her, Frida sank into the hollowed centre of the stool and gazed at the rug, gazed at it with all the absorption with which Narcissus had gazed at his reflection in the water, gazed at it as though the world had halted in this place, gazed at it with longing to know what it would reveal up to her, and weeping inside herself as she mourned those parts which were missing, and would never come again. A dog without a head, a cat-like creature whose body no longer touched the ground, a blank where a traveller entered, half a tent staked beside a wandering plant without roots.

As she sat there, for hours on end and unaware of any discomfort she might be causing to her injured body, Frida came to realize that the rug was asking her for answers, that she was to give to it the answers she would find somewhere inside her own self, not get the answers from it: or that, this process – giving, getting – was one. She reached out behind her and her fingers met a tray she could have sworn was not there earlier when her eyes had moved over every inch of the room. On the tray had been placed her pallet, her finest brushes and rows and rows of tubes of paints in colours as luminous and precisely brilliant as she had ever longed for and been unable to find. It crossed her mind that she could not weave with paints and that there would be ugly indiscretions between the old work of the rug-makers and the new work of her own, but she began anyway, as if in a dream, crouching now beside the rug and noticing that the border that ran around it was intact, was a weave of flowers which wound unbroken and loosely lying, as though put there slowly and as though having remained there in peace.

She bent low, so low that her face almost touched the rug, and saw, as Narcissus had seen in the water, the reflection of her own face caught in the heart of one of the flowers. Startled, she looked into the heart of the next flower and saw the reflection of a man's face whom she knew at once to be Trotsky. She sat back a little to sort out her surprise and then could see that buried in the heart of each of the flowers, in a chain without beginning or end, was, alternately, her own face and that of Trotsky.

Gathering up her brushes and reaching across the perfect border and into the half-worn heartland of the rug, she began to paint, quickly and vigorously and without need for deliberation.

Night fell but as swiftly as it fell the moon rose high and full in the sky and her spirits rose with it. Under the incandescent light of the moon Frida painted, noticing as she went that her work resembled stitches or that the stitches were easing into a resemblance of painted strokes; knowing that her hands were moving without effort or error across the rug and that where there had been half a life or nowhere to go there was, now, a whole life and, within her reach, a journey's end.

When her maid woke her, carrying to her the big decorated cup filled with milky coffee which Frida usually cherished, she looked into the opaque liquid and felt strong stirrings of disgust as a skin formed before her eyes, covering the hot liquid that lay beneath so she couldn't get to it without her lips and tongue touching something repugnant to her.

'Senor Rivera asks you to be ready to leave for the harbour at seven, Senora,' the maid said, standing beside the door and moving through it as soon as her message was delivered.

Frida set down the cup on a low marble table next to the big four-poster bed in which she slept alone. She looked at the old mantle clock on the dresser facing the bed. She was as tired as though she had not slept at all, yet today she must look her best or Rivera would fuss, intrude on her with nervous, persistent questions about her health or worse, her mood. He might insist on changing their plans and coming with her when all she wanted was to sit alone in the back of the big car, her eyes closed to block out the world, her ears filled only with the merging hums of the car's expensive motor and that of the cicadas, to retreat into that place she had been last night, the quiet cool room where she had painted as though the brush were part of her arm, where the paints had flowed like her own blood; where she – who was usually tossed into confusion by her search for meaning – was at peace with her answers; where she had seen her face in many subtle variations and had known them all to be true, and had seen the faces of Trotsky too, whose gaze so nearly resembled her own.

They waited five hours at the harbour before Leon and Natalya Trotsky emerged down the gangplank to be met. They were a small greeting party: Max Shachtman and George Novack, two American Trotskyists, and Frida. A message of welcome from Cardenas, the President of Mexico, had already been sent to the ship, had, in fact, been the necessary Open Sesame to encourage the cautious travellers to emerge. Of course the press were there too, in their hordes, as they had been everywhere to record how this man, and his wife, had been forced from one country to another for almost ten years, pursued, reviled, threatened, refused the basic human right of a place to call home.

It was Rivera, not Frida, who shared Trotsky's politics and it was only to humour him that she had taken an interest in the man. But he was a wandering Jew as her father had been, as well as a political exile. Frida as much as Rivera had come to follow their course, sharing an anxiety as if the two Russians were members of their family, and not only the man, and his wife, who in Rivera's view had answers for the world if the world could stop hounding and listen. In four languages they had followed garish newspaper accounts and had stared at muddy photographs distinct enough to show faces increasingly far from hope of inner peace. Rivera, and eventually Frida, had struggled hard for this solution. It was an important day for them all. Rivera was waiting with the President and the greeting party in the heat of Mexico City. It was perhaps no surprise therefore that Frida should have a dream in which Trotsky also was.

The blue house at Coyoacan in which Frida had been born was

231

given over to the guests. Frida and Diego were installed in their adjoining houses in San Angel, though they were almost as often at Coyoacan. That house was spacious and their guests were exhausted so it was some days before Frida became consciously aware that Trotsky seemed, occasionally, to be seeking her out, with a question that felt carefully prepared, about the climate, the foliage, the food they were eating, her experience of the world outside Mexico. His real questions – about world politics, about Mexico, about the degree to which this supporter or that one could be trusted – he saved for Diego Rivera.

It was Natalya who told him he should look at Frida's work, one evening as they all, except Natalya, sipped calvados, and cracked open the fine nuts which Trotsky relished. Frida, who spoke no Russian, did not understand what Natalya was saying though she sensed it concerned her and hoped that too much colour was not rising to her cheeks. She looked over to her husband for the consolation of a translation but his eyes were not on her and she couldn't catch his glance. She leant forward to move a great agate dish closer to Trotsky. As she did so he looked directly into her eyes, just as she had seen him doing out of the heart of the flowers, and said, 'Madame Rivera, my wife tells me that like your husband you're an artist and that I should know your work. Is that possible? I'd consider it a great honour.'

Frida sat up very straight and held his gaze. 'I must warn you, it won't be what you're used to. But the honour would be entirely mine.' She then smiled her large slow sensuous smile. The smile softened the formality of her words, and passed like a contract between them.

'I hope your wife will come too when I show you my studio? She's been kind enough to notice the work I have here in the house, but that's all she's seen. Please do extend the invitation to her also.'

Trotsky nodded, apparently in agreement, but he neither looked at nor spoke to Natalya and after a short time during which he cracked open a nut with more force than the simple act of extraction could ever demand, he turned to Rivera and, in English, began the kind of discussion which for Rivera made the months of wheedling, charming and negotiating for Trotsky's presence in Mexico worthwhile.

The women sat, apart from each other and from the men, in silence. One able to speak with any confidence only Russian. The other with no Russian at all. The voices of the men trickled between them.

After breakfast on the day on which Trotsky declared himself ready to view her work, Frida repeated her request that he extend the invitation to Natalya, but Trotsky frowned, shook his head and said that, really, his wife would prefer to rest. Their troubles had taken a toll on her; she was no longer young. And that anyway many years before each had decided they preferred to read separate books in silence, and to look at works of art alone. That way there could be no disquieting differences as to experience, or interpretation.

It was also in silence that Trotsky looked at Frida's work, first at those paintings which hung or stood against the walls of her studio then, by a gesture of his hand moving away from where it had been partially covering his mouth and beard, he indicated he wished to see those canvasses leaning against one wall, stretcher-side out. She, also silent, nodded yes and saw in her imagination what he saw as he worked through them, supporting them against his knees, gazing down into them, getting the worst possible view, withdrawing a few and placing them to stand alone, or almost alone as the large windows left little room for display.

'They are, indeed, not what I'm used to.' He had finished looking. Had taken a second slow walk around the studio, had studied one painting then returned to another, looking for connections between them. She was struck by the order in which he did this, noting the intelligence with which he apparently sensed how one had allowed, determined or developed another. He had not looked at Frida until he had taken in each painting to the full, and the body of the work as a whole. 'They're beyond me, beyond anything I've experienced. They're almost alive in their colours, and the feelings . . .'

After a pause and with some irony in his voice he said, 'I've been dry, dried out for what seems like years. I am fifty-seven. Sometimes I can forget I was ever young. Yet now, looking at your paintings, it's as though I've been feeling my skin lift outwards from my body to make room for the excitement they produce in me. Truly, they're like nothing else . . . so raw, Frida.'

He used her given name for the first time and the breath she was holding prisoner high in her body burst free to make way for more normal breathing.

'You possess a great talent, a marvellous talent. You are not just,' he stopped to check his words, 'not simply a beautiful woman, but very gifted too. And brave. I hadn't known. Forgive me.'

'There's nothing to forgive. I'm flattered, and touched, that you like my work. Not everyone does. You can imagine.' She stopped herself, looked around the room rapidly and went on. 'But it's hot and you're unused to our Mexican heat. May I fix you a small drink? Here, we could take it out to this patio. It's where I sit to ponder, or sometimes just to drift. I always intend to ponder but sometimes the pleasure of being alone is really all I want. It takes me into myself. Then, when I get up, I'm free to work again. Can you understand that?'

They stood, briefly, in silence. He did not answer her question but she knew he had heard her and had understood. They went to the patio and drank their small drinks in silence too and it was not until they were leaving the studio to return to the blue house that he spoke, as he took her hand into his own and traced a small mark on its palm and said, and it was enough, 'Thank you.'

They were alone the next time as if by chance. Natalya had been invited by the wife of a leading political commentator to visit some villages. The woman spoke Russian, was herself a scholar, and Natalya welcomed this possibility of fresh, intelligent conversation as well, of course, as being interested in the goal of their journey: to study the poverty of the rural peasantry at first hand. They had left early and would be back late.

Rivera was in San Angel. His day was to be interrupted twice: by a small delegation from a large and important trade union whose members wished him to perform a miracle of transformation on the ugly building they had erected as their headquarters, then, later, by a journalist from *Time* where it was argued that now, as host to the infamous Trotsky, he could be moved from the art pages to the front of the magazine.

Trotsky himself was to have been meeting a fellow exile, but a few days earlier a fever had gripped him during one night and alarmed by its intensity he'd had all engagements cancelled for the week, not trusting the experience and advice of Rivera that such fevers could pass as quickly as they came in Mexico. It had indeed passed, leaving him feeling a curious mixture of exhaustion and exhilaration, as though he had been cleansed and renewed by the bulldozer which had run over him.

Frida and Trotsky each had morning coffee in their rooms, perhaps only tangentially aware that they were, apart from the servants, alone in the house. By mid-morning each was in the garden, despite the rising heat, walking among luxuriant flower beds and each was a little surprised though of course charmed to catch a glimpse of the other, to walk towards the other and then to walk together back into the welcome cool of the house where more coffee was ordered, and drunk, and where Trotsky suggested he might see Frida's work again. It had been luring him back, he told her, and he would have no peace until he saw it for a second time.

Frida proposed they take with them a simple picnic lunch and when Trotsky agreed she hurried into the kitchen to explain what should be packed for she had already observed what her guest ate with pleasure and what he ate only because he was, in small matters, polite.

When they reached the studio they were silent, but not as before when the silence had been appropriate and even comforting. This time it separated them. Frida opened the large drawers in which she kept drawings and preparatory sketches. Perhaps he would like to look at these, she suggested.

Yes he would, he said, but did not. He looked at Frida instead, looked at her with such intensity she became confused as to whether she was seeing his own unexpectedly blue eyes, the much darker eyes of the Trotsky she had learned in her dream, or her own eyes, transposed into this man's pale, drawn face. She was extremely uncomfortable. He took off his small round glasses and rubbed his eyes. Sweat was beginning to roll down the hollow of her back and although she was leaning for support against a high chest of drawers, Frida's withered leg and injured spine ached horribly and she wondered if she might faint, though it was not at all the kind of thing that usually happened to her, despite the constant grip of pain in which her body held her.

Outside the room a wild cat screeched and this screech was taken

235

up by others. There was hissing and loud calling and then a woman's voice, her tone similar to that of the animals, screaming to the cats to disperse and as she screamed, repeating her desire that these miserably ragged no-creatures-of-God should be gone from her wretched life forever, Trotsky crossed the space between himself and Frida, put one hand on her upper arm, though keeping his body away from Frida's, then bent, slowly towards her, to kiss her. The only parts of their bodies that touched were their mouths and tongues and his hand burning on her upper arm, but then she feared she really was going to faint and she groaned into his mouth and he moved much closer towards her and held her along the length of her body and kissed her in one great unbroken kiss though his tongue moved and so did her own. She could smell sweet-sour desire rising out of her body and could sense the longing coursing up out of his. The weight of her tongue was in his mouth then the weight of his tongue was in hers and it tasted and was good so that even while having it she knew she would not have enough of it, it filled her mouth but made her feel empty in that heat-filled place between her legs which were parting as he helped her gently to the floor where they lay together still kissing, perhaps more quietly now, and then his hand moved towards her huge embroidered skirts and she knew that as much as she longed for him to reach beneath them she was ashamed, as though it could possibly have been her fault, that one of her legs would feel ugly to him, shrivelled forever by childhood polio, and she wanted to speak, to tell him to stop despite her own magnificent desire, but when she attempted to move her head, just slightly from under his, he increased the pressure on her mouth, and kept her there.

Her hands had found a path beneath his light linen jacket and were touching the cotton shirt next to his skin and through the shirt she could feel the movement of his flesh and her hands also traced his bones, and liked that. Rivera was very fat and his bones were not to be reached. In her mind's eye Trotsky was already naked and moving lightly above her. Flowers she had woven into her hair as she dressed that morning fell beneath her head and were crushed, releasing a sweet, sensual smell.

He had reached the hem of her skirts and his fingers were making their way forward, thank God along the stocking which covered the firm skin of her good leg, she should have trusted him, should have known, until he had reached the top of her stocking and was stroking the skin that ran above the stocking top up to her panties which usually kept safe the thicket of pubic hair but he had reached that too and was still kissing her. The sweat she had felt running down her back was running also down her front; she was wet everywhere but nowhere as wet as that dark place between her legs, not guarded sufficiently by panties or hair; he had circumnavigated both and was stroking, not quite there but nearly nearly, and she arched and he understood at once and touched her as she could only have touched herself then left her and moved his fingers inside her until she was filled as she had longed to be: mouth, vagina. Her hands moved to find her nipples, pushing up towards the sky. He brought his weight across and she was partially pinned beneath him. She wished to be wholly pinned but did not wish that he would move or move his fingers except as he was doing now, not only inside her but outside too, back and forth against her clitoris until she knew she was coming and shrieking and she couldn't stop though it was louder even than the cats and the windows were open and the neighbours would hear but still she couldn't stop nor stop moving against him until passion threw her way out of herself and then, finally, she was quiet. She lay still. Her face was very close to his though their mouths were no longer joined. After some moments he kissed her again, small, grateful kisses as though his passion too had been assuaged. Her eyes were closed but he touched them to open. When she did so, she felt at home.

It could not continue of course. And did not. It was an affair of the heart, not of state.

The first time Trotsky lent Frida a book, coming into the room carrying it before him like one of the three wise men bearing the perfect gift, beginning immediately to sing its praises, to say in such confusing detail how he'd been stimulated to believe she might enjoy it by their conversation when . . ., and how the author, in a way he hadn't met before could clarify precisely what . . ., and so on, and on, Frida's first reaction was of almost complete recoiling. Did he find her in some essential way naïve, an unworthy companion

237

even as rarely as they were, in any substantial sense, companions? She found it difficult to follow what he was saying and wondered why he was continuing without pause for interaction. A thin film of sweat covered his forehead and he wiped it away inelegantly.

When the recital was at last over she took the book he had continued to hold out to her and simply because she felt awkward and not only awkward but also hurt and self-accusatory, she left the room to escape with the book in her hand to the seclusion of her bedroom. There she put the book down on the marble table then lay on the bed, calming herself, turning her mind with effort to things and people other than Trotsky, reminding herself of what she knew to be solid and good in her life and refusing to indulge this lacerating speculation.

After some minutes she was calm enough to pick up the book, to look with some interest at its spine, and then to begin to leaf through it, looking for, she was not sure what, but certainly never expecting to find, on three single sheets of wafer-thin blue notepaper, tucked evenly between the sections, a handwritten letter from Trotsky to herself, a letter of lush lovely phrases which sang of such tenderness and good humour despite his own many troubles that her heart began to ache again, this time with longing to be with that man who seemed to have understood her, who had chosen phrases which exactly pleased her, whose insight made her feel she was visible, and within reach.

She read the letter again and again.

He called their exchange 'Frida's education programme' and continued to prefix the handing over of a book, several times each week, with a long elucidation of its contents, a knowledgeable portrait of its author, an analysis of why it would be useful to Frida. She would then hand back the previous book and he would ask if it had been helpful. Her replies varied and were splendidly imaginative. He and she both knew that she didn't read the books. She had no time, engaged as she was with his letters, returning to them as one might return to an image from a dream, until it is wholly understood, and can be trusted to a safe place within one's being.

When, eventually, cooled down and sensible – returned to himself – Trotsky asked Frida to return the letters, she was able to mitigate the pain, and her anger at his moment of choosing, by knowing she was handing back the husks only. The kernels would remain with her.

What also remained was her consciousness of the pleasure she and Trotsky had taken in their discussions of the purported reading: lengthy, animated discussions, in English, in the presence of her husband and his wife. So illuminating and intense had these discussions been that she was able almost entirely to ignore that, by contrast, Natalya sat far outside any light.

Of course Natalya did not understand the words which Frida and Leon spoke to each other but it would have taken a fool, and Natalya was not that, to fail to see how the two revelled in their exchanges.

What could Natalya do but be grateful for their ignorance of the darkness in which she sat, in which she inwardly hugged herself and nursed her pain, knowing it of old. Each time she had comforted herself: it will not happen again. And it had not, for so long. In this past decade of dreadful wandering he had needed her badly, mother of his grown sons, and kept her close. Yet even she could see Frida was different. Even she wanted to reach out towards, have some small part of that youth, that exotic beauty, that talent and radiance. Frida appeared to her like a creature from another world, full of warmth and light and promise. A creature of another world entirely, a woman of paradise, while she, Natalya— wife, comrade, confidante – often felt herself to be in hell.

Eleven

The phone may already have been ringing for some minutes before Gabriel became aware of its harsh sound. He was lying on his bed thinking about Sonja Beckermann with whom he had passed the previous night and most of today in that same bed in a state of pleasurable sensuality, a satisfying mixture of familiarity and novelty as she was a woman with whom he had, before he went to live in England, slept fairly regularly, but she was also the first woman other than Zoë to be in bed with him since his relationship with Zoë had begun, almost two years before.

It was not that Gabriel placed particular value on the practice of monogamy. On the contrary, he frequently argued a convincing critique against that limited lifestyle. But in fact rather than theory, he had little energy or desire to engage at the relatively intense emotional level which was, for him, a prerequisite to anything which would transcend basic physical relief. His life felt completely full. Not happy, or at least not often expressly happy these days, but filled up with his concern and longings for Zoë, his increasing sense of inadequacy in the face of the confusion she produced in him, his guilt about Christa and Stefan, and, of course, his work. He seemed to have been able to continue successfully with his work despite the personal unease in his life, and was grateful for this. While he was actually thinking about his sculptures, or working on them, everything else fell miraculously away. He was aware, with some sadness and even anxiety, that Zoë did not have an activity in her life which offered that kind of intensity of concentration, and the respite and recuperation it gave. He did not know how he would survive without it.

Sonja had left Berlin shortly after he had gone off to England. She was a photo-journalist and had correctly decided there would be more opportunity for her in Hamburg where both *Die Zeit* and *Der*

Spiegel were based. Her work was increasingly often appearing in both those prestigious publications and it had been obvious when she reappeared in Berlin for this brief stay that success had enhanced her natural confidence.

Sonja's looks were those a foreigner might assume are 'typically German': straight natural blonde hair, a tall strong body dramatically full breasted. But she eliminated the possibility of her appearance being in any way stereotyped by dressing in a bizarre, striking range of men's clothes – old pleated trousers with braces, collarless shirts in fine cotton, evening dress suits worn by day, larger than life-size tailored jackets – all cleverly adapted so her wonderful body was emphasised by their apparently haphazard fit. Her eyes were always, even in bed, surrounded by heavy lines drawn in kohl. Her long pale lashes were dyed black, making a dark contrast to her pale skin and hair. She had a lovely mouth, and laughed a good deal.

Gabriel had been only one of Sonja's several lovers. That had suited them both. She was a loyal friend with everyone she slept with regularly which made her inclusive style not merely tolerable but rewarding and remarkably freeing. Since her move to Hamburg she'd become more actively involved in the women's movement and, as she told Gabriel, less interested in making the effort required to deal with the not-so-subtle sexism of the left. She was sleeping almost exclusively with women now, and liked the change. Gabriel longed to question her about this but was afraid to, suspecting he was not only curious but titillated and knowing this would quickly be perceived and condemned by Sonja.

She had left him just an hour before, kissing him goodbye with warm affection and thanking him, sincerely it would seem, for a wonderful evening and night. Gabriel was stimulated by the episode and also somewhat healed of his anxiety that perhaps his relationship with Zoë had stripped him of the possibility of enjoying sexual and emotional intimacies with other women. Sonja had seemed gloriously *available* during their night together. He had been struck by that, and asked her as she was leaving if he could come to Hamburg to visit her. She laughed, said she'd intended to ask him; he'd simply asked first. She had really missed him, she told him. There were few men around who had learned to listen, and could comment intelligently on what a woman had actually said.

Gabriel's body and mind felt sated, and slowed to the pace of a contented slug. Nico and the Velvet Underground were singing to him out of his battered tape machine. It was a loud knocking on his door that jolted him into awareness of the phone which had, he suddenly realized, been ringing for some time. He switched off the tape abruptly and, calling to the person on the other side of the door to wait one moment, crossed the room, picked up the phone and as usual gave his name as greeting: Bongiovanni.

The voice at the other end was just recognizable as Christa's. She was sobbing and almost incoherent. The banging on the door was continuing. He spoke over Christa's voice saying to her, 'Please wait, don't go away. I must answer my door but I'll be right back. Do you hear me?' Once satisfied she had heard, he put down the phone and went to the door. There was Zoë, clearly about to launch into a speech of some kind and quite obviously displeased when he gestured towards the phone and asked her to wait while he finished talking to Christa.

'I'll walk around the block and be back in ten minutes,' Zoë offered, 'but please try to be finished by then as I haven't much time either.'

Gabriel nodded, anxious to get back to Christa and to focus his cloudy mind on her problem, whatever it was.

'It's your mother, Gabriel. I'm very sorry to tell you. Your mother, she died in the night.'

Gabriel's first reaction was one of relief: hearing the hysteria in Christa's voice he had, he now realised, been afraid that something fatal had happened to Stefan. But his mother, this was frightful too. He had spoken to her just a few days before. She'd been all right then, or had said as much, concerned only for the health of his father who was now permanently in a wheelchair and in need of more strength than his mother felt able to give.

'What do you mean, *dead*? I spoke to her only . . .'

'Gabriel, she had a heart condition for some years and didn't ever want to complain of it. You know how she is. Was. I knew of this only because she did tell my mother who of course told me but made me swear not to worry you with it. Though why my mother should wish to protect you . . . but anyway, she must have had a massive coronary in the night as this morning she didn't come to your father's room to help him out of bed as usual and when eventually he managed to get himself onto the floor to crawl to her room he found her already dead. He must have been appallingly shocked as I gather he lay there for hours. He phoned us only some minutes ago.'

'You must come, Gabriel, you must come today.'

'Of course I'll come. As soon as I get the time of a flight I'll call you back. Who's with my father now?'

'My own father has left for your house and I think some neighbours are already there. But he's gravely shocked. You can imagine. He'll be helped just knowing you're on your way.'

Gabriel replaced the phone and slumped on his bed. His mind, slowed by pleasure, seemed to have been utterly stilled by grief, or he assumed it was grief as he could not actually locate any specific feeling. Zoë's footsteps sounded on the stairs and then she was pushing open the door she had left ajar. She began to speak as she came into the room, then stopped as she saw his stricken face.

'It's my mother,' he immediately told her. 'It seems that she died last night. She had a heart sickness and I even didn't know this.'

Zoë stood in front of the bed gazing down at the top of Gabriel's bent head. She was aware of a sensation of fast-growing disappointment. She had always assumed that one day she and Gabriel's mother would meet. She had invested so much hope in this meeting: that Gabriel's mother would see in her the daughter she had never had, that she would see in Gabriel's mother some of the maternal qualities she had for so long been missing . . . Too late. The dream evaporated.

She pulled Gabriel's body slightly forward, cradled his head into her belly and held him for a few minutes in silence, rocking him very slightly.

'When will you go to Frankfurt?'

'I need to get the times of the flights, but it must be today if that's at all possible.'

'I'll do it for you. I can, you know.' She knelt down in front of him. His face was above her own as she smiled up at him. 'I don't have to be furious to speak German in your beloved presence these days you know.'

He touched the curls on the top of her head. 'I know.'

Zoë made the call, noted the details, gave Gabriel a piece of paper on which the information was written, and made them both strong coffee. As he didn't stir, nor seemed capable yet of doing so, she asked him, quite formally, for Christa's number, dialled it, asked for Christa, told her when she could expect Gabriel, wished her well, and hung up.

Gabriel had apparently been able to drink his coffee while remaining immobile. His cup was empty but he was carved into the same chunk of air as when she left him. Zoë sat beside him and for a long time rubbed his back, in large slow movements such as a mother might use to soothe her child as it approaches sleep. Eventually she spoke to him, gently but with sufficient force to move him. 'You must get ready now. Pack whatever you'll need. We'll leave for the airport in half an hour.'

As Gabriel was about to disappear through the doors that would take him along the corridor and to his plane, he appeared to wake up. He turned and hurried back to where Zoë was standing. 'What was it you had to tell me Zoë? You had a most urgent look about you as you arrived at my flat and I didn't give you one moment to spill your beans.' He shrugged, in apology, and looked at her for forgiveness.

She kissed him on the mouth, suddenly sprung out of her calm and near to tears. 'It can wait. Don't worry. Call me when you get there to tell me you're all right. At the *Kneipe* if need be, but do call.'

He nodded, hugged her briefly, muttered incoherently, and disappeared. Zoë left the airport building, hailed a cab and headed straight for her evening's work.

It was not until the journey was almost over that it occurred to her that neither she nor Gabriel had discussed or even contemplated the possibility of her accompanying him, of being the tower of strength at his side as he took his place in the shrunken bosom of his mourning family. He had simply gone; she had stayed behind.

When Zoë reached the *Kneipe* she went to the phone. She dialled Sibylla's number. There was no reply. She hesitated, but not for long. She dialled Frank's number. Surely he would forgive her weeks of neglect? This was probably unfair, but she couldn't face the entire night alone.

The phone rang for just a few moments before Frank answered it, cautiously. She heard his voice rise with pleasure when he realized who was calling him. He had great news, he said at once. His papers had come through for his return to the States.

Gabriel didn't tell Zoë when he would get back to Berlin. He took an early afternoon flight and from the airport went straight to his flat. Once there he made a couple of phone calls: to the foreman at the factory where he worked and to a former tutor whose astute advice had served him well in the past. Those conversations over he sat at his desk and attempted to work but today the concentration which he usually had access to by decision of his will eluded him. Instead his mind was flooded with pictures, stills from the two years he and Zoë had been together. They appeared in confusing array, sequentially cluttered, mannered, self-conscious, self and mutually congratulatory, tender, shy, exposed, loving. She was under his fingertips and in his bones; she was running through his veins and was imprinted deep into his memory; she was a figure of his dreams and the central point in his waking life.

He was going to leave her.

Gabriel paced and fretted. He drank countless cups of coffee and smoked cigarettes like a caricature expectant father waiting for a birth. But there was no birth. He was waiting only for the time to come when Zoë would arrive at work and he could phone her there.

There was a burst of excitement in her voice when she heard his own.

'God I'm glad you're back Gabriel, but why didn't you let me know you were coming? I'd have wanted to meet you, or organize some surprise in our grand tradition . . .'

He interrupted her. 'That isn't necessary at this time Zoë . . .'

Her mind flew to his mother. 'Oh God,' she repeated, 'I'm sorry. I didn't mean anything elaborate or festive, just, well I'm so pleased to have you back, that's all.'

Gabriel's voice, to Zoë's ears, was gentle as he said, 'How about if I go to your room and wait for you there? I'm not in much of a mood to see others at the *Kneipe*.'

She broke in, her tone buoyant with anticipation, 'Look, I'm longing to see you. Why don't I ask Peter if I can leave early for once and meet you sooner?'

'Fine, Zoë, do that. I'll hold on while you go and ask.'

She was soon back to tell him she'd be at her room in an hour, that if he could be there waiting for her that would be wonderful, that he should excuse the mess but she had been extremely busy. She couldn't wait to tell him all her news. He might even, she said after a moment's hesitation, be proud when he heard what she'd been doing.

Gabriel carried with him to Zoë's room the sculpture he loved most. It was made of bronze, something he could rarely afford. It portrayed a strong young woman poised to run, illuminated with the kind of excitement and anticipation Gabriel had not recognized as possible until he met Zoë. The grace and power of the piece were emphasized by the imminent movement of the small figure, but that was not its only source. There was a suggestion, only a suggestion but nevertheless palpable, that instead of the hollow centre which surely the metal must surround, that there was a living spirit inside it, animating the sculpture, and the spectator.

This precious piece, the most precious of all his work, was to be a gift for Zoë. Appeasement perhaps, or even an attempt to return something to her which may have been, unwittingly, stolen.

Zoë's room was indeed in a mess. It wasn't the heaps of clothes that caught Gabriel's attention as Zoë could empty a wardrobe-full in minutes when deciding on her outfit for the day – and those always eventually got put back. But now there were wire baskets laid out in a train across the floor. Piles of papers were obviously being sorted into them. Gabriel could not contain his curiosity.

He squatted down and picked up one or two pages, gingerly. They were poems, short descriptive poems and really not too bad. He went to the basket at the beginning of the line. There he lifted up a page or two, loose-leaf pages as though from a journal. His own name mentioned frequently. He put the pages back, feeling shy and embarrassed but not so inhibited that he didn't move to a neighbouring basket and found that the tall pile of papers there was made up of sheets on which were written quotations, copied poems, anagrams patterning down a page, aphorisms, sections of prose with source and date neatly noted. In the next basket were old newspaper cuttings. A quick glance suggested they were taken from New

Zealand papers, or British papers on matters that concerned New Zealand. In another basket were more newspaper cuttings but also clippings from magazines, this time of visual artists, women mostly, and here he recognized some pieces he himself had extracted for Zoë, though there were many others, in English and in German, which he was seeing for the first time.

Gabriel was stunned, and impressed. He would never have imagined. He felt ashamed. Why hadn't he known? Why hadn't he assumed that with her fine mind and robust energy she might have projects as worthy? He hesitated. As worthy as his own. There was a sense of purpose here. These papers were not the result of random collecting, nor of occasional writing. Why hadn't it been possible for her to tell him? Her own poems, a journal which had obviously been building for a long time, the diligent, thoughtfully chosen cuttings and quotes: all new to him. He had been urging her for ages, for a year at least, to consider further formal education. And all that time and before that time perhaps she had been building up a fund of knowledge in her own way. Self-made Zoë. And now was making something of it. That at least was clear.

With somewhat awkward movements Gabriel got up, looked down at the array of Zoë's work, backed away from it and sat on the edge of her bed. His hand searched for his tobacco tin in the breast pocket of his leather jacket. He rolled a cigarette and lit it.

Zoë's gift to him was a sense of a much larger world than that to which his previously unacknowledged Eurocentric vision had confined him. And the movement outwards was not simply geographical. Her vivid presence, her curiosity, her rapacious intellectual hunger, the different culture out of which she came: all these things have put demands on him which he relished.

By taking her seriously he has been richly rewarded by seeing her allow herself to mimic him and, at least intermittently, to take herself seriously also. Through her presence, her love, her apparently limitless confidence in him, as well as through her own sense of joy and possibility, he has gained access to an awareness of feeling and sensation at a level the most lyrical descriptions seemed only to have guessed at.

And he's given her? He heard an echo of her excitement in a torrent of words. 'A world I can *expand* in, Gabriel. Where I can believe in people and most of all you who are more like myself than I've yet become. Where I can push myself. Where trying things out is not "showing off". Where I can risk, and fail or win, and risk again.'

He understood better now, looking at the baskets, sensing there the effort, the persistence, the hunger for expression he's released in her.

Yet still his over-riding emotion, come undeniably into focus since the death of his mother, is a sense that they have failed each other. But no matter how diligently and even desperately he scavenges, he can break this emotion down into only some of its parts.

Into Gabriel's mind has come and settled an image of himself as hunter, as ugly as that and as powerful, but stalking a prey which has never been seen and whose invisibility cruelly mocks him.

Zoë's acute sensitivity to the world of feeling seems to have given her no awareness of how she now threatens him or of how he experiences himself as threatened by her: by the enormity of what is not spoken, by the distress which is the invisible prey in high grass. All his skill as a loving, careful listener counts for nothing because it has not and will not shift that crucial barrier of trust beyond which Zoë remains unknown to him: where she – or some essential part of herself – huddles, frightened and mute, turned inward to nurse her secrets.

He has been experiencing the panic of imminent submersion even while Zoë continues to smile, flatter, cajole, to speak with conviction of happy ever after, and to write – apparently in silence.

He senses a loss of control he can no longer bear. An infinite ache for her smacks up against bewilderment, frustration and a frightening anger he is without means to express. He is dizzy with exhilaration at the edge of a cliff; he is falling off it. He is reaching for a golden rope; he is hung by it.

At the great bay window Gabriel ceased his pacing. He stared at the tree where Zoë claimed she believed their good fairy rested. Perhaps she too has tumbled from her branch? His head ached. He reached for his tin. He rolled another cigarette, and lit it.

His agony was compounded by his awareness that he had led them both to an almost fetishistic sense of the extraordinary within

248

their relationship, unbound by the tempered horizons of everyday desires and expectations. What irony then that this cultivation of the extraordinary has, perhaps, disallowed them from realizing those most ordinary of desires: not only to love and be loved, but also to accept and be accepted; to trust into an indefinite future.

Zoë's entrance was announced by the rhythm of her boots on the wooden stairs. Her voice burst through the door before her.

'It's wonderful to see you Gabriel. I've missed you dreadfully. How was it? Was it frightful? Are you all right? You must be desperately tired? And your father, how's he managing? Did you get yourself something to drink already? Can I get you anything? It's so *good* to have you back. There's loads to tell you and I've been bursting with the waiting. I'm feeling great, you can see that, can't you? Better than for ages, and I have such *plans*.'

It would seem she had not noticed that he'd not yet said a word. His pale face was entirely predictable. His mother had just died and been buried.

Zoë poured them both some whisky. 'Come and lie down with me and tell me what's going on with you first. I have been thinking about you such a lot, wishing you well at this awful time.' She gestured towards the bed which was piled high with cushions.

'Not just yet Zoë. I'm feeling a bit restless. Do excuse me. You lie down. I'll bring up the big chair and sit beside you.' He pulled the grey armchair to the side of the bed and watched while Zoë settled herself down among the cushions. How lovely she looks, he thought. She'd had her hair cut much shorter and was wearing less make-up than perhaps she used to. The changes suited her. He saw Sibylla's face in his mind, with her short hair and forceful features unmodified by make-up, and then forgot Sibylla again as he cleared his throat to begin to speak.

'You've got me very curious about what's in those wire baskets Zoë. I was quite astonished to see them, a whole huge operation and a secret from me, eh?' He was trying to keep his voice light, his heart still and his sense of reality at least partially in-tact.

'That's part of what I've got to tell you, but only part. The really amazing thing —' she paused and sat up straight, 'is it okay if I tell

249

you my news first? It's not that I don't want to hear about Frankfurt.
I do. You must talk to me about that, I insist.'

Gabriel rushed in. 'Tell me your news. Please Zoë, I'm keen to
hear it.'

'Well, I can hardly believe it myself as it's so wonderful, but my
sister Rebecca is coming here to Berlin to see me with her daughters
and without her husband. You can imagine what this means . . .
It's been so long since I left and I can't face going back even if I had
the money which I don't, and of course in many ways I'm terrified.
But it will be wonderful, I know it will. It's my idea of bliss to have
you, Rebecca, and her little girls and me all on the same slice of
earth. I've told her everything about you, from the very beginning.
She's longing to meet you, Gabriel, though she says she's terrified to
face the paragon I've portrayed you as!'

Zoë took a hearty swig at her whisky. When she spoke again she
was looking down into her glass. 'It's funny, well, strange. I wanted
to tell you at once when I got her letter but when I went to your
room you'd just had the news about your mother and clearly it was
quite the wrong moment. And what made it even more sad, or odd,
I don't know which, is that the feeling I had when Rebecca's letter
came was that we'd all be together again. It was a strange elision
from the remembered "we" of our mother, Rebecca and me, to
Rebecca and me and you, Gabriel. That feeling passed but in its
place has come this lovely sense that I'm going to be part of a family
again. I know it won't be for long. Rebecca can stay a few weeks at
most, but just to have that family feeling again, after so many years
– almost all my life it sometimes seems – you've no idea how
important this is for me.'

Throughout this recital Gabriel had kept his gaze steady on Zoë's
face, struggling to keep his attention directed outwards. There was
a foul taste in his mouth which the whisky and constant nervous
swallowing were doing nothing to shift.

'I do know how important this is for you Zoë. Or at least I think
I can imagine it. And I'm delighted for you, really. How is it
possible though, with the money I mean? It's so far and surely most
expensive?'

'I gather from the bits written in invisible ink that she's having
an awful time with her husband. Well, that's not new. God knows

why she married him. However, for reasons best known to himself he's promised her and the kids this trip to see me, perhaps as some kind of compensation. My guess is that he's having some hot affair and wants Rebecca out of the way. But I've not suggested that to her and won't until I see whether she thinks it too, or cares. Anyway, whatever the reason I'm incredibly grateful.'

Zoë leaned forward to take Gabriel's hand.

'Gabriel, I wanted to suggest that we go to London to meet them and travel back with them here. A few days in London would be heavenly for Rebecca, and for us too, to return to our meeting ground. We could probably stay with Rosamund. Do you think we could afford it? Would you like such a trip?'

The worn mat at his feet offered Gabriel no comfort. He looked up at Zoë. The palm of his hand clasped inside her own was wet.

'I want to meet Rebecca very much. I'm most curious about this big sister, just as you can imagine of me. However, by then I'll not be living in Berlin. I've made a decision to return to Frankfurt.'

He stopped. She dropped his hand. After some moments when evidently he was not about to speak again, Zoë asked, in a small, composed voice, 'Alone?'

Gabriel looked briefly at her. 'Yes. Alone. Though of course we'll be constantly in touch Zoë. It's a change, not an ending. I'd hate you to think . . . you mustn't ever think there'd be a time when we'll not be in touch.'

'No of course I wouldn't think that.' Her face was stripped of the colour which had warmed it seconds before.

In place of the comforting fantasy of family life Zoë saw, as if the image had been projected onto the wall in front of her, herself as a leaf, lifted by a gale wind against which she had no defence and which would take her to a landing-place not of her own choosing. The slide changed. The image shifted. She was going nowhere. She was a pebble, of no consequence, about to be lost under the weight of a wholly moved mountain.

The fog was still with her, but she was learning to accept it. The bud of her sense of purpose had been breaking through the ice. Too late. She had driven him away.

'You'd better tell me why.'

He didn't speak.

251

Hope stirred in her. 'Is it Christa? Do you feel you should go back to Christa?' That at least would mean it wasn't something vile in her. And that it wasn't her fate always to be left.

She reached for a straw.

Gabriel rushed to say, 'No, it's not Christa. It is definitely not Christa.' The straw evaporated. Gabriel's voice had been momentarily stronger but when he spoke again it had fallen to a whisper.

'The point is, Zoë, I feel no longer adequate to you or perhaps to our relationship. We've given each other a great deal. I truly believe we've transformed each other's life and we'll never again be, nor want to be, the people who met each other. We've become infinitely richer than that. Yet something awful's happened to you. Or perhaps not awful. Today you look wonderful and are full of life.' He pressed his fingers against his forehead. 'Perhaps in my confusion I exaggerate. But you are, inside yourself, sad. I know that and my presence does nothing to alleviate it, no matter how much time we spend together and now we spend almost all our time together. On the contrary, I believe my presence makes it worse.'

He coughed. Nothing in his throat shifted. He rolled a cigarette and spoke again.

'Of course I can see your behaviour's not sad. You're as lovely and amusing as ever. But that makes it worse. Can you understand that?' He moved to the edge of his chair.

'No.'

'Forgive me. I'm very clumsy. But I must confess to you that I'm terribly afraid.'

Her face was frozen. She was waiting for him to continue. He did so.

'It's this I fear: that the same power which sprang from you into me, or perhaps into my work only – anyway there's probably no valid separation – that glorious power that vividly affirmed life, may also be power enough to end it. I am talking about the other side of what is apparent. You taught me – though I'll admit I've resisted this lesson – that one can look at almost anything and see either good or bad, hope or despair, beauty or treachery, and that this vision of what is seen depends almost entirely on the need or maybe the will of the viewer. It's you Zoë who taught me there's possibility in almost everything and rigidity only if one creates it out of one's own fear.'

Gabriel lit the cigarette he had been holding in his hand. He offered it to Zoë, who shook her head, and then went on. 'I saw you with such power for life. I named you as wild, spontaneous, full of joy. I believe this was true and goes on being true. But in the same powerful measure I also perceive a well of sadness which no matter how often or with what skill I send down buckets to find the bottom, I can never begin to reach and help to drain. I'm still seeing much joy but feeling more and more the sadness. This frightens me, Zoë. I'm afraid of that well and perhaps not only for you. I believe I'm afraid of what I'll see of myself by looking down into it as obsessively as I find myself doing. There's always one's own reflection to be found in water.'

He left the edge of the armchair and sat back, though he looked scarcely less uncomfortable.

'But I must insist that I see this well in a metaphorical sense only. I don't believe that literally you will die, or are dying, or will drown. It's maybe that I have a sense that something in you isn't living, or maybe is dying, I don't know. And of course it may be something in me, and not in you? Going to Frankfurt will help me find that out. From our beginning Zoë we've been so close it's hard for me to know what are my fears or feelings about you and what are my fears and feelings about myself. They seem almost inseparable. "I don't come to an end before you begin." You sent me that in a telegram to Frankfurt when I left you in London for the first time. Do you remember?'

She didn't reply, or move. He got up from the chair and returned to the same spot by the window where he'd stood some time before.

'Anyway, wherever this dying or partial dying is taking place, it seems powerful and I've become afraid of it. And I'm also afraid that somehow I've caused it, or anyway activated it. Yet I can't give you what's needed to stop this awful process. I see no choice but to go away. I can't be the stout wall to hold in the moat of sadness and stop it leaking.'

He laughed. It sounded odd. 'It's strange, I find myself when talking to you full of metaphors which never occur to me at any other time. Wells, walls, moats: I should evidently go into analysis.' He laughed again, ironically, unable really to envisage this.

'Zoë, there's so much yet you don't speak of to me. Even now perhaps we should try to talk of this sadness? Perhaps as to whether it belongs only to us, or rather that it comes from your mother? With my mother now dead I can maybe understand . . .'

With a swift gesture of her hand Zoë silenced him. 'I'm not, I really don't want to talk about my mother. I've told you all I can remember, which isn't much. There *is* no more . . .' She stopped, bitterly aware she'd just illustrated his point. His complaint. She struggled on.

'To be honest I don't understand much of what you've just said. You seem to have been talking for ages. I wanted to concentrate but my head's filled with fog and I could only hear you in bits, and those sound to me, I must confess, more than somewhat exaggerated. I *am* occasionally depressed, it's true. I'm very sorry about this, as sorry as I was the last time we discussed it, that dreadful time when you told me you'd been picking over me with Sibylla.'

She reached for his half-finished cigarette. 'This obsession of yours with my depression does confuse me. Partly because I believe I'm much more often cheerful than sad, but even more because I can't for the life of me remember feeling depressed before I met you, though in many obvious ways my life then *was* depressing. My dreams have changed. They've become quite frightening. And you remind me of my past which I'd perhaps sometimes rather forget. But I must insist that I am more often happy, or I would be if I had more confidence in you.'

He crossed the room and sat down at the edge of the bed. She relented. 'I'm sorry. That isn't true. I've had a great deal of confidence in you almost all the time, which is partly why it's seemed intolerable when anything's gone wrong between us.' Her voice picked up some pace and animation. 'What I don't understand is why my so-called unhappiness should affect you so much? Am I really to believe this or is it just the greased chute you're using to slide out on? I have to say I feel somewhat monstrous even if I'm only a pale version of this bottomless well of misery you describe. It isn't pretty. It's absolutely terrifying.'

She folded her arms tight across her body.

'You see I perceive you as strong, Gabriel, as someone who's real inside and possessed of independence. That's unusual, you know. Well I've certainly not met it before. And it attracted me. It goes on attracting me. "Knock, knock, someone's at home." You're real in there whenever I've needed that!

'But it seems inconceivable, or anyway ridiculous, that you could be so adversely affected by me? And quite frankly, what looms in my mind now is this appalling thought: if you can't take me as perhaps I am, then who could or ever would? Tell me that, will you? Who in the whole bloody world could?'

From his pocket Gabriel took an acceptably clean handkerchief and handed it to Zoë. She blew her nose forcefully but didn't cry. Gabriel took their glasses over to the whisky bottle and poured them each a second shot saying, as she had taught him, 'A bird can't fly with one wing.'

He handed her the refilled glass and returned to the chair.

'Zoë, there are many people who'd be easier than me. People who're much more accepting or maybe easy-going. I know how demanding I am and how critical you find me. And I have no prospects. A reliable husband could give you security, perhaps be someone to have children with.'

'Sure!' She didn't try to hide her scorn. 'And die of boredom with or go crazy with or take to the bottle with in an orgy of self-diminution! Marry such a person yourself if you haven't already.' She stopped herself. 'I'm sorry, but what on earth gives you the right to think I'd be better off with some dreary husband person? Who do you think I am? Mrs Donald Duck longing for her ducklings? Simperer for Mr Right, cooking his three-course dinners and ecstatic over the washing up? Spare me your sentiments Gabriel. They give me a pain in the arse.'

She downed her whisky in a single gulp then shuddered as it burned.

'You just said it yourself: "We'll never again be the people who met each other". Even before I met you my tolerance of your average Joe Blow was stretched to its limits by a weekend. It's not only them, the poor faceless sods, it's the idiot they expect you to be and somehow succeed in evoking. I could never go back to all that.'

255

Zoë thought about Frank. He was handsome, kind, undemanding, good fun.

A week would be too long.

'Believe me, I'd rather be alone forever. Or of course there's always the convent. I could repent publicly and they might take me in.'

He didn't laugh at her attempt at humour. He was staring at her oddly. She handed him her glass: 'The last one disappeared mysteriously and I need all the help I can get.'

As he walked back with her refill, stepping with care over the wire baskets, she asked in a quiet, apparently unemotional voice, 'Would you come to bed with me Gabriel? This has all been too confusing. You're not leaving tonight are you?'

'Of course not. But I plan to go fairly soon. I think anything else would be agony.'

'And this isn't?'

He stood, awkwardly, his usual grace lost. She turned her gaze away from him and addressed the plants.

'It's most curious but although I feel the prickle of many emotions it's as though they're muffled morse code rather than any decipherable message. Or like faint taps, meant for me but actually hitting the wall next door. Perhaps I'm in shock. Do you think so Gabriel? Perhaps I'll die of shock and save a great deal of trouble. "She passed away from shock, wearing her best frock." That would do nicely for a tombstone don't you think? Though to make it true I'd certainly need to change. Actually, the metre works better if it's "wearing her *only* frock". Please note that, Gabriel. Or of course I could try a little epitaph built around that useful word "schmuck". But no, with the Lord's help I'll resist that particular temptation.'

Gabriel felt dreadfully, almost overwhelmingly sick. He wondered if he should go to the bathroom and throw up. A light film of sweat covered his skin. He was cold and clammy. Perhaps he'd reached the bottom of the well all on his own? This decision to leave Zoë was, after all, entirely of his own making. An exercise of free will.

Of course it was important that his filial duty would be fulfilled by living with or near his sick, bereaved father. Of course it was a tremendous opportunity to look after his father in return for a great deal more time for his work. Of course it was fortuitous and remarkably well-timed that Christa's father had wrangled a civic commission for him which could feasibly begin to make his career and reputation. And it was undoubtedly true, as Christa had said, that if he didn't get to know his son now it would indeed be too late.

But none of that was actually the point.

The point was that he was following a compulsion, terrible and agonizing though it was, to leave this quite exceptional woman whom he had loved, whom he did love, whom he would always love. But whom he had come to believe he feared.

He looked at her, the inspiration and object of his love.

She was lying with her face turned away from him.

He loved her in a way that wouldn't come again.

But not more than he loved himself.

PART THREE

States of Grace

The past is not a husk   yet change goes on
Adrienne Rich, 'For Memory'

One

Once upon a time there was a court jester who could make no one laugh.

Not because her head was empty of jokes. On the contrary, it was all she could do to catch her breath as one joke after another coursed through her blessedly fertile mind. Wherever she looked, listened, smelt, touched, she found something wonderfully funny.

She was aware, as all born jesters are, that what she saw, heard, smelt and touched could as easily have been perceived as tragic. She believed it was all in the turn of your mind and was intensely grateful for the turn of mind that life had dealt her.

This gratitude was, however, mitigated by her frustration that she couldn't make others laugh as she laughed. Come to that – and it never did – she couldn't raise even a smile on the mostly downcast faces she saw around her. Didn't they know it's always possible to transform despair into hope, sadness into experience, grief into gratitude for what's been?

The jester's problem was this. When she opened her mouth, apparently no sound came out. The sounds were clear and melodious in her own head but they simply didn't carry to the ears of anyone around her, even when she was in the packed throne room and pressed closely by the crowds.

In fact, remarkable though this was, given the care she put into her appearance, no one seemed able to see her either. She planned her outfits to eliminate any possibility of being subdued or unobtrusive. But when she appeared in the throne room, timing her appearance with the instinct of an entertainer, she could see not a snicker, not a nudge, not a hand raised to hide a giggle.

Although she was reluctant to stoop to this, the jester even tried vulgarity. Over the top of her soft silk dresses she wore absurd brassieres. One had a miniature canary perched on each breast, another had large red nipples which, when tweaked, played 'Stand By Your Man' in a minor key.

During public sessions at the court there were frequently uncomfortable longueurs. People would mill around apparently waiting, but with no clear idea of what they were waiting for. The cats would also become depressed, or perhaps they became depressed first as the jester had noticed they were generally more sensitive to atmosphere than humans, though short on solutions.

The court jester would bounce up and down from the place where she was invariably stuck in the middle of the throng. If only she could make her way to the clear space in front of the throne. If only, once there, she could tell tall stories which would lift everyone's spirits so they'd believe they were flying, soaring above their daily problems until, looking down on them, they'd see how transitory and trivial they actually were.

Yet no matter how politely or persistently the jester pushed, no one would step aside to let her pass. She tried throwing her voice from where she was stuck, just easy catchy limericks to get things started, but people behaved as though she wasn't there.

One clear, sunny morning the jester woke up in her room which was filled with the many beautiful and amusing things she had collected over the years and noticed, not the things, but a thin film of dust which had settled on them. Her face tightened and when she got out of bed and looked in the mirror she was shocked. For the first time she saw her face transformed by a frown.

She also noticed that in place of the joke which usually filled her mind as she greeted the day there was an eerie kind of silence. More closely observed, this silence was sadness. She could identify this feeling from her reading as she doubted she'd ever felt it before.

She closed her eyes and concentrated on finding a good joke to get the day going. But as she had never had to search for a joke, she couldn't find one. Instead her mind kept returning to the sadness, worrying at it, enlarging it, even while she sensed she was going round in ever-smaller circles. It was almost like a rope which appears to have bound you one way so you turn the other way expecting to come free. Instead the rope binds you tighter and tighter. Your logical mind points out that you must then try the other way. There can be only two possibilities, after all. But when you do this the rope binds you even more tightly, so tightly you fear for the breath in your body, though your mind continues to insist that a rope which has gone around you can also be unravelled. And so you turn, and so the rope turns, and your breath is squeezed and your logic is mocked.

Without enthusiasm the jester looked at her wardrobe. Everything displeased her. The colours of her clothes were tawdry, the daring designs merely pathetic. She went to her mending basket. In the bottom and smelling rather musty lay a black satin dress covered with ludicrous feathers. If she plucked out the feathers the dress might do. She rubbed brown polish onto black boots and made up her pale face making it even paler. Her hair she left as it was: a mess.

After this exertion the temptation to go back to bed and pull the bedclothes over her head struck with such force she grew dizzy and nearly fainted. Could it be that she was suffering from joke deprivation? She had never gone this long without a good joke. And the morning had only begun.

As she passed the long mirrors lining the corridor that led to the throne room she looked around for herself. She usually enjoyed a lot of laughs on this journey. It was her habit to allow enough time to appreciate herself thoroughly and laugh herself almost into a heap as she caught the spectacular views offered by mirrors which lined the floors and ceilings as well as the high walls. But today all she could see was a drab, cringing creature – who was almost invisible.

The throne room was more packed than usual. Or perhaps she'd never arrived this late before so had never seen the population of the world from behind? It wasn't a pretty sight. In fact, it was thoroughly oppressive. (She gave thanks for the reading which had supplied this concept also.)

The jester stood close to the huge, ornate doors wondering if she dare leave and return to her bed. After all, who would notice, or care? Another late-comer stood beside her. She glanced at the person, a woman, and then stared.

Over the years, acting on her principle that there was possibility in even the most unlikely situations, the jester had taken full advantage of her apparent invisibility and had learned to stare wholeheartedly, free of the inhibition of possible observation.

This woman was old, and peculiarly familiar. She was dressed in a long grey outfit, rather like a monk might wear, with a rope-like belt around the middle of its thick folds and a hood hanging at the back. The fabric looked soft and comfortable, as did the woman's body. It was the kind of body that made you long to lay your head on her bosom, and be comforted. The woman's grey hair was caught up in a loose bun at the nape of her neck and her eyes were green and lively. Around her eyes the many lines went upwards. Her mouth, the jester noted, was like her own: slightly crooked and full and used to laughing.

For one moment as her heart stood still the court jester wondered if this woman could possibly be her mother who had, she assumed, died or disappeared soon after she was born, leaving the jester with only the faintest memories of being caressed and adored. But this was not a day for optimism and the jester chided herself for her foolishness.

Something foreign was running down the jester's face. She put her hand to her cheek and wiped it and when she took her hand down and looked at it she saw a tear, or several tears smeared together. She had seen people cry, oblivious to her efforts to help them. She had also read extensively about melancholia and depression. But the experience was extraordinary. There was something like a lump in her throat and no matter how often or with what force she swallowed, it wouldn't go away. Good God, people could die of lumps; it was a threat to her entire existence.

In her anxiety the lump rose and a sound pushed past it. The sound was unpleasant. It was a sob which became a long, thin wail although the jester was longing to turn in and make a ball shape of her body, with her head hidden and her heart too.

For the first time in her conscious life the jester was grateful for her invisibility. She could have a good cry (this was an expression she'd learned from women's magazines) and no one need know. She resolved to leave the throne room and creep back to the sanctuary of her bed, keeping her eyes downcast as she passed the mirrors.

This thought wasn't funny by even the most unrefined standards. And her joke deprivation was growing worse as her lungs filtered the same air for the umpteenth time since she'd belly-laughed herself to sleep the night before. But she did feel marginally better. She had made a decision, of sorts. However, the prospect of dripping her way to her room, of soaking her satin sheets until there wasn't a dry corner she could crawl to, struck her anew as terribly sad, and she moaned again, near to despair.

It was some seconds before the court jester realized she was being addressed. There was not only the sound of her own moaning filling her ears but also the total unexpectedness of this for someone almost resigned to her invisibility. She stopped moaning and listened carefully, to be absolutely sure. While she listened a hand touched her arm. At least she knew that's what it was when she looked down after registering something like an electric shock and saw a wonderfully well-used hand resting on her arm. This extraordinary experience halted her tears. The hand could only belong to the old woman next to her.

This was the court jester's moment. Contact had been made. At last she could share a lifetime's worth of great jokes. She could give her humour to this old woman and reveal all that was good about herself. The jester searched her mind. Where should she begin? But there were still no jokes. Not a single one. Only questions which weren't at all funny: who was this woman? why was she familiar? how had she noticed the jester when no one else in the whole world had? what did the old woman want to tell her? why did she feel this sad? who was she without her jokes?

The jester opened her mouth, and closed it again. The old woman was speaking but her words were a mystery. The jester abandoned her search for a joke and bent towards the sound, taking some moments to recognize that she wasn't hearing *words*, but only a single word. With infinite patience the woman said it, chanted it, made poetry of it, sang it with love, investing each repetition with the huge range of human emotion.

The jester began to move to the word. The woman's hand was still on her arm but as she swayed to the woman's word-music the jester took the woman's hands into her own or felt her own hands taken and the two moved together, the jester joining her voice to another's, experiencing for the first time the power of unity.

They were rocking with the word, shouting it, sharing it. The jester was opening up in places even the most riotous belly laughs hadn't reached, making her enormous with the word.

265

Tears were again rolling down from under her closed eyes but they expressed relief and discovery and joy. She wanted to open her eyes to look into the old woman's own, but was reluctant to risk breaking the magic and shy as to what the old woman might see.

The woman's voice rested on a single note and the jester's voice fell away. The note was like a lullaby: spinning love, compassion, strength. The court jester wanted much more of that sound but her feet were growing heavy and her head began to nod. She couldn't stop herself sinking to the floor though as she sank the old woman sank with her and their hands remained securely joined.

Suddenly and without premeditation the jester's eyes flew open and she looked into the eyes of the old woman. You're saying my name, she said, dispensing with any preamble. I've never heard it before, or I'd quite forgotten it. The old woman smiled and nodded. The court jester forgot in her excitement to register the astounding fact that she'd spoken and had been understood!

The court jester turned the name over in her mind. She loved it! There was life in her name and she continued to hear in it all the potential of the old woman's lullaby. The jester leant towards the old woman, kissed her, and put her head on the woman's breast to be held there.

When the jester sat back again, out of the woman's embrace but still with their hands joined, she was startled to notice that people had gathered around and were staring: at her.

The calm she had floated on or in as she lay against the old woman's breast fled from her. She searched her mind for a joke. These people were looking at her, could see her; she was visible to them and they were waiting. They must want to be entertained and as a court jester she should entertain them. She searched the old woman's face. Her moment had come and she needed help. In that face she saw wisdom and felt the beauty of wisdom, but there were no jokes. She had to hurry, she told herself in some desperation. Soon these people, her precious first audience, would turn from her in disgust, despising her as a dullard, scornful of her drab clothes and pale face, and mocking her for her tears.

Tell them who you are, whispered the old woman into the jester's ear.

You mean tell them a joke, asked the jester, almost frantic by now.

No. I mean tell them who you are, said a voice so close to her ear that it might almost have come from inside her own head.

The jester looked back again into the old woman's face, worrying at that familiarity which was so strong the old woman could have been some shamefully neglected part of her own self.

The faces of the people around her were growing blurred. The jester decided to concentrate on just one or two. She looked hard at those and was startled to see some familiarity in their eyes also. This gave her the boost she needed.

I am a court jester, she began, who wants to make you laugh.

The faces she was watching frowned, slightly.

The jester swallowed, and took a deep breath.

But, she continued, not without some difficulty, perhaps that's only the beginning of the story . . .

The faces relaxed and opened out.

The jester's attention was caught again by the old woman who was now very close to her. The jester wondered whether she might be soon overwhelmed by her presence, or even by the weight of that warm soft flesh. But she trusted the old woman. It was even easier than trusting herself.

The jester slowed her breathing as the lullaby had just taught her. Her eyes remained steadily on the old woman while she made herself larger and larger with the slow breathing, tentatively experiencing that breadth of emotion she had learned through her name: in, out, in, out.

There was a hush in the room. The questions the jester had seen forming on those faces near to her receded into the extending calm. The questions could wait. And so could the rest of her story. The present was quite unlike anything the jester had ever experienced, and it was enough; yet she believed she was ready for whatever would come next.

The jester noticed her breathing was growing even larger and deeper. Her chest and heart felt huge. There was now a roundness to her breathing as if a whole world was forming within her. The jester sensed she was watching her breathing and at the same time was centred within it.

267

The jester's eyes flew wide open. Her breathing momentarily stopped. Where was the old woman?

The old woman, who had been coming closer and closer to the jester, smiled at her as though leaving a gift and began slowly to disappear. She was not leaving the room but was moving into the jester's own self. The jester wasn't surprised. She might even have seen it coming. Or going. She giggled, just for a second.

The jester put her hand to her newly great heart which, considering the drama of these events, was beating remarkably steadily. Her breathing continued – regular, slow, deep – while the old woman, the wise old woman, found the space to settle inside her.

TWO

Zoë liked North Kensington. It was dirty, overcrowded and ill-kempt. It lacked clean sweeps of green between the battered, shabby relics of houses which might once have been as sprucely gracious as those of South Kensington, an area of London as different from North Kensington in appearance, population, status and price as the shadow is different from the shape that is its source.

There were glorious compensations. The so-called wrong end of Portobello Road market began towards Ladbroke Grove and offered the possibility of splendid bargains before the knowing began to sell to the gullible at the smart end of the market near Notting Hill Gate. There were delicious vegetables for sale grown in the warmed rich earth of the tropics. Huge bags of rice sagged next to dented tins of tomatoes. Loud reggae music throbbed like some great pulse of the streets. The bright colours on some of the buildings and many of the people defied the blanket grey of England. A stubborn hint of reverse colonialism prevailed, people refusing to 'fit in', instead importing their ways, their West Indian life and rhythms though not their sunshine to the stolid streets of London.

At the top of a house which had once been as elegant as any in the Royal Borough, Zoë was living with Archie Haines.

Her twice-yearly visits to the Home Office to renew her visa were becoming increasingly strained as it was ever more directly suggested she might return to New Zealand. She could, she supposed, if absolutely necessary, marry Archie. After all, they did share an address which would surely satisfy all but the most exceptionally diligent of the Home Office snoops.

It would not have taken that mythical, diligent snoop long to discover that Archie's passions changed with the days and were inspired by a string of heart-breaking men. Zoë's passions might have taken somewhat longer to reveal.

Zoë had met Archie at a party soon after she returned to England, six months after Gabriel left Berlin, left her, to return to Frankfurt.

It was the first London party she had been to for years, perhaps since that warm June night when she'd met Gabriel and, so she believed, changed her life for ever. She had given in to Rosamund's urgings only because it seemed churlish not to. Rosamund had been insistent in her misdirected efforts to get Zoë out, and thereby 'to forget Gabriel'.

Zoë was struck, after some minutes in the noisy, smoky room somewhere near Regent's Park, by how odd it had become to be surrounded by voices speaking English, any one of which, or even several of which, she could understand with no effort at all. She felt shy, stressed, gauche almost. During the weeks with Rosamund she had realized her style had changed and that she now found it difficult to be as amusing as she had once been, at least in memory. She ached sometimes to be taken seriously, to be direct, to be free to challenge opinions in an uncensored way without that being considered rude. But those were German ways. She was back in England and would once again need to change her coloration. She looked stiff and awkward, or so she feared. Her body seemed too big. Her mind felt both numb and under-nourished. She wondered how soon she could leave the party and return to the silence of her borrowed room without hurting Rosamund's feelings.

As soon as she had a job she would move out from under Rosamund's vigilant observation. She had been intensely grateful for the shelter Rosamund had offered when finally she had screwed up enough courage to leave Berlin and the painful, precious reminders of Gabriel. But Rosamund's world now pivoted around a rich, conventional married man Zoë was hard put not to despise; and Zoë's attempts to share her thoughts about Berlin, about the women's movement, and very tentatively about Sibylla, were unconsciously deflected by Rosamund whose image of Zoë seemed anchored in the past.

In the kitchen where Zoë wandered out to find some booze to lubricate the time she must endure before making her exit, two boys were standing by the table, tightly embraced and kissing passionately. Zoë's first reaction was one of embarrassment and she began to leave. Then, unable to face more of the party without a drink in her hand, she turned back. Bugger them she thought, inappropriately. They won't even notice, for heaven's sake. As she picked up the bottle to pour some wine into her glass she stared at them somewhat curiously. Instead of the blur she had first glimpsed they were now two separate but intertwined shapes. One boy was tall, broad, dark and dressed in what was, unmistakably, a sailor's suit. The other boy was tiny and blond. He wore high leather boots over the top of skin-suffocating jeans, a black string vest through which his pale body glowed, and on his head though not hiding the curls which cascaded beneath, was a bright yellow, authentically battered construction helmet.

Zoë giggled, then coughed, then lost her breath and continued to cough, and also to laugh until she feared for her loss of breath but couldn't any longer stop.

A faintly Northern voice was asking, 'Are you okay? Can I get you some water?'

Zoë was incapable of replying. She was bent double and concerned only to catch her breath between coughs and the laughter which continued to rise from within her as her mind's eye stuck on those two marvellously absurd outfits.

She felt a hand rubbing her back in strong soothing movements. That did seem to help and then to calm her. After some moments she was able to straighten up and to look down onto the top of the yellow helmet and into the blue eyes of the boy who wore it. She wanted to thank him with a moderately dignified face but instead she began to laugh again. The boy spoke. 'Here babe, you need a drink.'

He handed her a glass of tepid water which she gulped, gratefully, and then he gave her a glass of wine. 'Sorry there's nothing stronger. The beasts have emptied the troughs. Are you right now, do you think?'

She nodded, then without any of the forethought that might have kept her quiet, said, 'You both look ridiculous! I have to tell you this as it's done me more good than you'd believe. I might have coughed to death but at least I'd have died laughing. He's obviously not a sailor and you're no construction worker . . . or at least I presume you're not? So what's it all for? Please don't think I'm being critical. I love your outfits, but . . .' Zoë began to laugh again.

Yellow helmet laughed too. 'No. These aren't vocational adver-
tisements, that's for sure. To be frank, darling, and why not, I live
on the handbag.' Zoë frowned. 'You know, babe. The handbag. SS.
Social security. Government handout. Only while the world's first
truly meaningful gay novel gets written. It's a state subsidy to the
higher forms of art. Quite legit. And I also –' he paused for effect.
Zoë grinned. She knew the type. She *was* the type, or had been.
'Well, I also go in or should I say out for guest appearances of
various kinds. Entrances and exits, here and there. But more of that
later. After all, babe, I hardly know you. This is merely the opening
couplet in the possible epic of our friendship. Who are you anyway,
when not a dampener of passion?'

'Sorry about that. But you can always get back to it and no doubt
you will.' Zoë paused, for a split second. 'My name is Zoë, Zoë
Delighty.' She waited for the response she expected on yellow
helmet's face. She wasn't disappointed.

'For *real*? Delighty for real?'

'Not only for real, forever.' Zoë smiled and bowed. 'And you, and
your friend, Ocean Wave?' She winked at the face that rose, beaming
back at her, above the wide collar of the sailor suit.

'I, my dear Zoë, am Archibald Haines, and no jokes as I've heard
them all. And this gorgeous hunk is Emil. French, would you
believe. Fucks like an angel and not a word of English. But such
mime as you'd cross oceans to find. Hence the sailor suit. Got it?'

Zoë had, indeed, got it. She'd not felt this cheerful for months.
What a lunatic Archibald yellow-helmet Haines was. 'I had an
ancient great uncle called Archibald once.'

'Ancient? Well, not quite yet I hope. But uncle I may be. What
about a morsel of lunch tomorrow?'

'Great! Let me give you my address or should I just meet you
somewhere?'

'Come to *chez moi*. I'm in North Kensington, nestling with the
dustbins off the top of Ladbroke Grove. At least I'm there in the
meantime though more of that tomorrow.' Archie scribbled his
address on the back of a cigarette box which he hastily emptied,
then held out his hand to Zoë who raised it to her lips and kissed
it.

*

The flights of stairs that led to the top of the tall terraced house where Archie lived were drab and dirty beneath walls covered in graffiti but as Zoë reached the final landing she could hear Brahms' violin concerto resounding from an excellent stereo and could smell something promising a delicious lunch.

Without the yellow helmet Archie's cherubic curls were revealed full gleam. He was leaning against the door frame, dressed in a long, purple, possibly Moroccan kaftan and smoking a matching purple cigarette which emerged from the end of a Noël Coward cigarette holder. The scented smoke drifted up towards his curls and his eyes narrowed at the sight of Zoë, very much as Lauren Bacall's might have done at the sight of a resurrected Humphrey Bogart.

'You look quite wonderful, my dear, but I should have warned you, "No pets allowed".'

Giggles threatened Zoë once again.

'Well then, I shall simply have to explain to the poor creature she isn't wanted and lay her to rest outside your door. She can be guaranteed to lie quietly. She's been dead for longer than you've been alive.' Zoë took off her antique fox fur, stretched it out at Archie's feet, then stood up, bent down, and kissed him.

'It's just us for lunch. I've sent Emil off to the park. With warnings about strangers and their sweeties, of course. A drink?'

Zoë nodded, then handed him the bottle of champagne she'd splurged on. Archie lifted a single eyebrow to excellent effect. 'Bona! My absolute favourite for Sunday *déjeuner*. But what are we celebrating, other than our momentous meeting?'

'Nothing special. Or perhaps that meeting you last night had me laughing for the first time in I don't know how long.'

'Oh dear. A *tragic* history. Well let's eat and drink first and you can tell Aunty Archie all with the coffee. And I'll tell you my "all" too – never fear.'

The Brahms came to its magnificent close. Archie replaced that record with one of the Stones'. Then, seeing Zoë's brief grimace, he took it off and tried Joni Mitchell instead. 'No cock rock for you, eh?'

'Well, if you put it like that, no. But you should play whatever you want. This is, after all, your home . . .'

'Good God, Zoë, no need to be polite. The reason I've taken

you to my thin hairless chest is your glorious lack of *politesse*. So refreshing. I like Joni too. I'm a queen for all seasons. You'll see.'

Archie's risk was possibly greater than Zoë's when she accepted his almost immediate invitation to move into his much-loved flat. His previous flatmate had fled in unseemly haste to pursue a Brazilian lover to New York. Archie had been in despair of finding a congenial person in time to pay the next rent cheque and repeatedly declared that Zoë was *sans doute* the answer to his maidenly prayers.

Archie's flat had an immaculate, compact kitchen and bathroom and only two large rooms. The sitting-room was furnished in rococo Indian restaurant style: flock wallpaper in dark green, an over-sized chandelier, small standing lamps with chiffon-skirt shades, gilt-edged mirrors and ornately framed prints, French impressionists mostly, though also a solo Hockney and a cluster of Constables. Across one wall stretched a book case largely filled with contemporary novels though with one section devoted to books with titles like *The Making of the Modern Homosexual in North America*, and another section with a lavish array of virgin classics in fake leather bindings which had been 'donated' to Archie by an inefficient book club. The furniture included an old grandfather clock, two memorably uncomfortable *chaises longues* and a Georgian china cabinet crammed with ornaments and piled-up tea sets, some exquisite, some plain tat.

Photos of Archie's extensive Yorkshire family were clustered in silver frames, and a large smoked-glass cabinet, somewhat at odds with the rest of the room, housed the current couple of hundred favourites from Archie's immense and catholic record collection as well as the Bang and Olufsen stereo which had slid undented from the back of a slow-moving lorry.

Majestic in the centre of the second of the large rooms and liberally draped with snowy-white muslin was Archie's four-poster bed. It might well have been waiting for Sleeping Beauty herself and hinted at ghastly ceremonies of defloration. In one of the reproduction dressing tables topped with a cream crocheted doily, Archie kept his carefully tended costumes, and also his toys – sex aids of astonishing ingenuity – which were at odds with the white

274

muslin image but were doubtless partially responsible for the groans and pleas to which Zoë was to be an occasional reluctant witness.

The incongruities within the rooms reflected the breadth of Archie's personality. He was genuinely interested in pursuing the so-called finer things of life, and worked hard to maintain his faith that one day he really would produce a male gay novel worthy of its subject matter. He gave two nights a week to the Samaritans, though Zoë discovered this only by taking a chance message for him, and was an unfailing bulls-eye for every street cadger in the neighbourhood. He also found time to display his body in mock-macho attitudes of almost hilarious absurdity in magazines with names like *Strut*, *Butch* and *Straddle*. His 'entrances and exits' were shared not with his many devoted friends but with occasional 'paying guests' when the handbag was empty and also with an infinite succession of chunky pick-ups in whom he invested the most optimistically romantic hopes, but with whom it was usually obvious to everyone but Archie that he had nothing in common except vast sexual appetite.

At the far end of the flat was the small room which was to become Zoë's. This was more sober in appearance. The bed was shining brass, three-quarter size. A plain wooden table stood next to a single sash window through which a blank brick wall was loomingly visible. A single upright chair, a single comfortable chair, plus a commodious wardrobe in the wide hall outside, were all the room had to offer. It was quite different from the soaring splendour of Berlin, but Zoë had felt at home with Archie and believed that she could, once settled into his flat, begin at last to look forward.

Zoë answered a small, marginally promising ad which requested applications from women able to write fluently and type quickly who were interested in working in a 'large magazine department where human problems are our business'.

The offer of an interview revealed it to be the back-up service to one of Britain's best-known agony aunts whose weekly printed page flourished the promise 'Every letter answered personally'.

Sackfuls of letters arrived each day, searching for an individual experience of the universal wisdom which the agony aunt's beneficent face suggested. The wisdom actually received was, at best, partial. Poorly paid letter writers did what they could, which wasn't much. Any initial enthusiasm was soon constrained by the guidelines of the magazine. Wives were never to be advised to leave husbands, even the most persistently brutal. Pre-marital sex out of sight of the altar was not something to be endorsed for 'our readers'. Loneliness could be assuaged by more frequent attendance at evening classes. Those hardy few who whispered they were worried about their feelings for their best friend or for the lady next door were urged to visit their doctor, or their vicar if the feelings had already gone too far.

The service did help when specific information was needed: addresses of VD clinics, of Family Planning Association offices, or Alcoholics Anonymous or Weight Watchers. The less precise confusions, and apparent hopelessness of many thousands of lives, could not be healed or even relieved by long-delayed formulaic replies.

Zoë appreciated the irony of taking on a job where broken hearts and dreams were everyday banalities. She imagined writing her own letter.

Dear Miss X

After almost a year I am still passionately in love with a man who cannot live with me. Of course I am getting on with my own life but I feel I have a hole in the heart out of which my confidence seeps.

I do still see him and he continues to be attentive and loving. I am weepy and self-pitying on these occasions and, no doubt, terribly dull. But then he returns to a life which includes work that he loves and is brilliantly good at, a not-yet former wife who can forgive anything, a son, and, no doubt, to a horde of lovers . . . I return to a feeling of emptiness which is more familiar to me now than anything else.

There has been someone since, but it didn't work out.

I know I have much to be grateful for, but the loss is overwhelming.

Yours from the quagmire . . .

Zoë also imagined the reply which might leave her desk.

Dear Zoë
All good things come to an end.
Time will heal
Take up knitting.
The devil makes work for idle hands.
Be thankful for small mercies.
Think of the starving millions.
If there's been one person since then why shouldn't there be more?
Pull yourself together.
You have this man's affection. It could have been his contempt.
Take up sewing.

Yours in remorseless cheer . . .

The letters Zoë actually spent her days composing were inspected and signed by former letter writers promoted to the even more tedious task of checking that their successors were strictly attentive to the magazine's line and were not sneaking in unnecessary advice, nor being concrete enough that the supplicant could later claim she'd been told what to do by the famous Miss X.

The job was possibly an improvement on waitressing, but this wasn't the career Zoë had left Berlin to pursue. The letter writers worked in a shabby back-street building effectively separated from the glamorous premises with which the magazine was associated. Even the advertising sales people – as lowly as the letter writers but considerably better paid – were housed in the main building. There was no chance that Zoë could realize her motivation for taking the job: that reading her letters those in power would fall upon her talent with gratitude and whisk her off to put her opinions on the printed page.

The vigilantes who did read her letters were as isolated as she was, and were completely resigned to the lack of ambition which eliminated competitiveness from the lazy, amiable office but also crushed anything remotely resembling individual vigour.

Zoë was compelled by the frustrations of her working day to spend even more time on her own writing. This continued as entries in her journal, sometimes events written up factually, sometimes real or imagined events translated into fictional forms or into poetry. Then, without too much reflection, Zoë began work on a story based on the most recent of Archie's romances, but typical of them all.

She welcomed this new focus for her writing. She had not worked on a story about a friend before and it was necessary for her to quieten uncomfortable rumblings that perhaps she was plundering Archie's life from a position of privileged intimacy. Archie was unsparing in his descriptions of the minutiae of his affairs; Zoë sometimes felt like a participant herself.

The new story was quite short. It included a fairly explicit sex scene which Zoë was surprised to find was easy for her to write, given that she'd never been a man in love with another. She worked hard on the story, propelled by curiosity as to what flesh would settle on the bare bones she initially outlined, coming home quickly and shutting herself up in her room, acknowledging Archie's raised eyebrow of enquiry with only vague hints that she was 'trying something new'.

It was the world of the Archie character she found herself most interested in: a world that included at its borders women like herself who were witty and uncritical and usually heterosexual but who, for reasons that were surely individual, preferred the company of men with whom they would never be sexually embroiled. It was not the world Sibylla had introduced her to where sexual politics and acts were under perpetual surveillance. She had been drawn to Sibylla and through her to that world, but had been too unsteady in her sense of self not to be frightened by the challenge she believed it consistently demanded. Archie's world allowed Zoë to be a privileged spectator, and peripheral participant only if she chose. It was exactly the limbo she needed.

A week after she had finished writing the story Zoë grew impatient with her own hesitations and asked Archie to read it. She did so knowing she was risking the comparative contentment that had come from the security of their Ladbroke Grove life together. Archie's cheerful confidence in her, his casual support of her sexual uncertainties, above all his unreserved fondness for her, had gone a long way in quietening the barrage of self-criticism with which she had been at war since Gabriel had left her. And before. Living with

Archie didn't mean that she longed for Gabriel any less, but at a daily life level she was doing a little better than simply functioning.

Archie might hate the story, Zoë fretted, and be angry with her. He might ask her to pack her bags and take her piracy elsewhere. Or he might simply find the story dull, or pretentious, and she would shrink in his regard.

While he read the story — he lying on his four-poster with Madam Butterfly pleading through the walls, she tossing between brass rails in her own room — Zoë read it with him, running it through the screen of her mind, hating every carefully chosen word, writhing with shame that she could have exposed herself to him, bewailing her lack of satisfaction with the privacy of silence.

The door of her room was open and, like the cat she sometimes suspected she had once been, Zoë sensed through the silence, as Madam Butterfly folded her wings, when Archie had reached the last line, when he'd glanced back here and there, when he'd got up off his bed to pad noiselessly towards her, his Cinderella-small feet bare on woollen carpets.

'I hate it, Petal. I absolutely hate it.'

Archie was standing by her door, dressed, Zoë was surprised to find herself observing, in cream pleated trousers and a fetching dark blue silk shirt. She moved her eyes on up to his face. He was grinning.

'But *you've* got nothing to worry about. The only reason I can summon up for hating it is that it's really very good and here I am, *struggling* with my Great Work which had seemed to be going somewhere but now that I've read your slip of a golden tongue I think mine's mired in its antediluvian beginnings. Perhaps I should abandon it to become Alice to your Gertrude? Or even Leonard to your Virginia? No, too much angst and too little sex, *chez* Sussex. though why I couldn't have found a nice girl who wanted nothing more than to be a model or an air hostess . . . the clash of pens here could be *too* overwhelming.'

Archie crossed the space to the bed, put his arms around Zoë and hugged her with great warmth. 'It's a lovely story, Zoë. You can be very pleased. Mind you, I should hardly be surprised, given your inspiration!'

Pleasure and relief rushed through Zoë like a blast of amyl nitrate.

Burying her head in the pillow she beat her feet up and down at the end of the bed in a rampage of exultation. Which had still not entirely expired when, with Archie's editorial help and his addition of a few vividly authenticating details, the story got published, under a pseudonym of course.

Zoë wrote a tantalizing biography for 'Ronnie Giovanni' in a sidelong tribute to Gabriel to whom she did, after all, owe so much. The published story was startlingly illustrated showing tousled, swollen-mouthed boys with taut buttocks prominently centre page. Archie assured her they were lusciously attractive. The story was even featured on the front cover: 'Gay Fiction – Frank as Only an Insider Could Make It'.

As the story appeared in *Strut* it wasn't immediately obvious to Zoë how much good the publication of 'In the Palm of My Hand' would do for her still painfully embryonic career. But the gratification persisted.

Strut's editor, whose languid manner partially disguised his frenetic interest in domination, was pressing Archie to urge his 'friend in the country' to produce more stories. Zoë was flattered by his interest and did try, but couldn't again get beyond a few tepid pages. Clearly Ronnie G. was to be a one-shot. If she was going to write anything else of value she would have to move even closer to home.

Three

There was a woman who came often to Zoë, in her dreams. She wore many different faces. Sometimes she was old, sturdy beneath the patina of experience. Sometimes she was a young woman, a powerful, uncomfortable mixture of boldness and hesitancy very like Zoë herself. Sometimes she was a playful child aged three or four, but was usually the child in just a glimpse of a trusting, ecstatic laughing-girl's face.

Zoë had come to expect her, though she knew the woman had been visiting her long before she consciously recognized this and recognized too that her different faces and moods were facets of only one woman and were not many women as she had too readily presumed.

Occasionally the woman resembled Gabriel. There would be a gesture, a touch, a beautifully apt word which did more than evoke Gabriel: it was Gabriel. Or the woman would lean towards her, listening intently as she could only remember Gabriel ever doing. But when she stretched towards the image of the woman that sense of Gabriel would dissolve into a more mysterious sense which seemed evocative of Jane.

In her dreams Zoë would experience despair that she was wasting this listening, that it would be snatched from her before she'd had time to recollect what she needed to share. Occasionally, in the dream, she would be aware she was dreaming and aware too that if she could not gather her thoughts into some elusive coherence she would wake up, or that she might too soon wake up anyway to find herself without the woman, without Gabriel, without Jane. And when she did, inevitably, wake, she was always aware of the grief and loneliness which any unheard speaker might expect to feel.

But then the day would begin. Archie would call from the kitchen to offer greetings, toast and coffee. Or one of his naked, muscular lovers would be encountered with cheerful half-embarrassment en route to the bathroom. There would be the crush of the tube to endure and then on to the satisfying distractions of the office.

From time to time, even on the tube, Zoë would catch a glimpse of a face not unlike one of the woman's faces. She would look into a pair of eyes and read compassion there, or catch the tail-end of a smile directed at someone else but encompassing in its warmth; she would notice a hug, no sex in it but joy in closeness and comfort, and she would recall the woman or believe she could sense her close by.

There was a different office to travel to now. Zoë had left the letters and the letter writers behind her. The boredom had become so intense she feared she might smell of it like some awful mist that won't wash off, or down. Archie had tried to persuade her to join him on the handbag until something more inspiring turned up, but she was loathe to do so. Perhaps the Social Security people would inform the Home Office that she was a leech on the body-state and she would find herself tipped unceremoniously onto a plane and allowed to disembark only at Auckland. No. The worst boredom could be endured rather than an involuntary return to the home-lands.

She was determined to be satisfied with nothing less than a 'real job', a foot on a career ladder clearly visible in front of her. The few jobs she thought worth applying for seemed to wither in interest at the interview and when, once or twice, a carrot had been dangled that had seemed enticing, it had been whipped away in the final run to be given to a better qualified donkey.

The prominent ad in a national daily which sought a 'creative feature writer' for a new monthly magazine with an emphasis on current affairs seemed to Zoë so outstanding that she could hardly bear to apply. But pushed, cajoled and finally ordered by Archie to do so, she composed a letter of application of which even she was proud.

And when the call came, loud and clear like Brown Owl to her troops, it was for an interview the following day with copies please of her published work. Well, Zoë comforted herself, there was always *Strut*, perhaps without the illustration. Her emotions about that story had continued to vacillate between pride and self-consciousness. Several times she had sat down, begun and failed to finish a letter which opened:

Dear Rebecca

Here, at last, is my first published fiction. Perhaps not quite what either of us had in mind when we joked and plotted that I might become the writer in the family, but nevertheless . . .

Despite the letters which continued intermittently to pass between them, and the steadily increasing array of photographs of Rebecca and her two growing daughters which Zoë pinned to her wall, it was sometimes difficult for Zoë to summon up a convincing picture of Rebecca the woman. Her memories of Rebecca grew more vivid the further back in time she went. Rebecca the mother was sometimes as elusive to her as Jane the mother and when she sought specific images of either of them her mind would come up with cliché pictures: Virgin Mother with Child, Mother Earth, or the sanitized Doris Day mothers beloved of family planning brochures.

There was an increasing restraint to Rebecca's letters, and it had grown worse since their failure to meet in Berlin. Zoë suspected that it was born in part from Rebecca's perception of herself as a stay-at-home mother, and her perception of Zoë as the glamorous world conqueror with access to dazzling events and people. Zoë found herself in a considerable dilemma as to how to deal with this suspicion over half-a-world's distance. Were she to reveal the bleakness that sometimes threatened to dominate her life, Rebecca would be appalled and miserably anxious. But if she continued to describe only the glowing moments then Rebecca's misperceptions would further solidify to make an ever-chunkier wall between them.

Re-reading her story on the eve of the interview, Zoë realized she had almost no idea of Rebecca's contemporary attitudes to sex, sexuality or sexual politics. She tried to imagine Sibylla and Rebecca sitting in a room together and talking comfortably. She couldn't do so. She tried to imagine sitting in a room with Rebecca herself and talking to her about the changes and searching triggered by Gabriel but taken far beyond his expectations by her own needs. She couldn't do so.

Zoë put the story into a folder and placed it in her bag, along with some pages from her journals. These were reflections on Berlin life. They'd not been published, had not even been 'shown' before, but they would have to do. She had no desire nor material to show from her days at *Business World*, a million years ago.

Struggling hard to contain her misgivings, Zoë handed those journal pages to the editor first. He glanced through them without reading or pausing. Then put them down. She had only just arrived and already she was losing him. Where was her Guardian Angel when she needed her?

Zoë sat up a little straighter in her chair, and smiled. 'I do have published work of course but I've fairly recently got back to London after living in Berlin for some years and until I decide whether it's worth my while staying, I've not bothered to have all my things sent on.' She smiled again.

'Ah yes. I remember now. There was some mention of Berlin in your CV. What were you doing there, could you remind me?'

The young man leaned forward. His speech sounded to Zoë like a series of slides, attenuated vowels stretching between the precarious support of consonants. Long straight hair drifted into his eyes. He could have been very good looking in a well-deodorized northern European way but for a large birthmark which covered one side of his face, setting it into a permanent blush. This didn't appear to have affected his confidence.

'I went there initially to study art history. I'm particularly interested in modern sculpture.' Zoë stared into the man's pale eyes. There were few lines around them. He couldn't be much older than she was. 'And for anyone interested in politics over the last few years, Paris or Berlin were obviously the places to be. I chose Berlin because of the role Germans play in popular culture. I think I wanted to find out for myself what kind of place Germany really is, and who those "vile Huns" of contemporary myth really are.'

Forgive me Gabriel, muttered Zoë behind what she hoped was a face bathed in an inspiring aura of political wisdom and cultural sophistication.

'I guess it links up with a discomfort I've always felt with the notion of stereotypes and the assigning of sets of characteristics to groups of people, or to a nation in this case.' Zoë noted the attention the man was giving to her remarks. She went on, 'As you can guess,

I found pretty much the same mix of people there as anywhere else.' She paused and smiled. 'Maybe that's not quite true. At least my corner of Berlin had better than its share of glorious exhibitionists willing to turn themselves into living works of art. And of course there are also loads of people really engaged in left politics, or at least willing to discuss and argue and turn out for demonstrations.'

The editor looked considerably more animated as he began to speak again.

'My parents lived in Berlin for some time too. It looms rather large in our family mythology. That was before the war. They were, they are, Poles, but people of their class generally went to Germany to study though neither of them was there long enough to graduate. By 1936 it seemed wiser to get out.'

He picked up a dark blue, very slim fountain pen and began to play with its cap, partially screwing it off but never completing the act. 'Would you care for some coffee?'

Zoë nodded, then as the editor began to murmur into a phone she looked around the spacious room. The launching pad for this magazine was clearly well upholstered: understated comfort in a centrally located building. Books were housed on elegant shelving, well chosen lithographs hung on the walls. There was a single print by the door, a small Kirchner hugged in gilt.

'May I look at one or two of these pages?' The editor was waving his hand towards the pile of Zoë's papers he had previously set aside.

'Of course. I'd be delighted. And I'll explore your books if I may.'

Zoë stood in front of the books, retaining enough composure to extract one and feign interest in its illustrations. Her heart was beating fast and her palms were sticky. She wondered how she looked from behind. She had a heart-stopping moment of panic that blood might be showing on her skirt though her period wasn't due for days. Shit. She really wanted this job. She couldn't endure much more platitudinous letter writing. It really wasn't any better than waitressing. Nor was it in Berlin.

The coffee appeared, carried into the room by a Knightsbridge girl with a silk scarf knotted around her neck and an Alice band in her thick straight hair. Before leaving again she gave the man a long possessive stare and Zoë a brief, oblique glance. Zoë returned to her chair to drink her coffee and to leaf through a recent issue of the magazine, wholly aware that not 'one or two' but each page of her writing was coming under scrutiny.

'Don't you have anything with you that has been published?' Nick Green (that couldn't be his real name?) was coaxing Zoë now, willing her to do well.

She hesitated. She wanted this job very badly and was no longer protected from disappointment by the impossibility of it. If she didn't blow her response to Nick's question, could it be within her eager reach?

Without seeking her the woman in Zoë's dreams came into her mind. She was looking directly at Zoë and her smile was encouraging.

'Well I do have something. It's not an article though, it's a short story. And the problem is . . .' Zoë grinned at Nick but the grin slid too quickly from her face. To gain a moment's grace she bent down to retrieve her bag from the floor and as she sat up again she hugged the bag close to her chest.

'I had a story published quite recently in *Strut*. It's a gay . . .'

'In *Strut*?' Nick's wail of incredulity became hoots of laughter. 'Good God, did they know it was you? I mean, that place is genuine KY Corral, Boy's Own Country no less. You're not going to tell me now that you're a female impersonator are you?'

Zoë hoped she wasn't blushing. 'Not at all! I wrote the story under a pseudonym and the chap I share a flat with helped me get it published. He models for the magazine occasionally.'

From out of her bag Zoë pulled the obviously inoffensive publication and handed it to Nick, opened to 'In the Palm of My Hand' with its illustration still intact.

Nick's eyebrows disappeared entirely and he smirked as he skimmed the opening lines. 'I'm avid to read this but it won't do for the Board.' He put down the magazine and took up his pen. 'I tell you what. You stick to your story that your work's on its way via the Great Walls of China and Berlin and we'll get you started here in the meantime. I like these Berlin observations you've shown me. They're not journalism but we want people here who can write with a personal note to their work, especially for some of the longer pieces which we intend to make rather a feature. The tricks can be picked up as you go, adding to the *depths* of your previous experience.' He allowed his mouth to move fractionally outwards.

'We'll use your interest in art history, and I presume you speak German at least tolerably well?'

'Ah huh.' Zoë's mind was no longer turning. It was fixed on a neon light flashing a single, precious item of information. She had the job!

'Could you start at the beginning of next month? There will have to be a trial period, let's say three months with only one week's notice and no good reason for farewells need be given. Not by me anyway. After that you'll have the usual protection, for what it's worth.'

Zoë noticed that Nick had lovely teeth. They were small, white and even, very like her own. They were splendidly displayed when he smiled broadly. She gave him the pleasure of an equally pretty sight.

'You won't be sorry. So, until the beginning of next month then?'

Grateful though she was, Zoë was already edging towards the door, wanting to get home to Archie who would claim all credit for this coup and join her in the ceremonial whoops of joy she could feel bursting up which would be horribly out of place in this cool, assured office.

'Davina, my secretary, will drop you a line to confirm things. I've enjoyed meeting you Zoë. I do *like* a surprise.'

Nick walked Zoë to the door and leaned against its frame as he saw her out. A slim, elegant young man, a perfect young Englishman who was actually a Pole. An apparent heterosexual familiar with *Strut*. An ambitious perfectionist willing to take a gamble. Well, well, Zoë gloated, Deo bloody gratias.

FOUR

If Zoë dives quickly into the pool shattering its perfect surface then no one need see her tears.

At the bottom of the pool lies a blue glass bead. Gabriel has put it there for her. It's a test. When Zoë leans as far over the side of the pool as she dares she can see it glittering up at her, enticing her to go in to salvage it.

If others were to come to this pool which is almost hidden behind tall green trees they would see only the blue of the water. The more intense blue of the glass bead would remain hidden from them. But for Zoë it's as though all the colour of the pool has been drawn off to perfect the intensity of colour of that tiny beautiful thing far below her.

If Zoë were to dive in, sleek body moving down fast through the water, and come up with the bead she would have more than this treasure from Gabriel, hers to keep forever. She would regain Gabriel's respect, renew his admiration. There would no longer be any need for him to ignore her tears. They would be washed away by cool water. Her cries of triumph would drown out those sounds which linger in his ears of her strange, strained voice begging him not to go, pleading with him, promising him: anything, anything. (His bags are packed. He is already going. He is hurrying down the street and not looking back to where she stands and will stand for hours yet, at the window looking down onto a street along which he does not return.)

If she were to burst up from beneath the water, propelled by the strength of her moving legs, her lungs near to exploding, with her first breath she would call out to him, 'I have it, Gabriel, I have it!'

She would wave her clenched fist, closed tightly around her precious find. Her dark hair would be plastered around a face glowing with victory. Gabriel would stand beside the pool, dressed in white, smiling back down at her and she would hear him cheer, 'Bravo, Zoë, bravo!'

The bead could mean so much.

Inside it she might find a tiny key she could turn to unravel the mystery of how such a love could lead to separation and what she cannot help but call defeat.

Gabriel would have ready a huge white towel in which to wrap Zoë as she emerges from the pool shivering with excitement and waiting for his kisses as water drips onto him from her face and hair.

Then, while they stand together beside the restored calm of the water, Gabriel would take from his pocket a small object in which the blue glass bead could safely lie.

The object is the shape of an egg, and translucent. Only when she sees this perfect resting place can Zoë uncurl her fingers to reveal, shimmering on her hand, the bead.

If Gabriel tells Zoë to hurry and get dressed, concerned that she shouldn't grow cold, she will laugh and refuse him. She won't be hurried. She will never be cold again.

Zoë wakes.

Her pillow is wet. Her hair is dry.

Zoë has never learned how to swim.

Five

On the desk in her office Zoë kept a small sculpture which rose above the cloud of papers like a beacon. It was an early copper effort that Gabriel had wanted to abandon, and showed a woman turning, as if caught by a second thought.

It had slipped far from Gabriel's intentions until he could see only its faults. But to Zoë it had immediately evoked something hopeful and each day as she touched it and admired it she gave thanks she had been able, eventually, to persuade Gabriel to allow her to remove it out of his sight and into her safe-keeping.

She was holding the sculpture in her hand, caressing it with the unconsciousness of familiarity, when the phone rang. It was Nick, asking her to come to his office. Two productive years at *Issues* had convinced Zoë that Nick's summonses need not cause her mind to jump to the fearful worst. She felt nothing stronger than mild curiosity as she walked down the corridor from her office to his own.

Nick was fully occupied pulling the cork from a bottle of wine. It wasn't until he had succeeded that he straightened up and drawled, 'Ah Zoë. Have you ever heard of a woman called Imogen Modjeska?'

Zoë shook her head.

Nick poured them each a glass of wine then continued. 'I can't say I'm surprised. She was well before your time and even mine.' He smirked. They both knew he was six years older than Zoë, almost to the day.

'I know about her only because she's Polish. A rare *mistress* of the piano, or was. My parents have some ancient recordings, 78s, but even on those one can hear she played like an angel.'

He leant back in his large chair to admire his choice of wine, holding his glass up to the light and looking into it as he spoke. 'It seems her record company is bringing out a new set of LPs. They're lifting them from old recordings to get together a pre-mortem tribute before she's elevated to the great concert hall in the sky.'

Nick's gaze shifted from the glass to Zoë. 'I want you to rustle her up. You could interview her about the good old days. Does that interest you? She is, or was by all accounts, a remarkable woman. Knew everyone, did everything; was said to be sexually *progressive*. I know you admire that kind of thing.'

Zoë ignored Nick's last remark.

Except at work-connected functions where they played editor and star writer to perfection, Nick and Zoë rarely saw each other outside the office. Within their working world they got along together remarkably well. Nick had enough self-confidence to resist undermining his writers with unnecessary criticism. He also had enough confidence to ease out with great speed anyone whose work did not immediately satisfy his exacting standards. He was discreet and intelligent in his encouragement of Zoë and she rewarded him with her willingness to devote her considerable energy almost entirely to the magazine's continuing success.

On those occasions when they had inadvertently stepped onto the same social flagstone, Zoë had been in boys' bars with Archie.

The first time this happened Nick came close to losing his precious composure. Zoë and Archie were in the Coleherne, the heavy leather gay pub in Earls Court where neither Zoë nor Nick might reasonably have expected to find the other. Zoë was amused, on later reflection, to note that even Nick's leathers had been soft, subtle in colour and exquisitely tailored.

Archie was looking especially outrageous that night. His jeans were torn and patched to emphasize his crutch. He wore an oil-stained lime-green T-shirt under a studded black motor-bike jacket several sizes too big for him. Round his neck hung a silver phial in which was stuffed cotton wool soaked in amyl nitrate. Round each slim wrist was a heavy silver chain. He had cut off his curls until he had almost no hair left in a vain attempt to transform his sweetness into a look that was menacingly butch, and was leaning back against the bar, nursing his light-and-bitter and passing on wicked comments to Zoë about the many fellow leather lovers with whom he had, at one time or another, had 'trade', sex so casual Zoë was astonished he could remember the faces, let alone the arcane sexual preferences which were the substance of his stories.

Zoë and Archie were in a mood to celebrate.

Zoë had just returned from a weekend in Amsterdam with Gabriel. It had begun disastrously. Zoë had been met at Amsterdam airport by an unusually harassed Gabriel who had looked at her with some distaste and said, 'Zoë, Zoë, you English women have no idea how to make up your faces for the Continental light.'

She had stared at him, aghast, insulted, humiliated. And then had laughed. 'You're a pain in the bum, Gabriel. You really don't deserve me. Not even the *soupçon* of time we spend together. But since we do have this time together and since Amsterdam just happens to be a favourite city of mine, we are, let me tell you, my sweetheart, going to make the most of it.'

Gabriel had grinned, shame-faced. 'God, I'm sorry. Of course we should have a good time. It's not you, or your face, or even English women's faces, of which I know you don't have one. I just heard today I lost a commission which I was sure I'd get, but to hell with it. Actually, you look lovely. Let me look at you some more. And even closer.' He had pulled her towards him, kissed her with care and passion, and they had walked together tightly linked to a cab, and when they had reached their small, canal-side hotel, they had made love easily and with genuine pleasure on both sides, and then had talked without restraint, and although through the weekend they had not made love again, there had been an ease between them which Zoë trusted, and was proud of.

She had returned from the weekend feeling wholly intact and only mildly, indeed quite tolerably grieving about the inevitable parting, allowing herself to appreciate, perhaps for the first time, that as inevitable as their partings were, so were their increasingly rewarding reunions.

Archie's celebration had waited for her return. He had reached what he declared to be the magical half-way mark in the writing of his novel and was now working towards the end, no longer facing each new blank page with dread.

A letter from Rebecca had also been waiting for Zoë, and a copy of the magazine *New Zealand Arts*, inside which, the letter explained, Zoë would find published one of her own poems, sent to Rebecca some months before. Rebecca had been convinced it was good enough for publication and had made that happen. She implored Zoë not to think her presumptuous and at quite uncharacteristic length explained she had taken this initiative only because she was proud of Zoë.

The poem had no special merit but it expressed emotions which Zoë had felt deeply and she was gratified and touched by the added weight it gained through the imprimatur of the printed page. In the women's writing workshops she occasionally attended she made earnest obeisance towards and even half believed the line that it was the act of writing and not publication which mattered. But she was, she believed, too fragile to live out that credo. The visibility of her work confirmed her reality. She saw her name in print every month and the yardage of her words held up to the world like a sample from a weaver's bolt, from which more yardage would follow. Those few thousand monthly words were protection against retreat into that sense of nothingness which in Berlin had come close to overwhelming her and which occasionally still reminded her of its dark, persistent imminence.

The printed poem evoked something different from the initial thrill and reassurance, quickly followed by her search for improvement, which Zoë experienced as each month's new *Issues* slammed onto her desk. The poem was the excursion of a novice out of the recesses of a more diffident, inner self, inspired or certainly conceived out of the pain that ripped through Zoë when Gabriel wrote to tell her he was planning to live at least part-time with Sonja Beckermann. Her unspoken hope that he would, eventually, again find her a possible living companion, slammed like a door in her face, behind which, she believed, Gabriel and Sonja cuddled and laughed in constant harmony.

He wanted her to understand, he wrote. Though he didn't say quite what. He *needed* (he who never underlined, emphasized) to be sure that she would know it indicated *no* difference at all in his feelings towards her. He insisted that he would be as available to her as he had always been. She had hit the wall until her fist ached when she read that line, knowing nothing except how astounded he would have been to witness the passion of her distress. She had comforted herself over the months of separation with her petty beliefs that he needed more time for his work, needed more time for his child, needed more time for his father: all of which meant less time with Zoë. But it had, after all, been something particular in her which he couldn't bear. He had, after all, been fleeing from and not going towards. Though he had been stopped in his flight by the magnificent Sonja.

Even while he talked, Archie's eyes moved constantly and compulsively around the Coleherne's bar. It was he who noticed Nick first, nudging Zoë and asking, 'Isn't that the fabulous face gracing the contents list of your mag? The famous is-he-or-isn't-he Nikolai Greeny-witch?'

Zoë peered through the crowd to where Archie was indicating and there, indeed, was Nick who looked across at exactly that moment before she'd had time to hide her surprise, and saw Zoë gaping at him. Nick's birthmark had disappeared as his whole face blushed crimson but by the time he had squeezed his way to where Zoë and Archie stood he was at least outwardly calm again.

'And what's Little Red Riding Hood doing here among the wolves?' he opened.

'Protecting Snow White from the taller dwarves, of course.' She accepted Nick's shadow of a kiss on either cheek, and went on. 'This is Snow White, also known as Archie Haines, my famous literary midwife. Archie, this is Nick Green.'

The men eyed each other with practised skill. Nick insisted on buying a round of drinks but Zoë's glass was still almost full when he claimed an urgent engagement and disappeared.

Nick, Zoë and Archie next ran into each other at the end of a long night in a basement disco on Kensington High Street. Nick was less guarded and with little ceremony dragooned Archie off to the bar for what he wryly offered as 'man to man' drinks, though Archie later reported that their conversation had been almost entirely directed towards Nick's eventually futile goal of establishing whether the woman with Zoë was, in fact, her lover.

Zoë laughed aloud when she heard this. Had Nick confronted her with a direct question he would certainly have got a direct answer. As it was she took no pity on the studied indifference he refused to drop even momentarily. Ignoring his oblique hints, she deflected the curiosity that lay behind his attempts to provoke her into self-revelation. It had become a game between them, to be played only when they were alone.

Nick put down his glass of wine, half emptied, and picked up a plastic folder from his almost bare desk top. He handed the folder to Zoë. 'The faithful Davina's got this together. As far as I know Madame Modjeska lives in North London but you'll need to check that when you fix the interview. I think you'll enjoy it. You *deserve* a little treat.' He smiled somewhat smugly as Zoë finished her wine, took the folder and left the room.

It was obvious from the cuttings that Imogen Modjeska had inspired attention that bordered on the adulatory, for her musicianship most of all, but also for her dark beauty which was still strikingly apparent in the most recent clippings in Zoë's file from the post-war years when Mrs Modjeska was probably in her fifties.

None of her reading and staring at the photographs prepared Zoë for the woman who greeted her at an undistinguished Kentish Town front door. The eyes which looked up into Zoë's were bright and intent but across the face in which they sat were creases and tugs of pain and age which had obliterated the transporting vision that face had once been, and was to be again on the cover of the new boxed LP set.

The woman did not offer her hand but did give the suggestion of a bow with the smallest inclination of her head. The front door closed behind them and Zoë followed Mrs Modjeska, slowly, for the old woman moved with difficulty, into a sitting-room crowded with heavy, old-fashioned furniture, a closed grand piano, and a mass of books on shelves and in apparently haphazard piles on the polished wood floor. Facing the door on an occasional table was a tall vase crammed with burnt-orange chrysanthemums, just past their best.

Before suggesting they sit Mrs Modjeska offered tea. When Zoë accepted she explained Zoë herself would have to make it as she could no longer trust her hands with a hot kettle, so gripped was she by arthritis. She shrugged then, her small shoulders lifting gracefully under the heavy green woollen shawl that draped them, as though the arthritis were something she could scarcely comprehend and no part of her real life or self.

The tea things had been left ready in the small kitchen. Zoë had only to boil the kettle, make the tea and carry the wooden tray through to the sitting-room where Mrs Modjeska sat waiting.

By the end of that first meeting Zoë knew the tray would have been prepared by one of the two middle-aged daughters with whom Mrs Modjeska lived, but it was not until later meetings that Mrs Modjeska began to speak frankly about her daughters and to expand on her hints of what a weight of maternal disappointment she bore. Her remarks were usually accompanied by one of her dramatic shrugs, emanating the same sense of incredulity that these two plain, unremarkable women could be her own daughters as she had about the arthritis that had struck early enough to take her last priceless years of playing from her.

It seemed to Zoë that Mrs Modjeska judged her daughters too harshly, in poignant contrast to the generous enthusiasm she showed to her many friends and quasi-protegées. In no way did Mrs Modjeska seem willing to acknowledge what must have been an untenable burden: to live, without particular talent or beauty, in the shadow of a beautiful, talented and widely adored mother.

But Zoë sensed that to contradict Mrs Modjeska would be to risk her disapproval, perhaps even her withdrawal, and Zoë wouldn't take that risk. From the first moments when she had sat down with Mrs Modjeska and encountered her long, unguarded appraisal, her spirits had risen and gone out to the old woman.

It was very much like falling in love.

Six

Zoë wasn't able and didn't wish to stop talking about Mrs Modjeska in the days that followed their first meeting. Nor could she stop thinking about the remarkable impression the old woman had made on her.

She had taken a taxi from Kentish Town back to the office where she had burst in on an amused Nick to thank him profusely, even excessively, for his clever impulse which had led to the interview. With very little difficulty she prised Archie away from his plans in order to spend the evening with her so that she could, in the telling, re-live the afternoon. Gabriel had, by fortunate chance, made one of his rare, extravagant phone calls to her and she had revelled in the highly detailed curiosity that was his familiar response to her discovery. But it was Sibylla who had listened carefully when Zoë had phoned her in Berlin, and then asked, 'Is she the woman in your dreams, Zoë?'

The question took Zoë by surprise. She didn't react immediately and Sibylla spoke again, in English this time. 'I'm not asking if she's the woman *of* your dreams. I like to think this place is still open.'

There was the usual confident irony in Sibylla's tone but that remark too took Zoë aback. She could feel herself blushing and was grateful that distance protected her from Sibylla's cool scrutiny.

In the weeks that had followed Gabriel's departure from Berlin it had been to Sibylla that Zoë had turned, though more often she could face no one, not even Sibylla, and sometimes especially not Sibylla. For months she had known that Sibylla's interest in her was erotic as well as friendly. If she had failed to notice it then Gabriel's commentary would have forced her to acknowledge the small, persistent attentions Sibylla paid her, just beyond the bounds of close female friendship. There was nothing predatory in

297

Sibylla's manner. Zoë recognized with gratitude that it would never become necessary to exchange sex for Sibylla's continuing interest and support. Zoë was flattered by Sibylla's interest, but wary too. She held in awe the relationship which Sibylla had for years successfully maintained with Brigitte, an academic in her forties, married to a prominent state politician and author of several fat books which Zoë had never actually read but which she knew were held in esteem by no less a judge than Gabriel.

Sibylla exhibited little inclination to discuss Brigitte the woman or Brigitte the lover, other than to tell Zoë that monogamy had never been part of their understanding. She did, however, offer lively accounts of the activities they shared: meetings, discussions, writing projects. Zoë knitted these pieces together into a pattern that closely resembled the relationship she had dreamed of achieving with Gabriel. She envied Brigitte and Sibylla their intellectual equality, and lusted after it for herself.

Zoë kept silent about the erotic dreams and occasional fantasies in which Sibylla starred. She felt too far flung into chaos by Gabriel's departure to cope with the internal questions aroused by Sibylla's interest in her: about her own status in relation to the exceptional qualities she perceived in both Gabriel and Sibylla; about the significance of the shift from liking and feeling at ease with women, to desiring a particular woman.

It was Sibylla who persuaded Zoë to abandon financial caution and spend her last month in Berlin as holiday time. Zoë had never intended to stay at the Bogart so long but eventually the familiarity of the *Kneipe* had given her a sense of security more compelling than the boredom of the job itself. She had to cope with constant requests from Gabriel's friends and acquaintances for information of him but after a while she minded even this much less, seeing herself as a vital, living telegram stretched between Frankfurt and Berlin.

Sibylla was busy during that month preparing the index for the doctoral thesis she'd been working on all the time Zoë had known her, but this work was, for Sibylla, almost an act of relaxation, rather like adding flowers to the dining table after an elaborate meal has already been prepared.

She made no secret of her hope that there might yet be a change in their relationship significant enough to persuade Zoë to abandon her plans for a career in London and to stay in Berlin, to study perhaps. There had been no pressure from her. With cautious vigilance Zoë waited for this to come. It never had and so when they returned one evening to Sibylla's room after a day visiting the Egyptian collection in East Berlin and had sat down on Sibylla's cushions tired and relaxed with glasses of white wine in their hands and Mozart in their ears, it had been Zoë as much as Sibylla who had turned towards a kiss as they had done many times, but this time Zoë had not, after some moments, pulled back, but had moved her hands, tentatively but with excitement and curiosity over Sibylla's small breasts, and had then felt, for the first time, the memorable, lovely echo as Sibylla's own hands had crept under her shirt to tease, very lightly, her nipples.

That evening it had been Sibylla who drew away, sending Zoë home though Zoë hadn't wanted to go, but it was also Sibylla who had turned up at Zoë's room early the next morning with newly baked rolls and smoked ham to make breakfast for them, she said, though it was not until she had crawled into Zoë's warm bed with her and they had made love together, and then again, that they got up, made breakfast, and then returned to bed.

Zoë called on her dreams and fantasies to guide her and also her memories of her frustrated desires, even anger, that if only a male lover were in her skin he might think of doing this, or that, now, or later. Sibylla led their love-making discreetly and effectively and there were few surprises, other than for Zoë to find how quickly her suspicions were confirmed that she would feel at home with Sibylla's smooth face next to her own, with breasts which were delicate to touch but strong in their response, with the grace of a long curve from armpit to hip, with the warm, receptive wetness of another's vagina.

It should have been an idyll.

It was, Zoë kept telling herself, at least until a few days later when she heard her own voice blurting out that she would, anyway, have to return to England. Sibylla was too close to Gabriel, she tried to explain.

And Gabriel was still too close to her, she didn't have to explain.

*

Barely a week after their first meeting Mrs Modjeska summoned Zoë to return to her house. She had, in the meantime, read the copy for Zoë's interview and had been pleased by it, finding only an incident or two which perhaps she could elucidate a little more if only Zoë could spare the time.

With some difficulty Zoë had refrained from actually purring down the phone, instead assuring Mrs Modjeska that yes, of course she had time to see her; the following afternoon perhaps?

Zoë had always been scornful of those journalists who use an interview as an opportunity to talk about themselves. Yet she, who could keep herself effortlessly hidden, was unable to resist the clever, seductive questions Mrs Modjeska might almost have been honing in the days of their separation. Like someone reaching into the dark but knowing exactly where the switches are, Mrs Modjeska slowly turned lights on Zoë's writing, on Gabriel, on Berlin, on New Zealand, on Jane, and even on the woman who came to Zoë in her dreams.

Mrs Modjeska ceased to ask then and stared at Zoë most particularly. She got up, and with a small gesture of apology left the room. It was not until she had returned and with an effort that was painful to observe had seated herself, that she asked, 'Do you love women, Zoë?'

It became Zoë's turn to be silent, hot as she turned the unexpected question over in her mind, not wishing to avoid it but suddenly aware of how necessary it had become to find an answer, not for Mrs Modjeska, for her own sake. She experienced a rush of gratitude towards Mrs Modjeska and lifted her head, wanting to express that but finding instead that she was listening.

'Perhaps this is too blunt a question Zoë? You must forgive me – I've never become English. These matters are not strangers to me and I sense you as perhaps at a crossroads? But I'm presumptuous to ask.'

'No. No, please. I'm grateful, really. But can you give me a moment?'

Mrs Modjeska nodded but Zoë anyway began almost at once. 'I feel lots of things. Yet how to make sense of them all? Sometimes when I'm at women's events like dances or conferences I experience extraordinary waves of love and closeness to women at large. It's a lovely, inclusive feeling and takes in love for myself as a woman also. And those emotions are sometimes best expressed in an intense way with one specific woman. That seems easy for me.'

She paused. 'But there are other times, and maybe in just those same situations, when I'm as alone as I've ever been. The women's movement does offer something like a community feeling but along with that comes all the business of collectivity, of working with or towards a consensus. I agree with that in my head but don't feel comfortable with it and won't ever, therefore, quite fit in. Perhaps I'm even a bit stubborn about it now. I don't want to forsake what for lack of a better word I'd describe as my individuality, even though I'm unsure what it signifies – if anything at all.'

'I think I understand that. I was always grateful to be a solo performer, of course dependent in many works on the orchestra, but not part of the orchestra. I've not always admired this in myself; I simply accept it. Though your sense of individuality intrigues me.'

'Yes? The woman in my dreams . . .' Zoë hesitated. 'I know that here my perceptions are very much at the bare skeleton stage but my hunch is that she's drawing my attention to the possibility of wholeness. And that I'll achieve this through gathering together scattered or maybe unrealized parts of myself. Does that make sense?'

'To me, yes. Though it may be that it's more a process of ageing – with a certain awareness of course – and not something to be forced or struggled after, simply expected.'

'That would be a consolation! The woman's a beacon too, a kind of light above the emotions that Gabriel stirred up in me and I in him, though I perceive him as having been less changed . . . less needy and therefore able to stay on a more even keel. And yet there's something else about this dream woman that I can only describe as the woman herself, even while I know there *is* no woman, other than who I'm piecing together from her moods and faces and my responses to them.'

'Have you talked about this woman, as well as thought about her?'

'A bit. To Gabriel mostly as sometimes she reminds me so explicitly of him, and also to a woman friend in Berlin. Though

301

not much to either of them. She's felt very private, and maybe I've felt too raw. Or maybe I want to find my own answers. With Gabriel especially, we have a long history already of him explaining me to myself. He does it brilliantly, but if Confucius didn't say the eye that's dazzled sees no distance, then he should have! I've learned to be cautious. He means only to help me, and he does help me: but not always.'

Mrs Modjeska and Zoë sat in silence, until Zoë spoke again. 'But how does this woman in my dreams relate to my feelings about women in general? That's where we began!'

The pace of Zoë's words began to slow as if she were trying to make sense of thoughts she was expressing aloud for the first time.

'I know that it's women who interest me, and it's certainly women I need. When I got back to England, and even before, in that bleak time after Gabriel had done the impossible and left me in Berlin I did have some flings with men. What a word: *fling*. I flung my needs onto their corrugated-iron surface and any useful anger I might have felt was deflected back inside me where it curdled into the most awful depression which I couldn't even acknowledge. I hate depressives.' Zoë tried to laugh. 'Perhaps I was unfair to those men though frankly as they were so marginally present it's hard to believe that mattered. I looked for some tenuous similarity to Gabriel in each of them, something I could concentrate on and ignore the rest. It didn't work.

'But then after living with Archie I began to see that I was behaving rather as a moth might, hitting a window again and again, unable to believe there's no access to the light inside. Or even that the light itself was illusory. Archie likes me; really likes me. It was exactly what I needed, and a sense of normality about loving one's own sex which is certainly something he's given me.'

Mrs Modjeska noticed that Zoë's attention was deep inside herself, and that her hands were moving, from time to time, uncomfortably in her lap.

'There was a woman, even at that worst time in Berlin. She'd been a friend for ages and was and is always more of a friend than a lover, though we did become lovers. Her name's Sibylla.' Zoë looked up at Mrs Modjeska and a warm smile lit her face. 'She's wise and kind just as her name promises. I don't know how I'd have survived without her. And my feelings for her were definitely more passionate than simple gratitude.'

'She's a friend still?' Mrs Modjeska asked.

'Oh yes. Of course too far away and I see her very rarely. Which may be the story of my life . . . But definitely a friend. It's when she steps into the role of lover that I've more difficulty, or had.

'I think I can say I love women. Yes, I can.' Zoë's voice expressed her conviction. 'Certainly when I began to sleep with women I felt like a homing pigeon who'd been on the wing too long. I've never felt much awkwardness, and no shame either, but when I consider a passionate engagement with an individual woman I'm held back.'

'Because you're then too exposed?'

'Certainly to the possibility of loss. Love and death seem to me to dance in the same hot breath, and even hotter if the love is a woman. I've not dared. It took all the strength I had to survive the loss of Gabriel. I can only imagine it would be even worse with a woman.'

Zoë took a deep breath. 'There's my mother too, of course. The pain about her may be the only constant in my life but it's still extremely difficult for me to look at it, never mind confront it. Just to survive I had to sweep that pain under a carpet I called my wonderful life, and then I had to dance manically all over it to keep the edges from curling up to reveal whatever murk might have lain beneath it. I was like a wind-up doll. But Gabriel put an end to that. Fake feelings were not good enough for the beloved Gabriel. He wanted the *real thing*.

'But he left, and left me dangling. Apparently by choice. It wouldn't take too much of a genius to see how the confusions began, and grew. Gabriel was the first person to mother me, the *only* person to mother me, since my mother . . . and then he left as well. My image is that I burrowed under that carpet and left some ghost calling herself Zoë Delighty to dance on top. She did a good job for me too. I don't think anyone noticed.'

After some moments Zoë heard Mrs Modjeska ask, 'Do you remember much of your mother, Zoë? You spoke of her earlier with such warmth.'

'Fragments only. I *feel* lots of things. It's rather as though pins were left in my body so if I turn this way, or that, I might get an unexpected jab. Or shards of glass. Something bloody painful anyway. But people hardly ever talked about it, not only her death, her life even. It's so wrong.'

'Out of their pain perhaps?'

'I guess so. But they have their adult memories, and I do not. Just wisps: there's nothing for me to hold on to. I feel cheated. That's my overwhelming feeling: *cheated.*'

There were marks on the side of Zoë's face left by her fingernails as she had unconsciously scratched. Mrs Modjeska shifted her attention back to what Zoë was saying.

'I do remember, quite vividly even, that in the years just after she died I was terribly afraid she'd haunt me. I was full of saints and ghosts at the time, thanks to Mother Church. It wasn't so much the haunting that frightened me, though that was certainly part of it, but even more I was afraid that I would *shrink* from her, hurt her feelings and would then never have the chance to tell her how sorry I am. I was. I am.

'And now I *long* for her.' Zoë's words were emerging in a rush. 'Even for some minimal sign of her. It comes from those longings which the quality of Gabriel's love stirred up in me. I don't want to be looking for her in other women, not only because that's such a cliché, but also because it's unfair . . . to everyone. And anyway, I've never found her there, or anywhere, except perhaps in that dream woman, and Gabriel.'

'Zoë, listen to me. Are you listening?'

She nodded.

'You remind me very much of my younger self: not the facts of course, but there's something about the feelings, even the confusions which take me back perhaps more than I might like. But let me be an old woman for a moment who has learned that she knows very little but among that little is this: that you're opening up to much pain now only because you're ready to bear it. This is the beginning of healing, please believe me, Zoë. And maybe it's also the chance to learn something about compassion which I believe is the very opposite of pity. Compassion for oneself, and then for others. I can tell you these things and you may or you may not hear me or understand me.'

304

With some effort Zoë raised her eyes to Mrs Modjeska's face. 'I certainly do hear what you've said, and as for understanding . . . well, I hope so.'

Mrs Modjeska's hands parted, in a brief gesture outwards.

'You've come here today and we've found ourselves talking. And we will again. This meeting of ours has been a happy chance. Not only for you!' There was some irony in her tone, and she smiled at Zoë with the sense of self which usually only the consciously beautiful or successful are able to display. It was not only herself but also Zoë whom she flattered and reassured with that smile.

'*Are we of one mind?*' Mrs Modjeska asked this in German, and Zoë smiled, tentatively, and began to thank Mrs Modjeska, also in German, to worry that perhaps she had said too much, gone on for too long, taken more than she should of Mrs Modjeska's time.

Mrs Modjeska interrupted her in English. 'There will be cakes in the kitchen, Zoë. My daughters hide them to nibble on while they watch their endless television shows in the evenings. You'll find them in round tins on top of the cupboards where their old mother could certainly never reach!'

Zoë stood up and walked to the door. Her momentary embarrassment had left her. She felt light, almost exhilarated. 'And more tea, of course?'

Mrs Modjeska laughed. 'At the very least. We are in England, after all.'

The daughters Modjeska were called Angelina and Constantina, names chosen by a mother who had expected shining slivers off the matriarchal block. Their father had been a conductor of promise and a man of considerable sexual magnetism. According to Mrs Modjeska his talent had burned too quickly, too fiercely, and had fizzled. Along with it had gone, at least as far as she was concerned, the sexual allure.

Foreswearing joining him in the eating of ashes, Imogen Modjeska had left Poland, made a home of sorts in Paris and then in London, pursuing her career with a tenacity barely affected by the presence of her two small daughters. When they could be left she did that, first with a series of nannies, usually Polish emigrées down on their luck, and then at boarding school.

Angelina and Constantina were middle-aged when Zoë met them but were still inaptly referred to as 'the girls'. In some disquieting way they had stuck in adolescence, despite the ageing and thickening of their bodies. Perhaps it was at adolescence their mother had recognized that despite her genetic gifts and no matter how many or costly the tutors she hired for them, her daughters would never show more than a shadow of the talent or drive which Mrs Modjeska cherished as the distinguishing qualities of her own self. They had seemed foreign to her then, despite her powerful memories of their time in her womb and each agonizing journey out of her body. They had never entirely ceased to seem foreign, though the three women had lived together throughout the adult life of 'the girls' and were obviously to be together, in the Kentish Town house, in a symbiosis only death would end.

Because their mother had perceived them as jointly foreign, it was to her sister that each had turned for the comfort of familiarity. Through an exceptional act of over-compensation, they had made of themselves mirror images. It would have been impossible to say who was older, fatter; who smiled more often or laughed more shyly. It was sometimes impossible to remember which sister had just spoken until you learned to note the careful attention the listener gave to the rare public utterances of her sister. They'd never had paid work as when they were young Mrs Modjeska had been earning a great deal of money and there had seemed to be no work their mother considered them competent to undertake which she would not also have considered demeaning. They had left the house each weekday for many years to do voluntary work within the Polish community. Unless guests were present they spoke Polish to each other, although all their education had been expensively bought in France or England.

Imogen Modjeska had, unwittingly, made them unfit for a normal life of independence, despite the sacrifices she had willingly made to ensure the independence of her own life. Yet as increasing ill-health had forced her external world to shrink, eventually to be no larger than the walls of the terraced house, Mrs Modjeska had been forced to acknowledge her own dependence on the girl-women, and perhaps even her private gratitude for the devotion and good will which had miraculously survived her contempt.

Consta and Angel, as they were known, made Zoë welcome when she began to be a frequent weekend caller at their home. If they were jealous of the quality of attention she elicited from their mother, they didn't let Zoë feel that. Mrs Modjeska and Zoë would usually spend their afternoons alone but after some months the older woman occasionally suggested the girls might join them for the tea they had always prepared and Zoë began to discover that beneath Consta and Angel's appalling diffidence were two minds used to a very private, specific form of play. They skirted around Zoë like kittens taking their first steps, coming near only when they discovered she too spoke German, a borrowed language for all the women and one in which they could more safely approach the other.

Where the Modjeska daughters reigned confident and unchallenged was in the kitchen. This had never been their mother's domain and perhaps they had forgiven the scorn with which she had once regarded all domestic tasks and those people who spent voluntary time on them.

For years it had been difficult for Mrs Modjeska to accept social engagements out but she continued to give lunch parties, gathering in old friends and the occasional new one. Angel and Consta would be busy for days buying and preparing elaborate food and throughout the party would be occupied serving, replenishing and clearing, accepting the inevitable fulsome praise with modest surprise, as though genuinely amazed by what they had produced and the pleasure it gave.

Mrs Modjeska presided over these gatherings from her centrally placed, straight-backed chair. Her once lovely Siamese cat, Wolfgang, would sit on her knee, staking out its place within the household in an ostentatiously possessive manner and yawning occasionally to show its contempt for the gathered company by displaying its ancient, gummy mouth.

Zoë made sure she was always free for these lunches. She was grateful that her years in Berlin, even among less conventional leftists, had prepared her for the formal manners and ritualized social interactions of Mrs Modjeska's older guests. Some of them were more comfortable speaking German than English and always, with a little patient probing, Zoë would discover a segment of a remarkable personal history, the central events of which had usually taken place before she was born.

There was a small, shifting band of other 'young friends' invited to the lunches and Zoë noted how they too stared at Imogen Modjeska, absurdly gratified when she shared a word or a joke especially with them. Zoë recognized that her wariness of the 'young friends' sprang directly from anxiety about her place in Mrs Modjeska's affections. Had she dared, she would have flung aside poor Wolfgang to climb onto Mrs Modjeska's knee herself.

As successive luncheons passed, Zoë allowed herself the pleasure of realizing that if out of eagerness to be polite she tried to leave with the first or even the last wave of guests, Mrs Modjeska would delay her until there was no one left but herself, Zoë, Angel and Consta. Mrs Modjeska would then be at her most relaxed and amusing, bringing together all the conversations and allusions which had crossed the room, even those an observer might have sworn had taken place out of her eye or earshot.

Whenever one of her parties was mooted Mrs Modjeska would gently remind Zoë she was welcome to bring a guest. Zoë considered Archie for this honour, if only to reward him for the hours of listening he gave to Zoë's stories about the Modjeska household. Yet much as she loved Archie, and as genuinely as she believed she would have done 'anything for him', Zoë kept silent. She wanted Mrs Modjeska separate from the rest of her life. She had no choice but to share her with those people who were already part of the Modjeska circle, but it wouldn't be Zoë who would enlarge that circle.

At a barely conscious level Zoë was recognizing that to some extent at least she was creating Mrs Modjeska in response to a need of her own which had been near to exploding when the two women met. There had been no precedent for Zoë in speaking as freely as she had done to a virtual stranger, but that trust she had placed in Mrs Modjeska had not been ill-judged.

Zoë understood that when she was alone with Mrs Modjeska she was struggling towards 'truth' and an understanding of the shifting planes of reality in a necessary but painfully stringent way. She was enabled to do this by something in the woman herself — a need perhaps to re-examine her own history by eliciting Zoë's — though most of all by the qualities of wisdom and acceptance, which Zoë had projected onto the willing screen of Mrs Modjeska's being.

Seven

Draped over the less uncomfortable of the two *chaises longues* in the Ladbroke Grove flat was a Victorian mourning shawl, lavishly embroidered in shiny silk thread on a heavy, matt silk background, black on black. It had been discovered by Zoë and Gabriel during one of Gabriel's visits to Zoë in London.

It was one of their honoured rituals that they spend some Saturday hours at the Portobello Market minutely examining and comparing the wares of favoured stalls with Zoë resisting for only so long Gabriel's seductive promptings to her to buy. Of the two, and thanks to her success at *Issues*, Zoë was considerably the better off. In the years since his return to Frankfurt Gabriel had secured a few lucrative hours teaching each week. Adding that to a trickle of industrial and civic commissions allowed him to fend off the day when he would have to work for money only. His material needs had remained modest but the income he did receive disappeared quickly. Claiming the need to leave his place of work which was also his home, he ate out most evenings, with Sonja, or with many other friends who included his former wife, Christa, now married to a rich and relatively progressive periodontist and mother to plump twin daughters. They ate in cheap Italian or Greek restaurants mostly, but even those cost money. And there was Stefan-Georg, who involuntarily aroused in Gabriel uncomfortable guilt and in a futile effort towards appeasement Gabriel would too often fill the time he spent with his son buying the young adolescent clothes or books much more costly than he could or would buy for himself.

In appearance as well as clothes Gabriel had barely changed since Zoë met him. It was in vain that she half hoped he might turn up at Victoria Station after a long night of cheap train and ferry travel wearing anything other than the brown leather jacket

310

which exactly matched his eyes. Like a Dorian Grey stand-in, the jacket became more and more battered while Gabriel himself exhibited little outward sign of stress or ageing.

Gabriel loved to shop vicariously and in this at least Zoë knew herself to be his perfect partner. Their forays to the markets were tacitly understood by them to be effective distraction from all they didn't search for together: things for a home to be shared.

In his way Gabriel had been true to his word that he'd be no less available to Zoë after becoming more formally involved with Sonja. But no more available either. Zoë made strenuous efforts to take his visits casually but regarded herself as only partially successful. There was a stern familiarity to the heightened sense of loss she carried. She had admitted to Mrs Modjeska her recognition that with the brief exception of her Berlin years, since the age of eight the focus of her emotional life had been outside her daily existence. She had a recurring image of herself as a Martian-like woman with vast antennae growing out of her head. On one side an antenna stretched across the English Channel over Belgium to Germany. On the other stretched an antenna beyond the material world entirely to wherever her mother's spirit waited. For quite what, Zoë could not have said.

Zoë and Gabriel had spotted the shawl early on one of their expeditions and they, or rather Zoë, had bought it at once, contrary to their usual practice of surveying their entire territory first, enjoying the gamble that a treasure might be lost to them.

There was a small tear in one corner of the shawl. Gabriel had been quick to notice it and had muttered to Zoë in German that she should offer less than the asking price. Zoë was surprised at his suggestion but understood it to convey a convoluted apology that he could not buy the beautiful garment for her himself, as he would have wished, but could only share the pleasures of discovery and purchase. Gabriel's spending fault was to pay over the odds, though finding something that was already a bargain was as much a game for him as for Zoë whose small room overflowed with Portobello recycles.

That bleak, damp Saturday they had returned home laden with food and wine for the household, as well as the shawl and a small lamp showing a coy woman offering a glimpse of light from behind the swish in her long, full skirt. Gabriel had immediately settled in to mend the shawl. Watching him an hour or so later when the job was still far from completed, Zoë had remarked after only a moment's hesitation that he was displaying more obvious pleasure in this handiwork than he used to do in the drawings for his sculptures. He let the remark pass, acknowledging it with a slight grin and apparently under no compulsion to analyse it.

Lying on the shawl, playing with its long tassles, wearing only an old dressing gown made for a large Edwardian gentleman with a penchant for soft expensive material, Zoë contemplated yet another crossroad in her life.

The flat was quiet. She was not tempted to breach the pleasure of silence even with music. Her day had begun early. Coming home late and somewhat distracted the night before she had forgotten to pull the blind in her room and so was woken by early morning sun, recalling at once that today was Saturday, the day of one of Mrs Modjeska's parties, and also that she was alone in the flat and would be until Monday as Archie had gone to Bath for the weekend to celebrate the completion of a full month's ecstatic excess with Boy Blue, his latest love.

She had got up, made tea and toast and returned to bed to read for some time before getting up again to have a long bath and then not getting dressed but putting on the old dressing gown, feeling excited somehow, unwilling yet to be restrained by clothes, anticipating she was not sure what but perhaps something beyond the imminent and undoubted pleasure she would receive from Mrs Modjeska's party.

Gabriel's most recent visit had been for a long weekend just a month ago. Since his departure Zoë had been aware that yet again he had acted as catalyst, accelerating a small battle within her between a need to try something new, and a desire that the relative peace of her life should not be endangered by the push of her familiar lust towards the unknown.

For months Zoë had been working her way through the writings of and about the Brontë sisters. She had begun by searching for some understanding of how those women dealt with the imminence, and presence, of death through – or was it while maintaining? – their creativity. The more she read and thought about them the more separate each woman became for her until her feelings for Charlotte and Anne were interested, respectful and tender, but for Emily were almost passionate. In her contemplation of Emily, she felt as though she were reaching towards significant clues about her own self which were alluring, and possibly dangerous.

With the diffidence of a wife about to confess to adulterous desires, Zoë had revealed to Gabriel her interest in Emily Brontë and only because their dinner together had been delicious, their conversation relaxed and because she had drunk a little too much red wine did she also confess there were elements in Emily's life which she might attempt to explore and illuminate through something like a novel. She had laughed then and emptied her glass too quickly, uncomfortable with memories of Gabriel's scorn for her earlier passions and his damning of her insistence that there were many ways in which, to borrow Mao's phrase beloved of the sixties revolution, the past could serve the present.

But Gabriel hadn't been scornful. If anything he had been too insistent on what a marvellous idea it was, really just the thing, Zoë, and his voice had warmed as it carried to her his witty views on women writers in general and on the Brontës in particular, and on mystic writers of whom Emily Brontë was obviously one . . . but there was also, she thought she heard him say, the almost cruel super-realism of the characters in *Wuthering Heights* to be considered, as well as the double-edged power of exaggeration coming from an undoubtedly brilliant but perhaps somewhat *hectic* mind which must imagine everything, having experienced nothing. At which point Zoë realized she was a little dizzy and even while stressing how interesting she found Gabriel's comments and helpful too, she was getting up and leaving the table and making her way through the restaurant to the ladies where she sat on the lavatory seat, hunched into her body to prevent the anger within her from beginning to rise. And as she hunched the old fog began to wrap her in its clammy tendrils, settling her into the familiar state of hopelessness which she had believed she had left behind: that whatever she knew Gabriel would know more and better, and that whatever she might try it would be pale and imitative next to the gleam of his genuine originality.

In bending towards her subject matter with such erudition and enthusiasm, Gabriel was casting a shadow, creating shade in which her delicate idea could not grow.

Sitting in the cubicle, dully acknowledging the nearby sound of a chain being pulled, water flushing, a door banging, Zoë saw herself scrunched up like a piece of paper on which a partial message has been written, already discarded and heading for the bin.

She regarded this image for some moments before dismissing it. Then she got up, left the cubicle, carefully washed her hands and face and after a nod of resignation towards the mirror she returned to the table where Gabriel was waiting in a state of increasing bewilderment and concern. Zoë lit one of his cigarettes, looked down at the table which she noticed was covered with a linen cloth almost exactly the yellow of a dying gardenia, and then spoke.

'Actually, Gabriel, I think you're wrong about Emily. About what she experienced I mean.' She looked up at him. 'Or at least, you mustn't be too conventional in your use of that word *experience*. In my view her translation of experience into art was almost singularly direct because of the way she'd protected her unconscious life and even more, her sense of self, of who she essentially was, from childhood through to maturity. We can safely assume, I think, that her childhood was emotionally and erotically rich. And what you should understand is that her childhood grew with her; she never abandoned it.'

'I'm not sure that I follow you. Her masterpiece wasn't the work of a child.'

'Of course not. The point is though that the characters she created as a child for her Gondal poems grew with her. They're there in *Wuthering Heights*, born from Emily's voices and able to grow because she nurtured them. It's probable that all children hear voices but few adults have even a memory of that.'

'And you think there's something particularly significant about those childhood voices?'

'Not automatically.' Zoë took a deep breath. 'What I'm talking about is the honouring of something which comes from within, which isn't dictated from outside, which is, in perhaps quite a literal sense, true to the person's being. But let me go on. Maybe it'll then make more sense.'

314

'Of course, of course. I'm most curious.'

Zoë paused briefly, and frowned. 'It's her courage too. That amazes me. Well, actually it inspires me and I need all the inspiration I can find. She seems to have been unafraid of death in any conventional sense because for her death was possibly the culminating purpose of life. Not in the Christian mode of moving through this vale of tears to eventual heavenly rewards, but as a means to discard the constraints between herself and nature. Or maybe as a means to unite with the extreme passions of the natural world which she understood perfectly well, and had *experienced*.' Zoë allowed herself to smile. 'All that was quite contrary of course to the Christian insistence on separation which she must, as a clergyman's daughter, have been aware of, but was able to ignore, or anyway set aside.'

'And this desire for unity, is that something you experience too, Zoë? I'd not ever thought of you seeking communion with nature.'

'And you needn't start now. Though the longing for unity . . . somehow that, yes.'

The waiter arrived to take their order for coffee. As he moved away Zoë began again. 'What's astonishingly sad – at least to me it is, yet utterly consistent with a drive for privacy throughout her life which must have been necessary to protect this inner or essential self – is that publication may have killed her.'

Gabriel lifted one eyebrow, involuntarily. Zoë coloured.

'You must let me finish, and do bear in mind that I'm making the great mistake of airing thoughts that are new to me too. Emily knew the calibre of her work. I'm sure of that, and she knew that eventually it would be published. But that her *poems*, the very markings of her soul, should be made public at a time determined by Charlotte – who was much more conventional and comprehensible than Emily – apparently stultified her. Perhaps her voices left her, or anyway quietened to a whisper, and for someone who'd been hearing them at full blast all her life that would have been enough to make her feel half dead at least. It's that visionary force within that she addresses with such love in her poetry – and with such confidence in its staying power. It could make you weep because she apparently wrote almost nothing in the year following the publication of her poems and *Wuthering Heights*. Within two months of becoming ill, with TB — oh *great* surprise — she was dead. Aged thirty. She allowed it in, the TB I mean, after the death of her brother. Really, the pathos is frightful. There was Bramwell unable to go on living because he'd failed to find fame or even publication, and there was Emily, experiencing just those things — fame and publication — as bringing only the useless judgements of a world that was quite meaningless to her.'

Zoë's face was flushed with emotion. 'She was stubborn to the end, refusing medical help, refusing to stay in bed, insisting on feeding the dogs, even on the day she died. And one could say, oh what a waste, or, oh how tragic. Or one could say, this was a woman who was true to herself and was utterly self-determined.

'Virginia Woolf said she was heroic, not tragic. I agree with that.'

Gabriel smiled, and interjected. 'I'm sure Virginia Woolf would be very happy to have your agreement, Zoë.'

Before Zoë could respond Gabriel was speaking again. 'I'm struck by two things at least. The first is that there seems to be a pattern of sorts in the women outside your own life with whom you become intellectually engaged. Either they died early, or were terribly ill, or somehow death was a *leitmotif* within their life or work.

'The second point is that when I hear you talk about one of these women, tonight it's Emily Brontë and yesterday it might have been Katherine Mansfield or indeed Virginia Woolf, I'm certainly hearing you talk about them and I *am* interested in what you've got to say, but at the same time I'm hearing you talk about yourself. Am I right, Zoë?'

Her first reaction was to rush to her own defence. Surely she was being accused of something? But in her anxiety she could not immediately locate her fault and the moment's pause allowed her to say, 'So what?' She smiled broadly then, even flirtatiously.

'If that's an accusation then I plead guilty because surely we're all talking about ourselves all the time?'

Gabriel frowned. 'I wasn't in fact accusing you, Zoë . . . but talking about ourselves, I don't understand.'

'Our obsessions, passions, hobbies, call them whatever you like, surely they reveal us? And no less when they're a so-called objective area of interest. Why, after all, does one person choose God and another money?'

'There are specific material conditions . . .'

Zoë waved his words away. 'I know all that. Hang on a minute. We're talking about large strokes on a canvas, a sketch done with a house paint brush, crude clues only, but clues nevertheless.'

'Go back a bit.'

'Okay. Here we have two people. One is obsessed, let us say, with God. But who is her God? Which description or understanding of God does she latch onto? Here is the other person, obsessed, shall we say, with literature. But is it metaphysical poetry, or science fiction, or Carter Brown? Look, all I'm trying to say is that these things reveal something about how the person is asking their "meaning of life" questions, or avoiding them.'

Gabriel regarded Zoë closely. Had the evening really been saved, or must he continue to brace himself for painful accusations, caused no doubt by his own stupidity, but nevertheless. But Zoë was definitely smiling, was apparently quite buoyant as she lit another of his cigarettes, though this time not for herself but for him.

With an inward breath of relief Gabriel said, 'You're right, Zoë. "So what" indeed. This Emily Brontë business . . .'

'Is my business. But if it does come to anything I promise you'll be the first to know. But until then, silence! beloved comrade.' She laughed.

From across the table Gabriel leaned forward to take her hand, lift it to his lips and kiss it. 'Allow me to salute you, Zoë.'

The gesture was barely appropriate and probably patronizing. Zoë was aware of this and also aware that there had been an important shift in their interaction which she had orchestrated and with which he had entirely co-operated. She could afford to be generous. And besides, she loved him.

Archie's grandfather clock chimed with all the weight of its many years. Zoë turned to look at it and automatically added on the necessary twenty minutes. She had reached no conclusions during her hour of contemplation and was already late to begin her preparations for the Modjeska lunch.

Zoë earned enough money at *Issues* to buy expensive, flattering versions of the 1970s feminist uniform: designer jeans, pleated trousers in linen or wool, silk shirts, hand-knitted cardigans, severely tailored or velvety-soft leather jackets, occasional hats. She chose dramatic colours or wore the clothes in combinations that saved them from simple good taste. It was only for Mrs Modjeska that she wore dresses. Observing the delight these brought the older woman she scoured the markets for beautiful garments of the '30s and '40s which would amuse Mrs Modjeska, and make her exclaim what a loss it was she hadn't saved the many clothes abandoned over the years as fashions changed. Zoë never pointed out how hopeless it would have been for her to attempt to squeeze into the almost child-sized garments Mrs Modjeska must have worn, but she used her ingenuity to perfect each outfit, adding amusing accessories which might elicit a memory or a story.

Today Zoë wanted to present herself with special care. This was the lunch at which Claudine Denizet was to be guest of honour, though it was not this which was inspiring her but the eagerness she remembered in Mrs Modjeska's voice on the phone a few days earlier when she had laughed and told Zoë that she and the girls had been speculating as to how Zoë might surprise them this time.

Zoë chose to wear a black silk 1940s dress. Heavy cream embroidery framed the yoke down either side of a row of tiny, self-covered buttons. Padded shoulders flattered Zoë's figure, shrinking her hips as the dress fell to mid-calf, emphasizing the grace of her height. Over the dress Zoë slung a brightly embroidered short black jacket. On her feet she strapped black high-heeled shoes. Beneath the dress and a frail, silk petticoat, her seamed stockings were held up by a soft suspender belt.

In Archie's absence Zoë had to rely on the long mirror behind her door to tell her she was looking unusually smart, if somewhat consciously over-dramatic. She added an unplanned hat, no more than a small felt circle which sat on top of her dark curls and from which a black coarse-net veil fell, its symmetry broken by occasional sequins which mirrored the dark mauve beauty spot Zoë drew on her upper left cheek.

The sitting-room was already full when she arrived. She paused briefly at the door before going to kiss Mrs Modjeska, rewarded for her efforts by the approval and amusement in Mrs Modjeska's face as she evaluated the effect of Zoë's appearance.

'Zoë! You look marvellous, darling. How do you do it? Such a busy girl and still a new surprise every time! That hat too – it's quite perfect.'

Zoë laughed and kissed her again, enjoying the intimate smell of Mrs Modjeska's old skin and expensive perfume. Then she turned to look for Consta and Angel, and other familiar faces she should greet. As she turned she noticed a woman of about her own age pausing in conversation and staring at her. From behind her she heard Mrs Modjeska's raised voice saying, 'Zoë, I want you to meet Claudine Denizet, the daughter of my old friends Michel-Paul Denizet and Nadine Catusse, and of course a most celebrated artist in her own right.'

Zoë straightened up. On her high heels she was at least nine feet tall. The woman moving towards her was of *almost* average height but carried herself with the kind of self-assurance that let Zoë know she'd need to lean forward, sag at the knees, do anything to avoid the possibility that her height may make this woman feel small.

Claudine's face was porcelain fair. Her dark eyes looked borrowed in such pale surroundings. She had straight hair cut into a bob which would surely be full and free-swinging moments after she left the shower. Zoë hadn't seen anyone look this clean since she'd waved good-bye and found a genuine tear for Frank Gapes when he was released at last from the service of his country and the ingratitude of the German people.

The clothes Claudine wore were also pale, and expensive and understated. They could have been ordered by the dozen and were just the kind of clothes Zoë most disliked. Their effect, on Claudine, was as if she had 'lesbian' tattooed stylishly and unmistakably across her forehead. Zoë couldn't have defined what it was. Perhaps the collar of her silk shirt slightly raised beneath the matching cashmere sweater tied loosely over her shoulders? Perhaps the small gold chain, tight at her neck; or the single seed pearl in her left earlobe? Perhaps it wasn't her clothes at all but the way she tapped her cigarette lighter on her packet of Disque Bleu as she held Zoë's gaze longer than could be considered polite? Yet hundreds of women might have worn those clothes or used those gestures without investing them with the sexual presence which was causing Zoë to have urgent need of a place to sit down.

'Should we sit over there, by the wall?' Zoë indicated a pile of plump cushions stacked against a tiny section of bare wall and obviously intended for the younger, more supple guests.

'Why not?' The woman looked amused. She had noticed, though Zoë had not, their lack of customary greetings.

Zoë *had* noticed, even over those two brief words, Claudine's French accent. She was scratching at her brain like a chicken in the dust. 'Are you French?' was the cliché she found.

'Hell no, I'm a colonial like you.' Claudine was smiling as she folded herself into a relaxed, cross-legged pose. Zoë hated sitting on the floor. She was trying hard to disguise her discomfort when she heard Claudine say, 'I know all about you, you see. Mrs Modjeska's done nothing but talk of you since I got here last week. I've been wild with jealousy and ready to hate you. I might yet!'

Zoë glanced at her and blushed, remembered her veil and was thankful for it but gratified too, not only by Claudine's overt interest in her but even more by the news that Mrs Modjeska found her a worthwhile subject of conversation. 'Where are you from then?' she asked, listening to Claudine's answer even while she accepted a glass from Angel with a smile and a nod.

'Quebec. Montreal mostly. I've lived in Europe a good while like you have, but as Canada's that much nearer than New Zealand I'm able to go home fairly often, which I gather you're not? Our family's real close and I miss them. Also the Canadian government played money daddy to me for years and I feel I owe them. I go back to teach a little when they're desperate and give concerts there from time to time too. I play the fiddle.'

'Oh? Hey diddle diddle. *Miaow.*' Zoë remembered Rebecca. And giggled. Claudine was laughing too. Any awkwardness between them evaporated as both women's minds flashed to a single image of an unfortunate cow eternally suspended over the moon.

Zoë knew Claudine was a violinist. Mrs Modjeska had talked of Claudine also, of her super-refined gifts for interpretation and of her own compositions which were getting an enthusiastic response from the cognoscenti of the music world. What Mrs Modjeska hadn't told Zoë was that Claudine was beautiful and, even better, funny. Nor that Claudine was a lesbian. Or was she?

'How long will you be staying in London?'

'Long enough.' Claudine gave Zoë another impossibly meaningful stare. Zoë sank deeper into the feather pillow of her confusion. Claudine was astonishingly direct, but it could mean anything. What *had* Mrs Modjeska told her?

Claudine began again, her voice now marginally more serious. 'Really I'm here to learn, which is a treat beyond description when I'm forced to maintain the dubious authority of performer most of the rest of the year. An old teacher of mine lives here and she's sweet enough to let me return to her every now and then. As a matter of fact she's the person who got me together with Mrs Modjeska, though it turned out Mrs M. knew my parents years ago. They're singers. Well, he is and she was.' Claudine pulled a face. 'I'm likely to do some recording work while I'm here too so I guess I'll stay put about five weeks in all. Then the crazy balloon of my life fills with hot air and carts me off with it, first stop Tokyo. But I'm not even going to think about that yet. It's luxury enough to stay in one spot this long, I tell ya!'

Zoë's eyes were transfixed by Claudine's mouth. She'd not seen one like it since the last late-night screening of a Jeanne Moreau movie. It was apparently constantly in motion even when Claudine wasn't speaking and was the single feature on that lovely face which was not neat, and under control.

'Do you know London well? Where are you staying?'

'I guess as well as anyone might who's not actually lived here. I'm a pretty diligent tourist within the limits of my schedules. I've managed to discover the Gateways Club, for example.' Claudine named Chelsea's famous, scruffy lesbian bar. Zoë ignored this, or tried to, and repeated her second question.

'And you're staying?'

'In Hampstead.' Claudine darted Zoë a look of pure mischief. Zoë touched her veil, for luck. 'I've been lent a small studio flat there, right in the Village. It's up high and has huge windows which look out over the Heath. But you'll come visit won't you? I know very few people here who're not musicians and really we can be a hopelessly insular profession, talking of nothing but acoustics and fees and practically sleeping in rubber gloves.' She laughed. Zoë stared. Once again Claudine's tone changed. 'But I understand you write, Zoë. And have had poetry published?'

'My my, Mrs Modjeska *has* been talking! I'm a very mediocre poet and that's on my best days. No, that's just for fun, or more accurately as it's rarely fun, for private contemplation. But I've become a fair sort of journalist. I work for a glossy monthly which pretty unusually is aimed at both sexes. I write at least one long piece each month which has me frantic. You probably know the routine? Hours of slog and despair in exchange for a transitory moment of pleasure when the damn thing's finally done. Sometimes I wonder if I've developed a weird addiction to that kind of torment as I do notice that I try harder things with no particular feeling of virtue about that, but in response to a kind of compulsion.'

'That I can relate to! In my next life I've promised myself to be a beach bum, or a slug, or maybe a comptemplative. I've often suspected that those glorious hours in prayer could be a chance for many a long zizz. You're not a Catholic are you?'

'No. But I was. And you?'

'What else? It's not the fear of God they put in you as much as the fear of sloth! I've made a most unscientific survey and have come to the conviction that obsessives are all Catholics or Jews, haunted constantly and driven incessantly. Forget the Protestant work ethic. It pales in comparison!'

'I agree, though don't carry out too much of your research in the Mediterranean countries or your theory may get blown! Though you'd find lavish support there for the other favourite legacy of a Catholic childhood: heads constantly weighing up good against evil, making bets with God and laying off the Devil, and haunted by ghosts and creepy stories of the living dead.'

'Don't bring it back to me! Enough, enough already!' Claudine put her hands over her ears, 'Tell me what you write about. I'm keen to know that.'

'Oh, a whole heap of things: literary articles, interviews, some-times pieces on art — and they're not averse to a little feminist band-wagoning either. Within limits of course. It's an ideal place for me to work, though I'm still not sure that London's an ideal place for me to be. I lived in Berlin for some time, but I'm not sure about that either.' Her tone brightened. 'Still, while I *am* in London I'll certainly stay at *Issues* — that's what the magazine's called.' Zoë looked into Claudine's eyes, avoiding her mouth. 'I've even harboured notions that I'd like to be editor there, though that would mean doing without the chap who is, and I like him a great deal.'

There was a second's pause before Zoë went on to say, 'He's gay too.'

The Jeanne Moreau mouth stretched wider and wider. 'Well! That's a relief. Now I can drop my heavy-handed probing. I must confess doubts had begun to creep in that maybe I'd misunderstood Mrs Modjeska's marvellously discreet hints that you and I would get along together *terribly well*. Especially when I saw re-incarnated Rita Hayworth being hailed as the wondrous Zoë.'

Zoë's heart was beating fast. She was returned to an image of herself as a wild river, threatening to burst its banks, but sitting neatly on those banks as the water races towards them is a pair of shoes, side by side, abandoned there by Gabriel as he turned to run. To escape the flood. She felt like a river again, rushing towards the ocean, tumbling over stones without feeling the bumps, taking the light of the sun into herself, gleaming it back. The banks were high on either side of her, not keeping her in but keeping her safe. They were boundaries of her own size — and choosing. Or not boundaries at all. Perhaps arms to embrace her? Words came to her from a dream. *'Don't push the river. You are the river.'* Five weeks. And then she would be left. If only she could dare. The words went on, like an ancient chorus singing in her ears. *'You are not the stone over which the river flows. You are the river.'* The words faded. Claudine's voice was taking their place. She listened not to what Claudine was saying, but to the tone. It was warm, confiding, bright and alive. It was embracing. The river was life-giving. Zoë's attention focused.

'Please don't get me wrong. Your outfit's adorable and come to that, and it often did, Rita Hayworth gave me some pretty delightful moments in the privacy of my adolescent bed. It's just that it's quite unexpected in these days of hairy legs and baggy overalls among the sisterhood. I assumed you were going to be capital 'S' for serious as well as capital 'C' for creative. I'm glad to find . . .' she held the pause, and Zoë's attention, ' . . . I guess I'm glad to find you are as you are. If that makes any sense?'

Claudine laughed, at herself and at her own good humour. She took Zoë's glass, her hand skimming Zoë's as she did so. 'Let me get you a drink.' She bounded up with enviable grace then looked down at Zoë who continued to lean across the cushions on the floor. 'It all simply goes to show that one must never think in clichés. Even within the private sanctuary of one's own tiny mind.'

Eight

Zoë's face is buried in Claudine's neck. She is pressed closely against her. Claudine lies on her back, Zoë on her side. Their hearts warm up as though for a race. But there'll be no loser.

Their skin brightens with the glow of sex. Zoë's mind crowds with thoughts even while she's adrift with feelings: Can I please her? Does she really want this? Will she want me afterwards? How can it be special enough that she'll want me here, at her side, forever?

Zoë kisses Claudine, small nervous kisses on her throat, then longer ones, pushing into and sucking back from her skin. Her mouth takes its measure. She moves her body up a little. Some of her weight goes down on Claudine. As her mouth moves to make a trail of tiny kisses towards Claudine's open mouth, Claudine shifts slightly on the mattress. There is a sound outside. It's birds calling to each other: nature defying the constraints of the city. They laugh at the noise, then it disappears from their consciousness as they turn back to each other. Claudine's legs move apart, her left knee bends, her right leg is stretched to press hard against Zoë's. Her body asks Zoë to lie on top of her. Still slowly kissing her, soft and then hard against her wide open wonderful mouth, her tongue rubbing against Claudine's, biting, bumping against her teeth, Zoë moves to lie above Claudine. Her weight is on her elbows. Her left hand holds the crown of Claudine's head to guard that vulnerable place where feelings might escape or fears might enter.

With her hand Zoë touches the side of Claudine's face, soft lovely skin, no roughness, then she shapes that face, brailling it to remember always. She looks down as she strokes and watches Claudine run her tongue around her lips as though searching for Zoë who can see the fine glitter of sweat as Claudine's body continues to heat and can see how tenderly her dark lashes lie on her cheeks, and how her body arches to find more of Zoë. Along the length of their bodies Zoë feels Claudine drawing her in. She knows Claudine wants her hand to travel down her body faster faster, but Zoë reaches interminably slowly down her neck and past her shoulders towards Claudine's breasts and as her hand circles Claudine's shoulders, Zoë presses down to kiss her again. Claudine's tongue is high against the roof of Zoë's mouth, and still Claudine is pushing up from beneath. They are high on a cloud above a volcano. There's power in the air. They are dizzy with it.

Zoë moves away from Claudine's mouth although Claudine momentarily whimpers with loss as Zoë raises herself again on her elbows so it is not her hand that touches Claudine's breast but her mouth, wet from kissing. Her tongue moves back and forth, gentle sandpaper, each time a little nearer but not yet reaching the waiting nipple. She is every mother's child, nestling, nuzzling, nursing. She is Alice passed through the mirror. Her tongue moves to Claudine's armpit. She buries her nose and her mouth there, licks at the sweet sweat, until Zoë wants that nipple in her mouth and can't wait even while her tongue sweeps a final time across Claudine's breast and her mouth closes over the nipple and she sucks and sucks and then plays with it, plays with her memories of it, her tongue making circles around its edge as the small nipple hardens and Claudine calls her name and her body moves with the calling.

No questions clutter Zoë's mind. She has no consciousness of anything but Claudine and the exhilaration of her own self entirely present in this moment. Masks fall to the floor but their arrival there is muffled in the roar as through their locked mouths as Zoë returns to Claudine's face they tell each other how good, how strong, how tender this is. Two women opening wide to each other.

Claudine's head falls back. She cries out, 'Zoë, fuck me, Zoë.' Zoë is shocked to hear her ask like that but almost at once is not shocked at all but delighted and more excited and clear too that she's not ready yet and that Claudine will wait, will have to wait and will even love the waiting as they make an ancient journey across mutual passion.

Zoë stretches her arm to run her fingers up and down the insides of Claudine's thighs, scratching her, leaving red marks to show where she's been but knowing exactly what will not hurt Claudine and Claudine moves her legs wider apart as Zoë whispers to her, describing her wanting and her pleasure.

She is tickling her with words, teasing her, tormenting her, but they are not enough, not even in litany. Zoë feels her mouth drawn back to Claudine's. She moves her tongue as her hand moves closer to Claudine's labia, circling and stroking until she cups the neat shape of Claudine's pubic bone and Claudine twists her head away from their kisses to plead, 'Now, Zoë, now.' Then, as slowly as she dares, Zoë slides her middle finger down to part Claudine's pubic hair, caressing her clitoris as she passes it, slowly, to bend her fingers and, at last, to go deep inside Claudine, to slide in, loving it, loving her. Her hand finds its rhythms as Claudine shakes and sighs and cries out to God and so does Zoë in silent exultation knowing that her hand is amazing, delicate, sensitive, strong; is all and exactly what Claudine wants. Her fingers continue to move and her breathing guides her as her thumb bends, circles, passes and circles her clitoris, rhythm above matching rhythm beneath, memories of moon and tide changes stirring within her, unnamed, deeply felt. Her hand is soaked. Her own vagina is as wet. She remembers a single word: unity, and her desire to understand it. Zoë wants to kiss Claudine all over, wants a thousand hands and mouths, wants to be a millipede but, a snail instead, she crawls down Claudine leaving a shiny snail-trail of wet licks, tiny sucks, small kisses.

And when Zoë has slid all the way down the bed and her legs hang way over its end, she rests her head against Claudine's pelvis, gathering strength there though she's never felt so strong, breathing in the moment, breathing out her desire to return to the oceanlike salinity of the womb.

Zoë becomes aware of Claudine's moans and of Claudine's hand stroking the crown of her head. She is urging Zoë towards her clitoris, to push past the guarding pubic hair until Zoë's tongue moves against it in a rhythm to match her fingers inside Claudine where Zoë can feel the walls of her vagina changing in texture as they move in towards her, tighten, flood, then seem almost to dry out as, incredibly, Claudine's excitement continues to grow. She is in the whirlpool. The centre is very near. It is no longer Zoë's name that Claudine calls, nor that of God, but little wordless whimpers of pleasure, need, delight. Then around Zoë's finger she tenses and tightens. Zoë mustn't change her rhythm though she longs now to plunge. When Claudine begins to shake, to cry, Zoë holds herself steady. Claudine continues to come, circle after circle, then still more, and again. She is diving. The centre of the whirpool is vast. She is diving and still not surfacing. She floods Zoë's hands and now does call her name, telling her how good, how amazing, how loving she is. Then, as gradually she quietens, her hand again moves to Zoë's head, this time to pull her up, gently, until their faces meet to kiss, to take in the smell, the taste, the triumph of love.

Zoë is flying. She is Icarus, but unlike Icarus her wings are self-made and won't melt. She is completely alive, is turned on and turned out towards Claudine, her nerve endings tingling, alive with electricity she wonders that Claudine doesn't die of shock just to touch her. She is wholly present. Yet it is every moment of her past – good and bad, extraordinary and ordinary – which has brought her to this moment, which has allowed her this moment. There are no frogs, no princesses in the bed with them; no Sleeping Beauties, no princes gathering to haunt her; beneath their feather mattress no hard pea lies. There is Claudine, lying so close to Zoë that each could be breathing for the other.

Claudine slides one hand between Zoë's thighs. Zoë slows her breathing to postpone the orgasm which threatens even as Claudine's fingers begin their discovery. Claudine is whispering Zoë's name and telling her again and again in English and in French how much she wants her, while she strokes sliding and gliding until Zoë cannot tell how her fingers move. There is only sensation. She's lost, found, carried along, forging her own way, bursting larger and larger into life from a centre which is the place where Claudine's touching her and from this place Zoë can no longer push away her orgasm. She is coming, arriving, going beyond herself as she shakes and shouts into Claudine's mouth. There is a great shifting and heaving deep inside her: emotions emerging from long entombment.

While Zoë shudders, cries and shakes, Claudine rocks her and kisses her and whispers to her until Zoë is quiet. Until Claudine knows that Zoë is at peace.

They lie together, arms and legs entwined, their breathing gradually slowing. They are too tired or stunned to kiss. When the sweat is dry on their bodies and they begin to draw in against the cold, Claudine moves away from Zoë to hang over the edge of the bed and rescue the duvet from where they'd kicked it to the floor. She shakes it, then places it over them both. They lie on their backs. Only their hands touch. Their eyes are closed.

Zoë is completely happy.

It begins to grow dark. She is not afraid.

Nine

On a clear autumn day more people than usual were attracted to the largely uncultivated acres of Hampstead Heath, above crowded London.

Zoë and Claudine were barely aware of them. They sat with their backs turned towards the public paths, on carefully folded Sunday newspapers to protect them from the slight damp of the long grass. Beneath the woollen scarf Claudine had thrown over their knees they held hands as they huddled together.

'I'm walking towards a large area of ground which I know is an image for my life.'

Zoë's voice was quiet and Claudine stilled her breath to catch all that Zoë was saying.

'The ground's laid out in an entirely harmonious way, and that pleases me. The grass is smooth and that miraculous even green you find only in England. Neat paths radiate outwards with a sense of purpose. The plants and shrubs are flowering profusely and occasional artificial structures like statues or fountains seem to enhance a sense of "contained nature".'

'It sounds wonderful! Maybe you're glimpsing heaven? Zoë darling, could it be that I'm at last in the company of a holy mystic?'

'Wait for the next bit before deciding – and don't go placing any bets! Because when I'm actually *in* the garden, standing where I've just seen those orderly paths and pampered lawns, I begin to realize that I've lost sight of the controlled splendour and what I'm actually walking on is rough ground, newly turned, dug up and ready for planting with that lovely smell good earth has, but it's so far from the atmosphere of intense, *achieved* cultivation of the first part of the dream I could weep for sheer frustration at all that remains to be done. And my own misgivings as I face that. The earth's rich and alive, or at least eager to produce life. But in no way is it settled, or

330

ready for that glorious backward-sweeping appraisal which the first garden – the apparent mirage – invited. Does this all sound terribly weird?'

'Since when did you have a down on weird?' Claudine smiled. 'No. It doesn't, and even if it did? Go on, Zoë, you've stranded me in the mud.'

'Well, there's another level too to the dream. This time there are scarecrow-like figures in the formal garden which oddly enough are not incongruous with that highly cultivated sophistication. In this version the earth also eventually reveals itself as ready for planting rather than planted, but the scarecrows remain and when I wander among them, apparently unrecognized by them, I can see they're people from my life, though mostly people I left behind in New Zealand. My father James is there, and his wife Caroline, and I'm aware that when I look at them I've got to look up. They loom over me in that distorted way an adult must appear to loom over a child. I don't need to be Mrs Freud to conclude that my perceptions of them – and judgements too probably – are more appropriate to a child than to a woman pushing towards her mid-life crisis.' Zoë laughed as she moved slightly away from Claudine to watch her face more easily.

'Rebecca's there, often several times over at different ages, and her two young daughters whom I've never actually seen. Maria, who was my mother's best friend, is occasionally there though my mother never is. And I do search for her. I know that. Sometimes people from what I'd call my "real life" are interspersed among them: Gabriel, or Archie, or Mrs Modjeska, or Sibylla, or even some totally unexpected person whom I've never regarded as particularly significant but who fits in nevertheless.'

She paused before asking, 'Do you remember my telling you about the woman-of-many-faces from my other recurring dream?'

'Sure I do.'

'She steps into this dream too, though not as a scarecrow, more as a presence, with me in a non-physical way, pretty much as I sense her with me most of the time.'

'Why are you laughing?'

'I'm not. Well, yes I am. Maybe I'm beginning to resemble Joan of Arc! Any moment now I'll begin telling you what my voices are directing me towards. Beware the mutter of voices, Claudine. Beware the smell of smoke.'

Across Zoë's mind flashed a comic-book image of an armoured Zoë de Lighty leading hymn-singing troops into righteous battle, accompanied by a band which sounded suspiciously like the Salvation Army. She laughed again. Then she withdrew her hand from inside Claudine's and rubbed both hands over her face, hiding her eyes for some moments.

'I know I've got to go back to New Zealand, if only to bury the dead. Not only Jane, but whatever part of me cannot leave her in peace. I pursue her like a dervish and she who runs fast in circles must miss much else along the path. That's a saying from the wise old women, Claudine.'

'Mmm,' Claudine reached for Zoë's hand and once more tucked it into her own. 'Have you any idea what "leaving her in peace" would mean?'

Zoë was startled by the question.

'Not much. But surely at the very least I'd have more peace? Is it that the abandoned child would be placated? Anyway, I'd not be hanging on to the coat tails of memories, I'd just have those memories. Safe and sound. My memories serve me as a kind of measuring stick, an ideal I see no reason to avoid trying to live up to; a quality of love I'm determined to maintain. But those memories are also a barrier. To be free of longing for her — that would be something. Peace for me, and, who knows, for her too? Can you *imagine* the anguish of knowing you're dying and leaving your kids behind? It's insupportable. No wonder Rebecca spreads her feathers over her two like the proverbial Mother Hen.

'I've also clearly got to come to terms with Rebecca, and with James, though it's hard for me to imagine stepping into the land of the daddies which that'd entail. Of the two, Rebecca's obviously foremost in my mind. Despite all that intimacy which existed between us we've managed to live on opposite sides of the world for more than ten years leading quite separate adult lives and, I suspect, quite different ones. We do still hold onto something and I hope it's more than sentimental candle-burning for Jane. But listening to you talk about your family I've realized the extent to which Rebecca's joined Jane as a myth in my life, constantly being refigured, but only as *my* perceptions change. I've envied the relationships you've described. Their messiness and the fights and tensions, as well as the jokes and the warmth, are obviously part of facing the *reality* of another person – not my strongest suit to date.'

Claudine interrupted her. 'You've been present enough these last weeks, or if that was your ghost then get her an agent right away!'

Zoë kissed Claudine on the cheek. 'It was all in the inspiration.' She sat back. 'It might have been easier if Rebecca had come to Europe and we'd seen each other on territory that was free from childhood memories. But the one time that was possible I put her off. It was the hideous year Gabriel left me to go back to Frankfurt and I felt ashamed somehow. I'd gloated to her what a brilliant person he is and I couldn't stop picking at the suspicion that she might see him as clever enough to have got out. I thought she'd pity me, so I made some feeble excuse and she withdrew with such speed I guess she was really nervous about seeing me too.'

Behind them came the high-pitched wail of a child. 'Katy, leave my kite alone, leave it alone.' Claudine and Zoë watched as cruel Katy ran laughing down the slope, dragging the kite with her and awkwardly pursued by a much younger brother, close to tears.

'There you have it, sibling love in living colour!' Claudine smiled. 'But I'd not be without my lot for the world and with every word you've said about her I get more sense of what a giant Rebecca is in your imagination.' She hesitated. 'Actually, that could be the problem, Zoë. Who needs a giant when you could discover a comfortably normal-sized sister? I'd say, jump in, go find her. You can't find Jane now. But Rebecca's only a plane ride away.'

'I *am* closer to going back there, but after all these years it doesn't become easier. Am I a hopeless coward do you think?'

'Listen. I remember a real bad year I had when one of my sisters had got it into her skull that my lesbianism had caused Mom to be ill. She's got chronic arthritis and Celeste, who's one sister down from me, wrote me some pretty vile letters full of accusations. I was stuck in Paris for the year and all this went on and on until I could get back and she could see me, Claudine, her sister, not the Figment Dyke of popular imagination. And then, of course, she was able to get back her sense of proportion and recognize that Mom'd had arthritis for years, that our house has always been full of darling queens, and that Mom was far from unhappy about little Claudine, lesbian or not.'

Claudine paused. 'Do you get my message?'

'Maybe.' Zoë pulled a face.

'Good, because there's more. And I'd hate you to lag behind.'

'Okay. Break it to me.'

'That poem you wrote, the one about the water running in rivers and creeks across New Zealand, dissecting the islands but also connecting them to the ocean . . .'

'I know, it doesn't rhyme.'

'Rhyme, slime. What I'm interested in saying if only I could get the chance is that when I read it, it felt to me like you were evoking a place where a good deal of change and movement is possible. You weren't describing a static stage set only fit for tragedies.'

Again Claudine paused, as though slumped into uncharacteristic caution. 'Zoë, have you considered doing some therapy? There seems to be such a bonfire inside you. You send out puffs of smoke and they're certainly signals but I can't always tell what to make of these wisps.'

With a startling bound Zoë leapt up to kneel in front of Claudine, baring her teeth and roaring in imitation of a wild beast. Then she put one hand to either side of her head and rolled her eyes, shouting, 'See no evil, hear no evil, speak no evil!'

Leaving Claudine sitting and staring after her in considerable bewilderment, Zoë danced towards the nearest large tree, disappearing entirely behind its trunk before putting first one leg out, then a hand, then an arm, then her head, though withdrawing that almost at once, before beginning the nonsensical process all over again, this time augmented with even louder roars.

'Hey you fruitcake, come back here won't you? What in hell are you doing to me now?' Claudine was laughing at Zoë's antics but she was also concerned, and not only for Zoë. She was committed to leave London in less than a week and wouldn't be able to return for more than an occasional weekend for many months. It had been a long time since Claudine had wished to open herself in ways which had seemed simple and inevitable with Zoë. The imminent separation would, she knew, draw on all her inner reserves.

With the onset of rationality Claudine had understood she loved women. Indeed, despite her respect and love for her own sisters and mother it was almost incomprehensible to her that any woman with the privilege of choice might choose *not* to be a lesbian. What did trouble her was a depth of intensity she recognized within herself which if not turned almost entirely in the direction of her music, could threaten her music.

There had been a point of potential explosion some years before. She'd met a fellow musician, a pianist originally from New York, who was touring Canada while Claudine was there giving a series of classes. Ellen and Claudine apparently had all the essentials in common: lust, humour, music. Ellen's ten extra years and more diverse education had been powerfully attractive to Claudine who believed her mind would open to the woman with the same willingness her body had shown. In a way unprecedented in her rigorously disciplined life, Claudine day-dreamed of how she and Ellen could set up a base together so each would have her idea of 'home' intertwined with the other; of how they could juggle schedules to minimize separations; of how eventually they might play together, entrancing innocent audiences when their personal love was expressed through their public love for music.

Their first parting was all it should have been. They were wet with lust and tears in about equal proportions. Claudine couldn't face leaving their bed for a publicly constrained airport farewell but Ellen rang several times before the plane took off to reiterate her promises to remain constantly in touch.

When Claudine left Canada a week later she had already mailed a dozen letters, poems and cards to Ellen, but at her Cologne hotel there was only one brief scrawl: *Miss you madly. Writing soon. Always yours*.

She made excuses easily then. Ellen was much in demand. Her music must come first. But nothing followed until months after Claudine had forced herself with a supreme act of will to stop writing. Then the letter which did come gave lively accounts of successful concert engagements and gossip from the music world. To anyone else it would have seemed amusing. To Claudine, it stank. And went on stinking even after the tiny pieces had been flushed away.

It was a year before Claudine and Ellen met again, and then only by chance. They were separately invited to a dinner party in Basle by an acquaintance neither had known was mutual. They were polite to each other through the long evening and glittered to everyone else. When the time came to leave Ellen suggested they share a cab. It was raining. Cabs were scarce. Once in the cab Ellen gave the driver the name of her own hotel, assuming Claudine would accompany her.

Ellen led the way to her grand suite and into the great bed as though she were the puppet mistress and Claudine the puppet. Claudine was fascinated, and appalled, not least by her own passion which seemed uncooled by Ellen's prolonged rejection. They made love as though they were in love but when finally it was over and while Ellen was reaching for her first cigarette, Claudine got out of bed, dressed, and left. The following morning, in a panic of remorse and renewed lust, she phoned Ellen who was not, she was informed, accepting any calls.

Over time, and with help, Claudine won sufficient detachment to attempt to analyse the painful sequence of events, though her analysis remained uncomfortably partial. She trusted that during the weeks in Canada with Ellen she'd opened up to someone real. But then what?

The caution she identified from this time became part of a gradually changing self-image. In most cities she visited for more than a few days Claudine had friends, some of whom were also occasional lovers. She would go to lesbian bars, not to find sex but not turning that opportunity down. She was scrupulous about explaining that her commitment to her work meant she would flop as one half of a love match, and she was adroit at picking up the first hints of disbelief and moving on.

About a year before meeting Zoë, Claudine had, with difficulty, made a major change in her personal life. She stopped sleeping with anyone. She came to this decision not because she'd grown tired of sex. That was inconceivable to her. Her delight in women and curiosity about them was undiminished, and her sense of herself as a highly sensual woman was as important to her as ever. What did seem to have changed was a loss of comfort about her manner of sexual expression. She had become cautious to the point of minimal availability, generous only with her body and skills as a lover. In

336

taking the safe path she was increasingly aware that she had trapped herself into a pattern of inevitable repetition, denying herself that chance to grow which she believed could only come through an element of risk-taking. She had, on contemplation, two choices: to risk the possibility of real involvement by removing the barriers she herself had erected, or to embrace – she laughed as she chose the word – celibacy.

To fall in love continued to seem like a journey onto quicksand, so Claudine began to sleep alone, to make love alone, and to avoid people or situations that might tempt her back to passionate but ultimately meaningless sex.

It wasn't easy. She missed the comfort women's bodies brought her, and the verbal intimacies that usually followed love-making. Then her dream life surged to provide extraordinary compensation. Erotic dreams rocketed out from her unconscious, night after night, astonishing her with their intensity and inventiveness. With no special plan in mind she began to jot down the feelings the dreams evoked, using words or drawings or notes of music, then watching as carefully as an explorer might watch her map to detect what patterns were emerging.

After three or four months the nightly riots quietened, and eventually stopped, but their energy remained and found expression through her compositions. Her libido seemed entirely directed into her work yet when Claudine examined the possible incongruity between her self-image as a sexually free woman against the current reality of her life, she remained confident of her decision.

The afternoon Claudine met Zoë was something of a throw-back. Almost compulsively she found herself buzzing with the old sexual curiosity, even before the lunch party. Perhaps it was aroused by the emphatic way in which Mrs Modjeska had suggested the two young women might have a *great deal in common*. Perhaps it was the combination of factors that formed Mrs Modjeska's word picture of Zoë: a fellow 'colonial' with an adult life in Europe, a woman with a painful love affair in her history, someone with artistic ambitions in a field not Claudine's own. Then there was the energy and vivacity which Mrs Modjeska obviously relished and which Claudine could see at once when Zoë came into the sitting-room and could see, too, the love flashing between the older woman and the younger one.

Zoë had obviously dressed to please Mrs Modjeska and to parade for her amusement: Claudine applauded her for it.

She'd not planned to come on with Zoë like a lesbian Don Juan but had done it anyway and had very nearly trapped herself as she fell like a trouper into old routines even while she chided herself for their inappropriateness. Claudine had been relieved when she finally elicited from Zoë the expected revelation that she, too, was a lesbian. That could have been enough, cosy lining for a warm nest of a friendship while Claudine was in London. She knew she'd been sexually provocative, using her power in a too-easy way, but she was confident she could pull back without withdrawing the flattery she had sincerely intended.

Events had not followed Claudine's plan. Zoë intrigued Claudine, but there was also a sense of weightlessness about her which Claudine was both wary of and oddly drawn towards. It was as though Zoë were present only by chance, or held in the present tenuously. Claudine found herself dismissing involuntary images in which, with her own body, she weighted Zoë down.

Claudine noted Zoë's apparently casual allusions to a German man she had 'once been in love with' and her references to love affairs with women which seemed to lack some vital colour. She heard Zoë describe her reluctance to commit herself other than to her work, and with relief she assured herself that this situation too could be contained. But when Zoë, younger, infinitely less experienced, no baby but certainly no super-dyke, when *Zoë* had taken Claudine's glass from her hand, had refused to refill it and with the outward calm of Garbo's Queen Christina had said that really it was time they went to bed, Claudine had been unable to refuse, giving only a fleeting grimace of self-mockery towards the chorus in her head plaintively reminding her of how deliciously safe celibacy had just been.

Zoë reappeared from behind the tree, giving one final roar and enjoying the unsettled glances of an elderly couple out walking their mouse-sized dog.

She strode back to where Claudine sat, speaking as she went.

'The last person who suggested I needed shrinking was the

beloved Gabriel who, I might add, goes on suggesting it like a record stuck on an exceptionally boring crack. "Do it yourself, sweetheart," is what I say to him and will now say to you. It's taken me more than thirty years to get as big as I am and if I resemble one of T.S. Eliot's hollow persons as a result of stretching too quickly, then in time I'll surely fill up. I am filling up, believe me.'

Claudine heard an unfamiliar tone of defiance in Zoë's voice, and perhaps anger too. Zoë had not sat down again but was kicking the ground with force.

'It seems odd to me that you, and Gabriel too, should express such concern for my mental health yet — at least in his case — be unwilling to hold up the other end of the white sheet while I discreetly heal behind.' Zoë giggled. 'You'll think me hopelessly over the top and so I am and please swear to me on guide's honour that's why you love me. But before you do, listen to me, Claudine, as I assure you I'm slowly, slowly making sense out of my life. Without a therapist to lean on, without a new crutch which could be removed to leave me sprawling and howling. That garden I've been talking about, the one in my dreams, it isn't the mirage of completeness. It's the rough stuff. But remember I told you it was rich and ready for life? Can I take the analogy further and say I believe I've worked through the stones and rubble and weeds which might have covered the soil before planting could begin? I've lugged them aside and probably left masses of debris scattered behind me. But do you follow what I'm saying? Do I make any sense at all?'

Claudine nodded and put up her hand to pull Zoë back down beside her. She took a small bag of old-fashioned boiled sweets from the pocket of her jacket, gave one to Zoë and carefully chose one for herself. They sat in silence, cheeks bulging, mouths filling with a sickly sweet taste until Claudine asked, 'Do you remember Mother Sugar, Anna's analyst in *The Golden Notebook*?'

Zoë nodded, and sucked.

'I've got a Mother Sugar of sorts myself. She lives in Paris and as she speaks only French and Estonian there's no way you need worry I'm propagandizing for her in particular. But I want to repeat to you something she said to me. Will you sit quiet now and listen to your *Tata* Claudine?'

339

In a partial gesture of reconciliation Zoë put an arm around Claudine's shoulders and briefly hugged her, then sat back, staring out over the Heath.

'She likened the process of therapy to a dancer who takes herself seriously enough to return often to her studies at the barre. Of course even without this she can go on performing and the public might continue to clap and cheer, but the dancer should always know what the audience can't see and be willing to work on that in a quiet place. At the barre there is no audience to reinforce a fantasy. There aren't any kind lights; there's no one to applaud and no one to help maintain your soothing fictions.'

Claudine's accent, which could roll like mercury from North American to European, was at its most noticeably French.

'Of course you work constantly at the barre alone if you're a serious person, but with a teacher working there sometimes with you, there's more than one imagination present and more than one set of experiences. There's someone *outside yourself* ready to look inside with you. I'm assuming of course the dancer has chosen her teacher wisely and that this teacher understands what "the work" is for and has done serious work of her own.'

'And when she's too busy for you, or simply no longer there?'

'Then I guess if it was time to continue at the barre, or get back to it — and remember we're probably talking about something intermittent, not permanent — then you'd get up off your butt and find another teacher, though already this analogy with the teacher makes me uncomfortable. A therapist isn't a teacher in any usual sense, or shouldn't be. It's the *process* you undertake, with the therapist as a kind of guide, which teaches. And that process can proceed only as far as you dare allow it.'

Zoë noticed that her anger was dissipating and that she was listening with cautious curiosity to what Claudine was saying.

'What made the difference for me was that I realized, very slowly though, that for my work to succeed I must be able to distinguish all my emotions and draw on them. I simply can't afford to be tight or blocked off. I'd hear that in the music and to hell with whether anyone else could hear it: I could. Equally I can't afford to be a frightened little plastic duck bobbing around in a great wash of emotion which at any moment may submerge me.'

Taking Zoë by the arm and holding her in a tight grip Claudine said, 'Listen Zoë.'

Zoë interrupted her. 'Have you ever stopped to consider whether all musicians begin their sentences with "listen" and fine artists with "look" and writers with "I feel" or "I think" depending on whether they write fiction or non-fiction? Or sculptors, how often do they manage to squeeze "touch" into their sentences?'

'I can't say that I've noticed – but I'll let you know.' Claudine smiled. 'Where was I? Hmm, back to you and don't distract me again, do you hear.'

'*Hear* would, of course, be another entirely appropriate word for a musician . . .'

'Zoë!' Claudine shouted.

Zoë touched her forehead in a gesture of mock shame.

'That's better. Now you *feel* you want to be a writer, not a journalist. This means starting from the inside and working out. It demands a boldness and authenticity which as an observer of external events you can neatly avoid. I'm quite sure that the more you know about yourself the more you can observe in other people, and that's your *material*, Zoë, the stuff of your art! The journey inwards is simultaneously a journey outwards, or it can be. You'll need to hack at your old emotional brambles with a pen shaped like a machete. But you're so private about your old wounds I suspect you hide their effects even from yourself. And that's a kind of suicide. You're killing off your chance to use the past, to make something of it and also to go forward from it.' She glanced at Zoë. Had she gone too far? Zoë's face offered no clue.

Claudine's voice softened. 'Hey, dear heart, all I'm really suggesting is that like most of us you could use a little more support than you're getting. It's obvious that the issues therapy raises are the same issues you're dealing with on your own or peripherally with other people. I simply believe from my own experience that with the right therapist you could go further than you'd do alone. Why not think of it as an intense way of learning, not as a crutch, and then whatever happens it can't be taken from you?'

Zoë didn't respond.

Claudine's voice was pure North American as she said, 'Damn it, Zoë, should I go on?'

Zoë grinned. 'If you must darling. I'm no Canute to turn the tide of good advice.' She pulled a face of mock-resignation. 'I'm sorry. What an ungrateful beast I am. Mademoiselle Denizet, oh please do continue, pray.'

'I will, don't worry.' Claudine laughed, then grew serious again as she paused to collect her thoughts and choose her words.

'I like the bits of writing you've shown me and recognize the signs of someone eager to go hunting for new levels of understanding. But there are knots in you too and please don't pull those ridiculous crazy faces while I'm talking!' She laughed again. 'God help me Zoë, you'd try the patience of the proverbials, but I'm going to get this off my chest whatever you do because I have no doubts that you've tried to unravel those knots on your own and in great part you've succeeded, but I'd bet my Stradivarius if I had one that it's only in part. You can be like one of those weird flowers that close up when touched or even breathed on when I approach you on a subject that's too painful for you, or where you feel unsure. And the feeling I get then, Zoë are you listening to me, is of *loneliness*. And it makes me damned sad.'

Zoë spoke, cautiously. 'I am interested in what you're saying, and grateful . . . and of course I've been listening, but I'm not sure that I can be convinced. The things I *am* sure of seem pretty bloody negative, although generally I experience myself as a positive person, complete with an inflatable life-raft of a soul.

'Let me give you an example. I believe that everything's transitory, yet I can't accept that and I go on fearing the transitory nature of things. And how could a shrink change that? Except perhaps to make the pain smaller. Is that why they're called shrinks, by the way, or is it to make me smaller so I'll feel pain in proportion to my newly diminished size?'

Claudine didn't immediately respond. It was growing colder and people were heading along the paths towards the exits.

'Okay,' Claudine began, 'try this. Everything's transitory except, you could have added, the pain you feel about your losses: the death of your mother and the death of your hopes with Gabriel. They don't seem too transitory.'

'And nor do my feelings of being scared. At least I feel scared when I allow myself to remember you'll be gone too by this time next week.'

Zoë put her hand to her mouth as though bandaging over her words. 'Actually, I wonder about that. I do believe you want to be with me too and I'm asking myself if I really feel scared or is that simply so familiar to me that I'm taking a quick dive into old mud for a wallow?'

'Oink, oink,' the women chorused in unison, then shut their eyes tightly as they linked little fingers, made a silent wish, then recited aloud the name of a poet to ensure their wishes would come true.

'Rossetti, as in Christina,' said Zoë.

'Moore, as in Marianne,' said Claudine almost at the same moment.

Zoë went on. 'I've got to tell you that when I push behind my fear of your leaving and what that means I can just about identify less familiar emotions. Like confidence that you'll come back. That I'm worth coming back to. Or confidence that I'll survive, even if you don't. Oh I'd be miserable, of course . . but I've no sense of myself as hovering in your shadow. I experience us as equals. Well, you're a little more gorgeous of course, but I constantly put myself down in relation to Gabriel. With good reason. When we met we *were* unequal, at least in those areas we both thought were important. And it's hard to change that initial pattern.'

'Did he want it to change?'

'Yes, I'm sure he did. It quickly became such a burden to him. I needed an absurd amount of bolstering which can be tedious, to say the least. Yet of course, unconsciously anyway, he colluded in this notion of our inequality. I was always grasping towards him, Oliver with my bowl out, wanting more more more, and only in retrospect realizing that the reason that I hung in there, put up with whatever I did put up with in terms of pain and anger and so on, was precisely because I had and have so much from him. But how sad that I couldn't always feel that at the time. Whereas with you . . .'

'Yes?'

'It's vivid – in the present. I'm feeling everything *now*. Of course I'm older and, God help me, a modicum wiser. Gabriel had the rawest of raw apprentices to deal with. And his own disappointment

343

that I wasn't who he thought I was. But what I now know is that what you've given me already is greater than anything you could take away, even if you disappeared forever. Set that to music Claudine, like one of the great oratorios!'

Claudine kissed Zoë, slowly, oblivious to any homeward trudgers who might be offended by this sight. When they had sat back, and had recovered from the kiss, she asked, 'And your mother?'

'Just like Gabriel,' she broke off and made a quick gesture of impatience. 'Oh how we do reveal ourselves by opening our big mouths! Let me start again. I feel more than loss for her too. I am who I am because of Jane and Gabriel. All the things I like about myself.' She caught what she'd just said and smiled, ironically. 'Well, there are a *few* things I like about myself. On my better days. And it's thanks to them there's anything at all.

'In his way Gabriel has been outstandingly loyal, though I'd have wished a million times over that his way had been nearer to mine. At least until these last weeks. But if my fingernails were about to be pulled out I might admit that in the years since I believed he'd abandoned me we've spent a good deal of loving and purposeful time together. And even in the ways he provoked me – or enraged me – there's been substantial learning once I've straightened up from the shock.'

'I'd like to feel like that about Ellen, but there was such a brief good time and then a heap of distress, though what came out of that I am really pleased about. It wasn't Ellen herself though. It was, in my case, more the events.'

'Well, she has to have been some kind of fool. And unworthy to boot.'

'Though should you ever run across her, you may certainly boot her, with my compliments, of course!' Claudine's laugh was loud, and without malice.

'Can I say something else about Gabriel?' Zoë peered at Claudine.

'Sure. Why not? I'm really curious about the man. He's the first convincing male mother-substitute I've ever come across. Flawed, of course, but what else could you expect?'

'Anyway, it's only partly about him because what I wanted to say is that *our* weeks together, Claudine, have shown me that what I'm achieving now – or contemplating achieving – couldn't have

344

happened without those years with Gabriel, nor while I saw him as the mountain and myself as the molehill. Being on my own, away from him, has adjusted my horizons somewhat.'

She rubbed her cheek. 'You're right, Claudine, I am left with much more than loss.'

Claudine whooped with laughter. 'That wasn't *my* suggestion, Zoë, it was your own conclusion though it has to be valid as I wholeheartedly agree with you. Another hard-won learning from my Mother Sugar is that – and I pass this onto you whole – while we cannot always choose the events that shape our lives we can choose our reactions to them. I mean, whether they diminish us or whether they help us grow. Are you with me?'

'I think so. Mrs Modjeska's said something pretty similar several times. But we'll have to return to all this again, though not now. I've lost all feeling in my toes and the rest of me will soon be frozen over.'

'Good. I've got just the method for thawing you out!' Claudine was already jumping to her feet, then, as Zoë stood too, was reaching up to wind the scarf around Zoë's neck, before taking her hand and beginning to run.

As they passed the exit, panting from laughter as well as the exertion of their run, Zoë bent over, her hands gripping her knees, struggling to catch her breath.

'There's an image I want to share with you. Another one. Is it too much?' She was gasping as she tried to straighten her body. Claudine was shaking her head emphatically.

'You know how obsessed I am with the sea, not only the real sea but also "the sea" as metaphor for the unconscious and for the processes of continuity and renewal?'

'Yes.'

'Well, I've been worried for a long time by the gaps in my life. Between rare flashes of insight there are these great blocks of mystery. I don't know how to reduce them or reach around them to join up the clues I do have in understanding myself or anyone else.'

'Go on,' Claudine urged, aware that Zoë was struggling against an impulse to draw back.

'There's also a sense in which I find myself going over and over the same ground, worrying at it like a dog who's forgotten where she's

345

buried her favourite bone. It's not like running on the spot, there's more movement than that, but it is like going over and over the same ground, or in my case – because of the way I feel about the sea – the same bit of sand. I'm *loitering* next to what the unconscious can teach me. With intent. Though not always with effect.'

Claudine noticed that Zoë was nervously twisting the ends of the scarf around her hands. 'Because it's sand, I've perceived my insights as getting washed away by incoming tides, that is, by change or confusion or simply by time. I've had the despairing feeling that I've repeatedly had to begin afresh because there's always something I can't quite remember or hold onto. It's rather like the sensation you have when you wake up from a vivid dream and as you reach towards it already its content and colour are slipping away, refusing to be captured, and mocking you. But since we've talked today, just in these last minutes, I've been struck by an increasingly clear picture of the sea as not washing away my hard-won markings on the sand but taking them into her great watery body, storing them up so that eventually all those disparate thoughts or insights might come together and make new sense. Perhaps when I'm Mrs Modjeska's age, or perhaps not ever. But they're there, in the sea, not lost at all. There and safe.'

Without warning and to her own surprise Zoë began to cry, weeping freely but not diluting the sense of elation her revelation to Claudine had allowed her. Claudine held her close as Zoë dripped copiously on her neck. While they stood in the narrow Hampstead street the last of the light disappeared and the sliver of a new moon made a graceful, tentative début.

When Zoë was quiet Claudine offered her a pale green silk handkerchief.

'Seems a shame to blow my nose on this lovely thing, but here goes.'

Zoë blew her nose vigorously, then seemed to shake herself.

'I've got to go back to New Zealand, that's clear. And I'll do it too, as soon as I'm brave enough. I wish I could ask you to come with me but the first time at least I need to seek private audiences with my ghosts, those living ones as well as the said-to-be-dead. Then, who knows, maybe I'll want to find my own Mother Sugar. Or maybe not. No promises.'

From the pocket of her jeans Zoë pulled a small packet. She smiled at Claudine as she handed it to her. 'It's not the key to my heart. I'm hanging on to that. But it is a small token to mark new beginnings.'

Claudine moved to where she could catch the light descending from the lamp post and opened the beautifully wrapped packet with care. Inside, on a fine gold chain, was a seed pearl to match the one she wore in her ear. She touched Zoë's face, lightly, before moving closer towards her.

Again the two women kissed. Then, turning in the direction of Claudine's borrowed flat, they began to walk, arm in arm, in companionable silence.

Ten

There have been many greetings and departures in the lives of the two people searching for each other on the busy platform of a large German railway station.

When they glimpse each other through the crowds their faces open out with relief and pleasure. They smile widely and are no longer aware of the many other people hailing and farewelling between and around them.

The woman stops walking and stands still, waiting for the man to reach her. She is the traveller. She puts down the heavy suitcase she's been carrying. This is only her first stop. She is on her way to New Zealand, not forever and probably not even for long. If asked, she would say that it's her arrival there which matters, not her departure.

The man slows his pace. He is choosing to savour these precious moments of walking towards – but not yet reaching – this woman he believes he knows so well. By prolonging the anticipation everything can seem to lie ahead.

Through the crowd the woman appears to the man to stand out, to glow. He remembers the first time he saw her. She seemed wild to him then, untamed. Only the memory of that quality is with him now. He remembers too a poem he read as he sat on the floor of her soaring room in Berlin, where she once lived. In the poem she referred to herself as a lighthouse. He had exclaimed with the pleasure of recognition when he read those lines. She had silenced him with a reminder that a lighthouse directs its light outwards, and is hollow inside.

The glow is different now. He trusts it. A moth might scarcely notice it.

The woman has become impatient through the seconds' delay. She strides over the last few separating steps. Her suitcase is temporarily abandoned. She calls out the man's name as she reaches him, elevates it into an endearment as she embraces him, burying her face in his neck like a mole burrowing into a familiar hollow. Then she steps back, looks at him, to see just who he is.

They have known each other for a long time and have been reckless in their intimacy. Yet in this moment of greeting each is slightly embarrassed. This is the present. What they know best is already the past.

Walking towards the first few moments of a future neither would be foolish enough to want to predict, they leave the station and go into the cool winter night to hail a cab.

Their arms are around each other, their dark heads are bent together. In appearance they are so alike they could be mistaken for brother and sister. But they are not that, nor are they lovers. They are friends, comrades, fellow-travellers. They are each a hero in the compelling drama of the other's life. They are also, separately and together, survivors.